POSTCARDS
FROM
FRED

WUNDERFOOL

W/P

P R E S S

Also by Brad Whittington

Novels

Welcome to Fred

Living with Fred

Escape from Fred

Muffin Man

Endless Vacation

Non-fiction

What Would Jesus Drink?
What the Bible Really Says About Alcohol

BRAD WHITTINGTON

POSTCARDS
FROM
FRED

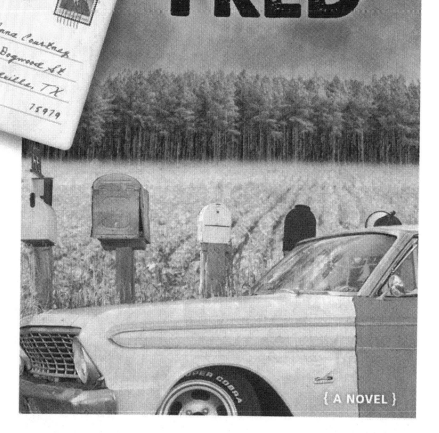

{ A NOVEL }

Copyright 2013 by Brad Whittington
All rights reserved

ISBN: 978-1-937274-20-7
Published by Wunderfool Press
Austin, Texas

Dewey Decimal Classification: F
Subject Heading: Fiction / Coming of Age

All characters appearing in this work are fictitious. Any resemblance
to real persons, living or dead, is purely coincidental.

Contents

What they're saying about Whittington

Whittington spins an enjoyable literary story
and is definitely a novelist to watch.
–Publisher's Weekly

Brad Whittington is an artist with a pen.
–Ethan C. McDonald, DancingWord.com

It is always a joy to find a new writer who knows what he's doing.
–Rick Lewis, Logos Bookstore

Whittington is a welcome new voice in the world of fiction.
–Cindy Crosby, author of By Willoway Brook

Who can resist a story of someone else's alienated youth if that
someone else is as talented as Brad Whittington?
–JT Conroe, author of The Blue Hotel

The pacing, humor, honesty, and believable characters made me
turn page after page in rapid succession until there were none.
–T Leigh

Brad Whittington paints some of the best word pictures I've seen.
–Cammi Ellis

What they're saying about the Fred books

What do you get when you cross Dave Barry and Garrison Keillor?
Two very irritated men. Besides that, you get a great talent like Brad
Whittington, whocan take the awkward moments of growing up
and turn them into something really ridiculous. But don't take my
word for it—visit Fred yourself."
–Robin Hardy, author of the Strieker Saga and the Sammy Series

I gobbled up the book in a couple of enjoyable evenings.
–Wanda Adams, Honolulu Advertiser

By the time I'd finished the first couple of paragraphs, it was as if I'd
found an old friend I never knew I had.
–Thom Lemmons, author of the Daughters of Faith Series

For Sarah

For giving me Claire

Let me not to the marriage of true minds
Admit impediments. Love is not love
Which alters when it alteration finds,
Or bends with the remover to remove:
O no! it is an ever-fixed mark
That looks on tempests and is never shaken;
It is the star to every wandering bark,
Whose worth's unknown, although his height be taken.
Love's not Time's fool, though rosy lips and cheeks
Within his bending sickle's compass come:
Love alters not with his brief hours and weeks,
But bears it out even to the edge of doom.
   If this be error and upon me proved,
   I never writ, nor no man ever loved.

—William Shakespeare, Sonnet 116

CHAPTER ONE

I was looking for stamps when I found it. I flipped the postcard over and read the poem that could have changed everything if only I had managed to get it postmarked March 30, 1973.

It was a plain white postcard like the kind you could buy in a post office, six-cent postage printed on it. It had no postmark and was addressed in my handwriting, the scrawl that looked like I was genetically predisposed for a life as a family doctor.

Finding it now in the back of a drawer in the rolltop desk I inherited from Dad, several decades too late, filled me with a kaleidoscope of emotions from nostalgia to speculation to resignation.

But as usual, I'm getting ahead of myself.

First off you should know that I, Mark Cloud, am a Southern Baptist preacher's kid, along with my sisters, Heidi and Hannah. PK as we call it in the business.

I hear you. You're saying there are preacher's kids and then there's preacher's kids. True, so I'll tell you straight up.

I'm not that kind. I'm the other kind.

The second thing we have to get out of the way is Fred. It's a town deep in East Texas about the size of a six-cent stamp. Right between Spurger and Caney Head. About thirty miles from the Sabine River. You know, the one with Louisiana on the other side.

That takes care of most of the big stuff. All that's left to tell is the story.

CHAPTER TWO

One thing about preacher's kids in rural churches is that they don't typically travel in packs like wolves or in herds like elephants.

In a small church, there's only one preacher, so it's not like the PKs can form a holy clique with membership cards and a secret handshake. Rural PKs are more like manatees or rhinoceri, animals of one kind wandering the landscape, or seascape, among the other species. And they don't hang with the deacon's kids on general principle.

I knew a few other PKs from school. Elrick from the black church in Warren, to mention one. But we didn't hang that much at school and not at all outside of school.

So when Heidi came home for Thanksgiving during her first semester at college and walked in with a PK named Hosea, it was a bit of a shock. Almost as shocking as Nixon getting reelected two weeks before.

Of course, seeing that she had gone off to a Baptist college where you couldn't swing a dead polecat without hitting half a dozen PKs, the odds were better than even that she would land one. Not that she went there for her MRS degree, but PKs have hormones too.

Hosea was a preacher boy, which is what they called the ministerial students up at the college. His dad was the pastor of the Baptist church in Woodville, thirty miles away, so of course Dad knew him. Dad knew everybody. And Mom made Hosea feel right at home, just like she did with everybody, sinner or saint.

Hosea was named after the minor prophet who preached doom and destruction. Provenance notwithstanding, you couldn't find a more complete opposite to his namesake than Heidi's Hosea, a pale redhead exuding Aqua Velva and a semi-bumbling, "aw, shucks" manner.

"I'm so proud to meet you, Reverend Cloud." He shook Dad's hand like it was a pump handle on a temperamental well. "I've heard so much about you."

The phone rang. Everyone froze, Dad still holding Hosea's hand, listening for the pattern. Two longs. That meant it was for us, not for the other three people on the party line. Mom stepped to the phone.

Dad realized he was holding hands with Hosea. "Mr. Cloud will do," he said as he extricated his hand from Hosea's iron grip. "I'm no more to be revered than the next man."

"Hold on, Catherine," Mom said. "Let me get it on the extension." She held out the phone to me.

I took it and hung up after Mom picked up the extension in the study.

Hosea shook his head. "That don't feel right, calling a man like yourself Mister."

"Can you live with Pastor?"

Hosea smiled and grabbed Dad's hand again. "Yessir, Pastor Cloud."

As Hosea brought in Heidi's suitcase and laundry bag, Mom emerged from the study.

"Matthew, could you talk to Roger? It's about Claire."

I watched Hosea depart in his sunflower-yellow Chevy Nova, trailing clouds of awkward sincerity, and wondered why Uncle Roger would call us.

Claire Foxe was my cousin, being Mom's sister's daughter, and was my age. She was rich and lived in a fancy section of Houston. Our families didn't hang out much. We played the poor country church mouse to their urbane city mouse lifestyle. They didn't frequent the gatherings of the less affluent family members anymore.

More to the point, Uncle Roger had little use for something as impractical as religion. I recalled some very pointed remarks at a Thanksgiving dinner—the last dinner, in fact, that our families shared. I didn't recall the exact substance of the conversation, but I definitely remembered the tone, which was blatant enough to register with a third grader. A long, awkward silence had followed, filled with tension and averted glances as the adults tried to make it disappear by ignoring it.

But even more clearly, I remembered the expression of contempt in Claire's eyes as she looked at Uncle Roger. The way someone would look at a bully, anticipating the day they grew big enough to visit upon his head all the meanness he had dished out to others.

And Claire had done so, turning herself into an instant karma machine designed for the sole purpose of torturing her parents. A few years back, when we were in junior high and I was consumed with assimilating into my environment by cultivating a hick accent, Claire was going to drinking parties with high school seniors. That got her a one-way ticket to an all-girls boarding school somewhere up in the northeast. Connecticut, I think. That was the last I had heard of her.

I lurked just outside the study door, hoping to acquire actionable intelligence, but I just heard Dad saying things like "You don't say?" and "Oh, that is unfortunate."

Then Mom and Heidi rounded the corner with a laundry bag and I had to pretend I was looking for something in the cabinet. I shuffled a few cleaning products around on the shelf, snatched up a superannuated sponge that had hardened into a slight smile over the years, and held it up like a prize.

Mom smiled, obviously not fooled but willing to play along, while Heidi continued the monologue that she had launched the moment the door closed behind Hosea. A play-by-play account of her first three fascinating months at college.

I fled before I got sucked into the narrative, ran some water on the sponge, and wiped down the stove to lend credence to my cover story. Then I tracked down Hannah in the living room where she listened to a Grass Roots album and labored over a freshman English composition.

"What do you think of The Hose?"

Hannah looked up in confusion. We had struck a temporary truce in our personal hundred years war due to a recent misfortune of mine that stirred her sisterly compassion. The calamity of which I speak is the devastating, for me, Sadie Hawkins dance debacle with Jolene Culpepper. But that is another story for another time.

4

"The Hose?"

"Heidi's new boyfriend."

"Hosea?"

"Hosea 'The Hose' Courtney."

"Who calls him that?"

"Me. And now you."

Hannah smiled. "I think The Hose is kinda sweet."

"Saccharine, more like."

"He has a sister. Sixteen, like you. Available, like you."

My pulse skipped a beat or two at the possibilities, but reality conquered my imagination. I'd seen Hosea, and DNA doesn't fall far from the tree. "Is she adopted?"

"Not that I know of."

"Let me guess. Her best asset is her great personality."

"That's what I hear."

It was ever the way of things. If they were available, there was a reason. If they were cute, they were either deadly, like Jolene, or taken.

I dismissed Hosea's sister from my consciousness and repaired to the kitchen for a Dr Pepper float and a Damon Runyon book.

But I was soon to learn the error of my ways.

Chapter Three

Black Friday dawned, if you could call it dawning, cold, wet, and windy. Facing the prospect of hunkering in the house all day, I opted to join the women on a trip to Parkdale Mall in Beaumont. Since there were four of us, we took the Galaxie, the greater of the two family vehicles. It was only nine years old and had air conditioning, not that we needed it today. Dad took the Falcon to visit folks in the hospital.

While Heidi chattered about The Hose in the front seat, in homage to the weather I huddled in the back and read "The Cask of Amontillado."

When Fortunato pleaded, "*For the love of God, Montresor!*" it sent a chill through me despite my jacket and the car heater on full blast.

I turned to the next story, but an occurrence in the front seat caused me to close the book, holding my place with a finger.

Heidi took an unscheduled break in the continuing oral history of the daily minutia of her college career for a question. "Why did Uncle Roger call the other night? Something about Claire?"

Mom took a while to answer. "She's been having trouble adjusting to the boarding school."

"You mean she got kicked out," Hannah said.

I glanced at Hannah. She spread her hands palms up as if the conclusion were obvious. And once she said it, it was obvious. What else could it be?

"Really?" Heidi said.

"Either that or she's pregnant," Hannah said as if explaining addition to a senior. "Or both."

"Hannah, try to be more generous," Mom said, chastising her with a pointed look in the rear view mirror.

"So Uncle Roger called to tell us she made the honor roll?" Hannah asked.

Mom gave her another look in the mirror.

"She's pregnant?" Heidi said.

"No, she's not pregnant," Mom answered.

A full fifteen seconds passed without Heidi saying anything, but we all knew it couldn't last. "So why did he call?"

"She was suspended," Mom finally admitted.

Hannah leaned back into her seat with a satisfied smile.

I didn't say anything. I knew I could count on Heidi to ask all the awkward questions.

"What for?"

"There's no need for us to gossip about the details. We just need to be praying for her."

I disagreed. I wanted details, and the more the better, but I maintained my policy of radio silence. Five years in Fred had taught me that only suckers asked questions. Better to remain silent than to admit ignorance. But I didn't despair. Instead I trusted the infantry to storm the battlements.

Hannah launched the first salvo. "So Uncle Roger called to ask for prayer?"

That was about as likely as ham on the Passover menu. In fact, I couldn't imagine a scenario in which Uncle Roger admitted any weakness to anyone, especially Dad.

"They're just considering all their options," Mom said.

Options? Hannah returned my frown of confusion. We rode in silence for several miles as we racked our brains for an option that would prompt Uncle Roger to place a phone call to the despised preacher in-law. Then I remembered how Mom had answered the phone.

"Aunt Catherine called," I blurted out.

Hannah nodded reluctantly, conceding a point to me. Uncle Roger wouldn't call for help if his face was on fire, but Aunt Catherine might call her big sister if she were at the end of her rope, no matter what her rich husband said.

"Aunt Catherine called for prayer?" Heidi asked.

"Actually, she did," Mom said.

Hannah saw my raised eyebrow and raised two. Things must be desperate indeed down in River Oaks.

"So what are the options?" Hannah asked.

"Nothing's settled yet," Mom said. "They're waiting to see how the next month goes."

I didn't have recent knowledge of Claire, or even a recent photo, but I had serious doubts that the Christmas season would bring good tidings of great joy to the Foxe household.

I returned to my book with the rumination that the next Poe story, no matter how macabre and angst-ridden, would likely end more pleasantly than the holiday season down in Houston.

At the mall I browsed through Spencer Gifts for presents for the unfortunates on my gift list and then blew an hour in the record store flipping through the pricey new releases before I moved on to the bargain cutout rack and picked up a copy of Buzzy Linhart's "The Time to Live is Now." Then I found a quiet corner to sip a root beer float and think about what I wanted for Christmas. A girlfriend.

In the past few months I had suffered two setbacks in the romance department.

Early in the school year, I had closed the book on The Sad Case of Becky Tuttle and the Dreaded F-word. Just as I had built up my nerve, screwed my courage to the sticking place, and come to school armed with dogwood blossoms to declare my undying love, Becky had uttered the one word no guy ever wanted to hear from the object of his affections. Friend.

That could shut down a guy faster than a cold shower during the winter equinox in Siberia.

Besides, she had trained her sights on number sixty-eight on the football team. At this point I was nothing more than scenery.

Then, at the Sadie Hawkins dance just two weekends back, I had allowed myself to be seduced into the delusion that Jolene Culpepper had secretly fallen prey to my indefinable charms.

With Jolene it was best to keep it platonic. Once things turned affectionate you became a target. The Big Thicket was littered with the hollow shells of guys who had been lured by her beauty into the kill zone.

Although it would require time travel or reincarnation or some other inconceivable mechanism, I suspected Keats must have been thinking of Jolene when he penned "La Belle Dame Sans Merci."

> I met a lady in the meads,
>> Full beautiful—a faery's child
> Her hair was long, her foot was light,
>> And her eyes were wild.

When it came to practical jokes, Jolene was indeed the beautiful lady without mercy. And though I had years of first-hand experience to warn me, I had fallen into her trap only to become the next in a lengthy line of hollow shells. Our saving grace had been a long-standing friendship, true remorse on her part, and a timely, or untimely as I thought at the time, sermon on forgiveness.

So that was two down and not many to go. Motown might think there were too many fish in the sea, but Fred was more of an over-fished stock pond.

I sipped my float and watched the great tide of Black Friday shoppers wash past. Scattered among the moms, grandmoms, aunts, sisters, and the occasional harried and confused male, females of a certain age traveled in packs. I pondered on how I could separate one from the herd and overwhelm her with my dazzling personality.

It didn't take long to recognize the flaw in my plan. Success depended on the dazzling personality.

Wisdom dictated that I fall back on Plan B. And I would, just as soon as I figured out what Plan B was.

Chapter Four

Sunday the temperature actually got up into the sixties, and anything seemed possible. I don't know what Dad's goal was for the standard-issue Thanksgiving sermon, but I was happy with it for the simple fact that it didn't pose any crushing moral dilemmas on forgiving your enemies. I was willing to experiment with an attitude of gratitude, at least for an hour or so.

After church, as Heidi departed back to college in the yellow-mobile with The Hose, my noble instincts overwhelmed by financial desperation, I sought out Deacon Fry for my monthly wages.

Last summer, as the Cloud family embarked on a pilgrimage to California, the Land of Ultimate Cool, the church janitor had become indisposed. Upon our return, Deacon Fry had offered the job to me at five dollars a week. It was slave wages, but it took half the time and energy of my weekly Grit newspaper route for the same pay. I jumped at the chance to double my income like a tick on a june bug.

Each Saturday I wandered through the empty gloom of the church like an ancestral ghost with a neatness fetish, sweeping and mopping the floors of the fellowship hall and classrooms, emptying the trash, and generally straightening up. On the last Sunday of each month, I collected my twenty or twenty-five dollars, depending on how many Saturdays there were in the month.

I caught Deacon Fry at the door of his black LTD. His expression as he turned toward me rocked me back a bit. It had a bit of Mr. Potter sneering at George Bailey caught in a tight spot with the bank examiner.

"I guess you'll be wanting your money," he growled, the thin autumn light glinting off his bald head.

"Yes, sir," I replied, feeling like George asking Potter for that eight thousand dollars before the bank examiner audited the book.

He dug in his back pocket for his wallet and pulled out some bills.

I looked at the money in my hand. Three fives. I looked back at him.

Deacon Fry loomed above me, his six-feet plus and considerable bulk dwarfing my short, spindly frame. "Only get paid when you work. We ain't running a charity here."

My momentary confusion faded as I recalled a Saturday two weeks ago. The day after the dance, when I had left the house, by passed the church, and wandered the back roads selling newspapers, hiding from civilization.

And I remembered what else happened that night. A call from Deacon Fry to Dad, accusing me of drinking and consorting with bootleggers. It was true, if you call one disgusting sip of cheap beer on a hunting trip drinking. Or if you consider sharing a Coke with a World War II veteran consorting with bootleggers.

And I also remembered what Dad had said about Deacon Fry, that he was looking for excuses to run Dad out of town, and that I was giving him ammunition, regardless of my intentions.

I worded my response to Deacon Fry carefully. "Yes, sir."

"Besides, our old feller may be coming back after the holidays. You were always a temporary replacement." He turned abruptly, climbed into his LTD, and pelted my legs with gravel as he raced home for Sunday dinner. Probably leftover turkey.

I spat out the taste of dust, shoved the fifteen dollars into my pocket, and circled the church without talking to anyone. I walked across the field and over the creek to the parsonage, considering my dilemma.

At the end of the summer I read a dangerous book. *In His Steps*. It looked harmless enough, a dusty old book from the last century, practically falling apart. But it had blown apart my world.

It had the nerve to suggest that the true follower of Christ should ask himself what Jesus would do before taking any action. My subsequent researches had revealed that if you had ten people in a room, you would get fifteen opinions on the topic, mostly self-serving. The question of what Jesus would do seemed to be the ultimate religious Rorschach test where people saw what they wanted to see.

One thing was clear. Dad and Deacon Fry had very different opinions on the answer to that question. Especially when it came to people who weren't the usual church members.

Like Vernon Crowley, a World War II vet who might or might not be a bootlegger but who definitely needed a friend.

Or like Parker Walker, a drunk who had stumbled into the church last summer during a baptism service and smashed a bottle of whiskey on the altar. Dad had converted him right there on the spot and had taken him under his wing. Parker had straightened out and started studying his Bible. At least for a while, anyway.

But Deacon Fry didn't welcome Vernon or Parker with open arms. In fact, he didn't welcome them at all. And he didn't want any pastor who welcomed such riffraff into his church.

As head of the governing body, Deacon Fry had the power and influence to make life impossible for Dad and even to replace him. Like he was threatening to do with me. By doing the gospel as he saw it, Dad could end up losing his job, and my antics weren't making things any easier.

I would have to watch my step. But I had vowed to walk in His steps. Should I appease Deacon Fry or follow the path I had chosen?

I remembered Dad's words that night. "If you choose that road, you had better count the cost. Because it will cost you everything."

Chapter Five

In mid-December Heidi returned from college and the whole family went to see a full production of Handel's Messiah in Woodville.

Compared to Fred, Woodville was the big city. Well, not Beaumont big city with a population topping six figures, but it was the county seat, so it had a courthouse and a county jail and the Dogwood Festival, where each spring they had a parade and crowned the Dogwood Queen.

The temperature had been in the forties for a week and the first freeze was rolling in. Not really the night you wanted to drive thirty minutes and sit in a church for three hours.

Now you might be one of those rare individuals who donates money to NPR during pledge week, who stops at a blinking red light at three a.m. with nobody visible for a half mile, and who sets aside an afternoon every Christmas season to listen to the Messiah. In that case, bless your heart and good on ya, mate, as various southerners say.

But if you're uninitiated in those ancient rites and think you might attend a full performance on the strength of the "Hallelujah Chorus," let me give you a tip straight from the stable: give it a miss.

The thing is, the "Hallelujah Chorus" is like the movie trailer that has all the good parts. It's sandwiched between a few hours of other stuff that never made the charts.

Oh, sure, the service started out nicely enough. I was sitting in an unpadded pew in my church clothes when the music minister came in from a side door and picked up his baton. The lights went down and I had the sudden realization that we were missing *It's a Wonderful Life* on the station out of Beaumont.

The orchestra cranked up the overture. It had a catchy tune and clocked in under three minutes, just like an AM radio hit. Not so bad.

Then reality set in. Hosea stepped up and sang, "Come for tea, my people." Very slowly. I checked the program and realized he was singing, "Comfort ye my people."

For the next seven minutes, he sang each line of the song four or five times, like the blues, only nothing like the blues. And every fifteen seconds or so he would stretch out a note forever, bouncing it around like an over-caffeinated mosquito trying to thread a needle.

Then the choir weighed in for a couple of minutes, and the next thing I knew, the bass stepped up and took his best shot for six minutes, then the choir again, then the alto. I got the little golf pencil from the back of the pew in front of me, placed there for the purpose of filling out offering envelopes and visitor cards, and started keeping score of how many times each phrase was sung. Heidi gave me a dirty look, but I ignored her.

After half an hour of this less-than-fascinating exercise, Handel finally threw us a bone with "For unto us a child is born," which was pretty catchy.

But it was a mere palliative for the next twenty minutes, which was basically more of the same until the director stepped down, everyone clapped, and I thought I was in the clear. I grabbed my coat and pulled it on.

"Where do you think you're going?" Hannah said.

I gave her a look like the Victrola dog confounded by his master's voice. She pointed at a word in the program. Intermission. Underneath, part two had more songs than in part one. I slumped onto the pew, defeated.

"Let's get up and stretch our legs," Dad said.

The deacons and others of questionable resolve went outside to catch a quick cigarette. I pulled my coat back on, followed them out, and looked down the street, blowing clouds into the night and wondering how long it would take me to walk the thirty miles back to Fred. At a brisk pace of three miles an hour, only ten hours.

Or I could blaze a trail through the woods to cut off the corner of the triangle. I did the math, squaring the thirteen miles south to Warren and the sixteen miles east to Fred and getting an approximate square root of the sum, which came out to a little over twenty miles cutting through wooded country that would slow my progress to less than a mile an hour, plus I'd need a compass. So it could take me a full 24-hour day, or maybe I'd never get there at all.

Compared to the last hour, which had felt like a month, getting lost in the woods for a week looked like a bargain.

I got my bearings to hike to the highway and take my chances thumbing it back to Fred when the porch lights blinked and Heidi poked her head out the doors.

"Come on," she hissed, and if you think you can't hiss a sentence with no sibilants in it, you're wrong. "They're starting part two."

I gave up on the great escape and followed the warden back to my assigned seat in the compound.

Part two eased in nice and mellow with the choir singing "Behold the Lamb," but then the alto started in with "He was despised and rejected," and we were back in the familiar groove. I tired of the counting game and inspected the choir for interesting characters. Just the usual collection of rural types—farmers, bankers, refinery workers, elementary school teachers, legal secretaries. Then on the back row of the altos on the lady's side, I spied an anomaly. A teenager. Female.

Despite the green choir robe, or maybe because of it, she looked like she had stepped right out of an Irish Spring commercial. Straight blonde hair, fresh and clean as a whistle. She sang "Surely he has borne our griefs and carried our sorrows" with a wholesome earnestness that made me wish she was singing about me.

I forgot about the counting game or hitchhiking back to Fred. Instead I thought back to Black Friday and my blacker thoughts of that Friday a few weeks ago after the dance. It seemed that there were fish in the sea that I knew not of. And providence was dangling one right above my net.

I watched her sing on the chorus songs. I watched her wait patiently while Hosea sang "All they that see him laugh" without a hint of irony. I thought of her in an Irish Spring commercial, whistling at me as I passed by with a green-and-white striped bar of soap.

Before I knew it, they launched into the "Hallelujah Chorus," and everybody stood like for the entrance of the bride.

That got my blood to pumping even more, and when they finished, I turned to get my coat, hoping to catch a glimpse of the Irish Spring girl up close, but everybody else sat down. I looked at Hannah, who rolled her eyes and shook her head and probably said "Tsk, tsk," but I couldn't hear it over the soprano singing "I know my Redeemer liveth."

I grabbed a program and flipped it over. There it was. Part three, nine more songs. They were going to power through without another intermission. I didn't bother to take off my coat. I just dropped back into the pew and consoled myself by watching the Irish Spring Alto, or Isa, as I called her in my head.

I compared her to Jolene, who was a study in contrasts—jet-black hair, fresh cream complexion, with a hint of strawberry in the cheeks and lips. Isa was more a study of shades and hues—flaxen hair and honey skin, perhaps golden eyes, although I was too far back to tell.

Then there was the brown-haired, green-eyed Becky Tuttle, whose charms I had recently abandoned after a careful cost-benefit analysis. She seemed a cat's-eye marble compared to Isa's opalescent glow.

These thoughts kept me sane, after a fashion, through the next half hour. After a stately "Worthy is the Lamb," the lights came up and everyone else stood. I carefully checked the program to verify that we had indeed come to the end of this trial by ordeal.

Hannah flicked the program with a pink nail. "I release thee from thy bondage."

I rocketed to my feet, pushed my way to the aisle, and threaded through the crowd to the front, where a sea of green robes obscured my target like a flock of mutant penguins.

Searching the faces of Sunday school teachers and building fund treasurers and Women's Missionary Union chairwomen and bus ministry captains for a fair maiden of Astolat, I quickly became disoriented. But I persevered. I had learned from experience that while the meek might inherit the earth, when it came to love, the timid inherited a handshake and an eternity of regret.

From the endless procession of robes, a hand emerged and grabbed my shoulder.

"Mark, what did you think?" The Hose stood before me, his green robe a compelling accent to his red hair. Before I could respond, he asked, "Where's Heidi?"

And then Heidi materialized and began gushing to a degree highly embarrassing for a sensitive soul such as myself. As I turned to continue my quest, The Hose snagged me again.

"Mark, why don't you come with us to Dairy Queen?"

"Uh . . ." I responded eloquently. The last thing I wanted was to become the third-wheel to a star-struck twosome. I cast about wildly for a plausible exit strategy.

"My sister is coming," The Hose said as if to supply added inducement.

That cinched it. Add to the current mix one Hosette in full bloom and my despair was complete.

"Well . . ." I shot back, not caring if it stung.

"Here she is," The Hose said, evidently immune to my rapier wit. "Anna, this is Mark, Heidi's brother."

I turned slowly, resigning myself to an evening of death by a thousand platitudes. Despite my debonair detachment, I could not in good conscience openly bruise a tender reed, regardless of her unfortunate gene pool of origin.

"Mark, this is my sister, Anna."

Isa, the Irish Spring Alto, held out her hand.

"Mark," she said in dulcet tones.

"Isa," I replied. "I mean, Anna." I wasn't used to being favored by divine intervention in the romance department. Or any other department, when it came down to it.

"What did you think of the concert?"

"Spellbinding." And I meant every word.

"Really?" She studied me through narrowed eyes. "Most people can't handle the Messiah in its entirety."

A sputtering laugh erupted before I could contain it, which seemed to puzzle her further. I recovered. "I found the chorus parts especially compelling."

"Exactly," Anna said. "I think 'Worthy is the Lamb' is universally underrated. Every bit the equal of 'Hallelujah,' don't you think?"

"Well, yeah." It was the best I could do on short notice, and it seemed to serve.

"Let's get out of these robes," The Hose said. "We'll be right back." He cast a long, sickeningly sweet gaze at Heidi and left.

I traded exasperated glances with Anna, pleased to see that she shared my impatience with this gooey interaction. She disappeared into the inner sanctum.

Heidi slipped her arm into mine and allowed me to escort her back to the family, where she informed the parental units of our plans.

"Hosea will bring us home."

"That's such a long way for him to drive home so late," Mom said.

"He doesn't mind," Heidi said.

Of course not, I thought. A thirty-mile return drive alone was a small price to pay for the thirty-miles out with the object of your affection.

"What about Hannah?" Mom asked.

"What about her?" Hannah said.

"Don't you want to go?"

"Seriously? Heidi and Hosea. Mark and Anna. Hannah and . . . Hannah."

"Point taken," Dad said. "We'll have hot chocolate and Parcheesi."

Hannah seemed satisfied with this arrangement. The three of them girded their loins and braved the elements.

I watched the doors close behind them and turned to Heidi. We looked at each other with a wild surmise.

"So, what do you think of Anna?" Heidi asked.

I wasn't about to tell her what I thought of Anna. There are things of which one does not speak, not even to one's older sister. But Heidi had been the one to intervene in the case of Becky Tuttle and the F-word. I owed her something.

"Does she like Led Zeppelin?"

Heidi frowned. "She has a poster of the Bill Gaither Trio in her bedroom. Is that good?"

CHAPTER SIX

I am told that in the olden days in England, the status of city was awarded to towns that had a cathedral. We have a similar ancient custom in Texas contingent on the presence of a Dairy Queen. The Woodville DQ was on the south end of town on Highway 69.

We emerged from the toasty interior of the yellow Nova and scuttled out of the freezing wind, into the aroma of fried food and Pine Sol. The Hose flashed some cash and bought the first round. He and Heidi split a banana split. Anna got a Dilly Bar.

Having had a long-standing aversion to the Dilly Bar based on the name alone, I preferred the old standard, a Black Cow, known to the proletariat as a root beer float.

In contrast to the Dilly Bar, which struck me as too absurd to actually say out loud, ordering a Black Cow sounded sophisticated, like a mixed drink—White Russian, Bloody Mary, Black Cow. They rolled off the tongue when ordering, and rolled down the gullet when drinking. Not that I had ever ordered a White Russian or Bloody Mary, much less drunk one. I had never even seen one.

But I didn't mention that when I stepped to the counter. I had one shot at impressing this girl from the big church in the city and I was going to make it count. "I'll take a Black Cow."

"What's that?" the girl behind the counter asked. "A burger extra well done?"

"No," I said in my most urbane tone. "It's a root beer float."

"Well, why didn't you say so?"

"Shaken, not stirred."

She stared at me for a few seconds before responding. "The machine makes them."

"Medium." I turned away, dismissing her to the mundane task of filling the order.

Heidi looked at me as if I had been possessed by an alien. I ignored her.

We found a booth, H and H on one side, Isa and I on the other, the girls on the inside as custom dictated.

The Hose assessed me. "So, Mark, what are you, a freshman?"

"Junior." Being small for my age, I was used to such mistakes, but I found it particularly galling after having gone to such lengths to establish my worldly sophistication.

"Oh, so is Anna."

"Yes, I know."

An awkward silence descended on the table, but it didn't last for long because Heidi couldn't abide dead air.

"That was a lot of songs to memorize," she said.

"No worse than memorizing the book of John," The Hose said.

"You memorized the entire book of John?" Heidi asked.

"Sure."

"I can barely remember my locker combination," Heidi said.

That seemed to be all there was to say on that subject, and the awkward silence returned.

I glanced at Anna. She still looked as wholesome as a bowl of blueberries in heavy cream. As I racked my brain for something clever to say, Anna caught me looking. She gave me a smile that didn't reach her eyes.

I smiled back with what probably looked like a grimace, reached past her to grab a sugar packet, and spun it on the table.

The silence metastasized and threatened to become terminal. Everyone watched the sugar packet spin.

It was unnerving knowing that the perfect comment could pull us out of the death spiral we had fallen into, that the one to make it would be the hero of the evening, and not being able to string two coherent words together.

All I needed was a running start and I could do it, but I couldn't beat the long jump record from a dead standstill. In the end, our salvation came from the most unlikely source.

"Mark plays guitar," Heidi said.

Anna turned her blue eyes on me. "Really?"

Until then I had not realized just how blue those eyes were. Not golden as I had imagined. Blue as the field upon which Betsy Ross had stitched thirteen stars. Blue as the Sunday afternoon before school starts. Blue as a day-old bruise. Blue.

I had to blink to keep from falling into them.

"Yeah," I finally blurted out.

"Anna sings at our coffee shop," The Hose said.

"You have a coffee shop?" Heidi asked.

"It's an outreach thing. Saturday nights in the fellowship hall."

"What do you sing?" I asked.

"'Day by Day.' You know, from Godspell."

"Cool."

"A few songs from the Love Song album."

"Hey, your stuff is ready," the girl hollered from the counter.

The Hose and I retrieved the order. I got an extra straw and shared the float with Anna.

"I can play 'By My Side,'" I said.

"I like that one. Maybe you can come next week and we can do it."

That sounded like a perfect plan to me. "How about 'Turn! Turn! Turn!' by the Byrds?"

"Who?"

"You know The Byrds. The band David Crosby was in before Crosby, Stills, Nash, and Young."

"Who?"

Could she really not know about CSNY? "There's no way you could listen to the radio without hearing CSNY. 'Teach Your Children.' 'Woodstock.' 'Almost Cut My Hair.'"

"Oh." She seemed to pull away from me without even moving. "I don't listen to secular music."

It was like all the air had been sucked from the room. How could it be possible that this beautiful girl sharing a Black Cow with me would voluntarily deny herself the transcendence of the Beatles, the Stones, Led Zeppelin, Jethro Tull, Simon and Garfunkel, Chicago, Yes, the Doobie Brothers, Elton John, Rare Earth, Janis Joplin, Cat Stevens, just to name a dozen.

"James Taylor?"

She shook her head, obviously clueless as to his countless accomplishments.

My PK brain searched for a way out of the hole I was digging. "Well, that's okay. Solomon wrote 'Turn! Turn! Turn!'"

"Solomon who?"

"The Solomon. King Solomon. Son of David and Bathsheba."

Anna frowned. "How is King Solomon on the radio?"

"He's not. But the words are from Ecclesiastes. 'To everything there is a season and a time to every purpose under heaven.'"

"Ah." She was back in her element. "Ecclesiastes, chapter three, verse one."

"Right." I didn't know the address, but I knew the verse.

"That's okay, then."

I glanced at Heidi. She shrugged. I sipped the float and pondered this revelation.

Evidently this was going to be tougher than I thought.

CHAPTER SEVEN

The weather warmed up the next week. Five days before Christmas, it was in the seventies again.

Since the weatherman on the Beaumont station said it would get colder for Christmas, I spent the afternoon on my bike doing my paper route. Each week I rode seven miles on back roads that would more aptly be called sand pits to net five dollars a week selling Grit, a family newspaper out of Pennsylvania.

First I biked past Parker's place. He and his pickup were nowhere to be seen, but one whiff of the scorched bones of the gazebo brought back vivid memories of his face illuminated by firelight, whiskey, and a renunciation of his newfound faith after his wife left him for being too religious. If the fire hadn't burned the thing down, his words would have.

That was barely a month ago. A month since Jolene humiliated me in front of the whole school. Thoughts of her quickly turned to thoughts of Anna and the coffee shop gig only three days away.

As I worked my way through the client roster, using the sentiments of the season to sell back issues to those who had missed them, I went over the chords to the songs Anna and I would perform. My fingers were still sore from multi-hour practice sessions. I wanted it to be perfect.

My efforts at up-selling paid off, making up for the lost five dollars of janitor revenue by the time sunset arrived. The temps had dropped into the lower sixties by the time I rounded a corner down in the bottoms. The familiar green Pontiac sat parked with the perennial tendril of smoke rising from a hand hanging out the driver's window.

I pedaled up to the passenger side, leaned the bike against the fender, dropped into the passenger seat, and tossed a paper in the back seat.

Vernon Crowley nodded and held out a dollar, his usual 300-percent tip, and a Coke. I would have preferred a Dr Pepper, but Coke was Vernon's soda of choice and I wasn't raised to look a horse in the mouth, gift or otherwise.

I'd picked up Vernon as a customer back in the summer, when I'd extended my route farther into the river bottoms. In the past five months, we'd established a pattern. I saved him for the end of my route, calculating my arrival according to the available light.

My aim was to catch him on the bare hill where he came every day to drink and smoke and watch the sunset. And watch the girl in the clapboard house across the road. It seemed to me that she draped herself across the porch swing like a cat taunting a dog on a chain.

Vernon was a World War II vet, his unlikely jet-black hair showing a trace of grey at the temples. The wide face, bushy eyebrows, and flat nose gave him a slight Eskimo air. The last three fingers on his left hand were missing a few joints, the story for their absence never the same twice. He held a Lucky Strike between the stubs of his middle and ring fingers so that when he took a drag the hand covered the bottom of the face like a man who has just blurted out an impolite term in mixed company.

I took a swig of the palate-cleansing carbolic called Coke and tilted the can toward the empty porch swing across the road. "This was the warmest day all month."

"I think she's skedaddled. Ain't seen her since the last time you were here."

That time Vernon had been well into his cups before I had even arrived. I had kept my distance for a month in deference to the threat of Deacon Fry, watching my step.

Vernon took a swig from his can, and the fumes of whiskey wafted across the space between us. I evaluated his condition from the corner of my eye. It was early and he was more alert and animated than last time. I should be able to keep my promise to Dad about being "wise as serpents and harmless as doves."

Yeah, I know, but that's how he talks. It was something Jesus said to the disciples before he sent them out two-by-two "as sheep in the midst of wolves." Maybe that was the problem. I always went out one-by-one. If I had a partner, it might make a difference, but a PK is more often than not on his own.

This time I would probably be able to make my exit without having to drive a drunk vet home and further jeopardize Dad's tenuous relationship with Deacon Fry.

"How's things with that little firecracker?" Vernon asked after a long silence. He had offered dubious counsel on matters of love the day after the Sadie Hawkins dance debacle.

I let the silence ripen before I answered. "We called a truce."

"Keeping yer distance, are ya?"

I grunted in the affirmative.

I thought of telling Vernon about Anna but couldn't think of a way into the conversation without an outright declarative statement such as "I got me a new girl now," which was not exactly accurate, nor was it consonant with our relationship or my grammar.

We were more for the occasional laconic observation separated by long minutes of reflection and sipping of our respective beverages while watching the sun disappear behind the world. Except for when Vernon got worked up and climbed up on his soapbox in precarious balance, usually fomenting about women and their capricious ways. That was not the conversation I desired at this moment. More something along the lines of the beneficent hand of fate and love at first sight.

Not Vernon's strong suit, I suspected. The first time I drove him home, his wife knocked him off the cinder block steps to his trailer, the next she sweet-talked him into the door and dismissed me to ride my bike home. He didn't seem qualified to provide encouragement or counsel in my present circumstance.

I finished off the Coke and opened the door. It was after five, and twilight was in full swing. "Better get home before it gets too dark."

Vernon took another hit off his augmented Coke and arrested me with a hand on the shoulder. "Don't you worry none, Mark boy. Yer time is gonna come."

I froze in the action of exiting the Pontiac and turned back to catch his glassy-eyed stare. "Which time?"

"There's a woman out there for ya. Choose carefully. Don't rush into it."

The aroma of booze and smoke intermingled in the cool air of the car. I came to a full stop and looked at him more carefully. Vernon was getting blurry around the edges. Not as bad as last month but definitely enough to advise a prompt exit in deference to my promise. "Okay."

He didn't relax his grip on my shoulder. "I never had a son of my own, but I'd like to think if I did, he'd be like you."

Like me? Confused? Tentative? Naive? What was he cutting his Coke with? "How do you mean?"

"Maybe you don't always do right, but you mean right, and that'll take you a fur piece down the road. You'll figure it out soon enough."

I chewed on this for a longish bit, his hand warm and damp on my shoulder. I looked into his broad, flat face. Despite the alcohol glaze, I saw something down in there, something real. "Thank you," I finally said.

Vernon squeezed my shoulder and pushed me out the door. "Now you git home and thank yer mama for what she done for ya."

"Yes, sir." I slung my Grit bag over my shoulder, mounted my trusty Spyder bike, and pushed off down the hill.

CHAPTER EIGHT

As I pedaled furiously down the dirt road in the falling dark, I came upon a Chevy pickup from the forties up on a jack. It looked more rust than Detroit steel. A large, lumpish figure crouched next to it, wresting a tire off the wheel. As I pulled alongside, I recognized Jimbo Perkins, called Jumbo Perkins by everyone except to his face.

We had been estranged since four years ago when one of my experiments had culminated in a pine log knocking him halfway into next week. Up until a few months ago when I had, as far as he knew, bagged a six-point buck single-handedly with a .22, earning his eternal respect.

I pulled the bike over.

Jimbo looked up. "Flat."

"I see that. Need some help?"

"Sure. Hop up in the bed and throw down that spare."

I climbed over the tailgate, dug around in a pile of chains and lumber and tow sacks and beer cans, and eventually found a tire. I wrestled it over the edge of the bed to Jimbo, who took it with one hand and tossed the other to me. I ended up atop the detritus in the bed with a flat tire atop me. By the time I clawed my way out and back to the dirt road, Jimbo was pulling the jack out and throwing it in with the rest of the mess.

"Hey," Jimbo said.

"Hey yourself," I replied.

"I don't care if yer pappy is a preacher, yer a okay guy."

"Thanks." What else could I say? He loomed above me like Sasquatch.

"I'm taking Lulu out this Saturday. Thelma's not doing nothing. Why don't you come along?"

The prospect took my breath away, but not in the way Anna did. I met Jimbo's sister Thelma at recess my first day at Fred Elementary years ago. She was hanging upside down on the monkey bars, her ponytail dragging in the dirt, two pudgy hands gripping her plaid skirt in a half-hearted attempt to cover her chunky thighs and large pink panties. She graced me with an inverted smile filled with crooked teeth like vandalized headstones in a neglected graveyard.

I found enough breath to choke out a reply. "I have a gig Saturday."

Jimbo frowned, shaking his head like a bull confronted by a particularly flamboyant matador. "You can't gig no frogs in December."

"I mean, I'm playing guitar in a coffee house Saturday."

Jimbo smiled. "Where at? Thelma loves guitar music. We can all come and go out for beers after."

I turned a full-body shudder into a shiver and grabbed my jacket from the handlebars, facing a serious dilemma on multiple levels.

First the obvious problem of burying this idea of a date with Thelma. Second, accomplishing the primary goal without being pounded into the sand like a tent stake, because I doubted that Jimbo's newfound regard for me as a stellar human would survive me disrespecting his sister by turning down such a generous offer. Third, going out for beers was not only illegal, given my age, but would, I suspected, violate my vow to Dad in the wise-as-serpents-and-harmless-as-doves department.

I pillaged my brain for some response and came up empty. I bought time with a direct answer. "Woodville."

"Woodville?" Jimbo replied in wonder as if I had said Paris or Katmandu. "All the way up yonder?"

"Yeah." My muscles relaxed from the tempered-steel level to ironwood.

"That's plumb in the middle of Tyler County. Miles from a beer store."

"Sad but true." For the first time I blessed the day I helped with Dad's grassroots effort to defeat the local option election and keep Tyler County dry.

"Maybe next weekend."

"I'll be busy through the holidays," I answered a bit too quickly.

Jimbo frowned. "Holidays?"

"Christmas. Monday."

Jimbo grunted.

"And New Year's. And Valentine's Day. Washington's birthday. Flag Day."

The frown didn't fade. "When is Flag Day?"

"I think it's on a Saturday."

"Football's over. We can do Friday too."

"It might be on a Friday."

"Well, Thelma's sweet on you. Got her heart set."

"Oh . . . Ah," I said as sincerely as I could.

"So Friday?"

"This Friday?"

Jimbo responded with a single, annoyed nod.

"I have Christmas stuff. Shopping and all that."

"Next Friday?"

"We're visiting family in Port Arthur."

"The next Friday?"

"That might be Flag Day. I'll check my calendar and let you know."

Jimbo smiled. "Okay. Can I give you a ride anywhere?"

"I'm going the other way."

He frowned again. "Don't you live t'other side of the highway?"

"Yeah, but I have to deliver some papers." I held up my Grit bag.

Jimbo grunted, perhaps not clear on what papers were and why I would deliver them.

I mounted my bike and headed back toward the bottoms, glancing over my shoulder until Jimbo's taillights disappeared around the bend. Then I turned around and headed home, unsure how long I could fend off the kind offer of a double date from hell.

CHAPTER NINE

On the eve of Christmas Eve, I pointed the lesser of the two family cars north toward the county seat.

Heidi rode shotgun. The guitar I had bought last year at a Western Auto store in Silsbee for $35, cardboard case included, lay in the back seat, daring me to remember the chords to "By My Side." Even when I remembered them, the F-sharp minor tended to sound less like music and more like someone dragging a corpse in a tow sack down a staircase, the head thumping on every step.

Heidi prattled in her trademark random-word-association style, touching on the dorm mother at Merle Bruce Hall who was a notorious stickler when it came to curfew and PDA, the difficulty of tracking the suitcases in *What's up Doc?*, whether Jackson Browne was a Christian based on the phrase "There's a seabird above you gliding in one place, like Jesus in the sky" from "Rock Me on the Water," and how eating pickled okra before going to bed gave her weird dreams. A mere sample. I didn't have the presence of mind to attend the entire thirty-minute peroration.

On the radio, the college station out of Beaumont offered Neil Young singing "Heart of Gold," but as we headed north, the Woodville station interspersed it with Mason Williams singing "You Done Stomped on my Heart and Mashed that Sucker Flat."

I remained silent, tapping the steering wheel nervously for a host of undisclosed reasons. In addition to the aforementioned troublesome matter of playing "By My Side" from front to back in one go, there was the detail of this being my first time to play in public.

Not counting the time a year ago when I played an original song at the high school talent show and my chord chart fluttered off the stand into the orchestra pit, and I improvised an amalgam of lyrics that, instead of melting the heart of Becky Tuttle as planned, had convinced the regrettably bovine Thelma Perkins that I harbored a long-standing and deep-seated love for her, with unforeseen implications that had ultimately flowered three days ago into an invitation from Jimbo to a double date.

I definitely wasn't counting that on my résumé. In fact, I was willing to undergo shock therapy to erase it from the collective consciousness in general and my consciousness in particular.

But my main source of disquietude lay in the uncertainty regarding The Inscrutable Case of the Irish Spring Angel, the prevalent question being "did she or didn't she?" Like me, that was. Was she interested in me qua me or merely in my offices as accompanist to her budding career as a singer of religious pop songs?

If it were merely the one, could I somehow leverage it into the other? My track record was less than promising on that score.

With these troubling ruminations played out against the soundtrack of "Don't Let the Stars Get in Your Eyeballs," overlaid by Heidi's uninterrupted monologue, we rolled into the thriving burg of Woodville.

The coffeehouse, if you could call it that, was really the church fellowship hall with a corner set aside as a stage and half the fluorescent lights unscrewed to cast the room into a dungeon-like gloom. A group of church kids turned to stare at us silently as we entered.

My guitar case granted us a bit of street cred as I approached the stage. The Hose emerged from a closet with a rat's nest of mike cables, spied Heidi, and shoved the mess into the hands of a pimply kid in a plaid shirt and jeans.

I steered clear of the lover's reunion, set my guitar by the scarred upright piano on stage left, and offered my services to the kid.

He regarded my latest fashion statement—baggy maroon-and-white plaid pants and a cranberry shirt, both with wide cuffs, finished off with navy-and-white patent-leather shoes—and hesitated.

I took the cables from his hands and began to create order from chaos as he beat a hasty retreat out the door without a backward glance. I contemplated my sartorial choices until Anna walked in.

She appeared to be dressed for Halloween as a hippie in a fringed leather jacket over a paisley shirt and bell-bottoms that could have doubled for the Liberty Bell. Her ears peeked through the strands of straight blonde hair held close to her head by an elastic Indian-patterned headband.

I had never seen anything more endearing.

She scanned the room, zeroed in on me, took in my outfit in a glance, and said, "Cool."

"Dig the headband," I managed to croak out.

She smiled.

To cover my ineptitude, I ran cables from microphones to the Peavy mixer on stage right. She sat down at the piano and played the opening chords to "Morning Has Broken." It sounded just like the record. I was out of my league on more levels than one.

Then she began singing. It was like hearing the first Bird on the first Morning fresh from the Word. I realized I had never heard her voice, just the choir as she sang with it. She could have looked like Thelma Perkins and at that moment I would not have cared. Well, not much.

I realized that all my tortured conjectures of "Did she or didn't she" were irrelevant. Only a fool would believe he could deserve this, or even aspire to it. I whispered a prayer of thanks that I had not also volunteered to sing. And that I had learned the truth before making any embarrassing overtures.

Anna finished her warm-up as I snapped the last cable into place.

I walked to the piano. "You like Cat Stevens?" Perhaps she had unplumbed popular music depths heretofore undiscovered.

"Cat who?" she asked.

"That song. 'Morning Has Broken.'"

"It's an old hymn."

"Oh."

Before the silence descended into a death spiral, The Hose rescued me by flipping on the mixer and creating an ear-splitting feedback somewhere above middle C. I leapt to the mains and slammed them down to zero.

"Now that I have your attention," The Hose boomed. Cheers and jeers answered him.

As I adjusted the line volumes to a more reasonable level and inched up the mains, the milling crowd dropped their hands from their ears and drifted to the folding chairs scattered in front of the stage, evidently regulars familiar with the drill. So much for the outreach thing. These were all church kids, compliant and domesticated. Not a bad boy in the crowd.

The evening progressed in a manner familiar to any habituate of institutional-based attempts at cultural relevance. Much like a white-bread choir singing spirituals, the dialect executed with perfect pitch and practiced precision.

I sat in with Anna on the two songs we had arranged to play, and I didn't completely disgrace myself, so I counted the night as an unqualified victory.

Afterward the regulars slunk away to their private pursuits. The Hose and Heidi faded into the background, engrossed in each other's charms.

Anna and I glanced at our respective siblings and quit the scene posthaste. We ended up outside on the front steps of the church. Despite the fact that it was two days before Christmas, the temperature had made it into the high sixties that afternoon. But now it was in the mid forties at best.

We watched the locals cruising past on Saturday night in search of good times. We huddled together against the cold, Anna in her leather fringe, me in my denim jacket.

"I think we reached some people tonight," Anna said.

"No question." I had no doubt because I was one of them. And here I was, still beside her. Alone. "You were amazing."

Anna bumped her shoulder against mine and smiled. "I was just a vessel."

A fine vessel. Fit for royalty. Like . . . like . . . "Your navel is a rounded goblet that never lacks wine."

"My . . . what?"

I had no idea where that came from. It seemed I had turned into Jolene's twin brother, Bubba, spouting off random verses at inopportune moments. "Song of Solomon. I think."

"Chapter seven, verse one," Anna supplied.

"Right."

"Why did you say that?"

"Well . . ." Why did I say that? It was just what came to mind. She was a vessel and . . . "If you're a vessel, then you're a vessel fit for a king. Like Solomon."

After a long silence, she said, "You think so?"

"Of course," I replied without thinking. There was more where that came from. Your eyes are doves. Your lips a scarlet ribbon. Your breasts—well, anybody who has read the Bible knows it's not PG-13. Far from it. I settled for something safer. "There is no flaw in you."

"Chapter four, verse seven," Anna whispered, her breath warm and moist and cinnamony in my ear, sounding as if she had carefully noted all of the intermediate verses that I had skipped. A cloud of condensation from her words clouded my vision.

I turned to face her and my lips brushed hers, she was that close. She leaned toward me. I did the same. The next thing I knew, we were kissing.

Now a gentleman doesn't kiss and tell, and my daddy didn't raise a boor, so I won't give a play-by-play account of the next epoch of my consciousness, with or without color commentary. All I can say is that I ceased to notice the traffic passing by, the temperatures diving toward freezing, or the motion of the earth spinning on its axis at a thousand miles an hour while simultaneously hurtling through space at sixty-seven thousand miles an hour.

I will satisfy your prurience to the degree of revealing that we didn't approach Song of Solomon levels, or even a PG rating, but for this PK, it was transcendent.

Eventually Heidi and The Hose discovered our lair. The Hose kidded us all the way to the car, where I stole a final secret kiss from Isa and drove the thirty miles home completely oblivious to inconsequential details like Heidi's running monologue, or the disintegration of the Paris Peace Talks, or the return of Apollo 17 with the last astronauts to walk the moon, or the posted speed limit.

One thought replayed in my mind, a condition unique in my experience. I am my beloved's and she is mine.

CHAPTER TEN

The next morning, I marked an item off my bucket list.

Played a real gig. Sort of.

Hey, I told you gentlemen don't kiss and tell. Not even to their diary.

In Sunday school, I positioned the front legs of the metal folding chair precisely two inches in front of the third scuffed salmon-colored tile, a spot determined by years of experience to allow me to lean back against the institutional green wall at the optimum angle, and took my place in the natural order of things as if nothing had happened the night before.

Jolene plopped down next to me. "Morning."

I grunted as per custom. Act natural was my byword.

"Yer looking mighty satisfied with yerself. What's her name?"

I jerked my head and almost upset the natural order of things. Settling the chair back into a sustainable configuration, I replied, "Whatever do you mean?"

"It's probably best to stick to yer own kind, anyway."

"I'm sure that means something."

"Preacher's kid. Birds of a feather."

As I attempted to formulate a deflectionary response, Scooter started the lesson. Scooter was the youngest deacon, with a pretty wife named Brenda and two preschool kids. His blond flat-top could rival a pool table for a precision surface, and he topped off his Sunday-go-to-meetings with a bolo tie. In my mental yearbook, I had voted him Most Likely To Go To Bible College.

The lesson was strictly boilerplate Christmas stuff, nothing everybody in the room hadn't heard a million times, which left me free to ponder Jolene's cryptic comments.

Somebody had been talking, and it certainly hadn't been me. I shot a piercing glance at Heidi. She smiled and winked. She clearly had not been discrete, but she and Jolene didn't mix. Obviously the word had traveled.

I shifted my visual interrogation to Hannah. She ignored me the way a dog avoids your gaze when you come home and discover the contents of the garbage can strewn about the kitchen. Evidently none of the Cloud women knew the gentleman's code. I wondered who Mom was talking to right now.

When the bell rang, I dropped my chair onto all fours and shot out of the room like an acrobat from a cannon, but Ralph caught me in the hall.

"I hear ya moved on up to a city girl. What's she like?"

I whirled on him and froze him with a stare. "How did you come by this information?"

Ralph rocked back on his steel-tipped boots. "Uh, Bubba."

Great. The news was spreading like a tumor. Next thing the paparazzi would spring up out of the baptistry in the middle of the sermon and start snapping photos.

"Was he wrong?" Ralph asked.

"Yes! I mean . . ." What did I mean? I hadn't done anything to be ashamed of. I just liked to keep my personal life exactly that. Personal. Fat chance for a PK living in the fishbowl.

"So he was right?"

"Look, I don't ask what you do with Squeaky on Saturday nights."

"Nothing. We don't do nothing."

"Ha!" I replied, and I meant it to sting. I suspected they did a lot more on Saturday nights than Anna and I had done, but I didn't press the point. I spun on my heel and found my regular spot in the sanctuary three pews behind Deacon Fry's regular spot.

I wondered if Anna was going through the same thing in Woodville. Probably not. She didn't have a sister to announce the glad tidings of great joy to all people. The Hose might be a dunderhead, but my money said he knew and kept to the gentleman's code.

In that moment, I felt an unlikely kinship with him. I closed my eyes and took deep breaths until it passed.

Mercifully, the service started before I was accosted again. The typical three Christmas carols and a hymn and then the sermon.

If the Sunday school board had chosen to stick with tradition in the quarterly, Dad took a different tack. His sermon consisted of a litany of all of the altercations between Jesus and the legalistic religious leaders of his day.

The teachers cry blasphemy when Jesus tells a paralytic his sins are forgiven. Jesus says, "What is easier: to tell him his sins are forgiven or to tell him to get up and walk?" And then heals the guy. Bam!

The teachers accuse Jesus of associating with sinners. Jesus says, "It is not the healthy who need a doctor, but the sick." Bam!

The teachers complain that the disciples unlawfully pick heads of grain as they walk along to eat. Jesus invokes the example of David eating the consecrated bread from the altar when they were hungry and says, "The Sabbath was made for man, not man for the Sabbath." Bam!

As the holy smack down continued, from my vantage point I watched the red rise up Deacon Fry's neck like a thermometer in July until his bald head looked like an Easter egg.

I wondered what Dad was at with this sermon. Not even two months ago he had told me to be careful of drawing Deacon Fry's ire and now here he was taunting the man.

Dad finished with the woman found in adultery. This was the ultimate example—a woman clearly guilty under the law and deserving the scriptural punishment. Death. But Jesus said, "Neither do I condemn thee. Go and sin no more."

That put the last nail in the coffin. Deacon Fry cleared his throat like a man on the verge of a heart attack.

Dad concluded with the knockout punch. "This is the gospel. Not a list of boxes to check to make sure you're okay. You are no longer subject to the law.

"The good news of the child in the manger isn't about a cute baby born in a stable. It's that this very child grew to be the only innocent man to walk this earth and then offer himself freely as a sacrifice to save you from yourself. When you open your gifts tomorrow, think of this ultimate gift of freedom from the law."

From the tensed tendons and trembling I saw in front of me, I thought Deacon Fry might just rocket up out of his favorite pew like Apollo 17 and proceed right past the moon without stopping for a single round of golf.

When Dad asked Scooter to lead the benediction while he took his position at the back of the church to shake hands, Deacon Fry pushed through the crowd, past Dad, and sat in his black LTD until his wife caught up with him.

As he tossed gravel on his way out of the parking lot, I waved and called after him. "Merry Christmas." Although the prospect seemed doubtful.

I turned back and looked the question at Dad.

He shrugged. "Just following orders, son."

CHAPTER ELEVEN

While Dad evidently felt free to smack Deacon Fry about the head and shoulders with the undiluted gospel, I was fairly certain this license didn't extend to me.

I continued with my assigned serpents-and-doves drill, surreptitiously monitoring Vernon Crowley as he supplemented his Coke and making a discrete exit when he slipped past the pleasantly-loquacious level to the feeling-no-pain level. I also avoided any double dates with Jimbo and Thelma to Hardin County beer joints, which was a bit easier as we never crossed paths except on occasions when statistical probability took the day off.

I invested in a long-distance call to Anna to sit through awkward silences as I struggled to dredge up clever banter. Perhaps some advance planning would have served me better, but with no older brother to initiate me into the sacred rites of the girlfriend thing, I had to wing it.

The day after Christmas, Mom got another call from Aunt Catherine, followed by an extended conference with Dad in the study. I had forgotten about Claire and her domestic crisis. The phone call renewed my speculations.

Word had it that underage drinking had gotten her kicked out of the private school in Houston. Maybe it was the same thing in the boarding school. Or maybe something worse. These things tended to escalate. Maybe she really was pregnant and her parents wanted to disappear her into Fred, out of sight from their rich friends.

After dinner Heidi and Hannah stood to clear the dishes, but Dad waved them off the chore.

"You can do that later. We have something to discuss."

The girls sat back down.

"Next week Uncle Roger and Aunt Catherine are bringing Claire up to stay for a while."

I perked up at this revelation. Had I guessed right?

Always first to grasp the implications, Hannah asked, "Where is she going to sleep?"

"In the study."

Dad's study was on the opposite side of the house from the other bedrooms. It had a bed and bathroom with a shower.

Hannah shrugged her approval, glad she wasn't going to have to share a room with what amounted to a stranger.

"Why?" Heidi asked.

"They're going through a tough time," Mom said. "We offered to give them a break."

"We thought Claire might benefit from a change of environment," Dad said.

"Wasn't that why they sent her to a boarding school?" I asked.

"Obviously it didn't take," Hannah said.

"An environment with a little more structure," Dad said.

"How long is she going to stay?" Hannah asked.

"She just needs someone to love on her," Mom said. "She's been through a lot."

She's put her parents through a lot, I thought.

"She'll finish out the school year at Warren," Dad said. "Then we'll see."

"Five months?" Hannah said, her voice rising.

"Don't worry," I said. "You still get a room to yourself."

"It won't be any different than having Heidi here," Mom said.

Oh, I bet it will, I thought. Very different.

On Thursday the temperatures climbed back into the sixties and I repaired to the Fortress of Solitude to ponder the unprecedented step of asking Anna on an actual premeditated date.

The Fortress was a rickety tree house built by the previous occupants of the parsonage. It jutted out over the creek that bisected the fourteen acres of church property at a diagonal. Walls on the two sides shielded the occupant from civilization (the house) and a half roof kept one moderately dry in a slight drizzle. A few improvised shelves and benches finished out the interior.

I had added some embellishments of my own over the years, most notably a secret compartment where I hid a waterproof ammunition case I had picked up at the Army surplus store in Beaumont.

In the Fortress, I mapped out the logistics like I was planning the assault on Troy.

Verify funds. Negotiate use of the car. Determine a destination consonant with Anna's preferences, of which I knew nothing other than an aversion to secular music and an apparent encyclopedic knowledge of the scripture.

That didn't suggest much. I considered falling back to the old standby—dinner at Pizza Inn followed by a movie. Finding out what was playing in the theaters posed a challenge, especially for a family that didn't subscribe to the Beaumont Enterprise.

I was startled from my intense strategizing by the appearance of a feminine head poking up through the scuttle hole in the middle of the tree house floor.

Heidi crawled from the one-by-twos nailed into the trunk of the tree and into the Fortress, hugging an available branch for comfort.

"I don't know how you can stand it up here." She peered over the edge to the ground a mere fifteen feet below and shuddered.

I suppressed my shock at seeing her. The womenfolk avoided the Fortress like a drunkard skirting a temperance meeting. "Nerves of steel." I awaited an explanation for this unprecedented visit.

"What do you do up here?"

I wasn't about to divulge such privileged information. "You're looking at it."

"You just sit around?"

"As far as you know."

"Well, okay."

She sat on a crate by the trunk. "What do you think of Claire coming?"

"It's going to be weird. I mean, we got along fine when we were in third grade, but that was a long time ago. And she's . . . put on some miles since then." Partying down with older guys, getting kicked out of two schools. I couldn't imagine what Mom and Dad were thinking.

"Yeah. And she's an only child."

"Okay." I was sure that meant something, at least to Heidi.

"She's used to getting her way, being the center of attention."

"And living in a mansion in Houston." The parsonage wasn't a dump. In fact, it was a four-bedroom brick ranch-style house with central heat and air on fourteen acres, but it wasn't a mansion by anybody's definition. And it was in Fred. On a dirt road. "And having her own car and stuff."

"You think she'll bring her car?"

I gave that a few thoughts. "That would be cool." Maybe she would let me borrow it for the alleged date I was scheming.

We sat in silence for a while, and then Heidi blurted out a question. "Hey, how would you like to double with me and Hosea?"

"Double what?"

"Double date. You and Anna. Me and Hosea."

My astonishment and relief at Heidi spontaneously providing the solution to my dilemma was diluted considerably by the realization that it came at the cost of spending an evening with Heidi and The Hose and their glutinous exchanges.

But one does not require that a gift horse step forward and assume the position. At least this one does not.

"Uh . . . okay."

And thus it was ordained.

However, the awkwardness began way before the date. The next day, Heidi tracked me down in my bedroom where I was finishing off the Poe short story selection with a rousing reading of "The Fall of the House of Usher."

She stuck her head in the door. "Phone."

A phone call for me was an event on the order of a solar eclipse. "Who is it?"

"Hosea."

I cannot say I looked forward to the conversation with any great relish. In fact, I was simultaneously filled with confusion and dread, and it couldn't be completely attributed to Poe.

"What does he want?"

"I don't know. He just asked me to get you."

I decided that whatever this conversation might consist of, it was best taken on the extension in the study rather than in the public forum of the den.

"Hello?"

"Mark? *Que pasa*, bro?"

"Uh . . . *nada, amigo*." Hey, I can hang with the best of them.

"I just wanted to have a little chat with you before the date."

"Sure, man."

"Anna is my little sister."

The man was on solid ground here. I found no point on which to contradict him. "I noticed."

"I just want to make sure you treat her right."

It took me a few seconds to dredge up a response to this one. "Okay."

"You should treat her like you would your own sister."

"I . . . uh . . . what?"

"You know. With respect and consideration."

The implications of his request struck me speechless. I had already kissed her, not something I would consider with my own sisters. And I was pretty sure The Hose had kissed Heidi more than once. Was this how he treated his sister? The thought gave one pause. More than pause.

The Hose filled the silence with more advice. "You know, just think what would Jesus do?"

I had spent the last few months contemplating that very question in a range of contexts, but this turned even my inquisitive head on its ear.

What would Jesus do on a date? A concept completely unknown in first century Judea, where genders didn't mix and marriages were arranged. There was no record of Jesus interacting with anyone romantically. I searched for some basis for extrapolation and came up empty.

Eventually the dead air weighed on The Hose like it did on Heidi. "You still there, Mark?"

"Yeah."

"So, are we on the same page?"

"Sure," I said while doubting, and sincerely hoping, that I would never find myself in the same zip code as any page The Hose might inhabit.

"Cool. See you tomorrow night."

"Sure." What else could I say?

I hung up the phone and walked away in a fog of speculation.

Heidi popped out of the living room. "What did he want?"

"Guy stuff."

"Did he say anything about me?"

"No." At least I hoped he didn't. If that treat-her-like-your-sister stuff included Heidi, I didn't want to know more about his family life.

I returned to my bedroom, but didn't pick up the Poe book. Unfortunately The Hose had led me into a line of thought that I found troublesome.

What would Jesus do on a date? It was not a context I had ever considered. For the average American teenaged male—not that I fit in that category in many respects—a date was a second-by-second negotiation in companionship versus hormones.

Dates were scored like baseball games. You struck out or made it to first, second, or third base. Or home plate, which was unthinkable for me, both in terms of aspiration and biblical morality. Applying this WWJD motif to dating didn't work against a baseline of first-century Palestine two millennia before baseball was invented.

Would Jesus kiss on the first date? Would he stop at heavy petting? Could I be struck by lightning for just considering such possibilities?

A verse sprang to my head like I was channeling Bubba. "Therefore do not worry about tomorrow, for tomorrow will worry about itself. Each day has enough trouble of its own."

I returned to "The Fall of the House of Usher" as the safer of the two options.

Chapter Twelve

For one inured to the scholarly routine of American public schools, a week of inactivity paled after a few days. I awoke on Friday with a pervading sense of ennui that faded when I realized this was the Day of the Date. I survived in a state of advanced agitation until the time came to dress for the evening.

I had outgrown, in sophistication if not stature, the white bell-bottom jeans, royal blue shirt, and flag-design socks I had amassed for my trip to The Land of Ultimate Cool last summer. And given the cultural mismatch of my baggy plaid slacks and cranberry shirt of the previous weekend, I settled on a Big Thicket staple—plaid shirt, Wrangler jeans, and my one concession to individuality, square-toed Dingo boots. I had derived a primary law of East Texas fashion. Plaid on shirts good. Plaid on pants bad.

Displaying his consummate grasp of protocol, upon his arrival The Hose came in to pay his respects to the reverend before whisking away the firstborn daughter to a night of debauchery.

Anna stood next to him, strangely shy and uncertain compared to her demeanor at the coffeehouse where she was on her home turf. Although I would have thought it impossible, it made her even more endearing, rendering me in danger of spontaneously combusting on the spot. Fortunately for all concerned, we made our exit to the sunflower-yellow Nova before anyone had to figure out how to respond to that catastrophe.

The Hose being a man of means by reason of his advanced years as a college freshman, we headed south past Silsbee to the wider social scope of Beaumont and the Red Lobster off I-10.

The drive down was an excruciating torture of proximity and inhibition. Here I was, inches from Anna but constrained by Hosea's admonition to consider this Irish Spring Angel as my sister. We had shared a moment of intimacy in the adrenaline aftermath of a gig and the sensuous words of King Solomon, but now we were back at square one-point-five, needing a running start to break out of earth orbit.

I settled on a sure-fire opener. "How 'bout them Cowboys?"

Heidi shot a puzzled glance over the headrest. I had a notorious disinterest in all things sports.

"I know, right?" The Hose exclaimed, almost swerving into on-coming traffic as he looked back at me. "Staubach comes off the bench in the playoff and totally pulls it out with two touchdowns in two minutes. Who saw that coming after the Giants cleaned our clock last week twenty-three to three?"

"Uh . . . yeah," was all I could manage since I had no idea who Staubach was, much less that we were in the playoffs.

"How do you see our chances against the Redskins Sunday?"

My gamble had taken a nasty turn and now was pointed directly at me with both barrels. "Uh, better than even I would say."

"Well, we're both even at ten and three. It comes down to whether Staubach is good enough to play after last week."

"Good point."

I glanced at Anna. Her expression said, No comment. I shrugged. She picked up the ball.

"So, Heidi, how did you and Hosea meet?"

"Oh, this is a hilarious story." Heidi turned in her seat to include us all in the conversation. "I was in the line at the cafeteria, and they had hot dogs with sauerkraut. I hate hot dogs and I hate sauerkraut even more."

In the long pause that followed this announcement I said, "That is pretty funny."

Anna giggled.

Heidi waved my comment aside. "I didn't get to the funny part yet. I asked what else they had and they said Reuben sandwiches and I said what is that and Hosea said it was a sandwich invented by the firstborn son of Jacob." She laughed like she had just delivered the punch line to a joke.

Anna and I looked at each other and then back at Heidi, not quite seeing the humor or following how this answered the question of how they met.

"He was in line behind me," Heidi added. "I didn't know him. He just said it out of the blue, right on the spot." She laughed some more.

That answered the question of the meeting, but I was still unclear on one point. "When do we get to the hilarious part?"

Heidi graced me with a glare that could have induced global warming without the assistance of chlorofluorocarbons.

The Hose chimed in, oblivious to Heidi's pique. "The funny part is that Reuben, son of Jacob, couldn't have invented the Reuben sandwich because it's not kosher. It has beef and cheese on it."

He engaged me via the rearview mirror, his eyes crinkled in a smile. I raised an eyebrow and turned to Anna. She shook her head, stopping just short of rolling her eyes. I turned back to The Hose.

"But Jacob was four hundred years before Moses and the commandments from Mount Sinai, four hundreds years before kosher laws, so his son could have invented the Reuben sandwich."

That shut The Hose down, most likely causing him to regret the idea of a double date. But Heidi's abhorrence for dead air obliterated any conversational lull. She started in on another hilarious story of how her roommate thought Hosea's kinky red hair looked just like a rusted Brillo Pad.

Heidi's monologue left Anna and me wordless, glancing at each other in an antiseptic environment that didn't offer us a path back to the romance we had stumbled upon in the aftermath of the coffeehouse gig. And so it went for the hour-long drive to Beaumont.

At Red Lobster, we worked our way through the cheese biscuits and shrimp scampi and cheesecake and then proceeded downtown to the Jefferson Theater for a showing of Sleuth with Laurence Olivier and Michael Caine.

I must admit that the subtleties of the plot escaped me as I remained fixated on one thought. I was on a date with a girl that no one, including me, would have predicted to be willing to endure more exposure to Mark Cloud than absolutely dictated by the FDA. Or the AEC, for that matter.

The drive home was like the drive down, only intensified by the realization that the window of romantic opportunity was rapidly closing.

In the darkness of the backseat, I ventured a hand between the seemingly infinite gulf of inches that separated Anna and me. My fingers found hers lying palm up on the seat. I released a sigh of relief and satisfaction when her fingers closed on mine.

My world became a swirl of sensation emanating from the warm, damp bliss of two palms pressed together. The drone of the tires on the highway became a mantra lulling me into a trance. I was aware of the chill in my toes contrasting with the warmth of my head, which could not be entirely attributed to the heater The Hose had blasting from the front seat. But my tunnel-vision consciousness focused on the few square inches of flesh in contact with the girl in the back seat.

Lost in the pheromone haze of prolonged premarital interdigitation, I barely registered the conversation from the front seat that concerned itself with people and events from that mythical land that Heidi and The Hose shared—college.

Anna and I sat side by side, staring forward like a teenaged, postmodern parody of Grant Wood's *American Gothic*, sharing a handclasp and occasional glances at each other. One thought emerged from the hormonal miasma swirling in my brain: no more double dates.

I was ready to solo. No, that wasn't quite it. I was desperate to solo. I was ready to brave the primordial seas like a latter-day Lindbergh.

But when I considered all the reasons why, it raised a most unwelcome question.

What would Jesus do on a solo date?

CHAPTER THIRTEEN

Saturday morning I cleaned the church, the fifth week making up for the five dollars I lost in November due to Jolene's perfidy. Then I set out on my Grit route and converged on Vernon Crowley's hill in sync with the setting sun.

We observed the ritual—toss the paper in the back seat, accept the dollar, pop the ring tab on the Coke, toast the dying day in silence, and take a sip.

The temperature had hit the high sixties and was still pleasant in the late afternoon. I settled back into the seat and watched the sun settle down on the chimney of the house across the road. The girl that belonged to the house lounged on the porch swing. Barely twenty by the looks of her, shorts retired for the season in favor of faded jeans and Dreamsicle-orange sweatshirt.

"She's back," I said after a few minutes.

"Guess it didn't work out."

"Or maybe she didn't run off. Maybe she just visited her grandmother for the holidays."

"Have it your way, then."

That settled things for a while. I drank my Coke and Vernon drank his Coke spiked with whiskey and smoked unfiltered Lucky Strikes and we watched the sun drop behind the world and felt the temperature drop into the fifties until it ran the girl back inside.

Long, comfortable silences were a regular item on the program in the Pontiac with Vernon. I didn't know what thoughts occupied him on these occasions. Maybe scenes from World War II, or his mercurial relationship with Gina, who was as apt to smack him with her fists as with her lips, or some other hidden pleasure or regret he had ferreted away during his five or so decades of roaming the skin of this planet.

I had a much more limited palette from which to select topics for reflection. I settled on last night and the drive back from Beaumont with Anna.

True, things seemed to be proceeding in a satisfactory manner. Contrary to all rational thought, she seemed agreeable not only to my company but also to the first stages of intimacy.

As a typical, red-blooded American male—well, perhaps not so typical, but at least possessing the usual hormones common to the species—I welcomed an escalation of affinities. But that raised an issue that I was not as eager to face head on.

Unbeknownst to The Hose, when he suggested I consider what Jesus would do on a date, he touched a nerve. In fact, I had been there before him, just not when thinking about Anna.

Back in the summer, I had run across an eighty-year-old book that suggested we should ask the question "What would Jesus do?" as we went about our lives. After much internal and external debate, I decided to take the challenge.

But now I wasn't so sure how I could reconcile that question with what I hoped would be the forward momentum of my relationship with Anna.

My experience had shown that most people interpreted their answer in a manner that coincided with their personal preferences, but no matter how I twisted my reasoning, I couldn't see Jesus in a make-out session with Mary Magdalene. Not even if he restricted it to heavy petting, as the booklets I had read on sexual purity mentioned with obvious disapproval.

Vernon interrupted my meditations before I achieved enlightenment.

"They been ramping things up in 'Nam. Bombing the hell out of Hanoi. Yer number comes up, you could be in a world of hurt. They'll need some fresh meat if they decide to ramp up for a ground invasion."

"Two fifty-eight." It was my number as of August. It meant that holders of 257 other birthdays had to be exhausted before they got to me. Even though I was at least fifteen months from having to worry about it, I kept track of such things.

"Yer okay, then."

"So far."

"It ain't nothing to hanker after."

I nodded. Despite any impression he may have formed to the contrary, I wasn't hankering after it.

"I heard tell that General Lee said it's a good thing war is so terrible or we would fall in love with it. Might be for the generals, but as one that spent months lying in trenches wondering when a bullet or a shell with my name on it would introduce itself, it ain't so lovely."

I grunted my agreement. I was much more likely to find myself on the same page with Vernon than with The Hose.

I wasn't sure what it said about me that I had more in common with a broken-down alcoholic World War II vet than a fellow PK, but I was okay with it. No matter what Deacon Fry said.

Chapter Fourteen

Sunday morning proceeded without incident. Everything was business as usual in Sunday school. And based on the sermon about taking stock of the past year and moving boldly forward for the faith into the new year, Dad had not received additional orders from headquarters to taunt Deacon Fry with the scandalous impropriety of grace.

I was thankful, as it simplified the task of collecting my twenty-five dollars without the awkwardness that arises when the paymaster has been scrambled into a frothing beast by a family member. Plus, it gave me ready cash in case I needed it for the evening.

Heidi and I had been granted a special dispensation to attend the New Year's Eve service in Woodville.

I expect you may not be familiar with the nature of such New Year's celebrations. They did not involve the traditional revelries you might associate with the numbers rolling over to zeroes at midnight. No champagne, no kissing of the most appealing individual in your immediate proximity, no drunken singing of Auld Lang Syne. Well, that might not come as much of a shock seeing as how it all went down in a Baptist church. But the reality was even more sobering.

Observations of the passing of the old and the coming of the new followed along the lines of the sermon Dad had preached twelve hours before. Singing hymns, reflecting on the past year and what you had accomplished for the Kingdom, committing to redoubling your efforts in the next twelve months.

I was an old hand and had no unrealistic expectations. But all of that paled in the light of spending the evening with Anna. I dressed in culturally suitable attire and after a drive that mixed the anticipation of the glories to come with Heidi's non-stop stream-of-consciousness monologue, I found Anna in the fellowship hall with the rest of the youth group, enveloped in the aroma of sugar cookies and red punch.

The smile that spilled across her face as she saw me from across the room could have illuminated the Dark Ages, and at that moment I felt that God was in His heaven and all was right with the world.

Together we navigated the usual elements of such an evening, singing songs and praying prayers and holding hands when the opportunity presented itself. As directed, on small squares of paper we wrote one thing we were thankful for about the old year and one thing we pledged to do during the new year, addressed them to ourselves with a note to be opened 365 days later, and stuck them between the pages of our Bibles.

That reminded me that a similar envelope nestled somewhere in my Bible. I flipped through the pages until I found it and read the note from my former self. As I scanned the vow to focus more on Jesus and less on the world, I recalled that it was written in the aftershock of Becky's strong declaration of undying friendship. At that point, I would have joined the Foreign Legion if they had staffed an East Texas recruiting office.

As appropriate as these traditions might have been, they held little significance for me by virtue of their familiarity. These were things I had done for much of my short life, and they seemed to have no more relevance than brushing my teeth every morning.

As the midnight hour approached and we all bowed our heads in the harsh fluorescent light of the fellowship hall to pray in the new year, I slipped my hand into Anna's, a gesture now blessedly familiar from a few hour's practice, and breathed a sincere prayer of thanksgiving for this recent development.

My mind wandered as it inevitably did during these extended prayer times, searching for something authentic to keep me centered on the purpose of the service, something rendered doubly difficult by virtue of my heightened awareness of Anna's proximity, the sensation of her fingers intertwined with mine, the side of my thumb sliding across her manicured thumbnail. This was not going to work at all.

Instead I forced my attention onto the one true moment I could lay claim to. Could it have been only six months ago, the night in a camper trailer park in Needles, California that I stumbled upon a crossroad of the soul? That night I faced a choice between the aloof Mysterious Stranger that Samuel Clemens had planted in my mind and the stranger in a strange land who had beckoned to me with the open arms of a sacrifice nailed to a cross.

That night I had chosen, with all due deliberation, the way of death-to-self that the cross symbolized. The death of the seed falling into fertile ground, the death of one who would find his life by losing it.

In the months since that moment, I had vowed to find out what it meant to walk in the Way, to ask the hard questions and stick around for the hard answers.

Despite all my flailing as a teenager, trying to discern how my little thread was woven into the warp and woof of the tapestry of life, all my fumbling attempts at romance and relevance, all my amateur experiments with faith, I knew that this was the real question.

What does it mean to act justly and to love mercy and to walk humbly with your God?

I felt my hand, sweaty and twitching in Anna's, and wondered if I was willing to hear the hard answer to my question of what Jesus would do on a date.

For a second a thought flitted through my mind of the irony of tradition, of all the cheesy exercises, platitudes, and catchphrases designed to bring us to the point of authenticity, which instead blunted the double-edged sword that divided soul and spirit and judged the thoughts and attitudes of the heart.

But only for a second, because even that cynical thought was nothing more than a distraction, a way of avoiding the painful discipline of facing the question without flinching.

Here I was in this unlikely inner sanctum of scuffed linoleum and institutional lighting, come solely for the opportunity to sit next to this girl with the hopes of taking it to the next level. Yet I once again found myself face-to-face with troublesome questions, required to make a decision with potentially unwelcome but inescapable implications. This time it came down to whether I was man enough to honor my vow to act as Jesus would act, even if it meant sacrificing everything I had hoped would happen between Anna and me.

Okay, I said to the man with his arms outstretched. My daddy didn't raise a coward. Do your worst. I'm in it for the long haul and you know it.

He didn't answer. He just smiled and nodded.

I let out a long breath, let go of something that I couldn't exactly put my finger on, and opened my eyes.

The room was a bustling activity of kids folding chairs and tearing down the PA. I blinked and looked over at Anna.

She stared back with a quizzical smile. "Hey."

"Hey." I shuddered and rolled my shoulders. "It's over?"

"Yeah, for a while now."

"Oh." I realized I was still holding her hand. Tightly. I relaxed my grip and stood.

"Come on," she said.

"Sure."

Anna led me by the hand out of the fellowship hall, out of the building, and into a stand of trees behind a school bus painted with the church logo.

The temperature had fallen into the forties and the world smelled as crisp and clean as an over-starched dress shirt. I could see her breath in the light of the mercury vapor lamp over the parking lot as she turned to me, pulling me closer. We were inches apart.

"It was a great service, wasn't it?"

The visible vapor of her breath enveloped me. Sweet, cinnamon.

"Sure." I responded from the mental fog that lingered from whatever had happened back there in the fellowship hall.

"The Spirit was so strong."

Something had been strong, of that I was certain.

I stared into her blue eyes, her straight golden hair rendered in sepia tones by the security light. A million love songs ran through my head.

As if by prior agreement, we moved into the shadows of the small grove. She leaned against a tree trunk. With a confidence I had never known, I brushed her hair back with my fingers, leaned forward, and kissed her. She kissed me back.

Life as I knew it ceased to exist. The only thing left in the world were the few centimeters of our lips touching, three strands of her hair rolling between my fingers, her cinnamon breath like a cloud around our heads. I pulled back slightly and luxuriated in the feathery touch of our lips brushing against each other.

After a minute or a lifetime, reality asserted itself.

"What did you pray for?" she breathed, her eyes still closed.

I didn't have an answer that would make sense, not even to her, one of the holy tribe set apart from our classmates. What could I say? That I had reluctantly re-upped for service? That I had agreed to the Way even if it didn't get me what I wanted right now? Maybe what she wanted too.

She searched my face, waiting for an answer.

I couldn't bear to voice the answer I had pledged just minutes ago. Instead, I stole a final kiss, my fingers tangled in her hair, and pulled away with a conscious effort.

"Me too," she said.

I doubted it.

Chapter Fifteen

It was a New Year's Day without precedent. I was suffering from a religious hangover.

A year ago I would have given a year's Grit and janitor wages for the chance to kiss a blonde-haired, blue-eyed girl in an oak grove at midnight.

Now I was in the Fortress of Solitude braving the fifty-degree weather with a thermos of hot Dr Pepper and lemon, the smell of a fireplace wafting across the creek from a house over by the church, the radio verging between "Kiss to Build a Dream On" and "It's in His Kiss" and wondering if I would ever kiss a girl again, much less what would happen on my date with Anna Friday night.

Only twelve hours ago, I had signed a blank check, pledging once again to do whatever Jesus would do without knowing what the heck that might actually be.

The sticking point was that I was determined to stick to it. I could cheat, go back on my vow, and no one would ever know, not even Anna. No one except me, and that was the problem.

And to make things worse, I had just foresworn an actual oasis after years of chasing after mirages in the desert.

I had spent the last two years planning the land-war-in-Asia campaign against the romantic defenses of Becky Tuttle, only to see it crumble all at once in a shower of dogwood petals.

I had been seduced by my own delusions into making myself a target for the incorrigible whims of Jolene Culpepper's carnival-house mind. In both cases, I quit the battleground in defeat without a single kiss to show for my considerable efforts.

Now I was on the inside track with a willing participant from my own tribe, a "walled garden," to borrow from the lexicon of King Solomon, who was the archival reference on such matters, and I had nobbled myself at the post.

Worse yet, in absence of a definitive answer to the question, I had resolved to pull back to a defensive position and play the highly attentive eunuch until I received conclusive directions from high command.

Or I could forget all that esoteric stuff and just play it by ear.

The Dr Pepper with lemon served to keep the nerve endings tingling and the mind focused on my dilemma. I had recovered from the point of despair and was engaged in negotiating a compromise, when Heidi materialized in the scuttle hole, clinging to the trunk of the tree like a cat dangling above a pond.

I jumped up, depositing the contents of my mug in my lap and squelching a cry of alarm. Companions in the Fortress of Solitude were rare. Female attendees were strongly discouraged.

"Hey," Heidi quavered.

"Hey." I shoved a crate in her direction, close enough to be polite but not far enough to encourage comfort.

She looked at it, gauged its distance from the tree trunk, and shook her head. "I'm good."

"Suit yourself." I tried to wipe the Dr Pepper from my jeans, but it had already soaked in. "To what do I owe this rare and officially discouraged visit?"

"Oh, nothing." She peered over the edge to the pine straw five yards below and renewed her grasp on the tree. "Just thought I'd come visit my little brother."

"Mighty neighborly of you."

"Why do you come up here?"

"To be alone."

"Oh," she said, evidently immune to the implications.

I poured a drink into the lid of the thermos and held it out to her. "Hot Dr Pepper?"

She considered loosing her grip to the point of freeing a hand to take the cup and declined.

I shrugged, poured the contents of the lid into my empty mug, and awaited enlightenment as to her true purpose for braving the dizzying one-and-a-half-story heights of the Fortress.

Once she reconciled herself to the security of her position, Heidi finally spoke. "So, Claire comes tomorrow."

"Oh, yeah." I had been so consumed by my own concerns that I had forgotten about the imminent arrival of the prodigal daughter.

"What do you think got her kicked out of school?"

"Beats me." The options were too numerous to enumerate.

"Maybe Hannah guessed it."

"Pregnant?"

Heidi nodded with a shudder. Perhaps wondering what it would be like to come home from school with an announcement like that. "If I was pregnant, I'd want to disappear too."

"Where to?" Where does the person who lives in the middle of nowhere go to disappear? "Maybe Aunt Catherine and Uncle Roger would return the favor and take you in."

"I wouldn't want to live in Houston."

"Not even in the richest part of Houston?"

"Especially not there. I'd always feel like everyone was staring at me."

"Which they might be, if you were pregnant."

She shuddered again and changed the subject. "What do you think of Hosea?"

"The Hos—I mean, Hosea? He seems like a nice guy."

"Yeah, that's what I think."

I certainly hoped so. Why else would she endure his company?

We sat in silence for a while. Or at least, I sat. She continued to cling to the tree.

"But how do I know if he's The One?" she asked.

"Which one?" I had heard the capital in her question, but wasn't ready to concede it just yet.

"You know what they say. Don't date someone you wouldn't be interested in marrying."

"Oh. That One."

"Yeah."

I took on my best fatherly voice. "You haven't done anything you would regret, have you, little lady? Should I arrange for Uncle Roger to take you back with him tomorrow?"

She nailed me with a glare. "That's not funny."

I thought it was quite funny, but I was willing to concede that not everyone in our area code shared my sense of humor. I returned to the matter at hand. "Well, if that's what they say, are you interested in marrying him?"

"I don't know," she said in a voice that made it more of a lament than a statement.

It hit me. Here I was, isolated in my fortress of self-doubt while she had been wrestling similar questions in her bedroom or wherever Heidi went for her wrestling matches.

I was within a frog's hair of asking her what she thought Jesus would do but reconsidered when I realized that the question hadn't brought me any closure. I didn't have any fatherly advice. Appropriate considering I was far from being a father. I hoped.

"He's nothing like Dad," she said.

I considered that the understatement of the millennium, but I was curious about her reasons for this confession. "In what way?"

"Well . . . he seems too . . . eager to please."

I found myself speechless at this encapsulation of all the nameless reasons I felt The Hose was an inappropriate companion, delivered with an economy of words unexpected from Heidi.

"Quite." I pulled the cap from the thermos, poured another serving of hot Dr Pepper, and toed the crate farther until it nudged her leg. I held out the cup.

Heidi eyed the crate and the cup, inched down the trunk like a gunshot victim sliding down a wall, sat on the crate, and took the cup. Perhaps she had found her unwelcome answer. If so, like a Cloud, she would make her peace with it soon enough. As we enjoyed the contrast of the chill afternoon and the warm Dr Pepper, I envied her that baby step closer to some kind of resolution.

Eventually Heidi filled the silence as it seemed she was put on earth to do. "Anna seems nice."

"Yep."

"And she's very pretty."

"Yep." If she wanted to start an argument, she was going to have to take a different tack.

"Do you think she's The One?"

The question had never entered my pea brain, at least not in the sense I sensed she meant. The One. The Mate. For Life. "Hey, I'm only sixteen. I'm not even eligible for the draft."

"You know what I mean."

Unfortunately I did know what she meant, and I suspected it was just a different form of the question I had been wrestling with for the last few days. "Yeah, but that doesn't change my answer."

She dropped her voice an octave. "You haven't done anything you'll regret, have you, little man?"

I choked on my Dr Pepper. This snarky young woman was not the Heidi I knew. Perhaps The Hose had effected an unexpected transformation upon the firstborn of the Cloud clan. "Not yet," I said after recovering from my coughing fit.

"Well, you better not."

"Yes, ma'am." I tilted my cup to her and drank deeply, afraid that I had already done just that with my New Year's Eve pledge.

Chapter Sixteen

Tuesday was a cold, drizzly day, what I imagined England must be like if it were covered with pinewoods bisected by dirt roads. I walked around the house with my bathrobe over my pajamas like Sherlock Holmes in his smoking jacket, until Mom made me get dressed because it was almost time for lunch and the arrival of the Foxes.

As I pulled on jeans and a flannel shirt, I wondered what Claire looked like now. I had last seen her on Thanksgiving in third grade, the year I had been dragged from Fort Worth to Ohio for Dad's first church after seminary.

Back then she looked kind of like that girl in *The Parent Trap*, but with a rounder face. Blonde and bouncy and innocent, like a little choir girl. While the adults sprawled in front of Uncle Roger's big TV to sleep off the turkey and dressing in the vicinity of the game, we kids spent the afternoon in Claire's room playing board games. Sorry, Life, Monopoly—she had dozens of them.

As we left one game after another strewn about the room in the orgy of competition that afternoon, one thing became clear. Claire hated to lose. And despite her angelic appearance, she didn't blink at using whatever means necessary, including inventing rules and cheating, to assure a win. Perhaps a harbinger of her future if anyone had known how to read the signs.

I buttoned my shirt and wandered around the house in anticipation of their arrival, painfully aware of the smell of roast beef and dinner rolls pervading the rooms.

An hour later, the doorbell rang. I knew it was a stranger because everybody we knew came to the garage door. Hannah emerged from her bedroom and followed me to the living room, where Dad opened the front door.

"Come on in out of that mess before you get thundered on," he said.

Aunt Catherine came in first. Her coat looked like it had been made by Cruella de Vil's tailor. You could see the resemblance to Mom right off, the slender build, the blue eyes.

Mom came in from the kitchen and gave her a big hug.

Claire walked in, avoiding eye contact by glancing around the room, as if counting the exits and preparing for an ambush. She wore a peacoat over a cashmere sweater and gray wool pinstripe bell-bottom slacks. Like a Lands' End model.

She hadn't changed but she had. She still had the short blonde hair, round face, and naive appearance, although now she looked less like Hayley Mills and more like Patty Duke. But she no longer seemed bouncy and irrepressible. More like a cornered animal hoping to slip away unnoticed.

"Hey," I said.

She glanced up at me with a fleeting smile. "Hey." She looked over at Hannah and Heidi, nodded, and then was obscured as Mom hugged her.

Uncle Roger came in last, wiping his feet and closing the door. "Matthew." He shook Dad's hand. "The traffic was horrendous. I think they set loose every fool between here and River Oaks and put them on the road." He ignored Dad's outstretched hand and tossed his coat on the couch. "Nice place." He surveyed the living room with a gaze that calculated the value of everything it scraped across. "I don't remember the last time I drove on a dirt road."

"We can certainly help you fill your quota in that department," Dad said.

"I'm sure you're hungry, and it's been ready for an hour, so let's go right in," Mom said.

Mom delegated coat management to Dad and then led everyone, not to the kitchen table, but to the dining room. The Foxes were completely unaware of the minor miracle of dinner on the dining table, which had been buried in detritus from the day we moved in five years ago. Mom gestured Heidi and Hannah into the kitchen to retrieve lunch.

Dad took the spot at the head of the table, Uncle Roger to his right and Aunt Catherine to his left. Claire took in the arrangement and chose the middle seat next to her mother. I followed her, taking the last seat on that side of the table.

The women came in with the rest of the food and filled the remaining chairs. Mom sat next to Uncle Roger, leaving the end of the table to us kids.

Uncle Roger reached for a dinner roll just as Dad began to pray. He froze for an instant, his fingers an inch from the basket, and pulled his hand back. The last time he'd said a prayer over a meal was probably around the last time he'd been on a dirt road. If ever.

Dad finished the prayer, and the food distribution began. Dad asked about the weather down in Houston, even though it was only a couple of hours away, and what route they took and such things. Apparently he was intent on keeping it light during the meal.

Unlike Dad, I didn't have the gift for small talk, or large talk, for that matter. As the silence on the kid end of the table grew to insurmountable proportions, I tried to think of some topic that wasn't fraught with land mines. The usual openers wouldn't work. How's school? A non-starter. What have you been doing lately? Equally unacceptable.

I thought about what I had been doing lately that could serve as a conversation starter. Let's see, I'd spent the last six weeks obsessing over a girl, stealing a few kisses, trying to discern what Jesus would do on a date, avoiding a not-so-gentle giant who wanted me to date his sister upon pain of . . . something certain to be unpleasant, and dodging the sights of a misanthropic deacon.

With such a wealth of material, it was hard to know where to start. Perhaps I should recite "Jabberwocky" or recount the plot of the latest episode of *All in the Family* or *Columbo*.

As usual, Heidi filled the silence. "Claire, what does your Dad do?"

Claire looked up, startled. "About what?" she asked quietly.

"For work. What's his job?" Heidi actually blushed. "I'm sorry, I should know, but it's been so long since we've seen y'all."

"Oh." She appeared to be relieved. "Besides make my life miserable you mean?"

I looked over at Uncle Roger. The adults were involved in their own conversation and paid us no mind.

"He doesn't get paid for that," Hannah said, smiling.

"No, he does it for free."

"A labor of love?" I asked.

"Hardly," Claire said with a cutting glance at Uncle Roger.

"So what does he do?" Heidi liked closure.

"Oil. As he likes to tell everyone, he has a gazillion patents on gadgets that oil people can't live without."

"Have you been to Paris?" Hannah asked.

Three teenaged heads turned to look at her at the foot of the table.

"What?" Hannah said. "I just wondered."

"Sure," Claire said.

"Venice?"

"Yeah."

"London?"

"Of course."

"You're so lucky."

Claire looked at Hannah for half-a-minute before responding. "Have your parents sent you to the psych ward?"

Hannah stared back.

"Just wondered," Claire said.

Conversation kind of withered after that. We finished the meal and had strawberry shortcake for dessert.

Dad leaned on his elbows over his coffee. "Claire, we're looking forward to having you here this semester."

"Thanks," Claire said without expression.

"It's a shame we haven't had the chance to know you well for the past few years, but we hope to remedy that in the coming months."

"Uh . . . okay," Claire said. "Me too," she added quickly as if she just realized how her earlier responses had come across.

"Good luck." Uncle Roger held his coffee cup up to clink Dad's cup.

"Roger," Aunt Catherine said. "That's not helpful."

"Or maybe I'm the only one willing to acknowledge the elephant in the room." He took a swig of coffee and stared at the cup as if reproving it for not holding something stronger. "Do you believe in miracles, Matt?"

"If you had seen this table yesterday, you would believe in miracles too."

"Unlike many of my peers, I have always been a rational animal." Uncle Roger killed the coffee, frowned at the cup, and turned to Dad. "Speaking of miracles, didn't Jesus turn water into wine?"

If the room was quiet before, it got twice as quiet now.

"So I have heard," Dad responded.

"But you don't have any in the house."

"Correct."

"Or whiskey."

"You're two for two."

"Damn shame." Uncle Roger glanced at Claire and back to Dad. "You might change your mind after a few weeks."

"Roger," Aunt Catherine said, louder this time. "If you can't be civil, maybe we should leave."

Uncle Roger stared at her for a few seconds and then turned to Dad. "Make a note of that, Matt. Honesty is not always the best policy. Having manners are nothing more than practicing the art of lying in a flattering way. Who said that? If somebody didn't, they should have."

Claire looked back at Hannah and whispered. "Still think I'm lucky? Just be glad it's me moving in and not him."

"Perhaps good manners is just leaving hurtful things unsaid," Dad said.

"Ignoring the truth, you mean."

Dad adjusted his Buddy Holly glasses and focused his most serious look on Uncle Roger. "That is not at all what I mean, Roger. For example, we all recognize the truth that you are acting like a jackass, but under normal circumstances it would not be necessary to point it out."

Whoa! I glanced at Claire. She looked at Dad as if, despite his receding hairline and budding paunch, she wanted to kiss him. Uncle Roger stared back at Dad like he'd bent down to pet a kitten and had instead been mauled by a tiger.

Aunt Catherine had a blank expression on her face as if Dad had suddenly started speaking in tongues. Mom looked at Dad with a small smile mixed with a hint of a frown.

Into this silence of staring, Uncle Roger burst out in laughter. "Matt, I take back everything I've said about you. You're alright." He patted Dad on the arm. "But you'd be even better if you had a liquor cabinet."

"To the contrary, I don't think anyone is better off with a liquor cabinet."

"You might be right, Matt, you might be right. I can't believe I'm saying this, but maybe religion is just what Claire needs. God knows reason hasn't worked."

"You say that as if you think reason and religion are opposites."

"Of course. Religion is irrational by definition."

"You've been reading the wrong dictionary. Christianity is the most rational response to the human condition. But you're not really interested in that subject, so let's not bore everyone."

"You might be surprised, Matt."

"I frequently am," Dad said. "How about you?"

"Rarely."

"That's too bad. The universe is a mystery that surprises anyone who is paying attention. You need to get out more."

Uncle Roger laughed again. "Maybe so. I drove out here to hear a hick-town pastor tell a world-traveled millionaire he should get out more. That's surprising."

Dad looked away from Uncle Roger with a trace of boredom and turned to me. "Mark, why don't you help Claire get her things into the guest room?"

I looked at Claire. She shrugged. As I stood up Uncle Roger tossed the keys at me. They hit me in the chest and fell to the floor.

"Don't get any ideas. I have the odometer memorized," Uncle Roger said.

I grabbed the keys and Claire followed me out to the car.

"Is Uncle Matt always like that?" she asked as we walked through the garage.

"No occasion for it down here. We may be hicks, but we have manners."

"Roger thinks everyone who wasn't born in New York City is a hick."

I hid my shock at her calling her dad by his first name. "He's always like that?"

Claire nodded.

"Why did your mom marry him?"

"Believe me, I ask her that at least once a week."

A silver Mercedes 280 sat on the wet sand of the driveway. I stepped out into the drizzle and opened the trunk. It held three large suitcases, two bulging garment bags, and a king-size makeup case.

"Do you have any clothes left at home?" I asked.

"Tons.

"I don't know if all this will fit in the closet." It was a guest room designed for weekend visits, not boarders.

"Seriously?"

I wrestled two suitcases out and half-carried, half-dragged them through the side door. Two more trips got the rest of it.

Claire stood in front of a closet about the size of a refrigerator. "We might need to order a wardrobe." She looked at the chest of drawers in the corner. "And an armoire."

"I'll ring Jeeves and have him send them right up."

That earned me a smirk. "I'll give Mom a tour of my new lodgings, and I'll have what I need by next week." She sat down on the bed.

I sat in the swivel chair at Dad's desk. "I thought you'd bring a car."

"I lost that battle. Mom was okay with it, but your dad vetoed it."

"Not your dad?"

She snorted. "Roger would have sent a fleet of cars and built a garage with an upstairs apartment for the driver if it would have got me out of the house before Christmas."

I tried to imagine what it was like to live in a war zone. Maybe like renting a room from Deacon Fry. I shook the thought off. I would be drooling on my straight jacket in two days.

Claire pulled a pack of cigarettes and a lighter from her purse. Virginia Slims.

"You can't smoke in here," I said.

"Seriously?"

"Serious as lung cancer."

"But it's raining outside."

"It'll be worse inside if you light that cigarette in the house."

She frowned. "Seriously? But Uncle Matt's so nice."

"Oh, he'd be nice about it, but by the time he was done you'd be crawling under the bed to make it stop."

Aunt Catherine walked into the middle of the room, stood between the desk and the bed, and surveyed the room. "Very . . . cozy."

"Looks like I'll be living out of suitcases," Claire said.

"We'll see what we can do, sugar." Aunt Catherine held out her arms.

Claire stood and dutifully received a hug while looking over her mom's shoulder at me.

A honk sounded from outside the driveway. Aunt Catherine pulled back from Claire and looked at her with misty eyes. "You take care, sugar, and be nice. Please." She turned to me and tousled my hair. "Good to see you again, Mark. You take care of my baby."

"Yes, ma'am."

Claire looked at me and shook her head.

As Aunt Catherine walked out, Hannah and Heidi came in.

Heidi stared at the pack of cigarettes in Claire's hand like it was a rattlesnake. "Uh, we thought we'd help you unpack."

Claire slipped the cigarettes back into her purse and pushed it aside.

"And pick something out for school tomorrow," Hannah said.

I stood up. "As fascinating as that sounds . . ."

"For starters, you can't wear pants unless it's freezing," Hannah said.

"Seriously?" Claire's incredulous stare jumped from Hannah to Heidi to me.

"Literally. Like thirty-two degrees."

I escaped to the kitchen.

Mom looked up from the sink. "Just in time to help with the dishes."

"They already gone?"

Mom handed me a plate. "Claire's going to need your help adjusting to school with all the hicks."

"And a bigger closet."

We washed dishes for a while.

"So, what did she do?" I asked.

"That's not the important question," a loud voice said from behind me.

I flinched and dropped a plate. It landed on another plate and they both broke. "Dang it!" That would probably cost me a week of cleaning. I turned around. Dad stood next to the kitchen table.

"It's what she does from here on out that matters." Dad stepped to the sink, assessed the casualties, and looked at me. "Guilty conscience?"

I looked at his feet. He had changed to his slippers. "Sneaky Dad." I dumped the fragments in the trashcan. "Somehow I don't think Deacon Fry is going to be a big fan of Claire." Especially if she went out to smoke with the old men between Sunday school and the service.

Dad smiled. "Maybe she'll drive him to drink."

"But what if she does the same thing that got her kicked out of school? Whatever that was."

"Then we'll deal with it."

"You don't care what Deacon Fry thinks?"

"Of course I do. But I care about the gospel more."

Somehow I didn't think that would cut much with Deacon Fry.

CHAPTER SEVENTEEN

On the third day of the new year, a suitably chill and dreary morning, Hannah, Claire, and I walked the three hundred yards through a misting rain to the elementary school to catch the bus.

The locals eyed Claire in her knit cap, peacoat, plaid wool skirt and white stockings, but she smiled at everyone we introduced her to. When the bus arrived, Hannah invited Claire to sit with her friends for the half-hour ride to Warren. Before I had even found a seat, she was chatting with the gang like they were old friends.

I dropped next to Bubba. I didn't chat with him, even though we'd known each other since sixth grade. I just nodded. He nodded back. Fog crept out in wisps from the unbroken wall of pine trees lining FM 1943 and shrouded the creeks under the five bridges. It was like riding the bus through Mirkwood.

My thoughts turned to the upcoming weekend. The standard off-the-shelf date in Tyler County consisted of dinner and a movie. For the marginally-employed teen, that meant the buffet at Pizza Hut followed by a few hours of hand-to-hand combat at the drive-in.

But in that way lay madness for a reluctant pilgrim such as myself. Might as well take the vow to turn vegetarian and then make reservations at Steak and Ale.

Paul had even warned against such things when he said, "Make no provision for the flesh." Or, as translated in the Revised Cloud Version, "Don't take a very kissable and accommodating chick to the drive-in when you have vowed to keep things on a sisterly level."

That was one of the many problems with being a PK. Disappointing verses popped into one's head at the most inconvenient times.

Postcards from Fred

In the fog-muted silence of the bus ride, painfully cognizant that the date with Anna loomed two days in my uncertain future, it occurred to me that Bubba might have some insight on the question that I had been kicking around for a week. And unlike my other classmates, he probably wouldn't use it as an opportunity to tease me mercilessly, despite being related to Jolene. Or maybe because of it.

A mere six months ago, Bubba had been a more or less typical Big Thicket teen. Except for that one thing, being the twin brother of Jolene, an accident of birth that had consigned him to a childhood as the target of Jolene's ceaseless practical jokes.

Then last summer Brother Bates had swept into town for the summer revival like an avenging army. By the end of the week, dozens of classmates that I had never suspected of harboring a single spiritual thought between them had fallen prey to his scorched earth campaign.

Even I had been sorely tested. I narrowly escaped by virtue of a healthy dose of faith from an early age, which served as a vaccination sufficient to safeguard against any serious case of religion, even when most of my classmates succumbed to the epidemic of revival.

Bubba was one of the casualties and took to quoting conversation-stopping verses at every turn like Poor Richard collecting aphorisms for the sequel. But unlike the typical convert of the hard-sell tactics of practitioners like Brother Bates, for Bubba the effects didn't wear off after a few weeks or months. Six months later he was still snapping out verses like a pan of Jiffy Pop on the stove, and the range of his knowledge was encyclopedic.

"Hey," I ventured.

"Hey."

"Remember that book about what would Jesus do?"

"Course."

After a longish moment, I finally blurted out the question. "What do you think Jesus would do on a date?"

Bubba considered me for a second, then turned to look out at the fog and consider the question. He didn't answer quickly, hampered no doubt by the complete lack of any reference to the romantic life of Jesus in the gospels.

72

"Well," he finally said without turning to look at me. "Like your daddy said a few weeks back, he didn't condemn the woman caught in adultery. But he didn't condone her behavior either, so he doesn't seem to be okay with fooling around."

"Not if you're married to someone else, anyway, I guess."

Bubba shook his head. "Or shacking up even if you're not. Don't forget the woman at the well."

Leave it to Bubba to hit all the points. "Touché."

"Then there's the dinner with Simon the Leper where a woman kissed his feet and washed them with her tears and dried them with her hair."

"You're saying that was a dinner date?" Anna's hair was long enough, but somehow I doubted she would be up for crying on my feet and kissing them at the Pizza Inn buffet. In fact, when you came right down to it, I wasn't sure I was up for it either.

"I'm saying there's not many stories about Jesus and women, and that's one of them."

"But how does that help?"

"You want me to make stuff up?"

"Maybe." At this point, I was willing to dig out the Catholic Bible from Dad's study and search the Apocrypha if it would settle the question before Friday.

Bubba cleared his throat and did a creditable impression of Dad. "And lo he came upon a hot babe at the Dairy Queen and spake unto her, saying, 'Verily I say unto thee, set aside thy Dilly Bar and let us go down unto the drive-in and steam up the windows.' And there was much rejoicing, and in the due course of time, he gave unto her his class ring and his letter jacket."

"What's that from? Second Permutations, chapter five?"

"I think it's the Acts of the Undergraduates."

I sighed and stared out at the fog. Evidently I was on my own with this one.

"Is it the girl from Woodville?"

I nodded without looking up.

"Preacher's kid, I hear."

I nodded again.

"She against kissing?"

"Not so as you'd notice."

He chewed on this a while. "So, what's your problem?"

That was a good question.

As I got off the bus in Warren, Jimbo loomed in front of me. I ground to a stop and Bubba ran into me.

"Friday," Jimbo said and gazed at me intently.

"Friday?"

"Yeah, Friday."

"What happens Friday?"

"Date. You, me, Thelma, Lulu."

Although it hardly seemed possible, I had completely forgotten about the Jimbo date dilemma.

I stepped aside and motioned Bubba on, but he just stood and watched. I turned back to Jimbo. "This Friday?"

"Yep."

"Two days from now Friday?"

"Yep," Jimbo said again, but with waning enthusiasm.

"I . . ." I was on the verge of explaining that I had scheduled a date with another girl, but just in time I realized that in this case honesty might not be the best policy. Particularly if I wanted to retain the basic arrangement of my physiognomy.

My practice of tucking away useless facts in the recesses of my cavernous brain rescued me. "Sorry. That's the twelfth day of Christmas." I ignored Bubba's snort, keeping eye contact with Jimbo.

"Christmas? That was last week."

I nodded. "The first day of Christmas was last week. The twelfth day of Christmas is January fifth. You know, twelve drummers drumming and all that."

"Yer doing something fur the twelfth day of Christmas?"

"Yeah, we usually do . . . uh . . . a drumming thing. Family tradition. Eggnog. Wassail. Turkey. The drumsticks, of course."

Jimbo's eyes, already too close together to be altogether pleasing, narrowed in an unattractive and menacing manner. "You messing with me?" He turned to Bubba. "Is that a real thing, what he said?"

"Oh, yeah. Very big with the Eastern Orthodox," Bubba answered.

I shrugged an apology to Jimbo and stepped around him.

74

Bubba followed me into the school. "Is that a real thing, what he said?"

"Which one?"

"You and Thelma."

"In Jimbo's mind, yes."

"So somewhere in your future is a date, either with Thelma or a paramedic."

I nodded and shuddered.

"So what are you going to do?"

Another good question. He was on a roll.

In Spanish class, I was working through the conjugation of a dozen irregular verbs when the door opened and an office assistant came in, followed by Claire. Every eye followed them as they walked to the front and talked to the teacher. The assistant left, and the teacher turned to the class.

"Class, we have a *nuevo estudiante*, Claire Foxe. And, as it turns out, she is *la prima de* Mark. Let's welcome her. *En español, por favor.*"

Claire smiled. A few students muttered, "Hola, Claire." The rest just stared at her as she took the empty desk behind me.

"I didn't know you were taking Spanish," I said.

"I was taking French. Until now."

"What's the rest of your schedule look like?"

"They gave me the same schedule as you, except for band, when I have something called Home Economics."

"Oh, you're going to love that."

"What is it?"

The bell rang before I had to explain it to her.

At lunch Claire followed me to my usual spot with the gang. She had already met Bubba and Darnell at the bus stop.

"Hello, boys," she said. "You're looking chipper today."

They looked at each other, then at Claire, then at me. We didn't typically enjoy the company of the delicate gender at our table. Before they could respond, C.J. arrived.

"Whoa! Mark, is this your new girlfriend from Woodville?"

I ignored Claire's questioning glance. "This is my cousin. Claire Foxe."

C.J. dropped his tray on the table next to Claire's. "How does a bozo like you end up with a fox for a cousin?" He sat down and turned to Claire. "How is it that we've been deprived of your company lo these many years?"

"I'm from Houston."

If she didn't have his attention before, she did now. "Where in Houston?"

"River Oaks," Claire said.

That stopped the normally irrepressible C.J. dead in his tracks. He stepped up the intensity of his inspection, taking in the Oxford shirt and plaid wool skirt.

"You've maybe heard of it?" I said.

C.J. held out his hand, palm up. "C.J. Hecker at your service. Also from Houston in a more humble ZIP code."

Claire reached to shake his hand, but he bowed and pressed her fingers to his lips.

"Your slightest wish will be my command."

"Hey, put a governor on it, C.J.," Darnell said. "You're going to blow a gasket before dessert."

"Right now I wish I had a cigarette," Claire said.

C.J. leapt from his chair. "I shall attend to it immediately."

"And a Coke," Claire shouted to his departing back.

As we ate, we watched C.J. bounce from table to table and then disappear into the hall.

Elrick arrived, pulled back C.J.'s chair, and dropped into it. "Is this the cousin I've been hearing about all morning?"

I waved a fork in his direction. "Elrick, Claire. Claire, Elrick. Spanish for 'The Rick.'"

Claire set down her fork and held out her hand. "Hey."

"Actually, it means 'noble ruler' but I don't usually mention it." Elrick shook her hand. "Are you a PK too?"

"A what?"

"Preacher's kid. Like Mark and me."

"Oh no." Claire laughed. "Far from it."

C.J. returned holding up a can of Coke and two cigarettes like winning lottery tickets. "I didn't want you to get lonely."

"Since when do you smoke?" I asked.

"New year's resolution. Try one new thing every day."

Claire stood, plucked a cigarette from C.J.'s fingers, tucked it behind her ear, grabbed the Coke, and slipped her arm in his. "Lay on, MacDuff."

Like a knight with his lady, C.J. escorted her out a side door, heading for the gate behind the band hall where the smokers congregated.

Evidently Mom's concerns about Claire fitting in at school were misplaced. She'd been on the premises four hours and she already had them lined up and taking numbers.

"How does a frog like you end up with a princess for a cousin?" Elrick asked as the door closed behind them.

I didn't like this recurring theme. "Have I ever mentioned how hideously ugly you are?"

"If she's from Houston, why is she going to school here?" Darnell asked between bites.

"She's living with us. Moved in yesterday."

"Maybe I should come out to Fred and visit you," Elrick said without taking his eyes off the door Claire had disappeared behind. "We PKs should stick together."

"You going to take up smoking too?" I asked.

"I got a corncob pipe stashed away somewhere."

"I'd keep it right where it is if I were you," I said. "Bad for your health."

Chapter Eighteen

Thursday started off with a touch of fog, but it cleared up by lunch, and in the afternoon it got into the sixties. After school I holed up in the Fortress to consider the morrow and my long-anticipated first date.

In an effort to make no provision for the flesh, I had amended the typical date agenda by substituting the seductive privacy of the drive-in with the libido-quashing exposure of the bowling alley.

The fact that in normal circumstances I would rather submit myself to Jimbo for ritual vivisection than go bowling was testament to my commitment to the vow.

I was thus engaged in reflection when a head poked up through the scuttle hole. Claire surveyed the glory of the Fortress before entering. "Whatcha doing?"

"Thinking."

"I didn't know you had a tree house back here."

"It's called the Fortress of Solitude." I put special emphasis on the last word.

"Like Superman." She took a seat on the crate by the trunk and pulled her Virginia Slims out of a pocket in her peacoat. After she lit the cigarette and flipped the lighter closed with a practiced move, she took in the view of the creek meandering through the woods between the parsonage and the church. "I like it up here."

"Who wouldn't?" It looked like Don Henley was right. You call someplace paradise, you can kiss it goodbye. First Heidi, now Claire. Next thing I'd have to mark off a parking lot, hire attendants, and charge admission. Add handrails so I wouldn't get sued when some idiot fell off the side.

Claire held out the pack of cigarettes with one sticking out.

That was all I needed, to get caught smoking in the Fortress. "No, thanks. I'm trying to quit."

She laughed and slipped the pack into her pocket. "You know, you're not half bad for a preacher's kid."

"Aw, shucks, ma'am, you're too kind," I drawled.

"Oh," she said, blushing. "I didn't mean that the way it sounded."

"Of course not."

"Well, I guess I probably did," she admitted and took a drag off the cigarette. "I was a little nervous about coming here, but anyplace is better than home."

"What, did you think we had three-hour prayer meetings every night?"

"Pretty much."

"You seem to be getting along okay at school."

"My philosophy is that no matter where you go, there's always someone ready to party. You just have to find them."

"Even in Fred?"

"Oh, yeah," Claire said. "You know Jimbo? He's cool."

"Jumbo Perkins? Cool?" Despite the mind-blowing vastness of the galaxy, I couldn't imagine it containing a planet on which Jimbo would be considered cool. Perhaps the planet Bluto, world of bullies.

"Jumbo? Is that what he's called?"

"Not to his face."

"He's sweet." She flicked ash over the side of the platform. "He's absolutely devoted to his sister."

I could vouch for the devoted part. Not so much for the sweet part. "How did you learn all this in just forty-eight hours?"

"Bumming a cigarette is the best conversation starter in the world. You can meet a lot of people if you smoke."

I hadn't considered this aspect of the habit, but it made sense that people bonded over a shared addiction.

"I have an idea," Claire said. "Let's go to Fred Grocery and buy a six-pack and bring it up here."

"We have Dr Pepper in the fridge."

"No, I mean beer."

I considered her through narrowed eyes, doing my best to conceal how close my head had come to exploding. "Not from around here, are you?"

"Does it show?"

"First off, Tyler is a dry county. Selling beer is illegal."

"Seriously?"

"Second, neither of us is eighteen, so buying beer is illegal."

"I have that part covered."

"Third and most relevant, you bring beer up here and that will be your last cigarette, just before they give you the blindfold and ask for any last words."

Claire frowned. "I thought you were cool."

"I'm cool. Just not suicidal. Baptists and alcohol are like . . . a mongoose on a cobra."

"I take it the two don't get along?" She tapped out another cigarette and lit it off the first one.

I couldn't find the words to express the unthinkable horror of Dad finding me in the Fortress with a beer.

"So you don't drink beer, then?"

"I tried it once. Wasn't my thing."

"You just need to find the right brand." Claire rubbed the first cigarette out on the floorboards and raised her hand to flick it over the edge.

"Hup," I interjected. I held out a hand. "You can't go leaving evidence lying around like that."

She looked at the butt. "Evidence?" She handed it to me.

I pulled out a coffee can from my stash of supplies and deposited the butt. "It's not like beer. But when you're a preacher's kid, it's better to fly under the radar whenever possible."

"But I'm not a preacher's kid."

"A mere technicality that I'm not sure Deacon Fry would recognize."

"Who?"

"You'll find out on Sunday. For now just remember the motto. Fly under the radar. Think of yourself as a spy behind enemy lines. Blend in. Don't attract attention."

"What happens on Sunday?"

"Church."

"Seriously?" Claire choked on her cigarette. "Nobody said anything about going to church."

I'm afraid I made no effort to disguise my incredulity. She might have been a player in her world, but she was an ingénue in mine. "You're living in a preacher's house. Tell me you didn't think you could skip church."

"It never came up."

"Taking showers probably didn't come up, either, but it is a requirement."

"Well, everybody takes showers."

"And everybody in a preacher's house goes to church. At least everyone in this preacher's house."

She smoked contemplatively. "Will I die of boredom?"

"That's optional."

A suppressed squeal startled me. "Oh, I know a little secret about you."

I didn't like the sound of that. "I don't have any secrets." Not many, anyway.

There was my little WWJD project that was causing me such grief. There was the little thing of helping Jolene play jokes on her dates. If that got out, I could be strung up on the flagpole while every male in three counties cheered on. Then there was the secret of how I bagged that deer with a .22 rifle last November, but nobody would believe the truth even if I told them. Which I absolutely was not going to do.

"You have a secret admirer."

"Thelma? A not-so-secret admirer, you mean."

Claire smiled. "Jimbo says you have a date with Thelma."

"Jimbo is delusional. Have you seen Thelma?"

"You'd make a cute couple."

"And you'd make a beautiful corpse, but I'm not wishing it on you."

I thought about Claire waltzing into Warren High, smiling and bumming cigarettes and making more friends in two days than I did in two years. Was it the money? I figured that no matter how much money Dad had, I'd still be the same geek. Or would I?

Did she do the same thing at her boarding school in the East? Just show up and own the place within a week? And if so, why did she get kicked out? If she did get kicked out. I realized I had taken Hannah's theory for fact without verifying it.

"So, what are you in for?" I asked.

Claire squinted one eye through the smoke and frowned at me.

"Well, you got sent down for something, and it wasn't good behavior."

"Ah." She took a few more drags of the cigarette. "It was a little experiment in free market economics."

"You're a casualty of capitalism?"

"There were a few other things, but my little venture was the thing that tore it."

"This is at the school up in . . ."

"Philadelphia."

"What was this little venture, exactly?"

"I sold copies of tests before they were administered."

"You . . ." My mouth kicked into neutral as my brain tried to wrap itself around the idea. "You sold tests?" It seemed Claire couldn't open her mouth without dropping another mind grenade. I wondered how long she would last in Fred.

"It's not complicated. People wanted tests. I sold them. Simple supply and demand."

"Okay, but how did you get the tests in the first place?"

"Social engineering."

"Which being translated means . . ."

"I knew a girl who worked in the office. Charity case."

She stopped. I motioned for her to elaborate.

"I had her bring me the trash from the teacher's workroom."

It was the simplicity of genius. I studied this rich girl in front of me in her rich clothes smoking her fashionable cigarettes. Round, genial face framed with thick blonde hair. A smile like she just won the spelling bee by spelling "ingenuous." Lose the cigarette and she looked as wholesome as fresh-baked bread.

"How did they catch you?"

"I'm a softie."

She was as bad as Dad about doling out information in chunks. I frowned and she continued.

"A business like this is only sustainable if it flies under the radar, as you are so fond of doing."

I acknowledged her jab with a bow.

"I limited the sales to one per class, at most two. But before too long I had girls lined up with sob stories of how they were going to lose their allowance or their scholarship or get kicked off the polo team or whatever if they didn't make an A on the test du jour."

"And you relented."

"You can guess the rest."

One thing bothered me. "But why start the business at all? You didn't need the money."

"You shouldn't underestimate the importance of financial independence. But it's not the money. It's the game."

Ah. It was about winning, whatever the cost. She hadn't changed that much since third grade. But neither had I if I thought about it.

"Well, if you straighten up and fly right, maybe you'll get time off for good behavior."

Her expression turned hard. "For what? To be sent back home?"

Well, there was that. One question remained. What would she do next? For some reason I didn't hold out much hope that it would stay under the radar.

I shivered in the gathering gloom. "Let's get back to civilization."

Claire stubbed out her cigarette and handed it to me. "You're driving me back to Houston?"

"Very amusing," I said as I stashed the butt in the coffee can.

As we entered the back door, Dad passed by with a handful of notes he had retrieved from his study that was now doubling as Claire's room. He stopped and tested the air.

"Have you been smoking?"

"Me?" I asked. "No."

He turned to Claire. "And you?"

She smiled and shrugged. Her first line of defense seemed to be a ready smile. She was cute enough that it probably worked more often than not.

But Dad wasn't a soft touch. He held out his hand. "I'm afraid I'll have to confiscate your contraband."

"Seriously? It's not drugs. Just cigarettes."

"And you are below the legal age for buying cigarettes. We're very happy to have you here, but in this house we honor the laws of the land, even the inconvenient ones."

Claire's smile faded as she stared at Dad's hand. Then she dug around in her pea jacket, pulled out the pack of Virginia Slims, and set them in his hand.

Dad slipped the pack into his shirt pocket and held out his hand. "And the rest."

I couldn't tell if Claire's expression indicated surprise or exasperation, but she reached into her coat pocket again and pulled out five loose cigarettes.

"Thank you," Dad said. "I'm sure you can find a much more profitable and satisfying use for your spending money."

"Perhaps," Claire said.

After dinner Claire, Hannah, and I repaired to the living room to listen to albums and do our homework. Claire brought a small elephant figurine with holes in it. She pulled the top half of the elephant off, dropped a cone of incense inside, lit it, and replaced the lid. Smoke crawled through the holes and a sweet, musky scent spread into the air.

"Cool." I put on the Presti and Lagoya guitar duets. "Music to do algebra by," I said.

Hannah rolled her eyes. Claire shrugged. I sat down to work algebra problems.

We were about halfway through side one of the album when the door jerked open and Dad strode in.

"I thought I made myself quite clear on the matter of smoking."

He stopped in front of the three of us on the couch and focused a steely stare, as if he had positioned us there for interrogation. As his eyes sought out the source of the sin, his expression morphed from outrage to confusion.

I pointed my pencil to the stereo behind him where the elephant emitted lazy tendrils of white smoke.

"As far as I know, it's legal for a teenager to buy incense," Claire said.

"And it smells pretty good," I said.

Hannah returned to her homework without commenting on either the legality or the aroma.

"Besides," Claire said, "don't they use incense in church?"

I shook my head and leaned toward her. "That's the Catholics," I whispered. "Not a good point."

Dad turned back around. "Well, at least it's a regular elephant, not Ganesha."

"Who?" Claire asked.

Hannah even looked up from her book.

"It's in the World Book under G." Dad smiled as he closed the door behind him.

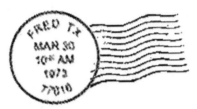

CHAPTER NINETEEN

The twelfth day of Christmas finally arrived, and my true love gave to me twelve pulses drumming.

During the week, the temperatures had bounced from the thirties to the sixties, but on Friday it got into the low seventies. After school I took a shower, dressed in traditional Fredonian-date garb, stole a splash of Dad's Old Spice, and pointed the Falcon toward the county seat where the object of my affection resided.

As a respectable citizen, I parked the car and went inside before whisking away the golden-haired princess in my chariot. Dressed in faded bell-bottoms and a turtleneck sweater, Anna introduced me to her parents.

Mrs. Courtney was short and plump with cat eye glasses, looking a little like an anthropomorphic hamster illustrated by Beatrix Potter. By contrast, Reverend Courtney was taken from the pages of Maurice Sendak, a tall, gregarious, rawboned, balding redhead, exuding more of the aura of a manic clown than one would necessarily look for in a pastor.

They enthusiastically endorsed the night's agenda, confirming my suspicion that nothing rivaled a bowling alley for obliterating romantic tendencies.

We escaped the house, and I opened the car door for Anna. She thanked me and kept a good three feet between us as we pulled out of the driveway, but when we hit U.S. 287 toward Beaumont, she scooted over and nudged my arm around her shoulders.

This didn't strike me as a violation of the sisterly principle. I would conceivably put an arm around my sister, say if she were freezing to death in the Arctic tundra. For a minute or two, anyway. Besides, the temperature had dropped into the sixties. Couldn't have her catching cold.

It was a pleasant, one-hour drive with her snuggling up against me. We didn't talk much, just listened to the radio. As a devotee of sacred music, every song was new to her. A song came on I didn't recognize at first, but then the lyrics kicked in.

Billy Ray was a preacher's son.

As was my custom when this song came on, I reached to change the station, but Anna stopped me. "Isn't that Aretha Franklin?"

I almost drove into the ditch. "You know Aretha Franklin?"

"Shh, I want to hear the words."

The last thing I wanted to do was hear the words. I hated the song, with its sexy, worldly-wise preacher's kid who seemed to have a Rasputin-like capacity for rendering young women grateful for his attentions. Plus, I was working overtime to keep the evening on a sisterly theme.

When the song finished, Anna said, "That was . . . different."

"Different from what?"

"Her album from last year."

"You have an Aretha Franklin album?"

"Of course. You haven't heard it? With Reverend James Cleveland? The Southern California Community Choir?"

"I missed it. How about 'Respect?' You like that song?"

"Never heard it."

We fell into silence as we approached Beaumont. I pulled into the bowling alley parking lot, killed the engine, and opened the door to get out, but Anna pulled me back in.

"I kind of liked that song."

"Which one?"

"About the son of a preacher man."

I stared at her in confusion, unable to decipher the puzzle that was Anna Courtney. She listened only to religious music but liked a song about a PK seducing one of the flock.

"Reminds me of you, a little," she said.

As I attempted to process this information, she leaned over and kissed me, and then slid across the seat and out the passenger door.

"Come on. I'm ready for a hot dog and a Coke." She slammed the door and headed to the entrance.

I scrambled out of the car and caught up with her in time to open the door for her. We navigated the bowling alley protocol, sizing and renting shoes, selecting a ball, finding our lane.

I got us some Cokes, by which I mean Dr Pepper, while Anna warmed up with a few goes at the pins. When I returned, she was already bowling strikes, and I realized the flaw in my plan. I knew less about bowling than I did about hunting, and as the opening of deer season last fall had demonstrated, I knew less than nothing about hunting.

My first half-dozen attempts were the bowling equivalent of hunting deer with a .22 rifle, which I had also done last year. I did a lot of damage to the gutters, but anything in the same county as the pins was safe from my assault.

Anna smiled and shook her head. "Here, let me show you."

You know those movies where the guy teaches the girl how to play golf by hugging up against her and guiding her swing? Yep.

If I had schemed for weeks to find a way to orchestrate physical intimacy between us, I couldn't have found a more effective ploy. I offered up a wordless prayer of apology and hoped that in this case the best of intentions wouldn't serve as paving stones for the road to hell.

Anna initiated me into the mystical rites of scoring the frames, and at the end of the first game she was topping 180 while I had a respectable 75. Not bad. For a golf score.

We continued in our lopsided pursuit, pausing for a hot dog, and decided on a tie-breaking third game. Tie-breaking in the sense that when we divided her score by two, I won the second game.

In the seventh frame, by virtue of some freak disruption of the natural laws of the universe, I bowled a strike. I looked around for an objective witness to document this miracle and caught sight of a figure that brought to mind something King David had jotted down one gloomy afternoon.

"I am poured out like water, and all my bones are out of joint. My heart has turned to wax. It has melted within me. My mouth is dried up like a potsherd, and my tongue sticks to the roof of my mouth."

Anna's squeals of joy faded as she looked to see what had turned my thrill of victory into the agony of defeat.

At the shoe counter, a familiar hulk grasped a pair of size four-teens. Next to him, an equally familiar hulkette reached for a similar pair.

Jimbo Perkins and his not-so-svelte sister, Thelma. On the other side of Jimbo I recognized Lulu, Jimbo's date from the Sadie Hawkins dance. Doubtlessly inspired by my piety, they had decided to celebrate the twelfth day of Christmas by drumming balls down the lanes.

And I had no doubt that if he caught sight of me with a rival to his sister's affection, Jimbo would rival twelve drummers drumming on my head. I found myself wondering if Thelma would join in or attempt to pull him off me, squealing "Mark, my darling!"

But matters of survival superseded such speculations. I sprinted to the score sheets, turned my back on the Perkins clan, and grabbed the pencil as if doing higher math.

I waved Anna over. "Hey, here's the thing." I searched for some suitable exit strategy and settled on a simple declarative statement. "We need to go."

"Why?"

I consulted my watch. "We have an hour drive and I promised your dad I would get you back before midnight."

"It's nine-thirty."

"There could be traffic."

"We could drive backward all the way and still get there before midnight."

"I was thinking of stopping by the DQ for a Black Cow."

Anna smiled. "That sounds nice." She surveyed the score sheet. "Let's finish the last three frames and go."

I chanced a glance behind me and observed the Perkins clan lumbering to a nearby lane to change their shoes, clearing our escape route.

"Let's go now!"

I ripped the score sheet from the pad, grabbed Anna's hand, and pulled her toward the shoe counter.

"Mark Cloud, what has gotten into you?" Anna demanded as I dragged her along.

I glanced up as we cleared the gateway leading from the lanes. Her cry of alarm had not gone unnoticed. Practically every head in the building turned our way, but I had eyes for only one.

To my horror, Jimbo turned, his boots in his hand, and locked eyes with me.

At that point my heart did indeed turn to wax and melt within me. My mouth might even have dried up like a potsherd, whatever that was, but my legs turned to pistons and propelled us out the front door, the guy behind the shoe counter yelling, "Hey!" as we rocketed past him.

In the parking lot, Anna jerked her hand out of mine and came to a stop with her fists on her hips.

"Mark Cloud, explain yourself!"

She had never looked cuter than in that moment, her eyes flashing with indignation, her hair disheveled. I wanted to break the vow, take her in my arms, and Jell-O-wrestle her to Nirvana. But preservation demanded otherwise, and I had a thing about priorities.

Instead, I danced between her and the car in a frenetic seizure of dread. "Sure. Be happy to. But let's talk about it on the way." I jerked the keys from my pocket and opened the passenger door.

"But what about our shoes?"

"Bowling shoes. It's the next big thing. Let's go!" I grabbed her hand again and dragged her to the car.

"But—but—" she stuttered.

A roar of rage emanating from the entrance to the bowling alley drowned out her objections. The crash door slammed against the wall into a spiderweb of cracks and Jimbo barreled out in his stocking feet. He cast his searchlight gaze in an arc. It came to rest on us and he glared, his nostrils flaring in and out like those of a bull catching sight of a particularly vexing matador.

His first step coincided with Anna diving into the car. I hit the lock, slammed the door, and vaulted across the hood like Mark Spitz diving into the 100-meter freestyle, just as Jimbo slammed into the fender.

As he charged around the front of the car, I clawed the door open and shot inside. I slammed the lock button down with my left elbow while starting the car, my foot on the gas, gunning the engine into a complaining whine.

Outside our glass-and-metal refuge, Jimbo grabbed the door handle and jerked. It came off in his hand and he stood there, looking from it to me. Before he could use it to batter through the window, I ground the stick shift into reverse with the engine roaring and spun the wheel to the left.

As we rocketed back in an arc of gravel and dust, Thelma raced out of the door into the parking lot. I stomped on the brakes, recovered from my head bouncing off the headrest, shifted into first, and floored it. We fishtailed through the parking lot, narrowly missing Thelma and several cars, and squealed onto the road.

The radio came to life with Jim Nesbitt's rendition of "Running Bare." We were a half mile closer to Woodville before Anna recovered.

She leaned against the passenger door and, with a glare, pinned me to the driver seat like a butterfly in an exhibit. "Who was that?"

My heart rate was spiraling down into triple digits. "Never seen him before."

She didn't react to this comment with the appreciation I felt it deserved, considering that it was first-draft material and I was working under substantial pressure.

"We almost got killed and I'm going home in bowling shoes. I want an explanation. Now."

What I wanted was a few hours, or perhaps days, to compose a suitable response, but I could see the schedule was not negotiable. I must deliver something to the point in the next few seconds.

Despite platitudes to the contrary, I had not always found honesty to be the best policy, but on short notice, it is the simplest alternative.

"Did you notice the girl who ran out in front of us as we left?"
"That was a girl?"
I nodded grimly. "Thelma. Jimbo's sister."

"And Jimbo is the Incredible Hulk guy who has your door handle for a souvenir?"

In that moment, my heart again melted like wax but for a new reason. I felt an inner tectonic shift from like, or maybe lust if I was completely honest, into something that might be love if I wasn't careful.

In ninety seconds, this girl had been hurled from a pleasant date into riding a whitewater rapid that had morphed from confusing to bewildering to disturbing to threatening. And she had already collected her wits to the point of a clever response. One thing was clear. She was smarter than your average bear, running or otherwise.

Of course, she was a PK. Members of our tribe had to be ready for just about anything. I didn't know how they did it in Woodville, but this episode was likely beyond the regular drill even at her big-town church. Spunky was the word. And cute. Did I mention she was cute?

Not only was the truth easier, and perhaps the best policy in some circles, she deserved it. "Well, here's the thing," I said. "Thelma is in love with me."

A smile crept into her initial expression of shock. "Well, who wouldn't be?"

Given my experience with Jolene, I willed myself not to take this as more than another clever riposte, with mixed success. The male ego is not good at balancing caution and desire.

But I realized I had not accurately represented the situation. "Actually, the thing is that she thinks I'm in love with her."

"And why would she think that?"

I could tell from her expression that she had switched into a foreign language. She was thinking like a girl now. Not a good sign, since no one could predict how her train of thought would derail everything. And by no one, I meant me.

"Well, uh . . . last year I sang a song at the talent contest, and she thought—"

"Ah. But you didn't."

"Absolutely not!"

"But her brother . . ."

It was like she had been reading my mail. Assuming that I had any mail to read, specifically mail about Thelma. "He's a protective sort."

"That's what brothers are for."

I nodded. "Admirable, when you think of it that way."

"What happens on Monday?"

She awaited my answer, her blonde hair glowing a ghostly green in the light of the dashboard, like a zombie queen in a comic book.

I frowned. "Monday?"

"When you run into Jimbo at school."

My foot let up on the accelerator as I contemplated this unwelcome line of thought. "Could you feel my forehead? I think I'm coming down with something."

Anna scooted across the seat and insinuated herself under my willing arm. "Did you mean it about the Black Cow?"

I stepped down on the gas. "Absolutely."

She snuggled closer. "Do you think we can go back for our shoes after?"

We had our Black Cow. Anna told me about Aretha Franklin's *Amazing Grace* album and I told her about my hunting trip with Jimbo, Ralph, and Darnell, with a few ticklish details omitted.

We returned to the bowling alley, and I trolled through the gravel parking lot like a shark, looking for Jimbo's 1940 Chevy pickup.

The coast seemed clear, but to be on the safe side, I parked on the dark side of the building, left the car running with the doors locked, slipped inside, and set Anna's shoes on the counter. The guy looked at me, confused.

I pulled off my bowling shoes and set them next to Anna's. "We had to take care of an urgent matter, but here are your shoes."

He examined me closer and the penny dropped. He looked over at the lanes. I followed his gaze. Jimbo, Thelma, and Lulu were engrossed in a game on lane seven. Somehow I had missed his truck.

I shoved some cash onto the counter. "Can we make this quick and quiet? You can keep the change."

He scanned the cubbies, grabbed some shoes, and dropped them on the counter.

I shook my head. "Dingo boots."

He got the right shoes. I shoved my feet into the boots, grabbed Anna's shoes, and turned to the door.

"Hey," the guy said. "You're short."

I pulled a five from my billfold. "Will that cover it?"

He nodded and I slipped out the door without suffering bodily harm.

We spent the hour drive to Woodville listening to the radio and talking about the songs Anna had never heard. I escorted her to her front door a good quarter hour before her curfew.

As we stood on her porch, the yellow bug light accenting her golden hair, I offered up a silent bargain.

I had acted in good faith, observing the sisterly principle, but we were not the same couple that had driven blithely south a mere five hours ago. We shared a bond forged in adversity. A handshake would not serve. I felt a kiss would not be amiss.

But the kiss I had in mind didn't exactly fall under the concept of the sisterly principle. I sent the petition into the universe. I didn't get a sign of angels singing me home. But neither did I get a flash of lightning and a crash of thunder. I took that as a yes.

I looked into Anna's eyes, rendered cornflower blue in the yellow light, and pulled her close. She melted into me and closed her eyes. I kissed her, my hand sliding up from her arm, my fingers entwining with her hair.

I knew that we were two teenagers with no clue as to what came next in this paint-by-number world, but I also knew that for the first time, I was with someone I thought—or at least I hoped like I had never hoped before—I connected to on every level.

We were from the same tribe, shared the same alienation from our peers, fellow teens who regarded us as a strange species, immune from and oblivious to normal human desires and reactions. The goody two-shoes that didn't get it.

But the big secret was that we did get it. We were tempted in every way just as they were, but were constrained by expectations to endure those temptations without sin.

For some the expectation was too great, and they spun off into the cliché of the wild-child PK. Others doubled down and owned the goody two-shoes image like the American colonists embracing the Yankee Doodle taunt from the British.

But there was no rule that dictated that the life of a PK must be a gutter ball racing to either side of the lane, was there? Surely we had the option of bowling a strike.

That was a lot to pack into a single kiss, and perhaps it was longer and more intense than I had been authorized for, but I felt that, in the aftermath of battle, Anna and I shared something deeper than the off-the-shelf post-date kiss.

I sifted her hair between my fingers as I pulled away.

"Yeah?" I asked.

"Yeah," she answered.

I ushered her safely into the bosom of her family and returned to the car only to find that I couldn't open the driver's door due to a conspicuous lack of a door handle.

I climbed through from the passenger side and drove the thirty miles home in a trance—from which I emerged when I found Dad in the recliner surrounded by reference books. Most likely preparing for the sermon while waiting up for me.

Dad looked up from his studies with an inquisitive stare.

"Uh," I said. "There's a little thing about the driver's side door handle."

"Oh?" he said, waiting patiently for the payoff, as was his custom.

"We don't have one anymore."

"Ah," he responded.

"But I left the window down, so you can open it with the inside handle."

I saved the explanation for the morrow, and he allotted a measure of grace sufficient for me to escape to my bedroom.

CHAPTER TWENTY

On Saturday the window of good weather slammed shut. The cold front the Beaumont weatherman had mentioned came in a few hours ahead of schedule. It started out in the mid-forties with rain and went downhill from there. My typical Saturday morning routine was delayed for a trip to a junkyard in Silsbee, where we bought a replacement driver's door. Or I should say, Dad bought it, and I put some money down on the repayment plan.

The color wasn't an exact match. More of a tan car, red door effect. Perhaps Mick Jagger would see it and paint it black. When we got home, I rushed through my janitorial duties and set out on my Grit route.

A few hours later, as the sun fell behind the pines, I turned toward the river bottom pedaling flat out with my head down, using the exercise to keep me warm.

I glanced up at the rattle of a vehicle approaching on the washboard road. It was a pickup. An old rusty one. Difficult to decipher the make and model in the failing light, but I was taking no chances.

I veered into the ditch, tossed my bike into the weeds, and vaulted over a fence into the woods, rolling to a lacerating stop in the undergrowth of a holly tree at the base of a monstrous pine. Then I waited for the sound of an old truck to whoosh past, preferably one driven by some river bottom farmer intent on a trip to the liquor store across the county line.

But that's not what happened. The rattle ceased abruptly and a door creaked open.

Risking permanent scarring, I wiggled through the branches and peered out, hoping that the rustle of the wind through the leaves would cover the sound and movement.

Backlit by headlights in the twilight, the bear-like silhouette of Jimbo stood on the edge of the road. He peered over the fence and I stared back, certain, or at least hopeful, that I was invisible in the gloom of the woods.

"I seen ya, Mark. Come on out and take yer medicine like a man."

I refrained from answering. How could he know for sure that it was me?

He turned and walked back to the truck, and I took the liberty of breathing. But he didn't climb back in and drive away. Instead, he fiddled with something next to the side mirror and the next thing I knew, a spotlight lit me up like a treed coon.

I scuttled into the brush until I was backed up against the pine tree. My left hand came down on a green pinecone, and it rolled aside, perforating me from palm to elbow as I tumbled.

Lying on my side in the pine straw, I choked back a cry. Then, over the sound of air whistling through my gritted teeth, I heard something that made me realize I had been sorely mistaken last night when I thought my heart had turned to wax. I suddenly knew what an authentic waxifying heart was like.

The sound of a pump shotgun racking a shell into the chamber.

Casting aside concerns for green pinecones, I abandoned my policy of cringing silently in the undergrowth. I rolled to my hands and scrambled behind the pine tree just as a blast split the air, ripped through the foliage, and converged on my right ankle.

An involuntary bark of pain burst out, but I bit it off and jerked my leg in, leaned my back against the trunk, and wrapped my arms around my knees to keep all of my appendages out of the line of fire.

A second pump, a second blast, and the bark peeled off the right side of the tree. Flakes fluttered down in the glare of the spotlight.

As I huddled into the tightest ball I could muster, a faint commotion bled through the white noise of the wind. The staccato cacophony of a vehicle held together by bravado and bailing wire traveling at a lunatic speed.

The sound of my salvation.

Without seeing it, I knew it was a truck that had been unwitting-ly camouflaged for a Mars expedition using the medium of Bondo and primer. And I knew who was behind the wheel.

It came to an abrupt stop in a symphony of rattles and groans. A cloud of dust drifted through the shafts of light shooting through the trees and settled on me.

"Say, doll. Spotlighting coons?" Darnell Ray asked Jimbo.

I had never been so happy to hear the voice of a classmate, even if he did have greasy Coke-bottle glasses and a Hitler haircut.

"On the ground?" he added, evidently confused.

"Hunting snakes in the grass."

"No percentage in that." Darnell's voice sounded suitably dubi-ous.

I heard a door open and close and then Darnell's voice a little closer. "Hey, is that Mark's bike?"

"Come out and show yerself like a man," Jimbo yelled.

"Hey, Darnell, *que pasa*?" I called from behind the tree.

"Mark?"

"Yeah."

In the long pause I could hear Darnell looking from the woods to Jimbo and back.

"What's going on here?"

"Just a little disagreement," I said.

"Just settling a score," Jimbo said.

"Now look here, Jimbo, you can't go shooting Mark."

"That's where yer wrong. I done did, and I'll do it again as soon as I reload."

"What's this about?"

"He's been toying with Thelma's affections."

Figuring Jimbo was distracted and hoping that he wasn't bluffing about being empty, I leaned onto my good hand and glanced around the tree.

The spotlight glinted off Darnell's glasses as he turned to Jimbo. "Thelma and Mark? Are you fur certain about that?"

"He sung her that song last year. Swore his love. You heard it."

Backlit by the spotlight, the cloud of their breath formed a halo around their heads. I leaned back against the tree and shivered.

Darnell kept his eyes on Jimbo. "What's he talking about, Mark?"

"The talent show."

"You sang a love song to Thelma?"

Although I had no desire to expose myself to ridicule by confessing my secret passion and ultimate failure, this was no time to nurse my wounded pride. "It was for Becky."

"Becky Tuttle?"

"The same."

"Then why—"

"It was for Thelma," Jimbo yelled. "She told me so herself."

"I wrote that song for Becky."

"That's a lie. She's dating a football player."

"It didn't exactly work out." If this went much further, I might just step out from behind the tree and beg Jimbo to shoot me.

"And that wasn't Becky you was with last night at the bowling alley. That was a blonde."

"Oh, that's okay. It was just his cousin, Claire," Darnell said.

"It weren't Claire. I know her." He shoved two more shells in the shotgun and yelled, "Now you come on out and we'll settle this like men right here."

"Wait a minute," Darnell said. "Jimbo, you can't go shooting people just because they don't want to date Thelma. You don't have that many shells."

For the first time, Jimbo turned away from me. He took a step toward Darnell. "What's that supposed to mean?"

"Well, Jimbo . . . there's a lot of folks who ain't dating Thelma. You can't shoot them all."

I squelched my overwhelming desire to shout, "Amen!"

"But she ain't sweet on all them other folks," Jimbo said.

"That's as may be, but you can't just shoot him. You don't want to go to jail. Again."

Again?

"It's just rock salt."

Just. What a relief. Somebody needed to inform my ankle.

"Doll, it's Saturday night. You got better things to do than stand here in the cold waiting for Mark to come out from behind that tree so as you can shoot him."

A set of headlights appeared from the other direction.

"And yer blocking traffic."

"All right." Jimbo tossed his gun in the cab of his truck. "But I'm not done with you, Mark Cloud." He shut off the spotlight, slammed his door, and roared off.

Darnell waved the other car on.

I crawled out of the brush, limped to the fence, and squeezed through the barbed wire.

"Thanks."

Darnell shrugged off my gratitude and tossed the bike into the bed of the truck. "Come on. I'll give you a lift."

I eased past the headlights, climbed into the passenger seat, flipped on the dome light, peeled back my bloody sock, and inspected the three holes seeping blood.

"He winged you."

"Lucky shot."

"No such thing with Jimbo. He can castrate a gnat at fifty yards with a .22"

"He's been in jail?"

"DWI. Last summer."

At home I explained my injuries with a story about being chased by dogs and getting tangled in a barbed-wire fence during the escape. It matched the wounds closely enough to pass muster. A hot bath and a pair of tweezers dealt with the rock salt.

I fell asleep pondering school on Monday, where I would discover what Jimbo had in mind for my immediate and possibly short future.

CHAPTER TWENTY-ONE

Since neither Jimbo nor Darnell attended church, my cover story for the injuries held for Sunday, but the red car door that Jagger had not yet painted black required an explanation. In this rare case, not only was honesty the best policy, it also was the best story.

I got as much mileage out of it as I could, but initiating Claire into the dark arts of Sunday school consumed most of my time. I gave her a primer during the two-minute drive to the church through the continuation of yesterday's meteorological reproof.

"First we go to Sunday school."

"School? Seriously? On Sunday?"

"Scooter will say a prayer and then choose people to read the lesson from the quarterly."

In response to her puzzled look, I held up my copy of the quarterly and flipped it open to the first Sunday in January.

"Then Scooter will ask the questions." I pointed them out. "And pick people to answer them."

"Seriously?" She grabbed the quarterly and scanned the pages. "How long does this take?"

"An hour."

"This is worse than group counseling." She slapped the quarterly back in my hand. "And you do this every week?"

I nodded.

"For how long?"

I shrugged. "As long as I can remember."

A chuckle from the front seat caused me to look up. Dad caught my attention in the rearview mirror, the crinkles around his eyes revealing the smile we couldn't see. I glanced over at Mom and detected a Mona Lisa smile on her profile.

In the Sunday school class, I took my usual seat next to Jolene, arranging my chair at the traditional angle against the wall. Claire sat next to me and smiled at everyone in the room.

"So, other than Jimbo mauling your car, how was the date?" she asked sotto voce.

"Satisfactory." I wasn't interested in a post-game analysis.

"Bowling, huh? You sure know how to show a girl a good time."

"It's all part of the plan." Never mind that the plan was to minimize the very thing that most people preferred to maximize on a date. It was too complicated, and Claire wouldn't get it, anyway.

"Okay," Claire drawled. "But what happens tomorrow when you find yourself trapped in a crucible with your antagonist?"

I frowned at her.

"Jimbo. You're going to be stuck in school with the very guy who recently ripped the handle off your favorite door. He might still have it in his pocket, saving it to beat you with."

I declined to admit that this very issue consumed my every waking moment. Well, at least every third moment. I also gave considerable thought to Anna and what was for lunch.

"You want me to talk to Jimbo?" Claire asked.

"No." What could she say that Darnell or I hadn't already said?

I was spared further embarrassment by Scooter and Brenda walking in. Scooter asked me to introduce Claire, but everyone knew her already from school. He asked Brenda to give Claire one of the spare quarterlies, opened with a prayer, and read the introduction to the lesson straight out of the teacher's book. It was about the battle of Jericho.

The reading of the verses proceeded around the room, covering the marching around in silence once a day for six days, then seven times on the seventh day.

Then it was Squeaky's turn. She cleared her throat and read. "When the trumpets sounded, the army shouted, and at the sound of the trumpet, when the men gave a loud shout, the wall collapsed; so everyone charged straight in, and they took the city. They devoted the city to the Lord and destroyed with the sword every living thing in it—men and women, young and old, cattle, sheep, and donkeys."

Squeaky looked up with a frown on her face. "Wait a minute—"

"Not now, Squeaky. Let's finish first." Scooter looked at Claire with a blank expression. "Uh . . . next."

"Claire," I said.

"Claire, could you read the next two verses?"

Claire picked up the quarterly. "Joshua said to the two men who had spied out the land, 'Go into the prostitute's house' . . ." She looked up from the quarterly with a surprised expression and glanced around the room.

"Go ahead," Scooter said.

She looked back down. "Uh. 'Go into the prostitute's house and bring her out and all who belong to her, in accordance with your oath to her.'"

"And the next one."

She read the verse about the two spies rescuing Rahab and her family.

I took the next two verses about burning the city and everything in it except the valuable stuff, which went into the treasury.

Jolene batted cleanup with the curse on anyone who tries to re-build Jericho.

"Okay," Scooter said. "Let's go back to the top and the instructions for battle. Why do you think God told them to—"

"But that ain't right," Squeaky said. "They killed the children and the animals."

"We'll get to that," Scooter said. "First let's—"

"But that ain't fair. The children didn't do nothing."

"We'll see in a minute that . . ." Scooter flipped a page in his teacher's book. "That this is a symbol of how we must be diligent to turn away from every sin in our lives and—"

"So it's just a story? They didn't really kill the children?"

"No, it's not just a story, but we're going to find out that . . ." Scooter flipped the page, ran his finger down the text, and read from the book. "That the people of Jericho were in total rebellion against God and in league with the occult, as the artifacts recovered from this period demonstrate."

"Well, of course they had to kill the children," Ralph said. "Didn't you see *Godfather II*? Don Ciccio kills Vito Corleone's father but Vito gets away, and guess who shows up twenty years later and kills Don Ciccio?"

"This ain't some stupid movie, Ralph," Squeaky said. "And the donkeys? Were they Satan worshipers? Or did he have to kill them so they wouldn't come back twenty years later and kill him too?"

"Squeaky, if we go back and start from the top, I think you'll get it." There was a hint of pleading in Scooter's voice.

"I don't care what happens at the top if at the bottom they kill everything anyway." Squeaky threw the quarterly on the floor and slammed the door on the way out.

As the rifle shot of the door bounced off the salmon-colored tile and puke green walls, another voice spoke up.

"What I want to know is what's going on with this hooker." All eyes converged on Claire. "It says right there that they made sure they got the prostitute out before they killed everything else."

"Well, that's back in an earlier chapter." Scooter rifled through the pages like a guy looking for a one hundred dollar bill he stashed in there during better times. "Here it is." He smoothed out the page. "Then Joshua son of Nun secretly sent two spies from Shittim. 'Go, look over the land,' he said, 'especially Jericho.' So they went and entered the house of a prostitute named Rahab and stayed there."

Scooter looked up with a proud smile, having found the verse so quickly.

Claire smiled back. "They're sent out to spy, and the first thing they do is go to a brothel."

Scooter's smile fractured. "They weren't there to . . . They were hiding from the king of Jericho."

"And when it comes time to attack, they make sure they smuggle out their favorite hooker first?" Claire smiled bigger.

I nudged Claire and gave her a small frown and a subtle shake of the head. No point in riling Scooter. No telling who he would talk to later.

"At least they have their priorities right." She turned to me. "This isn't anywhere near as boring as I thought it would be."

Scooter had gone from a frozen smile to a flushed face. "Now hold on a minute, you better be careful how you joke about the word of God."

"I didn't make it up. It's right there in the book." Claire held up the quarterly.

The buzzer saved us from further excoriation at Scooter's hands. We escaped before he could recover from his apoplectic fit.

"Way to stay under the radar," I said as we walked through the door and past the piano.

"That was never my strong suit." Claire scanned the pews in the sanctuary. "Now what happens?"

I led her to my normal spot. "We sing a few songs, have a prayer or two, take the offering, and then Dad preaches for half-an-hour or so."

We watched the people as they came in and found their spots. I pointed out a few characters she hadn't met yet.

"Who is that old buzzard?" Claire asked.

I followed her gaze. Scooter walked past the organ engaged in conversation with Deacon Fry.

"Deacon Fry."

"Oh, the one you . . ."

Her voice faded as Deacon Fry's laser-beam eyes focused on us. He said something to Scooter without looking away. Scooter looked at us and nodded.

"Wow," Claire whispered. "All he needs is a wheelchair and he'd be Mr. Potter from that Christmas movie."

Deacon Fry dismissed Scooter with a wave of his hand and approached us. Claire grabbed my hand and squeezed like she could make a sword pop out if she squeezed hard enough. But Fry turned before he got to us and dropped slowly into his regular pew a few rows up from mine.

Claire turned to me with the intensity of a kid seeing a roller coaster for the first time. "I want to meet him."

I stared at her, speechless.

"Come on. Introduce me."

"What about that flying under the radar thing?"

"Oh, that's just not going to happen." She dragged me into the aisle and up three rows.

Deacon Fry was reading through the announcements in the bulletin. When we lurched to a halt next to his pew he looked up with alarm that turned to a frown.

"Uh, Deacon Fry, this is my cousin, Claire. She's staying with us for a while."

Claire assaulted him with a beaming smile and an outstretched hand. "It's very nice to meet you, Deacon Fry."

Deacon Fry slowly studied Claire's Nordstrom wardrobe, thousand-watt smile, and extended hand. Then he took her hand. But he didn't shake it. He just held onto it and turned his withering gaze on me. "Which side of the family?"

"Mom's sister's daughter," I forced out.

He turned and bored twin holes into her head with his eyes. "Tell me, Claire, are you a Christian?"

"No, sir," Claire said without cutting the wattage on her smile even a fraction. "My dad's a scientist. This is the first time I've been in a church. But I'm enjoying it so far."

"Church isn't here for your entertainment. It's for the instruction of your soul."

"I'll certainly keep that in mind, sir." Claire tried to extract her hand from Fry's grip, but he didn't release her.

"It would be a shame for an attractive young woman to spend an eternity in hell."

Claire's smile faltered for a microsecond. "I haven't really thought much about it."

"Then it's time you did." He dropped her hand and returned to the bulletin as if we weren't there.

We shuffled back to our spot.

"I don't think he likes me," Claire breathed.

"Take a number."

"He doesn't like you, either?"

"Or Dad. Or a few other folks I know."

"Okay, but why should we care? Other than the nightmares, of course."

"The deacons are the ones who hire and fire the pastor."

"And he's a deacon."

"He's the head deacon."

"And he doesn't like Uncle Matt?"

"Can't stand him at any price."

"Then why are you guys still here?"

"He's working on it. He'll play his cards as soon as he gets a decent hand."

I told her about the phone call to Dad last November, about the beer on the hunting trip and hanging out with a bootlegger.

"That's not much. He's not even holding any trumps."

"Unless we hand him one."

CHAPTER TWENTY-TWO

By the time I got to school Monday morning, the story of the door handle and the shotgun had circulated to the masses. It afforded me some measure of protection. Not that anybody offered to throw themselves between me and Jimbo if he should attack, but they gathered to me in my hour of need, and the temporary entourage discouraged him from launching a full frontal assault. He limited his depredations to withering glares and wordless malevolence.

By lunch things were back to normal, or at least whatever that passed for in my world. The jukebox blared Bill Withers' "Use Me" as I walked into the cafeteria. I nodded to Bubba and Darnell, who had already established a beachhead on our regular table.

C.J. and Claire entered from the back door holding hands and joined me in line. Their clothes were redolent of smoke. Either she had renewed her supply or she was bumming. Probably from C.J., who seemed to have taken up the habit since last Wednesday. Either he had become a dedicated smoker in less than a week, braving temperatures in the low forties to get his fix, or he had become dedicated to something else. Three guesses as to what and the first two didn't count.

At the table, I set my tray between Bubba and Darnell. C.J. and Claire took the space across from us. I was pulling back the chair when a beefy hand grabbed my shoulder and spun me around.

"Hey," I snapped and then saw who it was and said hey again, but this time in a wavering tone that slid around the scale.

Jimbo grabbed a handful of shirt with his left hand and lifted me a mile or two off the floor. "I told ya I wasn't done with ya."

"Hey," Darnell and Bubba said in stereo.

"Easy, there Quasimodo," C.J. said.

"Jimbo, put him down," Claire said.

"Ain't no tree to hide behind now." Jimbo cocked his right arm back, his rump-roast-sized fist locking in the coordinates of my nose.

"Hey," Darnell and Bubba said, louder this time, but, I noted with some concern, remaining in their chairs.

C.J. jumped to his feet, but he was on the other side of the table.

Claire stood up next to him. "Jimbo, remember what we talked about?"

Jimbo glanced at her. "Sorry, Claire. He might be yer cousin, but Thelma's my sister. Ain't no excuse for what he done." He reared back for the punch.

So it had come down to this. First the door handle, then my ankle, and now my face. I threw my arms in front of me in an X and tried to duck.

Claire scrambled over the table, but she was hampered by the trays of mystery meat and mashed potatoes.

Jimbo flexed his arm, but it barely budged. He tried again, but it was as if it had been frozen in place by an anti-violence ray. He pivoted, swinging me in a squirming, kicking arc.

Claire leaned back to avoid my legs.

Jimbo looked over his shoulder.

Elrick stood behind Jimbo, his face contorted from the strain of holding the pile driver back. "Pick on someone your own size," he said through gritted teeth.

"There ain't nobody his size," Darnell said.

Jimbo tried to shake Elrick off. "You want to be next, Williams?"

"I'll take my chances. Put him down."

"Come on," Claire said. "He's not worth it."

I dropped to the floor as Jimbo released my shirt and spun around, leaning into a left-handed haymaker aimed for Elrick's head.

Elrick held onto Jimbo's right arm and pushed it to the left to increase the momentum of the turn. Then he leaned back, grabbed Jimbo's right arm by the wrist and elbow, and accelerated the spin even more.

As Jimbo staggered in a circle, Elrick dropped to the floor on his left hand and shot his right foot out between Jimbo's legs. Jimbo tumbled to the floor like Goliath on a three-day drunk, taking a few chairs with him as he tried to break his fall.

Claire jumped up on the table to avoid being smashed and knocked over her Coke.

Elrick popped up.

Before Jimbo could get to his feet, Vice Principal Timmons arrived. Tiny Tim, as we called him when he wasn't around, was five foot four in cowboy boots with lifts and was constructed entirely from spring steel and scorpions.

"Hey, what's going on here, gentlemen?"

"He tripped," Elrick said and held out his hand to Jimbo.

Jimbo looked at the hand as if it might be loaded, but eventually grabbed it and pulled himself to his feet. He looked down at Tiny Tim. "I tripped."

Tiny Tim looked up at Claire towering above him on the table. "And you, miss?"

"Me too."

Tiny Tim looked from Claire to Jimbo to Elrick to me. "I have one thing to say to the four of you. If you want to stay out of my office, no more tripping."

"Yes, sir," Elrick said. "You can count on it. Right?"

"Absolutely," I said.

"Yeah," Jimbo said.

Tiny Tim turned to Claire.

"Indubitably."

He looked at the Coke dripping off the table into Bubba's chair. "And clean up that mess." Then he left without a backward glance.

I accosted Claire as she climbed down from the table. "He's not worth it?"

"It works in the movies."

Jimbo turned to Elrick. "How did ya do that?"

Elrick smiled. "You don't grow up black in East Texas without learning a few moves."

Jimbo studied him for a few seconds, then turned to me. "I'm not done with you, Cloud."

"I think you are, man," Elrick said.

"This ain't no concern of yours, Williams," Jimbo said without taking his glare off me.

"PKs stick together, right Mark?"

I nodded so enthusiastically my neck popped. "Absolutely. It's the first rule of preacher's kids. Stick together. Ask questions later."

"What's the second rule?" Bubba asked.

"Never volunteer," Elrick said.

Sounded good to me. I filed it away for future reference.

"We'll see," Jimbo said and lumbered off listing slightly to the left.

"Thanks," I said.

"You'd do the same for me."

"Don't count on it," C.J. said and returned to his mystery meat and mashed potatoes.

I sat down between Darnell and Bubba.

Claire returned to her seat. Elrick took the chair on the other side of C.J. "What was that about?"

"Jimbo thinks Mark has been trifling with Thelma's affections," Claire said.

"True fact?" Elrick considered me as if recalibrating the pigeon-hole in which I resided in his brain.

"It's true that he thinks that," I replied.

"That's one mighty hunk of woman," Elrick said.

"Two hunks at least," Darnell said.

"Do I hear three?" C.J. asked.

"Do you ever actually listen to yourselves?" Claire asked.

"Can we change the subject?" I asked.

"I hear you scored a righteous babe up in Woodville," C.J. said.

Say what you might about C.J., it couldn't be denied that he was not overburdened with a superabundance of couth. Claire elbowed him.

"A member of the club," Bubba said.

"Club?" I asked through a mouthful of mashed potatoes without losing any, and if you think that's easy, just try it.

"The PK club," Bubba said.

"True fact?" Elrick asked.

I nodded.

Elrick continued his recalibration. "Anna Courtney?"

It was my turn to recalibrate. "You know her?"

"Great voice. Aretha fan."

The force of my astounded expression drew an explanation from him.

"We did a joint sunrise service with her church last Easter at the courthouse." He thought for a second and added. "A little . . . uptight."

"Not what I hear," Bubba said.

"Dude! Give me some skin." C.J. held out a hand.

I tossed an annoyed glance at Bubba and attempted to shut C.J. down with the classic Cloud countenance of censure.

"Bro, you can't leave me hanging."

"I think he just did," Claire said.

He dropped his hand. "Spill it. Details."

I turned to Elrick. "First rule of PKs."

His reaction made me realize that there might actually be an inner-circle club of PKs. As if I had coached him ahead of time, he changed the subject. "Have you met her brother?"

"The Hose?" I responded. "Now that is one uptight PK."

C.J. took the bait. "The Hose?"

"Hosea."

He recoiled as if he'd been slapped. "Who names their kid Hosea?"

"A guy named Beeri," Bubba said. In response to our astonishment he added, "The word of the LORD came unto Hosea, the son of Beeri. Hosea, chapter one, verse one."

"Beery?" C.J. asked.

It occurred to me that given Bubba's facility with verse retrieval, perhaps he should be dating Anna. I decided not to mention it. The mercy was that C.J.'s questions were successfully derailed and I was spared further interrogation regarding the intimate details of my romantic life.

Four hours later on the bus ride home, Bubba and I huddled in a seat close to a heater vent. The temperature hadn't been out of the forties all day long.

He was the first to break the silence. "Hey."

"Hey."

"What did you decide?"

"About what?"

"What Jesus would do on a date."

"Oh." What had I decided? "For starters, she didn't kiss my feet."

"Bowling shoes probably to blame on that one."

I nodded slowly. Good point. Despite the disinfectant the guy sprayed in them between customers, the shoes retained a certain enduring bouquet that didn't encourage excessive kissing.

"How long is her hair?"

I could see where he was taking this. "Long enough for the 'wash with tears and dry with hair' routine, but no."

"So . . . ?"

"So I decided Jesus would take his date bowling."

"Because . . . ?"

"It was either that or the drive-in."

"And you figured—"

"Exactly."

"She ain't against kissing, but Jesus might be?"

"Well . . ." I hadn't exactly worked out the details to that degree, but if you took the sisterly principle to its logical conclusion, that was pretty much it.

"No kissing before marriage, then?"

I looked at him in alarm. "You think that's what Jesus would do?"

It was a scary and depressing thought. I began to see the inherent flaw in the sisterly principle. If every guy treated every girl like she was his sister, nobody would ever get married or have kids. Unless they were from Arkansas.

The kiss on Friday night didn't feel wrong, but of course we weren't supposed to go by our feelings. That was exactly what would lead us astray. Desire. Lust. Sin. Death. Just follow the red-brick road that starts at the drive-in and ends in the flaming city of hell.

"No," Bubba said. "That's what you think Jesus would do."

"What do you think he would do on a date, then?"

"Got no idea. Not even sure the question makes sense. But I know what he wouldn't do."

"Do tell."

"He wouldn't follow some list of rules the religious leaders made up."

"Don't dance, drink, or chew, or go with girls that do."

"Exactly, doll."

That was helpful. Ignore the rules. Not an approach designed to commend me as a member in good standing of the Deacon Fry cabal.

I had a lot to think about before my next date. Unfortunately I had plenty of time to think because of an embarrassing shortage of funds, caused by the previous date combined with the payments on the red door.

CHAPTER TWENTY-THREE

Tuesday started off dark and raining. The mercury on the thermometer out the kitchen window was taking a nosedive to the thick red line that marked freezing when I stepped to the hook to grab my fleece-lined coat for the three-hundred yard walk to the bus stop. Except where my jacket should be, a bare bronze coat hook gleamed.

Some words I had heard in a movie crossed my mind, but I declined to give them utterance in the already obscene morning. Instead, I went to my closet for my backup, a denim jacket with no lining.

We three musketeers trudged through the near-freezing drizzle to the elementary school. I reflected on the capricious hand of fate. A year ago the three original musketeers had trudged this same path, probably under equally atrocious conditions. Now a fourth musketeer had replaced Heidi. Claire, our d'Artagnan.

Heidi had gone off to college and come home a few months later with The Hose, knocking over a string of dominoes that were still falling. Had she picked another college or another career path or another beau, I never would have met Anna. Never would have experienced the kiss on the church steps on Christmas Eve or the intensity of the last kiss (as I meant it) in the oak grove on New Year's Eve or the crazy-house roller-coaster ride that was our first date. Never would have found a companion in my own tribe.

That was only four days ago, but it seemed like an eternity based on the amount of time I spent thinking about her and how soon I wanted to repeat the experience.

I looked at the back of the blue peacoat on the trail in front of me. After almost a decade of radio silence, fate had also dropped Claire into my life. What dominoes would she tip over, and where would they lead?

Or what dominoes would I knock over in her life? Perhaps I was thinking about this whole thing wrong. Maybe it wasn't fate but God that had placed her here, not a year ago when I was wrestling with the Mysterious Stranger but now, after I had chosen a side and taken the vow to ask that confounding and often annoying question. What would Jesus do?

It occurred to me that Claire was the one sheep that the Good Shepherd left the ninety-nine to rescue. Wild child. Daughter of an atheist. Never had a chance until her unfocused struggle to pay back the bully who was her father landed her right here in the middle of the gospel. And she had chosen me as her companion and confidant.

Me. The most confused member of the tribe, feeling my way forward via the Braille method. I didn't welcome the assignment. In fact, I was sure it was a cosmic mistake.

I offered up a short silent prayer. Seriously? Me?

I received a silent answer with no way to gauge whether it was short or long.

I spent the bus ride to school finishing my algebra homework with a mental apology to whoever had the misfortune to try to decipher the ragged handwriting, then settled down to the problem of how to reconcile my desires with my finances. I wanted to drive to Woodville immediately and whisk Anna away, but that required gas money, and once the whisking was accomplished, some cover activity must necessarily follow that must necessarily require funds. And I lacked the necessary.

The bus ride and the day's activities at school failed to offer a solution to this dilemma. I was tortured by the knowledge that Anna went through her activities a mere eighteen miles north that might as well have been eighteen million miles for all the proximity did for me.

In the afternoon, we made the return journey under equally miserable conditions. I burst through the door anticipating some warm drink to return sensation to my extremities. Heidi was watching the *Dialing for Dollars* movie in the den. Mom was cutting onions.

Dad sat at the kitchen table and regarded us with a calculating gaze.

"Have a seat," he said.

"Who?" I asked.

"All of you."

We divested ourselves of our outer coverings and arrayed ourselves around the table.

"Does anyone here have anything to tell me about last night?"

I rolled back the log of my activities of Monday night. Dinner, homework, *Laugh In* on TV, and then *Tale of Two Cities* in bed until I fell asleep.

"No."

The girls shook their heads.

"Anyone care to offer a reason why I ran out of gas on the way to Beaumont today after filling up the tank last Friday?"

I declined to speculate on a possible leak in the tank. If it were that simple, we would not be sitting here under the interrogation lamp.

Dad pulled a small spiral notebook from his shirt pocket. The one where he recorded the mileage accrued on church business for tax purposes.

"Or why, since my hospital visits on Friday, over three hundred miles have been put on the Galaxie?"

The sound of chopping behind us faded. I saw Heidi glance over at us from the den and back to the movie she obviously wasn't watching. I looked at Hannah. Her expression told me she was as confused as I was. I looked at Claire. She stared at the notebook like a calf staring at a new gate.

"Mark," Dad said, jolting my gaze back to him. "I noticed you wore a denim jacket today. Unlined."

I nodded.

"A bit chilly for such a light jacket."

"I couldn't find my fleece jacket."

Dad reached down to the seat of the chair next to him, pulled my jacket up, and dropped it on the table. "Perhaps because it was in the backseat of the Galaxie." He pulled a few more things from the seat. "Along with some trash." He arrayed a crumpled Bugles bag, a shredded cheese cracker package, plastic from a Slim Jim, and two Coke cans on the table.

I eyed the jacket as I would a pit viper. "What was it doing there?"

"I was hoping you could explain that."

I shook my head. "I hung it up where I always do when I came home yesterday." I looked around for corroboration, but the girls ignored me. "I haven't been in the Galaxie since we went to church Sunday night. Plus, I don't drink Coke."

"Hannah?" Dad said.

"I don't have a license. Don't even know how to drive. And also don't drink Coke."

"In fact, nobody in this family drinks Coke. Except . . ." Dad turned to Claire. "Anything you would like to add, Claire?"

"No, sir," she said solemnly.

"You look a little tired."

"Up late studying for an algebra test."

I eyeballed her. There was no algebra test. In fact, she slept through the class.

"How did you do?" Dad asked.

"I think I passed it. Maybe a B. Math's not my thing. That's why I have to study more than other people." She smiled at me.

I was too stunned to smile back. The effortless manner in which she fabricated corroborating details and casually dropped them into her replies chilled me in a way Jimbo's raw violence had not. Only this morning I had felt, in the words of visiting missionaries, a burden to minister to this lost sheep. Now I felt gullible, or arrogant, or both, for making such assumptions. I wondered if she was a sheep at all, lost or otherwise. What if she was a wolf masquerading as a lost sheep?

Dad continued his interrogation. "So if we called your parents, they wouldn't tell us that you visited them last night?"

"Seriously?" There was nothing fabricated about that response.

"Or did you have a study partner? Someone, say, a hundred or so miles away?"

"No, sir. Just studied in my room. Until two or so."

"That was over six dollars worth of gas," Mom said from behind us in the kitchen. "It was supposed to last us for two weeks."

"I expect it's hard to find a gas station open in this area at four or five in the morning," Dad said.

While they talked, I found myself locked in an internal argument. Obviously Claire had taken the car somewhere last night, somewhere a half-tank of gas away. Downtown Houston was 125 miles away, quite doable on a tank of gas. And if she left at midnight, she could easily make it back by five a.m.

So what would Jesus do? Would he bust her or cut her some slack? He told the woman caught in the act of adultery that he didn't condemn her, and that was a lot worse than appropriating a car for a quick trip to . . . see your boyfriend, maybe? Despite the duplicity, she might have had a good reason, might have even been desperate and thought no one would understand.

And despite her genial manner, how many true friends did she have? Maybe all she needed to turn the corner was one person to show a little kindness and understanding.

"What if we chip in to pay for the gas? Say two dollars each?" I said.

"Hey," Hannah said. "Don't drag me into this. I can't even reach the pedals."

I shrugged. "Okay, then. Three dollars each." I looked to Claire for confirmation.

She smiled. "Sure."

I pulled three dollars from my wallet, over half of my current holdings, and set them on the table.

Dad studied me as if attempting to calculate my level of involvement in the incident.

"However, this should not be taken as an admission of guilt," I added. "Merely a willingness to do my part for the family."

"Exactly," Claire said as she extracted three dollars from her purse and stacked them on top of mine.

Dad stared at us for a long time before responding. I did my best to keep the stiff upper lip and united front. I thought he was about to reject the money, but before he could, Mom retrieved it.

"Let's be completely clear about one thing," Dad said. "There is only one car you can take whenever you want without asking, and that is the car you paid for." He stood. "Otherwise it's not borrowing. It's grand theft auto."

Dad left the room. Hannah spread her books out on the table and started in on her homework.

"You should know that your father had to walk two miles in freezing rain to find a gas station," Mom said.

"Wow," I said. "Bummer."

I went into the living room, put Iron Butterfly on the stereo, and started on my history homework. Claire slipped in, lit some incense, and joined me.

"What the heck, Claire?" I whispered.

"I just had to see Jeff," she whispered back.

"Who is Jeff?"

"My boyfriend. Dad hates him, so I haven't seen him for months."

"You've been here a week and you haven't said a word about him."

"And you haven't said anything about your girlfriend, so we're even."

She had me there. "But what about C.J.? Does he know about Jeff?"

"Why should he?"

"I would think that was obvious."

"Look at this." Claire held up her left hand. "Notice anything missing?"

All five fingers were present, complete with polished fingernails. "Like what?"

"Like a ring, jughead."

She swung her hand to slap me but I deflected it.

"We're not married. We're not even engaged. He hasn't even asked me out. So why should C.J. care what I do when I'm in Houston?"

"I bet he would if he knew."

"Another reason not to tell him." Claire gave me a hard look.

I wasn't sure I could let my buddy twist in the wind like that, but I declined comment.

After a few minutes of homework along with *In-A-Gadda-Da-Vida*, written by a guy who learned to play organ in church, Claire said, "By the way, thanks."

"You can't do that again."

"I know."

"So what about Jeff?"

Claire was quiet long enough for me to think she wasn't going to answer. "I don't know," she finally said.

She looked so forlorn there on the couch, her history book open in her lap, her short blonde hair half hiding the pudgy cheeks and square chin she got from her father. I wanted to reach out, hug her, and tell her it would be okay. But who was I to make such a statement or to presume to think I could deliver on such a promise?

Chapter Twenty-Four

The Hose organized a final coffeehouse event for the weekend before he and Heidi returned to college. Of course I jumped on the chance to split the gas money with Heidi for a ride to a kind of mini-date with no additional expenditures.

The weather had turned as nasty as a French bulldog waking you up with a French kiss. Claire had planned on coming along but decided instead to curl up with a good book and a cup of hot chocolate. Of course Hannah had no intention of attending irrespective of the weather.

The drive up was a dicey proposition with ten mile-an-hour winds and sleet. Of course I drove. For the whole trip, Heidi was as nervous as Casanova in a drawing room full of dorm mothers, but not once did she suggest we turn back. Good thing, as I would have refused.

Like last time, I helped set up the sound system and did a sound check. The Hose opened in his usual style. Anna and I did several songs together. Of course, as a preacher boy, The Hose couldn't refrain from "bringing a message."

When he was done, Anna stepped to the piano. The standard number for such occasions was "Pass It On" or the infinitely more odious "Amazing Grace" sung to the tune of "The House of the Rising Sun."

Anna sat down and knocked out a bluesy intro that I didn't recognize. But when she started singing, I was enlightened.

Billy Ray was a preacher's son.

She would do that. Sing "Son of a Preacher Man" right here, right now. I felt my ears glowing a nuclear red as everybody looked at me. Even Heidi. Even The Hose. Heidi was smiling. The Hose was not.

This was the ultimate humiliation, a betrayal beyond that of Jolene and The Horrific Case of the Sadie Hawkins Dance. Jolene had gone for the sight gag. You couldn't blame her for that any more than you would blame a dog for chasing a rabbit.

This was a betrayal on another level. In front of everyone, Anna mocked me with the one song that encapsulated all my inadequacies and threw them back in my face.

I stared at her, wondering how she could be so vicious, when it hit me. The girl at the piano leaned into every chord, every run on the keyboard, singing the words with her eyes closed, living every phrase. She was not mocking. She was confessing. In front of the world. Her world.

I blushed even deeper, struggling to cope with this revelation. I knew she liked me, but this seemed to be something more. Like she was saying I was The One.

Me? Was I ready to be The One for someone else? I was barely old enough for a driver's license. I couldn't join the army and fight in Vietnam, couldn't even buy beer.

This cast a new light on the night when she drew me into the oak grove by the church bus for a kiss. On her comments at the bowling alley about the very song she was singing right now. "Reminds me of you."

The only one who could ever reach me was the son of a preacher man.
The only one. The One.

I thought back to Heidi climbing up the one-by-twos into The Fortress of Solitude, clinging to the tree trunk like a cat forced by a predator to seek safety, asking the question.

Is he The One?

It seemed Anna had climbed into her own fortress, had asked the same question and, unlike Heidi, had found an answer. That was the only reason she had done those things, drawn me back into the oak grove on New Year's Eve, snuggled up next to me on the date, kissed me the way she did after the first date, and now bare her soul to the world. A girl like her didn't take those steps lightly. She did it with eyes wide open, with full intent.

Or maybe I was just projecting the whole thing.

In the midst of my one-man wrestling match, Anna finished the song with such force that the room erupted into spontaneous applause. The Hose stepped to the mike, took in the ecstatic reaction of the crowd, inspected me for signs of debauchery and dissolution, glanced at Anna who sat on the piano bench, winded and glowing, and turned back to the mike.

"Okay, then. Let's close in prayer."

This was the go-to preacher-boy response to just about every event, expected or otherwise. Baptists couldn't finish anything without a prayer, be it a church service or a garage sale.

We bowed our heads, and The Hose extemporized a petition for the occasion, liberally peppered with "Father" and "we just ask" after every dozen words or so.

I stole a glance at Anna. She was watching me. Our eyes met in an electric frisson. Something passed between us, but nothing that mere speech could clarify. It was what we had already shared, but in the words of the famous philosopher Homer Price of Centerburg, ever so much more so.

The prayer ended and the tear-down began. I went directly to Anna without passing go or collecting anything whatsoever.

I managed to choke out one word. "Wow."

"I know you don't like that song, but I couldn't resist," Anna said.

"What do you mean? It's my favorite song." It was true. No matter what happened in the next five minutes or five years or five decades, from this day forward, any time I heard that song I would remember the night the girl with no flaw in her sang that song about me and meant every word.

"Come on," she said, like on New Year's Eve.

I hesitated, thinking she meant outside and the oak grove where it was sleeting in the low twenties and dropping.

She grabbed my hand. "Come on, silly." She dragged me out past the piano and through a maze of hallways, through a swinging door into the sanctuary.

It was a gigantic room, more than ten times the size of the sanctuary in Fred. The only light in the room came from mercury-vapor streetlights filtered through stained glass, illuminating rows of white pews with blood-red cushions that stretched out before us and faded into the gloom at the back.

Anna led me around the organ, up the three steps that spanned the length of the front of the sanctuary, onto the platform. We came to a stop in front of the podium.

The security light by the oak grove threw its rays through the rose window above the baptistry and bathed us in its amber glow. We stood in silence for a long time, face to face, both hands interlocked.

I was beyond thought, caught in a dream sequence that could not possibly be real. I slipped my hands out of hers, slid them up the ribbed fabric of her turtleneck sweater, and wrapped my arms around her shoulders. She slid her arms around the waist of my flannel shirt. We pulled closer.

Our faces were now inches apart as we stared into each other's eyes, hers rendered an indigo blue in the half-light.

I wanted to kiss her. She obviously wanted to kiss me. But the realization that she thought she had found The One gave me pause. She was drunk on love or hormones or something. Was it fair to ride the wave of her infatuation knowing full well that I was not ready to claim her as The One? What would Jesus do?

I didn't welcome the question. In fact, I banished it from my mind. The past months had demonstrated that it couldn't be answered by anyone with certainty. As Bubba had said, the question didn't really make sense. There was no first-century equivalent to the twentieth-century practice of dating, and whatever rules the present-day Pharisees might conjure up were irrelevant.

Anna cut through my confused thoughts with a single word.

"Yeah?"

"Yeah," I replied and kissed her.

It was only a kiss, nothing more, but at the same time it was so much more than just a kiss. It was a declaration.

I knew, without knowing how, that it was a surrender without condition, without plea for quarter. That Anna had already given herself to me in her mind and heart, and how much more she gave was up to me.

Not that the kiss was visibly more sensuous than the few kisses we had already shared. It was a chaste, respectable kiss by any objective standard, rated PG in its restraint. But it ripped into me like a fist grabbing my soul and dragging it through the depths of my being before claiming it as a prize.

By surrendering, Anna had somehow emerged victorious, and I could either follow in surrender or walk away in defeat.

Once again, it was a lot to pack into a kiss, way more than I had packed into the kiss after the date, but she had done it. Or maybe I had just imagined it all.

I pulled back and searched her indigo eyes. "What just happened?"

"Nothing," she said. "Everything." She closed her eyes and leaned in for another kiss.

Who was I to deny her obviously heartfelt wish? Besides, it gave me time to think. But the moment our lips met, thinking was struck from the agenda by a motion, a second, and a majority vote of all operational systems.

This kiss was a mere distant relation to the first one, the grownup third cousin you'd heard about but never met. The one your parents didn't talk about. If you had to assign a word to the second kiss, that word would be "Yes."

Yes to what was happening. Yes to what might happen. Yes to the future with a certainty that this right here was the future. Now was everything and always would be.

It was the moment I discovered that a kiss, the right kiss, was a time machine. Not one that took you to the future or the past, but one that made right now all times, turning the next second into an eternity that encompassed the past and present, froze it in amber, and erased everything that had been or might be.

The sensation through my flannel shirt of Anna's hands moving up my spine to my shoulder blades one molecule at a time felt like an ice age of sensation. My fingers moved over the fold of her turtleneck to the space just behind her earlobes with glacial speed, a fraction of a millimeter per eon.

After a second or a century, I had no idea which, I heard voices, one voice in particular, and pushed Anna away gently. We looked at each other, our breath heavy and visible in the chill of the sanctuary, and turned to face the creak of the swinging door.

The Hose burst through, followed by Heidi.

"What are y'all doing in here?" he demanded.

"Looking at the moon coming through the rose window," Anna answered.

I decided not to point out that it was just a streetlight, not the moon.

"Oh, look at that, Hosea" Heidi said. "It's so pretty."

"Yeah," The Hose said, not taking his eyes off me to appreciate the view.

"And it hits right on the podium," Heidi said. "Aren't they cute standing right there in the light? Just like a wedding."

Those last four words had drastically different effects on the people in the room.

I felt like I'd been hit with an oversized semi truck just below where my ribcage ended. I looked at Anna. A raised eyebrow accented the lazy smile that crept across her lips. I turned back to The Hose. He wore the expression of a man who has just been forced at gunpoint to eat an armadillo three-days dead from the center stripe of Highway 69 at high noon in the middle of August.

"Mark, can I have a word?" He turned to Heidi. "We'll meet you at the car. Anna?"

At his implied command, Anna pulled away from me and followed Heidi through the swinging door. But not before squeezing my hand. It was like a secret handshake between conspirators, affirming a lifelong vow that outsiders would never understand. I squeezed back. Regardless of whether she or I were The One for each other, we were fellow time-travelers into another dimension. And I doubted The Hose even knew that such other worlds existed.

I walked down the three steps from the platform to the altar on the sanctuary floor, wracking my brain for some clever response, but my brain didn't report for duty. It was on indefinite leave.

"I want to hold you accountable to our agreement. To treat Anna like you would your own sister. Are you doing that?"

In that moment, fresh from a time-blurring encounter with an alternate reality, I scorned The Hose with an intensity that transcended a mere impatience with someone whose every thought was antithetical to my own instincts and interests. It was a new sensation, and I welcomed it.

"Let me ask you a question, Hose. Who is holding you accountable? Are you treating Heidi like you would your own sister?"

The Hose blinked his pale eyes. "Uh. Of course."

"Really? Then let me ask you this. Have you kissed her?"

He was struck speechless but recovered quickly. "I don't think that's any of your business."

"Exactly."

"Uh . . . what?"

"We agree. I'm glad we had this little talk." I turned on my heel and pushed through the swinging door.

The Hose followed close behind. "You didn't answer my question."

I didn't slow down. "That's only fair. You didn't answer mine."

"But . . ."

"But what?"

"But . . . what were you doing alone in a dark room with my sister?"

I stopped and turned around. The Hose ran into me, and I pushed him away. "I'll answer your questions about what Anna and I do when you answer my questions about what you and Heidi do. Not that I really want to know."

The Hose stood three feet away, breathing heavily through his nose and staring at me for what seemed like a long time. It was obvious that he wanted to say something, but he couldn't find anything that I couldn't turn back on him.

I decided to put us out of his misery. "Nobody can treat a girlfriend like a sister. It's a stupid idea. It comes down to a simple question. Can you trust Anna to do the right thing?"

The Hose stepped forward with a resolve that seemed to expand him to twice his size. In the tile hallway between the sanctuary and the fellowship hall he suddenly looked like a very different person, one who deserved to be taken seriously. I wasn't prepared for this transition and I stepped back, wondering what he would do next.

"No, it comes down to this question. Can I trust you to do the right thing?"

It was a good question. As I struggled to answer, I realized I didn't know if he could trust me, or if Anna could trust me, or if I could even trust myself.

"I could ask you the same thing," I shot back, but it sounded hollow even to me.

CHAPTER TWENTY-FIVE

The next day after church, The Hose showed up at our house to take Heidi back to college. We nodded at each other from across the den but didn't speak. He loaded up her luggage and her laundry bags and they disappeared out of sight.

But his question remained behind like the smell of cooked cabbage. Not the one about the sisterly principle. The one about trust.

In the third week of January, it got up into the seventies, warm enough to disappear into the Fortress of Solitude after school and wrestle with the question.

For months I had dedicated myself to the goal of doing what Jesus would do. But in that moment in the sanctuary, under the light of the rose window, I had abandoned the quest without a thought. In fact, thought had never entered into the decision. I had sensed a willingness from Anna and had followed her lead while she seemed to be following mine.

The more I thought about it, the more it seemed like the quintessential case of the blind leading the blind. More to the point, two willingly self-blinded souls following each other. Or leading each other. It got kind of complicated in a hurry.

After days of piecing out the puzzle, it came down to another question, of finding The One. If you found The One, then everything else followed. And if I was reading the signs right, that was the road Anna was on. As inconceivable as it might be, this golden-haired, blue-eyed vision right out of the pages of Song of Solomon had come to the bizarre conclusion that Mark Cloud was The One for her.

And like a complete idiot, knowing all this, I sat here a story-and-a-half above the pine-straw floor of the woods, debating the question of choosing The One. I was only sixteen, seventeen in a couple of months. Was I really in a position to make a lifelong commitment to another person, even if it seemed to be a no-brainer to the untrained eye?

As I should have expected, the answer came from the most unexpected source.

To my surprise and dismay, on a warm Wednesday afternoon in the middle of January, Hannah appeared in the scuttle hole of the Fortress. Unlike Heidi, she walked to the edge of the platform and looked down to the ground fifteen feet below.

"Cool."

She took in the glory of the Fortress, a six-by-ten piecemeal platform enclosed on two sides by scrap-wood walls, noted my position in the corner, and took a seat on the crate near the trunk. In a willow by the creek, a mockingbird flipped through the dial before settling on a station.

"No wonder you hang out up here."

"It's not as cool as it seems."

"Of course not."

"To what do I owe the honor?"

"Bored."

In vain I searched for some ruse to discourage her from making this a habit. A guy had to have some kind of refuge in which to ponder the verities.

"How's the ankle doing?"

"Fine." The scabs had fallen off after a week, leaving behind three small, pale scars in the pattern of finger holes on a bowling ball.

"It wasn't really a barbed-wire fence, was it?"

"What are you insinuating?"

"I'm not insinuating anything. I'm coming right out and saying it."

I looked askance at her bold statement and replied with my most cultured British accent, which unfortunately sounded more like Liberace than Lloyd George. "Whatever do you mean? I went through a barbed-wire fence."

"True, but not running from dogs."

I considered issuing a strong denial on the grounds that Jimbo might actually be classified as a dog on at least one level if not a dozen, but clearly someone had been talking out of school. Or more likely in school.

To my knowledge only three humans, using the word loosely, knew of the incident. I knew I hadn't told a soul, and I doubted that Darnell was the weak link.

That left Jimbo, but as wide as Hannah's social circle might be, it didn't extend to him. So who would he tell?

Thelma. And since Hannah shared Mom's social egalitarianism, my imagination didn't even have to break a sweat to see them talking in gym or home ec or some such.

"What's your point, Sherlock?"

She leaned forward on the crate like the town gossip in a quilting bee. "Did he really shoot you with a shotgun?"

"Twice. Missed the second time."

"Wow. What was that like?"

The term heart-meltingly terrifying sprang to mind. "Let's just say if they're passing a sign-up sheet to be next in line, I would give it a miss."

"So I guess Anna is really The One."

"Huh?" What was it with these women? When it came to boys they only had one thing on their minds.

"Jimbo attacked you, ripped the handle off a car door trying to get to you, even shot you, but you refuse to abandon her. That's true love."

Evidently even the clear-thinking Hannah wasn't immune to the dreaded ravages of that classic oxymoron, the romantic thought. I cut her some slack since she was a high school freshman, a mere child after all.

She had failed to consider the alternative that was ever present in my mind. Jimbo would not be satisfied until I was engulfed in Thelma's passionate embrace like a chihuahua embedded in the cushions of an overstuffed couch.

"Hold on a second. It might have escaped your attention, but we're not old enough to vote, much less get married."

"Juliet was thirteen."

"And we know how that turned out."

"So you're saying Anna isn't The One?" Her tone had turned decidedly unfriendly, bordering hostile.

I was getting tired of all the women around me speaking in capitals and hidden agendas. "I'm saying I haven't even known her a month yet, for crying out loud." I climbed to my feet, took a step toward her, and waved a finger in her general direction. "And, on general principle, I don't think people who can't legally vote for dog catcher should get a tattoo, sign up for a credit card, or declare someone The One."

Hannah stood and kicked the crate aside. It tumbled over the edge and splintered on the ground. "You mean you don't even love her?"

"How should I know?"

Actually it surprised me that, just like the question of The One, it had never occurred to me to wonder if I loved her. That probably said something.

"I like her. A lot. I think about her every second. I'm going to ask her to the Valentine banquet. But does that mean I love her? You tell me."

"With your track record, you can't be too picky."

"So you're saying I should just take the first girl who doesn't run away screaming? That I'd be lucky to have Thelma?"

Hannah shook her finger in my face. "You . . . you . . ." She spun around, grabbed the trunk, and disappeared through the scuttle hole.

I took three deep breaths and threw myself back down in the corner.

Hannah's head suddenly popped up through the scuttle hole. "Next time I hope he gets you good," she yelled, and disappeared again.

I had barely sat down on the crate when Claire's head poked through the scuttle hole. "She hopes who gets you?"

Was there a sign on the trunk of the tree or something? Torment the monkey, three for a quarter. "Jimbo."

"Ah." Claire reached past me, flipped open my secret compartment, and extracted a copy of Moby Dick that I had never seen before. "The shotgun incident." She turned back the cover of the book, removed three items from inside the book, and set them on the surviving crate. An elephant incense burner, a box of incense, and a pack of Virginia Slims.

I was about to ask her how she knew about the shotgun but realized Jimbo was her smoking partner. Or one of them, at any rate. However, there was something else on my mind at the moment.

"What the heck, Claire?"

She looked up from lighting the incense. "I knew it wasn't from barbed wire. Jimbo told me the whole story the next day at school."

"You violated my secret compartment and hid cigarettes in there? What if Dad had found those?"

"Seriously? How long have you lived in this house?"

"Uh . . . five years."

She used the same match to light a cigarette. "And how many times has he come up here?"

"Never, as far as I know."

Claire blew out a stream of smoke with a satisfied sigh. "This is what we in the business call a low-risk proposition. Or what you would call flying under the radar."

"I would call not smoking at all flying under the radar."

"That's not flying. That's hunkering in the bunker."

She moved the elephant to the floor, sat on the crate, and leaned against the tree.

"So, Mark Cloud, tell us about this secret lover that drives you to risk being drawn and quartered by Jumbo Perkins."

"It's not a secret. She just goes to a different school, so nobody knows her."

"Except Elrick."

By the creek, a mockingbird and a blue jay staged a reenactment of a World War I dogfight over possession of a branch. "Do you think Jeff is The One?"

Claire blew twin streams of smoke out her nose like a dragon. "What?"

"You know. The one for you. That you are meant for each other."

"Seriously? I didn't realize you subscribed to *Seventeen* magazine."

"How long have you been dating?"

She took a while before answering. "It's complicated."

"Well, you stole a car and drove three hundred miles in one night to see him. Why would you do that if he wasn't The One?"

She stubbed out the cigarette viciously. "Look. First off, you can't expect me to carry on a serious conversation with someone who talks like a teenybopper with a crush."

I held out my hand for the cigarette butt. She threw it at me. As I added it to the collection in the coffee can in my secret compartment, I considered her reaction. Perhaps this obsession with The One was limited to the females in my immediate family. Maybe I had projected the whole thing on Anna, although when I thought about Saturday night, I didn't think so.

"So you don't think there is one person out there for you and you'll know it as soon as you find them?"

"No, I don't think there's some Prince Charming who will sweep in on a white horse and rescue me."

"That's not what I said."

"Right."

Perhaps I could have been wrong, but I got the distinct impression that I had possibly approached the subject from the wrong direction. "How did you meet Jeff?"

Claire lit another incense cone and another cigarette. "I was at a party in Montrose the day Janis Joplin died. Just two weeks after Hendrix. I was kinda bummed out. I mean, Janis, she was ours, you know."

She looked up at me, this preppy, fresh-scrubbed girl wearing gray wool bell-bottoms and a white Oxford shirt with a red scarf draped over her shoulders, sitting on a crate in a tree house as if she were on the veranda of the country club drinking a mint julep, mourning the passing of one of the most radically counter-culture icons of our generation. So far.

Claire, who grew up in one of the most affluent neighborhoods in the nation, claiming kinship with Janis, who grew up in a working-class family in a refinery town.

"Yeah," I said. "Port Arthur."

She snorted a puff of smoke. "Go ask Janis about finding The One."

Not only impossible, but considering the lyrics of her songs, ill advised. With a shudder I wondered if that was the point of kinship Claire shared with Janis. Which led me to reflect on the daily example of a romantic relationship she grew up with. Aunt Catherine and Uncle Roger.

In the light of this revelation, I looked at Claire with fresh eyes and a fresh dose of pity. Lucky for me, she was staring into the past and didn't notice, or I might have earned additional scars to nurse.

"I was sitting on a couch by myself and Jeff came over and sat next to me. He knew what I was thinking without even asking. He brought me a beer and we sang 'Mercedes Benz.'"

My first impulse was to ask if Jeff taught correspondence courses. He could be rich if he wasn't already. My second thought was to do the math. She was fourteen at this party. My third thought was to wonder why she could meet a guy who understood her so well and not think he was The One.

But I picked a safer question.

"So you started dating?"

"Roger, in his infinite wisdom, wrecked it by deciding that the climate of Pennsylvania suited me better."

"He didn't like Jeff?"

"Roger doesn't like anything. Except patents. And scotch."

"So you haven't seen Jeff since you went to Philadelphia?"

Claire graced me with a sly glance. "I didn't say that."

"So . . . ?"

"He drove up to see me last year."

"Seriously?" I bit off the word, realizing I'd been around Claire too long. "That's like a thousand miles." How could she not think he was The One?

"He picks up cars at auctions and takes them back to Houston to sell. He found a pristine 1963 Nine Eleven in Boston and stopped by Philadelphia on his way back."

"A nine eleven?"

"Porsche," she said with a smidgen of condescension.

"Right," I said, more than somewhat peeved at breaking the cardinal rule of East Texas. Never ask questions. "Wait. He bought a Porsche?" A lifetime of cleaning the church and selling Grit wouldn't even make a down payment on a Porsche. "A teenager?"

"Jeff is twenty-four."

"Your boyfriend is twenty-four?" I'm afraid I may have stuttered. He was twenty-one when he bought a fourteen-year-old girl a beer. What a sweetheart he must be.

Claire took a final drag off her cigarette and rubbed it out. "I told you it was complicated."

"And the boarding school was okay with that?"

"I didn't exactly ask them." She handed me the cigarette. "Remember when I said there were a few other things they were upset about?"

"Yeah."

"I kind of disappeared for a weekend with Jeff."

"A weekend?" I squeaked.

"You're starting to sound like Roger."

I dialed it down a bit. "What did you do for a whole—" I decided mid-sentence I didn't want to know the answer to that question. "If you really like him, you're old enough to get married without your parent's consent. And it sounds like he can afford it."

"Who said anything about getting married?"

"But . . ." I was clearly out of my depth. I had no idea where to take the conversation. She steals our car to drive half the night to see this guy, but she doesn't want to marry him. "Then what—"

"Hey, Beaver Cleaver!"

I couldn't be sure, but lightning may have sparked from her hair as she jumped to her feet.

"It might be hard for someone from Fred to wrap his head around the idea, but not everyone has an Ozzie and Harriet life. If they ever did. Which I doubt."

I wanted to shout back that I had been some places and seen some things myself, but the force of her declaration electrified my skinny frame. She had given me a small glimpse into another world, maybe the world the rest of the population lived in while I blithely concerned myself with such mundane matters as how to placate

Deacon Fry and whether to kiss my girlfriend the next time I could scrape together enough cash to finance a date and how to avoid becoming a martyr to love at the hands of Jimbo Perkins.

Claire fumbled for a cigarette, drew one out with a shaky hand, and tried to light it several times. She let loose a few choice syllables, turned her back to me, and leaned against the tree. "I don't want to talk about this anymore. Why don't you just go polish your stamp collection or something." Smoke billowed out as she finally got her hands to cooperate.

I waited for the adrenaline to drain from my system and then asked, "So, if I hear you right, you're saying Jeff might not be The One?"

Claire jerked her head around and looked at me for a second. Her expression could have been love or hate or both. I wasn't versed in such nuances. I thought I saw moisture gathering in her eyes. She turned away. Her shoulders shook, and she made a noise that could have been laughing or crying. Or both.

A thought or a voice slipped into my head and asked the question that seemed to haunt me these days, so much that I almost wished I'd never read that book, had never asked myself that seductive but altogether too demanding question. What would Jesus do? Right here, right now, for this lost lamb who might be a wolf underneath? For this girl who was my age but at the same time so much older and yet heartbreakingly younger. It was complicated. Or maybe it was simple. So simple that it was hard to believe.

I hoped she would get what she wanted, but I didn't know what that was, or even if she knew, when it came down to it. I wanted to hug her until it all went away and she was as trusting and wholesome on the inside as she looked on the outside when she wasn't trying to act tough.

"Hey," I said softly. "No matter how or why, I'm glad you're here."

She turned enough for me to see the glistening tracks of the tears on her round cheeks and the ghost of a timid smile.

I continued. "Not just up here in the Fortress right now, but here in Fred. With us."

After a long while, she said, "Me too."

CHAPTER TWENTY-SIX

The weather held until the weekend. Saturday morning I had my usual breakfast, a Pop-Tart and the chocolate milkshake with a raw egg that Mom had taken to fixing for me in an effort to fatten me up beyond the look of a Bangladesh refugee. So far it had produced no visible results, but I wasn't complaining.

As I prepared for my assault on the church for the weekly cleaning, Claire decided to tag along. I wasn't opposed to assistance, and we made short work of it. We returned to the parsonage for a leisurely lunch of a slice of bread, a slice of cheese, and a slice of tomato stacked in that order and sprinkled with diced onions, fresh from the toaster oven, with a side of chips and Dr Pepper.

Thus fortified, I set out on my Grit route with a companion for the first time. Claire used Heidi's long-abandoned bicycle. Since we were braving the back roads and the river bottom, she had made a wardrobe concession with a plaid shirt borrowed from my closet, a pair of Levis harvested from her suitcase, and tennis shoes. Being a quick study, it didn't take her long to master the sales pitch. I let her do the talking and our sales increased accordingly.

A good half hour before the winter sunset, we arrived at the hill where a can of Coke awaited me. I hoped Vernon had an extra. When I veered off the road away from the house with the leggy girl on the porch swing and toward the Pontiac, Claire hesitated.

"What's this?" she asked.

"Don't worry, he's cool," I answered. "But I get shotgun."

As we passed by in front of the car, Vernon's head didn't move, but his glistening black eyes followed us. I leaned my bike against the front fender, got into the front seat, and tossed a paper in the back. I reached for the Coke he held in his hand, but he pulled it away.

"Mind yer manners, Mark boy."

I inspected his face. Eyes slightly red and gleaming. A smile sliding off his face. Looked like he'd got an early start.

When Claire climbed in the backseat, he offered the Coke to her. "You must be the rich girl from down south that's staying at Pastor Matt's place."

I shrugged in response to Claire's questioning glance. I hadn't mentioned her to Vernon, but there were no secrets in Fred. Not for long.

She held out her hand. "Claire Foxe."

Vernon lodged his cigarette in his lips, twisted in the seat, and offered his left hand, the one constructed largely of half fingers. "Vernon Crowley at your service, Miss Claire," he said with one eye squinted shut against the smoke.

"Pleased to meet you." Claire nodded at the cigarette hanging from his lips. "You wouldn't have another one of those you could spare, would you?"

Vernon glanced at me. I nodded. I always smelled like smoke when I came home from the Grit route, so it was probably safe.

He gave her a Lucky Strike, held the lighter for her, and then flipped it shut. "If yer feeling neighborly, you can dig a Coke out of that cooler for Mark boy, here."

I peeled off the tab and dropped it in my pocket for Hannah, who made chains of the things for some inexplicable reason. I tilted my Coke toward the girl draped across the swing in short shorts and a plaid shirt tied together across her stomach. She reminded me of Raquel Welch in *One Million Years, B.C.* "How much longer you think she'll hang around?"

"Till she traps another one," Vernon said.

Based on recent conversations, I wondered about her position on The One. Was she waiting for a white knight to charge through the river bottom and carry her away to Graceland?

Claire broke the silence. "Mr. Crowley, is this a 1960 Bonneville?"

Vernon studied Claire in the mirror with lidded eyes. "I reckon she's 'bout as old as you." He took a sip of his Coke. "You got a good eye, Miss Claire. She's a fifty-nine."

Claire ran her hand over the upholstery. "She's in great condition."

"That she is. A car is like a woman. You pick the right one, treat her right, you won't have no regrets. At least on her count."

I glanced at Vernon's profile as he took a drag from the cigarette wedged between two half-fingers, his hand cupped over his mouth the way he did when he was feeling no pain. Did he subscribe to the philosophy of The One? I didn't know much about his marriage other than that sometimes Gina showered him with kisses and other times showered him with fists. Why would he stay with her if she wasn't The One? On the other hand, could a woman who took a swing at you as the mood took her really be The One?

"So you've had this car for fourteen years?" Claire asked. "One owner."

"That's what the math works out to."

Claire hesitated before asking the next question. "And is there a Mrs. Crowley?"

"That there is for certain. Had her for bout twice as long."

"I think Mrs. Crowley is a lucky woman."

"Don't know how lucky she is, seeing as how she has to put up with me."

Claire patted the seat back. "I know someone would give you a good price for her."

Vernon chuckled out smoke signals. "I don't see as how Gina would cotton to that idea."

"The car. I know a collector in Houston who would give you whatever price you asked."

"Well, now, I'm the one who wouldn't cotton to that. Couldn't sell her no more than I could sell Gina."

"I understand," Claire said.

The sun settled on the chimney of the house across the street. The girl had disappeared from the porch without us noticing. Vernon pulled a flask from between the driver's door and the seat and dispensed a few ounces into his Coke can. The sickly sweet smell of whiskey wafted through the car.

"You wouldn't be willing to share some of that, would you?" Claire asked.

"Claire," I said before Vernon could react. "You can't go home with whiskey on your breath." I turned in the seat and looked at her unapologetic expression. "Besides, after Monday night you have a good reason to fly under the radar."

"Or maybe I have a good reason to fly. Period."

We stared each other down for a few seconds before Vernon intervened.

"Miss Claire, I ain't got no objection to sharing, but I wouldn't do anything to hurt Pastor Matt, and I know he would take it amiss."

His consideration for Dad took me by surprise. We hadn't talked that much about my family or Dad's profession. I didn't figure on a bootlegger holding a Baptist preacher in high regard.

"Fine." Claire got out of the car, slammed the door, and walked thirty yards off to the edge of the pine woods. She knelt down to tie her shoe, but when she stood up she had a cigarette she had evidently smuggled out of the house in her sock. She smoked it while meandering between the trees.

"Got a bit of a fuse on her, don't she?" Vernon said.

"Don't take it personally. She's got it pretty rough right now."

"Oh, I don't object to a bit of spunk in a woman. Keeps things interesting."

We watched the sun disappear behind the house across the road.

"She's cute as a bug's ear. You two make a right fine couple."

I choked on my Coke. "She's my cousin!"

"Ain't no reason to keep you apart."

"First cousin," I said with deliberate emphasis on the first word.

"Them royals do it all the time. Ever heard of kissing cousins?"

"Ever heard of the phrase 'mad as a lord?'"

Vernon chuckled. "Well, I might be wrong, but I do believe she fancies you."

If he kept talking like that, I might even ask him to spike my drink. But his drunken conjecture burrowed into my mind like a screwworm and laid its eggs. What did I have to offer a girl like

Claire? Or, to be brutally explicit, what did a penurious, skinny, naive, provincial nerd have to offer a rich, pretty, experienced, cosmopolitan player like Claire? Or was that just what she needed?

I slammed the door closed on such conjecture. This was the exact thing that had got me into trouble with Jolene two months ago. Vain imaginations and speculations. Besides, she was my cousin, for crying out loud.

But I had more pressing issues, and I thought Vernon might be drunk enough for me to slip a personal question over the transom.

"Do you think there's one perfect person out there for everyone? I mean, you've been married to Gina for close to thirty years. Did you see her and think she was The One?"

Vernon lit another cigarette, took a long drink from his Coke, and blew out a lungful of air. "Well, Mark boy, that's a big question."

I hoped he had an equally big answer.

"It's kinda like a rainbow. Looks like three or four or five colors, but it's really millions of shades that blend from one to the next. Let's say yer perfect match is one particular shade of blue. There could be a thousand colors so close as so you'd never know the difference unless ya saw them right next to each other."

"So you're saying there might be a thousand girls who could be The One? But if there are thousands, how can you call her The One?"

"There's four billion people on the planet. Think them thousand girls are all piled up in one place? Ya might only meet one of them in yer lifetime. Or never at all."

"Is that what happened to you? You found The One?"

Vernon didn't answer. He pulled out the flask, but instead of spiking his drink, which I figured by now was close to eighty percent whiskey, he just took a long swig of pure whiskey. Then he wiped his lips with the back of his hand, screwed the cap down with great deliberation, and slipped the flask back between the seat and the door.

"Yessir, Mark boy," he slurred in a voice barely louder than a whisper. "That I did."

I didn't say a word. I barely breathed. I felt like I was in the presence of something special, almost holy.

Just the math alone was staggering. What if there were only a thousand girls out there who could be The One for me? That would mean that any one of them would literally be one in four million. For me right now, that meant maybe fifty in the entire country, one per state. Somewhere in the almost two million square miles of Texas, one girl was the one for me. What were the odds that her name was Anna and she lived only thirty miles away? Ridiculous.

But Vernon had found his one in four million. He was one of the lucky ones. The rest of us had to wander the face of the earth wondering if we would ever find The One. Wondering if we should just settle.

I was jarred from my meditation on probabilities and providence by the back door slamming shut.

"Mr. Crowley," Claire said. "I want to apologize for being rude. You've been very gracious and I have no excuse."

An aroma of incense eased through the air of the car. I turned to look at Claire, unsure of what it could be.

"Missy, don't you worry yer pretty little head about it," Vernon said without turning around. "Yer always welcome at my house."

I realized Claire was shrouded in the gloom of the twilight. More time had passed than I realized. We needed to get home before it got completely dark. But Vernon was in no condition to drive home.

"We have to be getting along," I said. "But how about we drive you home first?"

Vernon was slow to respond. "Yessir, Mark boy. I reckon that would be best."

"Okay. You can slide over while we put the bikes in the trunk."

I grabbed the keys from the ignition and jumped out.

Claire joined me at the back of the car. "Does he always get like this?"

"Not usually."

I opened the trunk. A dozen or so jugs glinted from the shadow of the trunk. I pushed them to one side to make room for the bikes, loaded them in, and slammed the lid closed.

We drove the half-mile to Vernon's single-wide and helped him to the cinder block steps. The door opened and Gina looked out, her black hair glistening in the mercury vapor lamp at the end of the driveway.

"Vernon, how have you come to be as this?"

She slipped down the cinder blocks like a duchess descending a marble staircase and helped him into the house. From the door she looked out on us. "Thank you, Mark boy, for taking the care of him. He is the little boy sometimes."

"Yes, ma'am."

I extracted the bikes from the trunk and delivered the keys to Gina. She thanked me, and Claire and I pedaled off into the gloaming.

"Wow," Claire said. "You really know how to party."

"Just another day in my Ozzie and Harriet life."

"Look, I'm sorry about—"

"That's okay. We all have our things we're dealing with."

"Yeah."

We ate up a mile or two as the Milky Way stretched itself across the sky like a cat in front of a fire.

"See that tree over there?" I said.

"Yeah."

"That's the tree I hid behind when Jimbo shot me."

"No kidding?"

"The historical plaque is scheduled to be installed next week."

A half-mile later, I pointed to the right side of the road. "Two months ago I watched Parker burn down that gazebo he built for his wife right after she left him because he was too religious."

"Who's Parker?"

"A guy with an eyepatch and a wicked scar running down the left side of his face. Not something you want to see in the firelight."

When we got off the sand roads and onto the highway, the going was easier. Claire pulled up next to me.

"Did you see all those jugs in the trunk?"

"Yeah."

"Was that what I think it was?"

"Moonshine."

"So Vernon is a moonshiner?"

"Pretty much."

I could feel her gaze in the moonlight. "So who's flying under the radar now?"

"It ain't Ozzie and Harriet," I said.

At home we parked the bikes and went inside.

Dad got up from his armchair where he was working on his sermon with a stack of notes. "Claire, I'd like a word with you."

She looked at me. I shrugged.

Dad pointed the papers toward the guest bedroom, followed her in, and closed the door.

I looked at Mom, who was watching *All in the Family*. "What was that about?"

"You'll have to ask them," she said.

The next day, between Sunday school and the service, I followed Claire behind the church where she usually sneaked a cigarette.

"So, what was with the secret meeting?"

"Uncle Matt evidently reads every line of his phone bill."

"Of course."

She blew out a stream of smoke. "Roger doesn't."

"Sure, but he's a millionaire. What does the phone bill have to do with you?"

"I called Jeff a few times. It didn't even come up to a hundred dollars." She obviously had no clue how much a small town preacher made. "I'm grounded until I pay it back."

"Of course."

Claire wheeled around and took a step toward me. "Stop saying that. It's not 'of course' to me. I didn't grow up in a . . . in this—this . . . concentration camp."

"You didn't grow up at all," I yelled back. "When I call Anna, I pay for it. When I want an album, I pay for it. When I use the car, I pay for the gas. That's not a concentration camp. It's just pulling your own weight."

"No, it's just how your family does it. Not everybody does it the way you do."

"You can always go home where everything was perfect." I felt bad as soon as I said it, but I was too mad to take it back.

"Maybe I will," she snapped. "Maybe I will," she said again to herself. "Or maybe I'll . . ." She threw down the cigarette, ground it into the dirt, and stormed off.

I didn't ask about the other option. I didn't want another secret on my conscience.

Inside Claire smiled at everyone and carried on like it was her favorite place. Go figure.

CHAPTER TWENTY-SEVEN

I spent the next three weeks amassing funds. I nursed the relationship along with occasional phone calls, the content of which is best left to the imagination since we might have been guilty of straying into the realm of Heidi-Hosea levels of glutinosity, if I can use that word. While helpful in the romance department, the calls were of the long-distance variety and therefore counterproductive in the finance department.

I still didn't know if she was The One, but I did know I wanted to meet her at midnight in the light of the rose window and take another trip in the time machine.

On Wednesday, February 14, the day ordained by greeting card companies for obligatory expressions of romantic sentiments, I came home from school and arrayed myself in a blue blazer with brass buttons, maroon shirt, white bell-bottoms, and maroon and white patent leather shoes. I topped the whole thing off with a neon paisley tie wide enough to serve as a landing strip for a C-130 transport aircraft.

Having been granted the dispensation of the greater of the family vehicles for the occasion, the one with the factory-issue monochromatic color scheme, power steering, and air conditioning, I drove the thirty miles to Woodville through a chilly drizzle with the anticipation of a kid who has discovered that Christmas, a birthday party, and a trip to Disneyland will all be magically bestowed in a single tap of a wand custom-made for that purpose.

Reverend Courtney answered the door and pointed to the den. "Have a seat. They're engrossed in the endless feminine process of gilding the lily."

He settled into his armchair, and I dropped onto the couch wondering how long this would last. Due to my inexperience, I had not prepared for an extended conversation with the paterfamilias, although now I saw it must be a traditional element of the pregame show.

I started to toss out the default "How about them Cowboys?" gambit, but stifled it just in time as I remembered how that turned out on the double date. In vain I racked my brain for some suitable topic.

Fortunately, Reverend Courtney's inability to contain his pride saved me the effort. "You probably haven't heard down in Fred, but our little punkin is in the running for the court for the Dogwood Festival."

"I'm not surprised," I said, although I was. Or more accurately, the festival hadn't crossed my mind.

In February of each year, the festival committee selected candidates from each of the five area school districts to make up the court of the Dogwood Queen. Over the next two months, they narrowed the field to five queen candidates and ten princesses.

As a junior, Anna was a candidate for princess from Woodville. I had no doubt that Jolene was a candidate from Warren. I also had no doubt that they both would end up on the court.

"We're very proud of her."

I nodded, and the room settled into a predictable awkward silence that lasted an eternity of a few minutes.

"How's your folks?" Reverend Courtney finally said.

"Fine. They're doing fine." I crossed my legs and tapped my fingers on my patent leather shoes.

The tick of the pendulum clock on the wall filled the silence like the deathwatch beetle in Poe's "Tell-Tale Heart."

I was saved from leaping from my seat and declaring my guilt by Reverend Courtney dragging himself out of the armchair and saying, "And here she is."

Anna entered in a shining midnight-blue satin formal draped with a lace shawl that rendered both her father and me speechless. I presented the corsage Mom had bought in Silsbee, and her mom helped her pin it on. Then we mercifully escaped.

I don't recall what we talked about on the drive back to Fred, or if we even talked at all. In the early twilight, I steered the Galaxie on the glistening ribbon of road, through the fog-shrouded woods, like Odysseus sailing home to Penelope. Except that Penelope was already nestled next to me against the chill of a fading winter, already mine without having to fight my way through dozens of suitors.

And I realized I was insane. Crazy about this girl. Crazy to debate whether she was The One. Forget Claire's name-calling or Vernon's lesson on the math of romantic compatibility. Anna was clearly the one with the most sense, able to recognize the obvious truth while I floundered in a fog of indecision and self-doubt.

Dogwood princess or not, we were made for each other. Members of the same tribe sharing a common tradition. Each fascinated with the other, unable to think of anything other than the chance to share the same space, the same time, the same breath.

As we passed over Toodlum Creek, I panicked at the thought of how close I had come to wrecking the whole thing with my endless and pointless second guessing. Whether you were six or sixteen, when you found The One, you didn't hold back for the opportunity to comparison shop. You snatched up the deal, sold everything to buy the pearl of great price, and considered yourself lucky.

I squeezed Anna with the arm I had draped over her, and she burrowed closer to my heart. We traveled the final ten miles to Fred in silence.

The fellowship hall was decorated for the occasion with garlands of red and white cardboard hearts punctuated with red and white balloons. The tables were arranged in a giant horseshoe with the chairs on the outside and a podium at the open end. Candles flickered above white tablecloths and name cards. Chamber music played softly on a portable stereo in a corner. I recognized it as the Telleman album from our collection at home.

As we entered, everyone turned toward us and the room fell silent. I flattered myself that we made for an imposing couple, but I knew that the ensemble draped over my skinny frame, something I had cobbled together from the available material in my closet, played no part in the effect on the crowd.

It was all due to Anna, her blonde hair turned burnished gold in the candlelight, the lace shawl spelling out hieroglyphics against the midnight blue of her gown, the sheen echoed in her eyes that were the color of desire and regret.

Then the conversation returned, unnaturally loud to compensate. Jolene approached, accompanied by a victim I had not seen before. Evidently she had been forced to reach beyond the stock pond of Fred for a date to the banquet. He was big and dreamy, as the girls say, and seemed suitably oblivious to his fate, like a spellbound sailor without the foresight to pack beeswax for the trip past the Sirens.

"Hey Mark. And you must be Anna."

"This is Anna," I said unnecessarily, suddenly self-conscious about introducing this conversation-stopping stranger into my natural habitat.

Jolene ignored me. "I'm Jolene."

"Nice to meet you," Anna said. She looked to Jolene's date for an introduction.

He didn't notice. His attention was focused on Jolene. He would fall hard before the night was over, all the more because he seemed the type that had girls eating out of his hand from the moment he said, "Do you come here often?" Tomorrow he would perhaps be wiser, and probably more cynical, for the experience.

I considered the two girls, both beautiful in their own way, one deadly to the male ego, the other as sincere as a blank check, both as rare as a winning lottery ticket.

Bubba was there with Mary, Ralph with Squeaky. I made the rounds with Anna, getting approving nods from the guys and insincere smiles from the gals. Then we ran into Claire and C.J.

I stared, momentarily speechless. Claire hadn't said a word about coming to the banquet and C.J. had never been to the church.

"How did you get past security?" I asked C.J.

C.J. gave Claire a one-arm hug. "Turns out whoever comes with the prettiest girl gets in free."

I hugged Anna. "Then I guess we're getting a refund." To C.J. and Claire I said, "Too bad for you guys."

Claire stuck out her tongue for a microsecond and then turned to Anna. "Hi, I'm Claire, Mark's cousin. This is C.J., which is short for court jester."

I put an arm around Anna. "This is Anna, which is short for princess."

C.J. grabbed Anna's hand, bowed low, and kissed it. "Your wish is my command, your majesty." He turned to me and whispered loud enough to be heard to the farthest corner of the room. "Dude! You said she was hot, but you didn't say she was this hot."

Claire elbowed him. "You'll have to excuse C.J. He was dropped on his head—"

"Five minutes ago," I said.

"I see no need for ze apology." C.J. said in a mangled French accent and gestured to Claire. "As you can see, I am ze, how you say, connoisseur of beauty."

Anna and Claire exchanged glances and a whole conversation seemed to take place in three seconds, very little of it about C.J. It was like watching a wireless Vulcan mind meld. I would have paid six months of church cleanings to get a transcript of just half of it. I resisted the urge to pull Claire aside and ask, "Did she say anything about me?"

At the signal, we found our seats and the program began. Opening prayer, a song, and the meal to the tune of the Telemann album.

As we attacked the garden salad with Italian dressing, Anna said, "Can you believe what Hosea did last weekend? Unforgivable."

"What?" Keeping abreast of the latest transgressions of The Hose didn't rank high on my list of priorities.

"Heidi didn't tell you?"

"She hasn't come home since the semester started. It's only been a month."

"He stood her up for a date and then blamed it on her."

I finished off my salad, pushed the plate aside, and snagged a bread stick to keep me company. "How do you know all this?"

"She told me."

I stopped with the bread stick halfway to my mouth. "She told you about her date? When?"

"Last weekend on our phone call."

"Your phone call?"

"We chat every Sunday night. Girl talk."

"You do?" I found this odd and a little disturbing. Anna was in regular communication with my sister? What information was Heidi feeding her?

"Of course, silly."

"Okay." I took a bite of the bread stick and munched it slowly while I tried to figure out in which universe this was obvious.

"They were supposed to go to the Friday night campus movie in the chapel. Heidi got all ready and waited, but Hosea never came. She found out the next day that he went bowling with a bunch of guys from the dorm."

Bowling. Evidently it ran in the family. I wondered what his handicap was. "Maybe she got the day wrong."

Anna tilted her head and studied me. "That's what he said."

I shrugged. "There you go."

"They don't show the movie on Saturday."

"So maybe he got the day wrong."

"But everybody knows the movie only shows on Friday."

The servers came through with the main course. Our server turned out to be Hannah. She very carefully removed Anna's salad and set down a plate of Chicken Parmesan and asparagus. Then she jerked my salad plate away, dropped my entree on the table, and strode off.

The chicken had flopped halfway onto the table. I pushed it back on the plate. "Evidently The Hose didn't."

"The Hose?" Anna asked.

"Hosea, I mean."

Anna set her knife and fork down and released a loud breath through her nose. "He just forgot, but he wouldn't admit it. He tried to make her think she was the one who forgot."

"Okay," I said slowly.

"Sometimes he can be such a jerk."

I didn't doubt it. Except for the sometimes part. Pretty much all the time was my guess. "Well, consider the source."

"Just like a guy to act selfish and then try to make the girl think it's her . . . Wait. What do you mean consider the source?"

"Well, it's The Ho— It's Hosea we're talking about."

"And?"

"He is a bit of a goofus."

Her eyebrows arched in a manner that wasn't altogether flattering. "Is he?"

"Just look at his car. You can't take a guy who drives a canary-colored Nova seriously."

"What else?"

I had been reticent in Anna's presence about the many aspects of Hosea's behavior and personality that I found objectionable, and now that I found that she shared my opinion I let loose the full arsenal.

"Have you ever noticed how he chews with his mouth open? It sounds like a hunter field-dressing a deer. And he digs his little finger into his ear and wiggles his hand like a cellist playing vibrato. And then he smells it. And don't even get me started on his driving."

Anna's gaze pinned me down like a beetle in a zoology collection. "So Hosea is a goofus?"

"Well, you just said . . ."

"Sometimes he can be a jerk."

"Yeah. I was just agreeing with you."

"I never called him a goofus."

"Yes, but . . ."

Anna's expression didn't lull me back into the idyllic reflections I had experienced on the drive down, but I couldn't imagine why. Surely in the discipline of comparative terminology, jerk ranked higher than goofus in the precedence of pejoratives.

"Is there anything else you would like to add? Something about his dental hygiene? Perhaps he kicks puppies and drowns kittens?"

The knife and fork dropped from my hands onto the plate with a clatter that drew everyone's attention. "No . . . I mean . . . I was just—"

"It's not like your sister is any great catch. Have you heard the way she laughs? Like a sewing machine choking on a piece of sheet metal. And her makeup."

"She doesn't wear makeup."

"Exactly! Some people should have the presence of mind to realize that they can't get away with that."

To say the least, which I rarely did, the evening had taken an unexpected turn. I looked around at the fascinated faces pointed in our direction and desperately tried to put my finger on the exact cause of this disastrous development. Claire caught my eye from her spot around the corner a few seats away and made a "What gives?" expression. I shook my head and looked away.

Anna had introduced the whole Hosea-bashing theme. I was just trying to be supportive of her view and somehow it had turned into an ad hominem free-for-all.

"But you just said that—"

"So it's my fault that you hate Hosea?"

"No, that's not what I meant."

"Then what did you mean?"

"I just thought—"

"You thought what? That Hosea is some kind of bozo preying on your poor innocent sister?"

Somehow this conversation about Hosea's shortcomings had morphed into a hit piece on Heidi. Acutely aware that the scene was being played out on a public stage, I struggled for some kind of response that would serve to stem the tide of accusations.

"Maybe we could talk about this later?"

"I don't want to talk about it at all."

She stabbed her Chicken Parmesan so viciously that it squawked. Or maybe it was me who squawked. I couldn't swear either way. But at least she quit talking. For the moment, anyway.

I shrugged and cut a slice off my chicken. I didn't get it. Whatever Heidi and The Hose did was their own affair. I didn't see why I should concern myself with the vicissitudes of their relationship or why Anna would care either. And I really didn't see why I should be blamed for agreeing with her.

We ate in silence. I occasionally glanced at her and noted the furrowed brows, the bulging of her jaw muscles as she chewed the chicken with a focused deliberation. It made her look like a completely different person. A person I didn't know.

What had happened to the Irish Spring Angel of two months ago? The girl who had transformed "The Son of a Preacher Man" from a catalog of my failures to a celebration of my finesse?

What had happened to The One who had chosen me as The One?

My reflections were interrupted by the introduction of the dessert course. Strawberry cheesecake made from a box mix by the Women's Missionary Union. Hannah served it with the same asymmetric finesse as she had the main course and left in a completely symmetrical huff.

Cheesecake was my favorite, but it might as well have been half-cooked oatmeal. The world had turned a uniform shade of oatmeal grey as far as the eye could see and probably farther if I cared to investigate beyond the horizon, which I didn't.

Bubba closed the evening with a reading of I Corinthians 13, ending with the classic verse.

And now these three remain: faith, hope, and love. But the greatest of these is love.

I shook my head. The greatest might be love, but in my opinion, none of them remained.

Bubba's voice had barely died out before Anna said, "It's a school night. I have to get home."

I stood. "Okay."

I followed her without speaking to anyone, or even meeting their eyes. Outside I opened the car door for her and she got in without a word.

The temps were down in the thirties, and as I got in the driver's side, I noted that she shivered against the passenger door, putting as much space as possible between us. Once the engine warmed up, I turned the heater to max.

It took the seventeen miles to Warren and half the twelve miles to Woodville for the car to warm up and for me to come up with a way to assault the fortress of silence.

"Anna, I was just agreeing with—"

"I don't want to talk about it."

"But—"

"Don't. Want. To. Talk."

"Okay."

Ten minutes later we pulled into her driveway. She was out of the car before I even got my door open. I sprinted to catch up and walked her to the door.

She hesitated on the porch, threw a furtive glance at me, and rushed inside.

The walk back to the car took as long as the drive out, as long as the entire evening. I sat behind the wheel with my hand on the key and wondered what had just happened. After an eternity of bewilderment, during which Reverend Courtney looked out of the curtains three times, I cranked the car and escaped.

Hannah and Claire were waiting for me when I got home. Unlike Anna, Hannah showed no reluctance in the talking department. Her green eyes looked like a storm at sea. One that sailors didn't come back from.

"What did you do?" she demanded before I had the door closed behind me.

"Nothing." I headed straight to the fridge. It was time for the hard stuff. I pulled out a can of Dr Pepper and a jar of pickled okra.

Hannah cornered me in the V of the open fridge door. "I've seen nothing before. It didn't look anything like that."

I pushed past her and sat down at the kitchen table. "I don't know what it was."

Claire sat down next to me. "This is the princess to your Prince Charming? More like the wicked stepsister."

Hannah shot her a wicked look and loomed over me. "What did you say that made her so mad?"

"They were talking about somebody named Hosea," Claire said.

Declining to comment, I cracked open the Dr Pepper, took a long slug, and ate a pickled okra whole, including the little cap I usually discarded.

The gesture was not lost on Hannah. She raised an eyebrow, pulled out a chair, and sat down.

I chased the okra with another slug of Dr Pepper and wiped my mouth with the back of my hand. "She was mad at Hosea for standing up Heidi on a date. She said he was a jerk. I agreed. Then she went ballistic."

Hannah flopped back in her chair and stared at me like I had announced I was pregnant. "Well what did you expect?"

"From what I could hear, he was a jerk," Claire said. "Forgot about the date and tried to make Heidi think it was her fault. It's like a scene straight out of *Gaslight*."

Hannah's reaction arrested an okra halfway between the jar and my mouth. "What did I expect? A thank you," I said.

I gave her a hard look, swallowed the okra after a level of mastication well below the recommended minimum, and choked.

Hannah observed my coughing fit without comment or concern for my well-being. Claire used the opportunity to take a sip of my Dr Pepper.

After I recovered, I posed my question. "Would you care to explain what in the name of Peter Piper's pickled peppers you're talking about?"

"Never agree when a girl complains about someone she cares about," she said as if explaining to the Galloping Gourmet how to boil water.

"So I should have disagreed with her?"

"Duh," Hannah said. If she had rolled her eyes any further, she would have been looking out the back of her head.

"I think you should ditch her," Claire said.

I dismissed Claire's comment with a wave of a dripping okra and turned to Hannah. "Okay." I nodded, filing away her completely irrational and bewildering advice for future reference. "Disagree when she—"

"No, Twinkie-brain. Never disagree with her, no matter what she says."

"So I don't disagree with her."

"No!"

"And I don't agree with her."

"No!"

I took a strong hit of Dr Pepper straight from the can, feeling like I'd sampled Vernon's can of Coke by mistake. I began to suspect that Hannah would only make sense if I had been drinking. A lot.

It was like coming across a proof in algebra where A equals not A. "Can you work that out on paper?"

"Could you be any more stupid?"

I thought I probably could, but I didn't see any profit in pursuing that line of inquiry.

"Anna's the one who's stupid," Claire said. "She can't call her brother a jerk and then get mad when someone says the same thing. That's a double standard."

"Yeah," I said. "That's a double standard. What ever happened to women's lib and all that?"

"Does Anna seem like a girl who is into women's lib?" Hannah demanded.

"No," Claire and I said simultaneously.

"Okay, then."

I decided to concede the point in the interest of time. "So, how do I not agree and not disagree?"

"Just be sympathetic."

Claire threw up her hands, and went to the fridge, and pulled out a Dr Pepper.

I gave this some thought while I munched an okra and washed it down. "So I sympathize with her without agreeing with her."

"Exactly. It's not brain surgery."

Perhaps not, but I was fairly certain I would require brain surgery to do it. "That's all good," I said, although it was far from good. "But it's too late. She won't even talk to me."

"She'll talk to you if you apologize."

"Wait." I held up a hand to stop the madness. "Apologize? But I didn't do anything wrong."

"Yeah," Claire said.

Hannah's sigh of exasperation spawned several tornadoes in the kitchen. "Of course you did something wrong. She's mad at you, isn't she?"

"Oh, right. I agreed with her." Obviously the wrong thing to do. How could I have been so dense?

"You think sarcasm is helpful at this point?"

"What sarcasm?" I didn't understand it enough to be sarcastic about it. I would settle for being able to make a single statement that Hannah would accept. "Okay, let me see if I have this right. I apologize for agreeing with her, but then I don't agree or disagree, just be agreeable."

"Sympathetic."

"Or you could just cut your losses, dump her, and consider yourself lucky," Claire said.

"Be sympathetic. Got it," I said, not getting it at all or even having the faintest idea what "it" looked like.

"There," Hannah said. She stood. "Now go and sin no more."

I shook my head. "How about you just stone me now and we get it over with?"

CHAPTER TWENTY-EIGHT

Here's the thing about Dr Pepper and pickled okra. Heidi was right. It gives you weird dreams.

Anna appeared as the Red Queen in Alice in Wonderland, running around with a flamingo tucked under one arm and yelling "Off with his head!"

The Hose showed up as the Red King and shook his finger in my face. "Rule forty-two. Think of her as your sister. It's the first rule in the book."

Hannah faded in as the Cheshire cat. "Sympathetic," she said, and then faded away.

"Simply pathetic!" Anna said. "Off with his head!"

I woke up and swore off Dr Pepper and pickled okra. At least until the next time.

I barely made the bus and took a seat in the row behind the driver where nobody ever sat. I was in no mood for conversation or company. I maintained my policy of radio silence through the first four periods, fending off questions from the usual crowd with a wave of my hand and "Everything's fine."

At lunch I hunted down Elrick. Although the Jim Crow laws had been abolished for almost two decades, no Supreme Court decision could abolish the natural inclination of teenagers to minimize the risk of rejection. As a result, a defacto Jim Crow law split the cafeteria along color lines on either side of the jukebox more effectively than any legislation could.

But for some reason, perhaps because he was from Dallas, Elrick moved between the two worlds as easily as Alice stepping through the mirror. From day one, he sat with whichever group of friends he chose, white or black, football or debate team, student or teacher.

I found him in the section of tables the black kids had staked out at the west end of the cafeteria and sat down next to him. I ignored the inspection from the surrounding diners and launched directly into my attack.

"Dude, we need to talk."

Elrick sized me up for a few seconds before responding.

I glanced around the table and said, "Hey" in response to the panoply of expressions of the surrounding diners.

"Okay, man. Hit me," Elrick said.

"Not here. PK club stuff."

He cocked his head to one side. "So it's a club, now?"

I had envisioned things moving faster. "What do you want, a secret handshake?"

"No, man, just a chance to eat lunch." He picked up his fork.

Evidently Elrick lacked the sense of urgency required for the situation. "Dude, we're at DEFCON One here."

Erick frowned at me, his fork poised over a pile of green beens. "Nuclear?"

"Post-nuclear." I turned to the crowd. "You guys will look after this for him, won't you?"

"Oh, yeah," Elrick said. "They'll watch over it like one dog waits for another."

"Hey, we don't want your tired little green beans," a girl said.

"I counted them and everything else on the plate. It all better be here when I get back." Elrick stood up. "Just like I left it," he added with more emphasis than one would expect in reference to Salisbury steak and green beans.

I led him next door to the library and the orange and black armchairs by the magazines.

"Last month you said Anna was a little uptight. What did you mean?"

Elrick frowned. "This is DEFCON One?"

"DEFCON Zero," I answered with enough force to set Elrick back in his chair.

"Man, you need to chill and tell me what is the haps."

I gave him the story of the night before with full-color commentary. When Miss Thermopolis shushed me from the checkout desk, I switched to a forced whisper that still drew censorious glances.

When I was finished, Elrick sat in silence for several minutes, studying the magazines on the coffee table before responding. "So you really dig this chick?"

"Yeah."

"Even after last night?"

"Well, yeah." Last night was an aberration, some kind of misunderstanding that I still didn't understand.

"Then you have to call her."

"Sure, but what do I say?"

"You apologize. Chicks love it when you do that."

"But I didn't—"

Elrick held up a hand to silence me just as Miss Thermopolis sliced her death-ray glare in my direction.

"This isn't about who was right or wrong. It's not about thinking. It's about feelings. Her feelings, not yours. You want her back, that's what you got to do."

Elrick stood up. "And I got a lunch waiting on me."

He walked out the door. I stayed behind, uninterested in lunch—his, mine, or anyone else's.

When I got home, I went directly to the extension phone in the master bedroom.

Anna's mom answered the phone in her signature drawl-laden greeting. "Courtney residence. God bless you."

"Hey, Mrs. Courtney. Is Anna there?"

"Is this Mark?"

"Yes, ma'am."

"She doesn't want to talk to you, honey."

"Could you tell her I want to apologize?"

I waited, but the only answer I got was a dial tone.

It was too cold to disappear to the Fortress of Solitude, so I dropped down on the chaise lounge Dad had inherited from Grandmother.

I thought about the first coffeehouse gig, where I quoted Song of Solomon and we accidentally kissed. Of the double date where we held hands silently in the backseat. Of New Year's Eve where we had our first real kiss in the oak grove. Of the first real date where we almost got clobbered by Jimbo. Of the second coffeehouse gig where she claimed me with a song. Of the time-machine kiss in the glow of the security light streaming through the rose window.

And then the disaster of last night. Could that really be part of the narrative of our relationship? It was like a scene from *The Three Faces of Eve* had been edited into a screening of *Love Story*. Before the part where Ali MacGraw gets sick.

I thought she was The One. Still did, despite the last twenty-four hours. She thought I was The One. Until last night. Now she seemed to see me through the eyes of The Hose.

And as I thought back on the sequence of events, I realized that was the turning point. If I had just kept my mouth shut about The Hose, I would still be The One.

And I wanted to be The One more than anything.

CHAPTER TWENTY-NINE

Friday afternoon on the walk home from the bus, we ran across Dad in the woods near the house. It was rare to see him out of uniform. Instead of the usual black slacks, white shirt, thin tie, and black jacket, he was wearing coveralls, a corduroy jacket, and a straw hat.

He squinted up through tree branches at a pruning saw he had lashed to the end of a ten-foot pole. He pushed it up, but it fell short of the dead branch he had marked with orange paint back in the summer.

When he heard us, he dropped the pole down next to his foot, pulled off his hat, and wiped his brow with his sleeve. "Mark, why don't you hand your books to Claire to take in? I need you to climb up to that first branch and saw off the one with the paint on it."

It would be tricky, but I figured I could make it to the first branch and the rest would just be a matter of balance and sweat. I handed off the books and climbed the tree while the girls continued on to the house.

Dad handed up the pole. "Rest the blade on the branch a few inches from the trunk and pull the saw back and forth."

I maneuvered the blade into place. "I may not be a carpenter, but I do know how to use a saw." I leaned against the tree and grabbed the pole with both hands.

"No, don't push down on it. Hug the tree with one arm and just use the weight of the saw to get it going."

"Huh." I did as he said. It took a while, but eventually I had a groove going.

"Okay, now you can use both hands if you want, but be careful and stop when you get about an inch from the bottom." He stepped back. "If you fall, I'm not going to catch you. I'm going to be running from the saw."

"Thanks for your support."

I sawed on the branch for a while, working up a sweat in the afternoon heat, which had reached the low fifties.

"How's Claire doing these days?" Dad asked.

"Okay, I guess." I stopped at the one-inch mark. "Staying out of trouble. Mostly."

"That's good. Okay, this is the hard part." Dad stepped closer. "Flip the saw over and cut up from the bottom opposite of the groove you have going. We want it to break off without peeling the bark off the trunk."

"Now you tell me. How about we have Hannah take over?"

Dad chuckled.

"Claire?"

In the silence that followed, I flipped the blade and tried to saw upward without falling off the branch. I was working against gravity and wasn't happy about it. After a minute, I let the saw swing down to rest my arms. "How's that?"

Dad squinted through his Buddy Holly glasses. "Give it another thirty seconds if you got it in you."

I drew a deep breath and went at it again.

"I saw she took C.J. to the banquet. Are they dating?"

I was a little puzzled. Dad knew as well as I did that, not counting the banquet, Claire hadn't been out on a date since she moved in. I answered between breaths. "Just. Hanging. Together. At. School."

"That's good." He backed up. "Now we can finish it off from the top."

"We?"

"And by we I mean you."

"Yeah." I flipped the blade, dropped in the groove, hugged the trunk, and let gravity do the work.

"Is she serious about him?"

There was a loud crack and the branch fell to the ground. I lost my grip on the pole and it landed on top of the branch.

"I don't think so."

"Where does C.J. live?"

"In Warren."

"Where in Warren?"

"Right off the highway a few miles toward Woodville."

"Hop on down. I want to ask you about something."

Since I was about ten feet off the ground, I didn't do any hopping. I climbed down, and Dad led me to the garage. On the way, he stopped at the corner of the house and pointed to traces of mud in the grass. "That look familiar?"

I frowned. "No." Sure, there was some mud, but so what?

He continued around the corner and stopped behind the Falcon, which was parked in the garage as it normally was.

"Notice anything unusual?"

I glanced at the car. "No."

"Take your time. Walk around it."

I walked between the two cars and noticed mud smeared on the tires and fenders. I continued around the car and even saw some on the front bumper. "It's been off-road." I kicked at the hardened mud. Clay. "Down in the bottoms by the looks of it."

"That wasn't there last night when I went to the deacon's meeting. But it was there this morning when I came out to go visiting at the hospital."

He let that fact marinate for a while. I knew I didn't do it, but I had a good idea who might have.

Dad finally spoke. "I'm pretty sure I know the answer, but did you take the car out last night after we went to bed?"

"No, sir."

He gazed at it a while longer, glanced at the door, and said, in a voice that wouldn't carry. "She tried to cover her tracks this time. But what I can't figure out is how she got the key." He looked at me. "Since the last time, I've been keeping the keys in the drawer of my nightstand. And I'm not a heavy sleeper."

"Where do you think she went?"

"I was hoping you could tell me. Who does she know down in the bottoms?"

"She's pretty good friends with Jimbo." Not good enough to stop him from trying to pound me, though. "She bums cigarettes off him."

Dad cocked an eyebrow.

I shrugged. "I figure she needs a little space to keep from feeling too crowded in."

Dad conceded the point with a nod. "Why would she visit Jimbo in the middle of the night?"

I couldn't imagine the permutation of combination of atoms in the universe that would lead to such an eventuality. "Oh, and Vernon."

"Crowley?"

"Yes, sir. Last month she went with me on the Grit route and met Vernon."

Dad's eyes narrowed. He pulled his keys out, opened the trunk, and searched through it. Then he opened a back door, looked under the front seat, popped the backseat out, and looked under it. He climbed out of the car and walked to the door. "If that girl has brought moonshine into this house . . ." The door slammed behind him.

I did my own search of the car but found nothing. I put everything back, pulled it out, and gave it a proper washing.

Inside I found Mom fixing supper and Hannah doing her homework at the table. They looked up when I came in. I raised an eyebrow. Mom nodded toward the guest room that now served double duty as Dad's study and Claire's bedroom.

"Need some help, Mom?"

Mom smiled at me. A sad little smile. "It's sweet of you to ask, but I have it covered."

I went into the master bedroom and tried calling Anna again, with similar results. Life was just firing on all cylinders. In the living room, I put on Led Zeppelin and did my homework until dinner was ready.

Mom poked her head into the guest bedroom and came right back. "We'll go ahead and eat."

I didn't see Claire again that night.

CHAPTER THIRTY

Saturday the temperature never got out of the forties, supplemented with fog and freezing rain, so I didn't make the Grit rounds. Instead, I limited the agenda to my impression of a mournful ancestral specter vacuuming and mopping the Sunday school rooms, dusting the piano and the organ, and generally haunting the place.

The gloomy afternoon suited my equally gloomy mood, and as I worked, I hummed all the melancholy songs in my repertoire: "Hazy Shade of Winter," "Fire and Rain," "Love Hurts," "One is the Loneliest Number."

I'm ashamed to say that such was the intensity of my grief that I even sang Bobby Goldsboro's "Honey." But if you repeat that to anyone, I'll deny it.

In the silence of the sanctuary, I was about to break out into "Red River Valley" when a voice sent me into spasms. I recovered, picked up the hymnal I had dropped, and turned to the sound.

"Need some help?" Claire asked.

"Do you have a defibrillator?"

She didn't laugh.

"You can take that side." I pointed to the pews on the organ side of the sanctuary. "Clear out all the trash in the hymnal racks. Straighten up the hymnals and stuff."

She complied. We worked in silence for a few minutes until I couldn't take it anymore. I stood up and turned to her.

"What the heck, Claire?"

Her eyebrows formed a vicious V. "Not you too."

"Really? After he let you off last time, you had to do it again?"

"I didn't do anything."

"Besides take the Falcon down to Vernon's place and buy some booze, you mean?"

"It wasn't me."

This absurd denial was even crazier than stealing the car in the first place. "Is that what you told him?"

She stared at me.

"And you expect anyone to believe that?"

"It's the truth."

I slammed the hymnal I was holding into a rack and dropped onto the pew. "We go a few decades without anyone taking midnight drives in the car, and then after you show up the car is taken out twice in two months." I stood and went to the next pew. "That we know about. Maybe you covered your tracks better the other times you stole it."

"I didn't steal it," Claire yelled.

"Okay. 'Borrowed' it."

"It wasn't me," she whined.

"And then you go buy moonshine off of Vernon. When you know how Dad feels about it. Not to mention Deacon Fry."

"Now you're just being ridiculous."

"I'm being ridiculous?"

"Where could I hide a jug of moonshine?"

I froze. "No, you didn't. Not the Fortress."

"No, because I didn't buy any moonshine. It's like drinking lighter fluid anyway."

I calmed down because that made a little sense. But I made a mental note to check the Fortress on the way home. "Claire, think of what you're asking us to believe. That some complete stranger sneaked into the garage, stole the car, went off-roading with it, and then brought it back."

"Why is it everybody automatically suspects me?"

"Really? If we set aside the lone carjacker theory, what do we have left? Here's your lineup—Hannah, me, you. All we have to do is look at the rap sheets of the suspects. The case is open and shut. Even you should be able to see that."

"Look, I admitted I took it the first time."

"To me. Not to Dad."

She waved my interruption aside. "But there's no way I could have done it this time. Uncle Matt hid the keys. You should know. You have to ask for them every time you go anywhere."

She had placed her finger squarely on the weakness in my theory. It was easy enough the first time when she drove down to Houston to see Jeff. But this time, not so much. Sneaking into the master bedroom was too risky, even for her. Maybe . . . "You hot-wired it," I said, louder than I meant to.

"Seriously?" Claire shook her head and went back to cleaning up.

"Sure. I bet Jeff taught you. He knows about cars." Wait a minute. Jeff sold used cars. And that meant . . . "You got Jeff to make you a copy!"

Claire snorted. But there was a hesitation, a fluttering of the eyelids just before the snort.

"You did! And what's more, it was premeditated. Copying in the first degree. You drove the Galaxie to Houston, but you drove the Falcon to the bottoms. You took both sets of keys to Houston and made copies. I'd bet three months of cleaning on it."

"Wow," Claire said. "Sixty dollars. Big spender."

I ignored her continued inability to understand the economics of the finances of a small-town preacher and his family. "Okay, I'll bet you sixty dollars right now that if I search your room right now, I'll find keys to both cars."

"And you would lose. Uncle Matt searched my room last night. Confiscated my cigarettes. No keys."

I thought about this for a while. "Did he search you?"

"Me? Of course not."

"You could have had them on you."

"So what are you going to do? Search me right now? Is that what you want to do?"

"I don't have to. We both know you took the car. The only question is why." Why she took it. Why she was lying to me now when I didn't rat her out the first time.

"I'm sure you have a theory for that too. Just like everyone else."

171

Suddenly I wanted Claire to be gone. Back in Houston. Back in Philadelphia. Anywhere but here. "Hey, I got this. I'll finish up. Thanks." I went back to cleaning out racks and straightening hymnals.

"Oh."

I could feel Claire staring at me. The air suddenly felt colder than the forty degrees outside. I glanced at her.

She stood, a blue hymnal in one hand, looking at me like I had just killed her favorite puppy.

I fumbled for a response. "I have to mop the classrooms and there's only one mop." It was a lie. I had already mopped the classrooms. Besides, we had several mops.

"Okay," she said. She dropped the hymnal and left without looking back.

I finished up in the sanctuary, feeling like the jerk that ate New York City. I locked up, peered around to make sure Claire was out of sight, and walked back across the field and over the creek.

I stopped at the Fortress and checked, but no jugs of moonshine. Not even a flask. Only the elephant, incense, and spare pack of Virginia Slims.

I slipped into the house via the sliding door in my bedroom. On the way home, I had come up with an alternate approach to the phone call embargo at the Courtney household. I sneaked into the master bedroom and dialed the number I knew by heart.

This time when Mrs. Courtney answered the phone, instead of announcing myself or asking for Anna, I pitched my voice lower than usual and said, "I'm sorry."

"I beg your pardon?"

"I'm sorry."

"Who is this, honey, and why are you sorry?"

"I want to apologize to Anna."

"Mark, is that you?"

"Yes, ma'am, and can you tell—"

"She doesn't want to talk to you."

"But can you just tell her I'm sorry?"

Once again my only answer was a dial tone.

For the rest of Saturday and all of Sunday, things were strained between Claire and me. She tolerated my presence and I hers, but the camaraderie had faded.

On Sunday the temperature got into the mid fifties. After church I made my Grit rounds, arriving at Vernon's Pontiac half an hour before sunset.

The sun showed as a dull glow behind the thin layer of clouds as it dropped behind the chimney of the frame house across the road. The porch swing was empty. We sipped our respective drinks.

Back in November, after my public humiliation at the Sadie Hawkins Dance, Vernon had offered an in-depth analysis of the battle of the sexes, and in his version, it was indeed a battle.

His theory included the assertion that beauty and cruelty were directly proportional. Not having studied mathematics in his youth, he didn't put it in those words, but that was the essence of his rant.

I had discounted this theory at the time. Given his domestic situation, I suspected he had a bias when it came to romance. That can happen when your true love alternates between assaulting you with fists and seducing you with kisses.

But in the aftermath of the St. Valentine's Day Massacre, I was willing to reconsider the possibility.

I took a bold step and asked a direct, but fairly safe, question about his personal life.

"Vernon, do you and Gina ever have arguments?"

Twin puffs of cigarette smoke from his nostrils signaled his answer.

"Does she ever refuse to talk to you after, even if it wasn't your fault?" I thought about how I had trashed The Hose and added, "Technically."

"Mark boy, one thing ya got to learn 'bout women. It's always yer fault, even when it ain't. There ain't no technical 'bout it."

"So you apologize every time?"

He grunted in the affirmative.

"What if she won't talk to you?"

Vernon studied me from the corner of his eye without turning his head. "This 'bout that Culpepper girl?"

"Somebody else."

"Already feuding?"

"It just came out of nowhere." I told him the story of the massacre and her refusal to talk either in person or by phone.

Vernon nodded knowingly, grunting at the right places to show sympathy. At the end, he sat silently in the gloom left behind by the setting sun, took a long pull from the Coke, and turned to me.

"Mark boy, I got just the ticket for ya. Notes."

I frowned. High notes? Low notes?

"It's like what the Brits did to the Krauts back in '40. The Jerries bombed the stuffing out of the Tommies, but the RAF just kept cranking out planes and pilots and wore them down. You just keep at it, like Churchill said."

"Notes?"

"Little notes. You leave them around the house in funny little places. In the breadbox, in the medicine cabinet, in the coffee can, wrapped around her toothbrush. You just keep 'em coming till she's overrun."

"What kind of notes?"

"The kind women like. Tender words. Sappy sayings."

Vernon writing love notes to Gina. Who would have guessed?

"Do you remember any of them?"

A shy smile crept across Vernon's lips. "Well, there is one I like particular. It said 'If I had'a knowed what yer love could do, I would'a started sooner loving you.'"

He wasn't kidding about the sappy part, but even from what little I knew of the female of the species, I had no doubt that the woman who read that might roll her eyes, but she'd still say, "Awwww" in that way they did when they saw a puppy or a baby. Even a woman who has knocked you out the door with a skillet the night before.

But there was one slight problem. "I can't sneak into her house and stash notes all over the place."

Vernon crushed his Lucky Strike into the overflowing ashtray and stroked the stubble on his jaw as if he could summon out an idea like a genie from a bottle.

"I see ya found the catch to it."

I finished off the Coke and tossed the empty into the back seat as per tradition. "Thanks anyway. At least you tried."

The temperature had sunk down to the forties. I zipped up my jacket before climbing on my bike. I wheeled away with a wave, but before I got to the road, Vernon called out from the Pontiac.

"Hey, Mark."

I put a leg down and turned back. "Yeah?"

"C'mere, I got a thought."

I coasted over to him and put a hand out on the mirror to hold myself up. "Yeah?"

"Postcards."

"You mean write the note on a postcard and mail it?"

"Zactly."

"But why not a card in an envelope? Everybody can read a postcard."

"There ain't no percentage in being timid when it comes to love, Mark boy. Let her know ya ain't ashamed to tell the world."

There was a certain logic to it. After all, Anna had certainly gone public last month at the coffeehouse.

"Okay. I'll do it."

Vernon waved me away. "Now go write a good 'un."

Chapter Thirty-One

Monday the temperature got into the mid sixties. After school I rode my bike to the Fred post office and bought a stamped postcard. In the Fortress of Solitude, I set out to pen the perfect note.

After a couple of hours, I settled on the optimum combination of sentiment and economy of words.

> Yee-ha! I love you, baby,
>   but could you please take off those spurs?

I copied it from my notebook to the card, addressed it, and was admiring my work when Hannah poked her head up through the scuttle hole.

"Whatcha doing?"

I normally wouldn't divulge such private information to Hannah, but I had resolved to follow Vernon's motto—be bold in love. Or something to that effect. Plus, she had already been read into the case.

"Writing a card to Anna."

"Nice. Let me see."

She scanned the card and looked at me like she would a three-headed calf. "What is this?"

"A confession and a plea wrapped in humor." I considered it the literary equivalent of a bacon-wrapped fillet. Toss out everything but the best parts and wrap what's left in a belt of savory goodness.

"It's idiotic, is what it is." She flipped the card into the air and it fluttered to the pine straw below.

"Hey, that cost me six cents!"

"Well, it's worthless now that you wrote that stupid sentence on it."

"It's perfect. It starts off telling her I love her. She's got to love that, right?"

Hannah sighed and shook her head like a daycare worker watching a three-year-old spill his milk for the tenth time.

I pressed on. "And then it asks her to dial it down a little, in a humorous way."

When she didn't relent, I pulled out my notebook and showed her my backup note. "What about this?"

Could I live without you?
    Possibly, but what would be the point?

She raised a hand to her head and massaged her temples with her thumb and middle finger. "I gave you two things to do. What were they?"

"Apologize and . . ." What was the other one?

"And where in that note is the apology?"

"It's an implicit apology. Nuanced. She's smart. She'll get it."

"The only thing she'll get is that you were dropped on your head as a baby."

Tuesday afternoon the temps held, so I biked down to the post office, bought another card and retired to the Fortress to try again. After a few hours, inspired by a recent comment by Nixon's press secretary, I forged a winner, inscribed it on the postcard, and read it aloud.

I misspoke myself, I think you know
    I could have said it better
I wish I could unsay those words
    Like an unraveled sweater
If you can find it in your heart
    To give me a do-over,
I'd gladly take you in my arms
    And roll you in the clover

177

But the longer I looked at it, the less it seemed to capture the required elements of apology and . . . something else. Sympathy. That was it. I shoved the card in my notebook and went in for dinner.

Wednesday I was back at it in the Fortress when Claire popped up the ladder, retrieved her contraband from the secret compartment, fired it all up, and sat down on the crate by the trunk.

"This your new homework spot?" she asked as if nothing had happened.

"Not exactly," I said, playing along.

"Oh. So what are you working on?"

"You know this whole thing with Anna?"

She blew out a cloud of smoke like a giant caterpillar sitting on a mushroom. "You haven't dumped her yet?"

"No," I said, stretching it through three pitches to indicate my incredulity at such a suggestion.

Claire shrugged her commensurate incredulity at my persistence. "It's all just a misunderstanding."

"I sure don't understand it." She blew smoke at me and grinned.

I waved the smoke away. "Thanks. Now I'm going to have to sneak in the house and take a shower."

"So what are you doing with that notebook?"

"Vernon said I should write a postcard to Anna. He writes notes to Gina when they argue and he said it works every time."

"Hmm," Claire said. "Let's see what you have." She held out her hand.

I reluctantly gave her the notebook.

She read it while smoking, smiling here, frowning there, then handed it back.

"You have some good stuff. I like the one about the spurs."

"Exactly! But it won't do. There has to be some kind of apology in there."

"Seriously?"

"Sorry, but we're outvoted. Hannah says it's absolutely required."

"What does she know? She's just a kid. Has she even had a boyfriend?"

"She's not the only one. Vernon said the same thing."

"Hmm," Claire said through another cloud of smoke.

"And Elrick."

That got her attention. "Really? Elrick?"

"Oh yeah. He insisted on it. Said it was all about feelings. Hers, not mine."

"Must be nice," Claire muttered.

I agreed, but it was obvious that this was the required approach. "That last one is . . . better, but not quite right."

"How about this? Roses are red. Violets are blue. I'm so sorry I agreed with you."

"Catchy."

We sat in silence while I scribbled down some lines and then scratched them out.

"Hey," Claire said. "Maybe you could write one for me."

"How about I just say I'm sorry and forget the postcard?"

She stared at me blankly for a while and then looked away, blinking. "Wow," she said, looking out at the weeping willow by the creek. She turned back to me with a softer expression, one I hadn't seen for days. "Thanks, Mark. But I should be the one saying I'm sorry."

The feeling was like those times when you hear the national anthem at a game and all of a sudden it gets through the confusion of people asking if that seat is taken and the whiff of something vaguely unpleasant coming from under the bleachers and the million other things going on around you and you suddenly get it.

The song asks, "Oh, say, does that star-spangled banner yet wave?" And you answer from somewhere deep down inside, "Yes!"

It was a lot like that. I blinked away the moisture rising in my eyes and looked down at my notebook, flipping pages for something to do.

I didn't know if she was apologizing for lying to me or for taking the car the second time or for being rude or whatever. And I didn't care. I was just glad that the banner still waved.

"But that wasn't what I meant," Claire said.

I looked up, confused.

"I meant that maybe you can write a postcard for me to give to C.J."

As I stared at her, the tumblers fell into place and unlocked the mystery. She hadn't had lunch with the gang at school for several days. Evidently I wasn't the only one she was avoiding.

"We had a little argument. Maybe Vernon is right. Maybe a note will fix it."

"What happened?"

"Nothing. Just an argument about Houston. I told him he didn't know jack about the city. He didn't have much of a sense of humor about it."

"There's a lot of that going around," I said.

"Don't I know it."

"Okay, well, let's see what we can do about it."

I opened the notebook up to a fresh page and set my pen down on the first line. Nothing came. I smoothed the pages and set the pen down again. Nothing. I looked out over the floor of the pine forest, scanned the creek bank, regarded the elementary school a few hundred yards away, the church on the opposite corner of the property from the parsonage.

Then it came to me. I scribbled it down and read it aloud.

All I need is a watch, a hammer, and you.

Claire tilted her head to one side as if somehow the sense of it would filter down into her brain from her ear. "What does it mean?"

"You want to be together for all time. In a place where time doesn't exist."

"Ah." She nodded appreciatively. "That's good, but I don't think he'll get it."

"He's pretty smart."

"So am I."

I nodded.

"But you won't be there to explain it. Plus, it might be overstating things a bit. What else you got?"

I cranked the engine up again. It complained about the lack of a union break, but I lashed it into submission and wrestled another gem out of it. It took a little longer this time. I read it to her.

You know I love you, baby,
    There's no question that it shows.
About that I would never lie.
    Ask Pinocchio, he nose.

Claire laughed. "You should get a job with Hallmark."

"I couldn't stand the commute." I pulled out a postcard. "So, is it a keeper?"

"Well." She drew the word out. "Could you make it less funny and more . . . sexy?"

Sexy? Not my strong suit. "Not with Pinocchio."

"You can lose the puppet."

"You realize this is going on a postcard, right?"

"I have faith in you."

I set to it once again. After a few minutes, Claire lit another cigarette. Still I labored with no visible evidence of doing anything at all. Then I started writing furiously. After a minute, I put down the pen and read it.

It is not possible for me to express
The whole of my feelings for you
And still keep it suitable
For a postcard.

Call for more details.

"Perfect!" Claire gave me a little royal finger-to-palm clap.

"Okay. But you should write it in your own handwriting. If I write it, he might get the wrong idea."

Claire took the postcard and copied the poem from my notebook.

I retrieved the pen and notebook and prepared to address my own poetic needs. "If you hurry you can probably get it to the post office before it closes."

"You're a gem." She kissed me on the cheek and scampered down the ladder.

"Use Heidi's bike," I hollered over the edge of the Fortress. "It's faster."

If I needed proof of the efficacy of Vernon's scheme, I found it when by Friday Claire was restored to C.J.'s good graces and to her seat at the lunch table. But I had a feeling that C.J. was an easy mark compared to Anna. I would have to be at the top of my game to create the card that would assail her fortress.

After lunch, Claire and C.J. left by the back door for the smoker's compound. I steered toward the bathroom for some quality me time. I was about to address the porcelain portal when a voice behind me said, "Say doll, you know that card you wrote for Claire?"

The resulting spasm could have had serious consequences had it occurred five seconds later. I turned to face my stalker. "Dang it, Ralph, there's such a thing as an expectation of privacy."

Ralph nodded. "That's why I come in here. So nobody could listen in." He walked down the row of stalls, checking to make sure we were alone, turned on a faucet, and faced me. "So about that card."

I frowned. "How do you know about that?" I had no interest in going public with my little project.

"She told me. Said that after that blowout at the Valentine banquet, you were writing a postcard to patch things up with Anna."

Claire had been distressingly chatty. I thought I might get her a World War II poster for her birthday. The one about lips and ships. "So?"

"I got the same situation. Maybe you noticed Squeaky didn't set next to me in Sunday school or church this week."

Since my policy had always been "If it didn't happen to me, it didn't happen," I hadn't noticed, but I just nodded and Ralph continued.

"Been over a week since she talked to me. Or done anything else."

"What happened?"

"Said I spent the whole time at the banquet looking at Anna." He nudged me. "By the way, good work there, doll. Your daddy would be on that like a June bug on shore leave."

"Uh . . . thanks."

"So, you think you could come up with a card for me to give Squeaky?"

"It's not that easy. You can't just turn a crank and drop them out like a gum ball."

Ralph pulled out his billfold. "I can pay. What's the going rate? By the word or by the card?" He held out a bill. "How 'bout five dollars for the lot? Been a long week."

I glanced at the door and pushed the money back at Ralph. "You want someone to come in here and see you giving me money in a bathroom?"

"What?" he demanded. "We ain't doing nothing illegal."

"Never mind. Let's get out of here." I got my notebook from my locker and found a table in a back corner of the library. I pointed him to a chair and took the one opposite. "So, what are you looking for?"

"A card. Like what you wrote for Claire."

"Did you see it?"

"No."

I didn't think so. "You want to apologize? Something romantic? Funny? Serious?"

"Yeah, that sounds good."

"Which one."

"All of them."

I shook my head. I looked at Ralph like I was memorizing his face to describe to an FBI sketch artist. Something simple. Light verse. Doggerel. I opened the notebook to a fresh page and waited.

Ralph watched my hand like I was a magician about to astound him with a feat of prestidigitation. After three minutes of silence passed he said, "So, when are you going to start?"

I slammed the pen down on the notebook and slid it in front of him. "She's your girlfriend. Why don't you do it yourself?"

He flinched away from the notebook like I had asked him to sign a deal with the devil. "I ain't no good at that kind of thing."

"Okay, then. Either keep quiet or go somewhere else."

I addressed the blank page again, letting my mind roam freely through the ether, grasping at random words and phrases and throwing them away. Sooner than I expected, something flashed through my brain like a gunshot, and I wrote it down.

I picked up the notebook and read it to myself. I glanced at him over the notebook. Perfectly suited to the psychology of the client and his audience.

"Yeah?" Ralph said.

I read it to him.

One potato, two potato, umptysquat.
    You're my little sweet potato. I'm your tater tot.

Ralph squinted at me. "That's not worth five dollars. Not even sure it's worth a quarter."

"I guarantee, you send this to Squeaky, she'll come running back like a lost puppy."

"Umptysquat? That's not romantic. And she don't even like tater tots. She's a McDonald's fries girl."

I ripped the page out, balled it up, and bounced it off Ralph's face. Then I picked up the pen and again cast my line out into the primordial soup of the great unconscious. He wanted romantic, I'd give it to him in spades. Or better yet, in hearts.

I scribbled down word pairs. Heart/smart. Cupid/stupid. Valentine/Clementine. Romantic/pedantic. I slashed through the list and started again. Heart, cardiac, coronary, corazon, aorta. It sneaked up on me slowly, but when I saw it, I gasped.

"What?" Ralph said.

I wrote one word down. Earthworm.

"Earthworm?" Ralph demanded. "I'm not paying for an earthworm card."

I held up a hand to silence him and closed my eyes until it all came together, then I wrote it down and read it out immediately.

The earthworm has a bunch of hearts
    Which makes him romantic, sorta
I would have to be one giant heart
    To love you like aorta

"Aorta? What's that?"

"Latin."

"Here, let me do it for ya." Ralph grabbed the notebook from my hand, ripped out the page, and tossed it over his shoulder.

"That's going to be worth something someday," I said.

"Well, it ain't worth nothing right now." He shoved the notebook across the table.

"Look, why don't you just drive down to the mall and pick out something from the Hallmark store?"

"Ya think I ain't already tried?" He pulled the five out of his wallet and slapped it down on the table. "That's a tank of gas right there. It's yours if ya quit messing around and write something good."

It was the price of four hours of cleaning the church. It was also harder than four hours of cleaning the church. I smoothed out a page, picked up the pen, and prepared again for the deep dive into the ether in search of the one sparkling word that would explode into a supernova of metaphor and simile and allusion. That rhymed.

A word surfaced. "Sweet," I whispered.

"What's sweet?" Ralph asked.

"Shut up. I'm working." I closed my eyes and asked myself that same question. What is sweet? Lots of things, but which was the thing for me? For Ralph? For Squeaky?

Another word surfaced. I looked at it, shook my head, and threw it back. It returned. I rejected it. It refused to be ignored, so I picked it up, turned it this way and that, and suddenly realized what it could do.

I scribbled down a short list of words, studied them, and wrote two lines. I stopped, stared at nothing in particular for a few seconds, and wrote the last two lines.

"There." I threw down the pen and shoved the notebook to Ralph.

He picked it up and read aloud. "Some pickles—" He looked up at me. "Pickles? Forget it." He threw the notebook down and grabbed the fiver.

I reached out, latched onto his wrist, and held it there. "Just read it all the way through once."

Ralph glared at me for several seconds. Then he released the five and I released his wrist. He retrieved the notebook and began again.

Some pickles they are kosher, some pickles they are sweet
    But you are far, far sweeter than any pickle I may eat
I eat dill on my sandwich and bread-n-butter too
    But I'd be in a pickle, sure, if ever I lost you

He set the notebook down slowly, raised his eyes to mine, and cocked an eyebrow. "I don't know but what it might do at that." He picked the notebook up and skimmed the poem. "Yeah. That's a doofer."

I grabbed the five off the table, pulled a postcard from the back of the notebook, and tossed it at Ralph.

"Last step. You write in your own handwriting. The card is part of the package. No extra charge."

I ripped the page from the notebook, handed it to him, and walked out of the library. On the way out, I picked up several books of poetry, something I had to that point avoided like one avoids a rabid dog. Burns, Byron, Coleridge, Keats, Shelley, Wordsworth. Despite my success with Claire and Ralph, I had no doubt I needed to up my game to tackle Anna.

In the next few weeks, I pored over them, looking for the magic formula. I choked on Blake, concluding he was an acquired taste.

I started dozens of abortive attempts, none of which made it to a postcard. Then one day I looked up and it was spring and I was seventeen and it seemed possible that I was closing in on a candidate deserving of postage.

But before I got it down on the card and into the mail, I took a few broadsides in the serpent-dove war. The first salvo involved a serpent with the sharpest tooth of all.

Chapter Thirty-Two

On the afternoon of the Ides of March, I discovered I had filled the notebook with my endless attempts at rhymed, metered brilliance. When I got home from school, I went to my closet to file the spent notebook on the shelf and get a fresh one.

I pushed back the sliding door, but when I raised the notebook to the shelf, I happened to brush the inside trim. To my surprise, it flipped up and then fell back into place as I pulled the notebook away. I poked it again with the corner of the notebook. It swung up like it was on a hinge. I let it drop closed, set the notebook on the shelf, and pulled my desk chair over to the closet.

When I stood on the chair, I was at eye level with the trim. I looked along the top edge and sure enough I found a small silver hinge at each end. I lifted it up. There was a four-inch gap above the two-by-four supporting the sliding-door track before the paneling started, running the full length of the door.

Two packs of Virginia Slims and a Bic lighter nestled in that gap. But the thing that stopped my heartbeat was the four baggies filled with a green leafy substance lined up like a miniature soul train with Zig Zag rolling papers serving as the caboose.

No! She wouldn't! But she did. After I wrote her a card in her hour of need. After I apologized. After I covered for her on the Houston trip. I realized with a shudder that this might have been the reason for that trip. How long had I been sleeping a few feet away from a stash of a controlled substance that could qualify as possession with intent to distribute for all I knew? That was a guaranteed prison sentence.

There was no question now. She was not a lost sheep. She was a wolf in drag.

I slammed the trim closed and held it down as if I could weld it shut permanently through the sheer force of my panic. I jumped off the chair, rolled across the bed, and locked the door. Better to have to explain why the door was locked than to be discovered in possession.

What to do with it? Turn it over to the cops? Burn it? I could just take it to Dad and wash my hands of it. And change my name to Pontius while I was at it. Or I could give her a chance to do the right thing, to repent and change. But right now I had to get rid of the stuff before I got dragged into it.

I could smuggle it across the hall to the bathroom and flush it all down, but that didn't seem right. I didn't know the street value of four lids of pot. Heck, I barely knew the term "lid" from Cheech and Chong routines. But I did know that it couldn't be cheap, at least by my standards.

I didn't know why I felt it was wrong to flush something that was illegal, something Claire shouldn't have and that I had no intention of returning to her. It just seemed too . . . final.

But I did know I couldn't leave it where it was. I opened my underwear drawer, donned two socks like gloves to guard against fingerprints, pulled a backpack from under the bed, and stashed everything in it, even the cigarettes. It was time for the scorched earth policy. As I made the transfer I realized one of the baggies was half empty. Or half full, if you were one to look on the bright side.

I ditched the socks and unlocked the sliding door that opened onto the back yard, but stopped with my hand on the latch.

Sometime, probably soon, Claire was going to sneak in here to retrieve a bag, or at least a joint or two. For the first time since I opened the secret compartment, I smiled as I imagined her shock at finding the hidey-hole empty. But I wanted more. I wanted her to know who had done this. To know that if she thought she could play me like a stringed instrument, she was as mistaken as Nixon when he thought he could do the same to the citizens.

I set the backpack down, tore a sheet from a new notebook, and wrote a note. Short but trenchant.

What the heck, Claire?

I smiled, folded it up, and stashed it where the dope used to be. Then I sneaked across the yard to the pump house, climbed on top of the concrete cistern, and dropped the backpack down into the gap between the round cistern and the square corner of the building. For good measure, I grabbed an empty feed sack from when I had pigs for an FFA project and covered the backpack. It would serve in the short term.

I slipped back into my room, unlocked the door, walked through the house with my fresh notebook, and out the back door to the Fortress.

On this beautiful spring afternoon I had planned to continue my pursuit of the perfect postcard, but Claire's treachery trumped that project. I climbed the ladder and leaned back into the corner that afforded me a marginal level of privacy.

The first order of business was to search every inch of the Fortress for more contraband, but I found nothing of Claire's other than the elephant, incense, and cigarettes. I left them alone and turned to the matter of a more permanent solution.

Obviously the best solution was to destroy the weed, but I had already ruled that out. Second would be to get it off the property so it could in no way be associated with Dad or the church, but that option also put it out of my control. Not a fan. Third would be to conceal it in a place nearby that would not be discovered by any search, not by Claire, not by Dad, not by the authorities.

A thought occurred to me. Should I tell Dad? This was pretty big. Bigger than the cigarettes. Even bigger than "borrowing" the car. This was jail-time big. But what would be gained by telling him? I had it under control. I was pretty sure I had the whole stash, so it was contained. She wouldn't hide anything in her own room now that it had been searched, and she couldn't use the hidey-hole in my room anymore. And even she should realize that she couldn't risk running up the mileage again for a trip to Houston to replenish supplies without serious repercussions.

That led to another thought. If she got the weed on her trip to Houston, the trip she told me was to visit Jeff, if he even existed, then the weed was already in the house when Dad searched her room. Which meant she had created this secret compartment before the search, not in reaction to it. Who knew how long I had studied and slept and dressed and read novels in that very room without ever realizing it was there? Over a month. Maybe two months. She had been playing me from the beginning.

The hiding place Claire had created was pretty good, but it wasn't foolproof. I had discovered it, and a drug-sniffing dog would probably find it too. Same went for the pump house. The attic? The garage? Not secure. Hannah's room? I smiled briefly.

The longer I considered it, the more I appreciated Claire's twisted mind. She might think she was the master twister, but I was determined to out-twist her.

As I pondered these things in my heart, my eyes came to rest on a cylindrical hole in the woods about seventy yards from the house. A hole three feet across and six feet deep. I knew exactly how deep it was because I had dug it a few years back. Not willingly. It was one of those forced-labor details that teenagers get conscripted for.

Fred wasn't a proper city and as a result didn't have garbage service. There were a few dumpsters scattered along the dirt roads at strategic points that citizens could use for their trash, but the closest one was a couple miles away. Rather than drive to a dumpster, Dad elected to dig a pit where we could burn our trash. Or rather he elected to have me dig a pit.

It took a few months of hard labor to dig down through the clay to a depth of six feet. And once I dumped the trash down there, it was tricky to light the stuff on fire. I couldn't just light a match and drop it in. Even if it didn't go out, which it usually did, it didn't do much more than burn out on top of a wad of aluminum foil or a waxy milk carton. And obviously some things wouldn't burn at all, like tin cans or chicken bones.

For the first few months I had to dump the trash, climb down inside the pit, light the fire, and climb back out. Eventually I developed a system of arranging the trash so that the most flammable items were on top where a splash of gasoline and a dropped match would do the trick. After a while it was only five feet deep, and then four.

The good news was that it was easier to light. The bad news was that the pit became a gauge ticking down the months until I would have to dig a second one. The final good news was that I had calculated the growth rate of the garbage and I would be in college before a second pit would be required. However, I suspected I would come home for Thanksgiving one year and Dad would meet me at the door with a shovel and a wheelbarrow.

But now I looked at that trash pit and blessed the day Dad had possessed the foresight to provide me with the perfect place to stash four bags of weed in my time of distress.

However, I required a more durable container. The backpack would not serve. Besides, I liked that backpack. I didn't want to bury it under two feet of garbage. It only took a second to flip open the secret compartment and pull out the metal ammunition case. It was big enough for the deed at hand. It seemed Dad hadn't been the only one with magical foresight against my hour of need.

As I placed the case back in the compartment, Claire climbed through the scuttle hole. I slammed the lid down on the compartment convulsively.

"Working on your postcard for Anna?" She sat on the crate by the trunk. "While you're over there, could you hand me the stuff?"

"What stuff?" I blurted out.

"Elephant. Incense. Cigarettes."

"Oh." I sat on a crate, picked up the notebook, and flipped it open. "Get it yourself. I'm working on a postcard." I started writing down random words.

"Well, excuse me."

As she leaned next to me to retrieve her paraphernalia, I caught a whiff of the aroma I smelled in Vernon's car when Claire came back and apologized for being rude. I had a pretty good idea what that smell was now. Evidently she'd taken a walk in the woods to smoke a joint before she joined me in the Fortress. How many times had she smoked a joint and I never knew? How many baggies had she brought back from Houston?

I blushed at my naïveté, but it wasn't my fault I'd never smelled pot. Where would I get the chance?

I watched from the corner of my eye as she went through her ritual. "You know, one of these days you're going to get caught."

"It's just a cigarette," she said as she blew out a cloud of smoke.

"It's still illegal."

"Technically, it's illegal for a store to sell me cigarettes. It's not illegal for me to smoke them."

"But you know how Dad feels about it. Don't you care about that?"

Claire studied me for a second. "What's up, Mark?"

"Well, I just think you should consider how what you're doing affects others. You know, do unto others and all that."

She thought about this for a while. "We could also say that maybe he should consider how I feel about it. It's not like I'm hurting anyone."

"Except yourself."

"Nobody lives forever. So I die a few years sooner. Better than living like a nun and wishing I was dead."

"But look at all Dad's done for you."

"Like interrogate me about phone calls and stealing cars? Confiscate my property? Force me to sneak out to this tree house to smoke like a criminal?"

"Like giving up his study so you could have your own room. With a private bathroom. Regular meals."

"I had that at home."

"If it was so great at home, why are you here?"

Claire frowned at me. "What's going on? I thought we were good."

"I just think you should be more grateful. Maybe pay back something for what everyone is doing for you instead of acting like . . . like you deserve it all and then disrespecting the ones who are helping you out."

"Wow, Mark. You're getting all heavy on me all of a sudden."

Before I could think of a response, Hannah's head poked up from the scuttle hole. "Hey, guys. What're you doing?" Then she caught sight of Claire's cigarette. "Oh."

She turned to me. I held up my hands to show I was not party to this insurrection. She shrugged and climbed up, taking a seat on the last crate.

"Nice day. Thought I'd come hang out with the upperclassmen."

Claire dismissed the comment with a wave of her cigarette. I scribbled something in my notebook.

"Does Dad know you smoke up here?" Hannah asked.

"Did you?" Claire asked.

"I figured you did. The incense isn't fooling anyone."

"Then I guess he does."

"Does Uncle Roger let you smoke at home?"

Claire flicked ash over the side of the tree house. "I quit using the words permission and Roger in the same sentence a long time ago.

In my estimation, she'd quit using the word 'permission' period.

I glanced up at Hannah. She looked back at me with the expression of one who has just discovered that pigs do indeed fly, that Santa Claus is fake, and that holding your breath doesn't cure hiccups, all on the same day.

"Why do you do it?" Hannah asked in a quiet voice.

"Why does anyone do anything? Because they want to."

"Don't you care about your health?"

Claire sighed. "We've already covered that one. Ask Mark. He might share his notes with you."

I slammed my notebook shut and stood up. "I can't get any writing done with all this talking. You can stay here and do whatever it is you feel like doing without permission from anyone or regard for your health or how what you do affects the very people who are trying to help you if that's what you want to do. It's your nickel."

I climbed down, went to my bedroom, and locked the door. I tried to write a poem for fifteen minutes, gave it up, and threw the notebook across the room. Then I tried to read Keats, but Grecian urns held no appeal for me. I threw that book across the room too.

I muddled through the rest of the evening and went to bed, locking my door as a precaution. Around two a.m. I grabbed a flashlight and slipped out the sliding door to the pump house. I climbed on the cistern and, with the aid of a hoe, I fished out the backpack without incident, if you don't count the heart attack when the pump kicked in like a freight train blasting through a barn. Somebody must have flushed a toilet.

I grabbed a shovel, crept out to the Fortress, and poured the contents of the backpack into the ammunition case without touching any of the contraband, thankful that the walls shielded the flashlight from the house.

Then I proceeded to the trash pit by the light of a waning fingernail moon. Pretty much by the Braille method is what I'm saying. Once inside the pit, I leaned the flashlight against a soup can, dug through two years of burnt trash down to clay, dropped the case into the hole, and spread the trash evenly in the pit.

My scheme thus accomplished, I tossed the shovel and flashlight out, climbed to the surface, and screamed like an Edvard Munch painting when I came face-to-face with a wandering armadillo that jumped three feet straight up in the air. By the time I had restored my heart to its proper location, the armadillo had scurried away in search of a more peaceful dining location.

Back in bed, mission accomplished, I wondered why I didn't feel a sense of accomplishment. The whole thing just made me want to join the Foreign Legion and disappear to Mauritania.

Chapter Thirty-Three

Friday afternoon I was back in the Fortress working on the postcard. Encouraged by my success—Ralph and Squeaky had reunited—I pressed forward, knowing those meager efforts would not serve in my dire situation.

I repeated the words over and over like a mantra. Apologize and sympathize. Apologize and sympathize. First apologize, then sympathize. I took a shot.

> I repent me of the things I said
>> And how they made you feel
> I must have been clean out my head
>> To act like such a heel

I scribbled over it until the page was a shredded black mess. I took another go at it.

> Most folks don't get what they deserve
>> Lucky for them it's true
> I don't deserve you, that's for sure
>> I'm lucky to have you

Rather than scratch that one out, I just threw the whole notebook over the edge.

"Hey!" a voice called from down below.

The next thing I knew, Claire stood next to me in the Fortress waiving a scrap of paper in my face like a trader on the New York Stock Exchange with a hot tip. "This is not funny! Where is it?"

"What's not funny?"

"This!"

I stood up and plucked the paper from her fist, ripping it in the process. It was the note from the hidey-hole.

"You're right." I shoved it back in her hand. "It's not funny."

"Where is it?"

I sat back down. "I . . . disposed of it."

"You flushed it? That was one hundred dollars of . . ." She glanced around nervously. "Of stuff."

"Oh, is that all? No problem. That's just a phone bill for you. Pocket change."

"I'm serious, Mark."

"You think I'm joking here? You plant illegal drugs in my room and then have the nerve to get mad at me?"

In response to my escalated volume, Claire peered around the corner toward the house. "Not so loud. Look, nobody's going to search your room. At least I didn't steal your property."

"You really want to go there with the stealing thing?"

Claire spun around, threw the paper over the side, and paced the short length of the tree house, hyperventilating. "I can't believe you flushed my whole stash. The whole thing. You don't know what I went through to get that."

"I never said I flushed it."

She whirled around. "Where is it, then?"

"First you answer some questions. Sit down."

"I can't." She paced back and forth a few more times, then dropped on a crate, almost flattening it.

"Where did you get it?"

"Why? What are you going to do?"

"If I was going to do something, I would have already done it. I just want to know."

"I can't tell you."

"Fine." I climbed down the ladder.

"Where are you going?" She ran to the edge of the platform.

"To get my notebook." I grabbed it, climbed back up, and began writing.

Claire opened the secret compartment and pulled out the Virginia Slims. "At least you didn't steal these."

I rolled my eyes and kept writing. The words on the paper were complete nonsense, but she didn't have to know that.

After she had smoked half a cigarette, she blurted out. "Okay, if I tell you, will you give it back to me?"

My answer followed a leisurely show of considering her question. "Let's just say that you will be given the opportunity to recover your . . . property."

"Mr. Crowley."

"Vernon?" The notebook fell off my lap. "He sells pot?"

She shook her head. "No, he's just a bootlegger. But he knows a guy." She shivered. "Some scary wigged-out river rat."

"So that's where you got the mud on the Falcon, buying weed from some river rat."

She grabbed my arm. "But you can't tell anyone! He'd probably kill me!"

"Right." I shook her hand off.

"Seriously. That's why I couldn't tell anyone. Even you."

"How did you get the keys to the car?"

Claire looked away. "You were right. Jeff made me copies when I went to Houston."

The fact that I had guessed it didn't minimize the shock at her cold, calculating strategy from the beginning. "Seriously?"

"Okay." She turned to me. "I answered your questions. Now where is it?"

"First you have to tell me about the hiding place."

"It was when I was grounded. You were cleaning the church or selling papers and everybody else went to Beaumont shopping. I stayed behind. I noticed the gap over the closet—"

"How exactly did you come to notice a gap on the inside trim in my closet?"

"I noticed one in my closet first, but realized I couldn't use my room because it might be searched. I checked your room next."

"And the hinges?"

"You know that old chemistry set in the garage?"

I nodded.

"I drilled the brads out of the hinges on the chemistry set, pulled the nails out of the trim, and used the hinges to hang the trim back in place."

"You broke my chemistry set?"

"That was two months ago and you haven't noticed yet."

"It's the principle of the thing."

Claire rubbed out her cigarette and stood up. "Okay. Through with the questions?"

"Just one more," I said from my seat on the crate. "Why?"

"I don't get it. It's not as big a deal as you're making it out to be."

I just stared at her, shaking my head.

"I mean, you were never in any real danger of getting caught."

I jumped to my feet. "Did you even hear anything I said yesterday?" I gestured wildly at the house that was hidden behind the two flimsy walls. "A family takes you in when you're in trouble and you repay them by hiding marijuana in their house?"

"You're starting to sound like Roger."

"Well maybe Uncle Roger is actually right about a few things." My voice rose to an unflattering screech. "What do you think would happen when Deacon Fry picks up his copy of the Silsbee Bee and reads 'Pot found in home of local preacher?' Dad would be out of a job and we'd be out of a home faster than you can tell a lie. That's not a big deal to you? Seriously?"

"That would never happen."

"Of course not. Just like you would never get caught selling tests or driving to Houston in the middle of the night. Because the laws of nature don't apply to you."

Claire looked away, blinking back tears, but this time I didn't care. The last time she used that trick, she knew she was hiding a ticking bomb in my closet.

"So, are you going to tell me where the stuff is?"

"What are you going to do with it?"

She surveyed the woods.

"Don't look around here. It can't be anywhere within a mile of this place."

"I don't know. Maybe C.J. will keep it for me."

"C.J. smokes pot?"

She shrugged. "He tried it. Once. Or maybe I could ask Jimbo. He's cool."

"Jimbo smokes pot?" It seemed I was surrounded by potheads and never knew it.

Claire looked at me calmly. "There's a lot about Jimbo you don't know."

"And I'd like to keep it that way, if you don't mind."

"I'll figure something out."

"Gone. The minute you find it."

"Okay! I get it."

"I haven't told Dad anything about this, but if I see or smell as much as a single joint, I'm going straight to him."

"Thanks, Benedict."

"I'm serious."

"Got it."

"Also, I want the keys Jeff copied for you." I held out my hand.

She gave me a long, hard look and dug two keys out of her pocket. I had guessed right. She wouldn't leave those anywhere that they might be discovered in a search.

"Okay." I picked up the notebook, tore out a page, and handed it to her. "Here you go."

She read it out loud.

The pot, she called the kettle black
    The kettle, he was stainless
She set the kettle on the boil
    By treating him as brainless
The pot, she fell into the pit
    Of fire we call Gehenna
But there's a place in heaven yet
    For one repentant sinna

Claire looked up at me. "Is this a joke?"

"It's a riddle. Everything you need to find your stuff is right there on the page."

"Seriously?"

"Serious as a search warrant." I sat back down. "I guarantee that if you show that to Dad, he'll know where it is before he gets to the last line." I picked up my pen. "But I wouldn't recommend it. He might not take it as calmly as I did when he finds out what you've done."

She read over it again, whispering the words. "Gehenna? What is that?"

"The Hebrew word for hell."

"This is crazy. I can't find it with this."

"It all depends on how bad you want it. But I guarantee that nobody, not you, not the cops, not anyone, will ever find it without the clues in that riddle. So don't worry. It's not going anywhere."

Claire crumpled the paper and threw it at me. It bounced off my forehead and fell to the ground. "This isn't fair."

"Strange, I know just how that feels. Welcome to the party."

She speared me with a final glare and disappeared down the scuttle hole. A few seconds later I heard the crinkling of notebook paper and a voice saying softly, "The pot, she called the kettle black."

That had not gone as I had hoped. She wasn't repentant, she was indignant. No apparent intention or even desire to change her ways. But at least she didn't have the stuff anymore, and she never would, if my guess was correct.

I turned back to my postcard construction project, confident I had defanged the serpent, averted disaster, and restored the Shire to its accustomed tranquility. But I had not anticipated the second salvo in the serpent-dove war.

It started innocently enough with an invitation to a church service. But somewhere along the way, it took a left turn off a cliff.

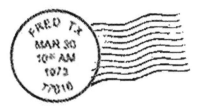

Chapter Thirty-Four

The next Sunday, I endured Sunday school in my usual position tilted against the wall. Scooter dutifully plodded through the routine,
forcing random kids to read parts of the Sermon on the Mount with
all its 'blessed are these folks' and 'woe unto those folks' and 'love
your enemies' and 'do unto others.' Then he tortured us individually
with the questions at the end of the lesson.

As usual, Squeaky couldn't just let the dreary lesson play itself out
against the backdrop of bored teenagers and their laconic replies. She
had to ask a question.

"What I don't get is verse thirty-one. Everybody always says do
unto others as you want them to do unto you, but that doesn't always
work. Like when I see Mark sitting by himself in the cafeteria."

I jerked out of my stupor and frowned at her. I was just sitting
here minding my own business, pondering the unfairness of life and
the inequitable distribution of moss-covered three-handled family
gredunzas. How did I get dragged into this? I grunted my displeasure.

Squeaky didn't even notice. "If I was eating by myself, I'd want
someone to come keep me company. But every time I sit down next
to him and try to have a conversation, he just snaps my head off."

"Wait a minute," I interjected from my quasi-supine position. It
was true that I had been less than cordial on the one occasion that
Squeaky interrupted my lunch, but I was trying to compose a sonnet,
and you can't have some girl doing her angry squirrel impersonation
in your ear when you're trying to construct iambic pentameter. But
my objection didn't slow Squeaky down.

"So ya can't just do what ya want someone to do for you, can ya? I mean, if I want a diamond bracelet for Christmas, it doesn't mean I'm gonna go out and buy Ralph one."

"You ain't getting no diamond bracelet, and I for sure don't want one, I can tell ya that right now," Ralph said.

Squeaky ignored him. "So, this ain't the Golden Rule, it's the Stupid Rule." She tossed the quarterly aside. It flopped to the tile floor with a splat.

"You can say that again," Claire said from her corner.

Several people looked at her curiously. It was the first thing she'd said all morning.

Scooter, ever the defender of the faith once delivered unto the saints, said, "Now look here, Squeaky, I think you better be careful how you go calling God's Word stupid."

"I agree," Hannah said. "Based on what Mark does to me—"

"Hey!" I dropped my chair down onto all fours. "I don't remember seeing my name in the lesson."

"It seems that what he wants others to do unto him is correct his grammar and pronunciation every five seconds."

I shrugged and leaned back against the wall. What could I say? Who wouldn't want to know the right way to pronounce something?

"It's only stupid if you use it stupid," Bubba said. "Of course Ralph don't want a diamond bracelet, and the rule didn't say he did."

"It says do unto—" Squeaky started.

"What you really want is for Ralph to find out what you want for Christmas and then get it for you."

"Don't hold yer breath," Ralph said.

"So that's what you should do for him," Bubba concluded.

"What about correcting me all the time?" Hannah asked.

"I'm not getting into the middle of that," Bubba said.

"Wise man," I muttered.

Jolene elbowed me and almost disturbed the cosmic balance of my chair.

"I still think it's stupid," Squeaky grumbled.

She was spared further rebuke by the buzzer signaling the end of Sunday school.

That evening Bubba and I drove to Warren for a little cultural exchange experiment. It all started when Elrick invited me and Bubba to his church. Well, dared us to come is more accurate. He said that we had no soul and you couldn't have proper church without soul. I asked him what real church was and he said we should come to his dad's church if we wanted to find out.

So we did. And sure enough, if that was real church, we weren't doing it right.

To start off, there was the matter of the wardrobe. As usual per Sunday night, we wore jeans and plaid shirts. Elrick wore a blue, double-breasted pinstripe three-piece suit. And he wasn't the one who looked out of place. Everyone was dressed to the nines, possibly the tens if anyone was counting.

Then there was the band. Yep, band. In Fred we had Mom on the organ and Judy on the piano. In Elrick's church they had guitar, bass, drums, and a Hammond B-3 with a Leslie cabinet. And they played like they had been teleported en masse from Muscle Shoals, Alabama.

They took three offerings until the total reached a satisfactory level. Then a guy who looked like Medgar Evers with Malcolm X glasses got up and preached the varnish right off the pulpit. Elrick's dad, the Right Reverend Williams.

Brother Bates, the guy who had cut a righteous swatch through Fred the summer before, had nothing on the Right Reverend Williams.

Bates ranted and raved and sweated and spit and ranged around the platform like a caged animal looking for a weak spot so he could leap out and devour the cowering congregation and singlehandedly transport them directly to heaven.

Williams played the congregation like a virtuoso, hitting the full spectrum of dynamics from a hoarse whisper to a glory-hallelujah shout, alternately seducing, then thrilling, then terrifying us poor souls as the rhythm of his plea required.

Both delivered the knockout punch, but it was the difference between Hulk Hogan and Muhammad Ali. And for my money, there was no question who would win in a fight. I had already drunk the Kool-Aid.

When the service was over, without consulting me, Bubba invited Elrick to try out our church in Fred. Elrick smiled, like he found the idea amusing, but said nothing.

On the drive back in Bubba's rag-top eggbeater I said, "Dude, what were you thinking inviting Elrick to church?"

"Why not?"

"Well . . ." I thought the answer was obvious, but it seemed indelicate to come right out and say it. Elrick would likely not get the same reception we enjoyed at his church, where everyone treated us like honored guests and escorted us down front to the second row on the organ side. "It could be . . . problematic."

Other than his confidence, popularity, smooth dance moves, slick wardrobe, and athletic prowess, it wasn't that I had anything against Elrick qua Elrick. During my four years of Yankee Exile in Ohio in the sixties, my closest companion and soul mate had been M, the black kid who lived across the alley. I had spent the last four years in Fred searching for a friend like M, without success.

But there were no minorities in Fred, and as far as I knew, never had been. As I thought about it, I speculated that my family was the closest thing Fred had to a minority family simply by virtue of having spent the four years of the Johnson administration in the North.

"Because he's black?" Bubba asked.

That was putting the cards on the table. "Well . . . yeah."

"There is neither Jew nor Greek, there is neither slave nor free, there is neither male nor female: for ye are all one in Christ Jesus."

In theory, sure. "Tell that to the girls in that church that got bombed in Birmingham ten years ago."

"This ain't Alabama."

"No, it's East Texas." I had heard that Vidor, forty miles south, was the home of the Grand Dragon of the Realm of Texas. Maybe it was true, but not hanging in those circles, I had no way to know for sure.

I let it go. Elrick seemed indifferent to the invitation, and I had a postcard to perfect and mail.

But my complacency proved ill-founded.

Chapter Thirty-Five

In the interim after my previous failed attempts, I had read in the Tyler County Booster that Anna had been selected for the Dogwood Festival court, as had Jolene. That raised the bar, so I turned from the romantics to Shakespeare. I ran across Sonnet 116 in a collection, and it spoke to my plight. At least it seemed to once I dug down past the Elizabethan language.

> Let me not to the marriage of true minds
> Admit impediments. Love is not love
> Which alters when it alteration finds,
> Or bends with the remover to remove:
> O, no! it is an ever-fixed mark,
> That looks on tempests and is never shaken;
> It is the star to every wandering bark,
> Whose worth's unknown, although his height be taken.
> Love's not Time's fool, though rosy lips and cheeks
> Within his bending sickle's compass come;
> Love alters not with his brief hours and weeks,
> But bears it out even to the edge of doom.
>> If this be error and upon me proved,
>> I never writ, nor no man ever loved.

I was with old Bill. You couldn't call it love unless it could go the distance. Others might be willing to slap that word on the first infatuation that walked past in a short skirt, but in my book, love was not a feeling. It was a commitment. You can't call someone The One and then casually move on to the next pretty face. What would you call the second one? The Two?

And given my youth and inexperience, I had been reluctant to make such a declaration, to go all in with the whole pile of chips, based on nothing more than a few dates. A few transcendent dates, to be sure, but a few dates nonetheless.

But on Valentine's Day, before the massacre, I had seen clearly that Anna was indeed The One, that when it came to the land of love, the timid need not apply for a passport.

I was ready to declare with a sonnet, as she had done with a song, that I would claim this girl, this woman, this princess in the Dogwood court, as The One, my One. And like her I would do it openly with a postcard, not sneaking the proclamation to her door hidden in an envelope.

So, a sonnet I must write. Fourteen lines in iambic pentameter, four quatrains with an alternating rhyme scheme followed by a rhyming couplet on the end. I'm here to tell you that's not as easy as it sounds.

I took a shot at the first quatrain.

> Don't treat a speed bump like a barricade
> We can get past this misunderstanding
> If life gives you lemons make lemonade
> We can walk away from this crash landing

I read it through, ripped the page out of the notebook, and threw it over the edge of the Fortress. I would get nowhere with these ridiculous lines about lemonade and crash landings.

I closed my eyes and returned to that night in January, standing in the sanctuary in the light of the rose window. Yes, it was a kiss, but not just any kiss. Not the kiss your Aunt Eulah gave you on Thanksgiving, the one you squirmed away from.

This was the kiss that kisses had been invented for. The whole reason why the word kiss had been created. It went beyond the meeting of minds to the meeting of souls. It was throwing a message in a bottle out into the universe and receiving the unbelievable answer through her lips on yours.

Yes. Unquestionably yes. Always yes.

Perhaps I had been so slow to embrace it because I couldn't believe it was true, that this answer was meant for me and not the result of some screw-up in the cosmic postal service.

But now I was ready to open the bottle with its return message, ready to believe. Something like this, it couldn't happen twice in a lifetime, of this I was certain. If Vernon's math was right, there was only one sliver of the rainbow for me in Texas. Two if you calculated by square miles instead of states. You didn't toss it aside because of some silly disagreement about how goofy your brother was.

That was what I had to pack into fourteen lines, one hundred forty syllables. I started on Monday when it was in the seventies and clear. I continued on through the rest of the week up in the Fortress of Solitude, bundled up against the drizzle that crept in, soaking my clothes and my soul.

After dozens of false starts and complete misses, I finally settled on The Postcard. The one that would win back The One. I copied it out confidently on a stamped postcard, addressed it, and read it back to myself out loud.

> A speed bump need not be a barricade.
> A detour need not lead to a dead end.
> Too much has passed between us to persuade
> Me that it is over, or to pretend
> That what we shared was just a common thing,
> A lark, a crush, a phase we leave behind
> And not a ticket for a time machine
> To take us to a place where stars align
> And worlds collide. If you can look beyond
> The words that, spoken, cannot be unsaid,
> And not take offense, but instead respond
> Not to the past but to what lies ahead
>> Then we can lay to rest what has been done
>> And see that each of us has found The One.

The sound of solitary applause jerked me out of my creative cocoon. I leaned over the edge of the platform of the Fortress of Solitude to see Hannah fifteen feet below, clapping.

She looked up and caught my eye. "You finally got it."

I shrugged and leaned back into my corner. A few seconds later, she joined me on the platform.

"Took you long enough," she said.

"Hey, let's see you learn a foreign language in a month."

"It's good," she said. "She's lucky to have you."

"You might have that backward."

"If you both think that, it might just work."

As hopeful as I was, I still had my doubts. Perhaps Anna had just used my comments about her brother as a convenient excuse, an exit strategy. "You don't think she's out of my league? She's a princess in the Dogwood Festival."

"Well, you're not completely hideous."

"How kind of you to say so."

We sat in silence for a while, listening to the mist drip off the pine needles onto the planks of the Fortress.

Hannah stood, brushed off her jeans, and stepped to the ladder. "You don't get it, do you?"

"Excuse me?"

"You have no idea what a poem like that can do to a girl."

I pulled the card out of the notebook and scanned it. It looked pretty good to me, but I didn't know that it was some kind of ultimate secret weapon, a literary love potion capable of captivating random unsuspecting hearts and bending them to my will.

Hannah grabbed the trunk and stepped down a few rungs. "If you send it to Thelma, she'll be yours forever."

I grabbed a nearby pinecone and rifled it at her, but she was too fast for me. Another pinecone lay near to hand, but when I looked over the edge, she was out of range. I tossed it aside and checked my watch. With luck and a good tailwind, I might make it.

I scrambled down the ladder, grabbed my bike, and made the half-mile trip to the post office with minutes to spare. I burst in the door, dug the card out of my notebook, and slapped it on the counter.

The postmistress looked at the card, then at me.

"Local?"

"Woodville," I gasped out between breaths.

She picked up the postcard, skimmed both sides, drew in a quick breath, and looked up at me with a raised eyebrow and the ghost of a smile. "It'll get to her tomorrow."

"Thanks," I breathed and staggered out to my bike. No doubt it would get to the rest of Fred tomorrow too, but I didn't care. I had hoisted my flag, burned my bridges, and steamed full speed ahead, heedless of torpedoes or consequences.

CHAPTER THIRTY-SIX

Despite my best efforts to fill the time, Saturday passed with all the alacrity of a glacier with a limp.

I cleaned the church and set out on my Grit route alone. Claire was playing it cool these days. I couldn't tell if the weather created my mood or if it was the other way around, but the gray afternoon seemed to be an extension of the weather in my head. I slogged down the wet sand roads, selling limp papers when I could, walking slump-shouldered back to the bike when I couldn't. Maybe I should have brought Claire along after all.

Despite Hannah's pronouncement of the brilliance of the post-card, on the ride back from the post office, I had begun to doubt whether four sentences split into fourteen lines and sprinkled with rhymes could undo what had been done. I was out of my depth, punching above my weight, living in a fool's paradise, and otherwise indulging in all manner of delusional activity.

I had spent the rest of the night and all the next day reflecting that I had wasted the past weeks trying to reassemble Humpty Dumpty without the aid of horses or men, whether from the king or contracted out for the purpose from another source.

So when I finally rounded the corner to Vernon's Pontiac Saturday afternoon, I was as gloomy as the twilight around me and twice as morose.

I tossed the paper in the back seat with the air of a drowning man letting loose of a severed rope and accepted the Coke Vernon handed me like it was a blindfold and a final cigarette.

Vernon studied me from the corner of his eye as I wiped the ice from the top of the can, peeled off the tab, and took a long, slow pull.

I ignored him and looked across the road to the house. The girl was back, this time swinging on the porch swing and singing some song we couldn't hear. It was the first time I'd seen her do anything but lounge against the south arm of the swing and stare at nothing in particular in a sultry manner.

"What's got into her?" I asked.

"Got a new beau, I figure."

"Poor sucker."

Vernon slapped his left hand over his mouth, took a long drag from the cigarette lodged between the stubs of the second and third fingers, and blew the smoke out through his nose like a bull preparing to charge. "She'll school him soon enough, I reckon."

I grunted and sipped my Coke. Why did we bother? It was like trying to break an unbreakable code. Or breaking the code only to discover that the hidden message was written in a dead language.

But then I realized that if Anna were to show up right then and say all was forgiven and we could pick up where we left off, I would abandon Vernon to his Coke, whiskey, and cigarettes and follow her off a cliff.

I shook my head and took another sip of Coke.

Vernon studied me for a few seconds, but maintained radio silence. Then he turned back to watch the invisible sunset, and we sat in silence until all I could see of him was the glow of his cigarette.

Vernon interrupted my ruminations. "Why didn't ya bring that cousin of yours this time?"

"She's busy trying to decipher a riddle."

He nodded as if that made complete sense.

Since he had introduced the subject. "Speaking of Claire, she said she came to you for some . . . product."

I sensed Vernon's unease. He was as true a friend as I'd found in this strange land, despite the decades and experiences that separated us, and I wanted to hear it straight from him instead of filtered through Claire.

"Well . . . that she did, but I didn't give her anything."

"But you directed her to someone who would," I shot back in an instant.

The silenced stretched between us until I thought neither of us could span it, but he finally answered.

"She's an uncommon determined woman."

"That she is."

"And uncommon fetching."

I grunted my agreement.

"Powerful combination."

"That's what I hear." I wasn't going to cut him any slack. Given my current predicament, he had a lot to answer for.

"Powerful combination," he repeated and took a strong swig of his concoction. "Look, Mark boy, I wouldn't do nothing to disrespect yer daddy, nor you, but I reckon she got the best of me this time."

She had a way of doing that. "Maybe so."

"Got a lot of good in her fur the man who can handle it."

I hadn't considered this angle. But a different question pestered my mind. "Who did you send her to?"

"Now, Mark boy, I can't tell ya that."

"You told her."

"True, but you ain't near as determined." He fired up another Lucky Strike. "Or as fetching," he added.

I couldn't argue that.

"So, what ever became of that gal ya got crossways with? Write her a postcard yet?"

I waited half a minute before answering. "Yep. Mailed it yesterday."

Vernon's smile seeped through the darkness. "What did it say?"

I quoted the sonnet.

When I finished, I heard Vernon unscrew the cap to his flask and freshen his Coke. He took a long pull and said, "Maybe I can get ya to write some notes fur me in advance against the next time I get crossways with the missus."

"You think it will work?"

"Son, that dog'll hunt."

"Would it work on her?" I pointed my Coke out toward the invisible porch swing with the invisible girl singing to herself.

Vernon took my meaning without seeing my gesture. "It would if she had a lick of sense. But we both know she ain't got none."

A metallic click and a snick came from his side of the car, and his lighter flared up in the dark. The flame illuminated his vaguely Eskimo-like features from below as he fired up another cigarette.

In the glow of the lighter, Vernon looked full at me and said, "If it don't work, she ain't the girl fur you." Then he flipped the lighter closed and we were plunged back into darkness.

But she is the girl for me, I thought. And I'm the guy for her. So does that mean it will work?

"Tell it to me again," Vernon said.

I quoted it again, this time with more force in the right places.

"Mark boy, that Shakespeare feller couldn't of done any better if ya paid him fifty bucks. That's what them Brits call a corker."

"I hope so."

"Ain't no hope about it. If she's the one, that'll melt her right into a puddle on the floor."

Maybe so. Maybe she would see this was my "Son of a Preacher Man" sung in front of anyone who would listen. Written out loud for anyone who happened to touch that postcard between Fred and Woodville, and anyone else nearby. I began to wonder how much it would cost to get it up on a billboard right there in Woodville for everyone to see.

"Yeah," I said loudly. I ran through it again in my head. "Heck, yeah," I said even louder.

Then it hit me. The post office was closed. The mail had been delivered. Anna could be calling me right now, telling me to come home, that all was forgiven. And here I was sitting in the dark in an old Pontiac with a half-drunk World War II vet.

I pushed the door open and the light came on. "I'm going to go home and call her right now."

Vernon held his Coke can up to me. I knocked my Coke against his, finished it off, and tossed it in the back seat. Then I took a closer look at Vernon. He was getting decidedly fuzzy around the edges. "You want me to drive you home?"

Vernon sat quietly for a minute. "Maybe ya should."

"Will do." I got out and put my bike in the back seat while he slid over to the passenger side.

It only took a few minutes to drive to his place. As I helped him out of the car, the door of the trailer opened and Gina appeared, her dark curly hair glinting blue in the glow of the security light.

"Vernon, what is it you have been doing so long?" she called from the doorway.

"I been thinking of you," he replied.

"He has, ma'am," I said. "He's been talking about you for the past half-hour." I led him to the cinder block steps up to the door.

"Oh, he is ever the sweetheart," Gina said.

Her accent was definitely European, but I didn't have the knowledge to isolate a specific country. "Yes, ma'am."

She helped guide him into the door. "Let us get you some supper." She looked to me. "Thank you, Mark. You are a good friend to him."

"Thank you, ma'am."

She closed the door.

I got my bike from the back seat and started on my way home. It was four miles back to the house if it was an inch. I'm pretty sure I made it in half an hour. I burst through the door and yelled, "Did I get a phone call?"

Mom turned toward me from the kitchen where she was making dinner. "Not that I know of."

Dad looked up from the recliner where he was polishing his notes for the sermon tomorrow.

I didn't wait for an answer. I sprinted back to the master bedroom, closed the door, picked up the phone, and dialed Anna's number. I put the phone to my ear and heard one of our neighbors cussing.

We had a party line. The protocol was to make sure the line was free before dialing, which I usually did when I wasn't running on hope and adrenaline. I hung up without comment so they wouldn't figure out who had just walked all over their conversation with the clicks of a long-distance number on rotary dial.

I waited for an eternity, or perhaps ten seconds. It was hard to tell. When I picked up the phone and checked for a dial tone, the same voice said, "No, we ain't done yet, so hang up." And I did.

I went to the bathroom. Then I grabbed a National Geographic from the nightstand and flipped through every page, taking plenty of time to read the title of every article and glance at half the pictures, and then tried again.

"You got some kind of emergency?" the voice asked.

I hung up without answering and switched to Plan B. I raced to my bedroom, poured out the contents of my change jar, stuffed it into my pants until they looked like the bulging cheeks of a hamster, and raced outside, ignoring the puzzled glances of those I passed and Mom's call of "Dinner will be ready in ten minutes."

At Fred Grocery I skidded up to the pay phone, shoved a fistful of coins into the slot, and dialed Anna's number.

Mrs. Courtney answered on the third ring.

"Is Anna there?"

"Who is speaking?"

"Did she get the postcard?"

"Mark?"

"Yes," I admitted reluctantly, hoping that this time my name would be welcome in the afterglow of my magnum opus.

"She doesn't want to talk to you."

If her words didn't convince me, the rifle-shot click of the receiver slamming down should have, but it didn't either. I loaded the box up with coins and dialed again.

When Mrs. Courtney answered I blurted out, "Did she get the card?"

"Please quit calling."

An equally definitive click slapped my eardrum against my reeling brain. I stood there watching the traffic whoosh past on Highway 92 and tried to connect the dots.

Did she or didn't she? Only her postman knew for sure.

Chapter Thirty-Seven

The next day at church, I discovered just how wrong I was about the cultural exchange experiment.

I led the pack from Sunday school to the sanctuary. Claire trailed in the also-rans, still not reconciled to the disaster of the dope confiscation.

When I saw Elrick step into the sanctuary in his pinstripe suit, scanning the room for a familiar face, I hurried past the piano and the pews to meet him.

"Hey," I said. "You came."

"Figured it was only fair." He smiled like the joke was on me. He looked around the room at the jeans and shirtsleeves. "Guess I should have taken my cue from what you wore last week."

"Yeah, we're not so . . . formal."

"That's okay. I can hang."

Bubba joined us and shook Elrick's hand. "Glad you came."

Claire joined us. "What are you doing here?" she asked.

Somewhat indelicately, I thought.

"I'm here by popular demand," Elrick answered.

I scanned the room. We hadn't attracted much attention. Yet.

Dad caught sight of us from the front where he was consulting with Harlan Johnson on the song selection for the morning. His eyebrows rose a foot or two, but a smile quickly broke out on his face, and he strode down the center aisle with such purpose that all heads turned to follow him.

He held out a hand to Elrick. "I'm Pastor Cloud."

Elrick took his hand. "Elrick Williams."

I rushed to explain. "Elrick's dad is—"

"Pastor of the church in Warren," Dad said. "I've had coffee with him."

"Really?" Elrick said.

"You have?" I said.

"Is there anybody Uncle Matt hasn't met?" Claire whispered to me.

Bubba just laughed.

"Fine man," Dad said, still shaking Elrick's hand. "We're happy to see you here, Elrick."

Other than the revelation that he knew the Right Reverend Williams, I wasn't surprised by Dad's reaction. As far as he was concerned, the world was just a repository eight-thousand miles in diameter of potential friends.

I led Elrick to my traditional seat a few rows behind Deacon Fry, who was already seated and hadn't bothered to look back. Elrick sat between me and Claire. As a PK, I had a radar finely attuned to the sensation of people staring at me, and I had no doubt that Elrick's radar was even more acute, but he showed no trace of discomfort.

"Where's the band?" he asked.

I just grunted. He knew there was no band.

The service began and we powered through the first few songs. Elrick turned to the proper pages in the Broadman hymnal and gamely sang along to the first, second, and fourth verses. We always ignored the third verse like the crazy aunt in the attic that nobody ever talked about. I never knew why.

The third song was "Nothing but the Blood of Jesus." Elrick leaned over to me and whispered, "Man, we do this one so much better."

It was true, but there was no rule that said I had to admit it.

Then, as per custom, Harlan asked if there were any visitors.

My heart rate kicked up a few hundred beats per second. I had hoped to fly under the radar, but had not taken into consideration this normally rhetorical question in the order of service. I panicked, holding my breath and glancing at Elrick from the corner of my eye.

As the member with a guest, it was my job to stand up and introduce him.

Dad preempted my hesitation by standing and saying, "Mark, introduce your guest."

All eyes turned toward me as I stood. "This is Elrick Williams from Warren."

Deacon Fry swiveled slowly in his pew. When his eyes fell on Elrick, they hardened into anthracite.

"His dad is the Right Reverend Williams," I added in a lame attempt to sway public opinion.

Harlan broke the silence that followed with his usual line. "Ever body be sure to welcome Elrick while you greet each other." He stepped back from the podium and looked to Judy, who banged out "I'm So Glad I'm a Part of the Family of God" on the piano.

It didn't take long for the camps to declare their position on the visitor question. A goodly portion lined up to greet Elrick with genuine smiles, but there were plenty who didn't bother. With great deliberation and pique.

Deacon Fry sat solidly in the second camp. Literally. He stayed seated in his pew and didn't greet a single soul, friend or foe. If anyone had the slightest doubt as to his leanings, their confusion could be dispelled by a single glance at the bright crimson hue of his hairless scalp.

If Elrick was conscious of the undercurrents ripping through the sanctuary, he showed no sign. He flashed his award-winning smile and shook hands and was generally more charming than allowed by federal law for a teenager.

We sang another song, took the offering, only one, and then settled in for the sermon.

As fate, or the Spirit, would have it, the sermon Dad had prepared was about Phillip and the Ethiopian eunuch. Or maybe he decided to ditch his prepared sermon on the spot and wing it.

For the uninitiated, here's the scoop. Phillip was rocking a big revival in Samaria, casting out demons and healing paralytics, when an angel showed up and told him to go out on this desert road, which if it wasn't the end of the world, was at least in the same ZIP code. Even though Phillip was killing it in Samaria, he hit the road.

On the way he came across an Ethiopian eunuch. I thought it was a bit cruel that not only had this poor African dude been deprived of some of the more essential bits one values as a man, but this particular fact was recorded in the story so even now, two millennia later, all we knew about him was that he was black and castrated.

Kind of like Rahab the harlot. Despite all the good she had done, including being in the lineage of David and Jesus himself, thousands of years later you can't say the name Rahab without immediately thinking "the harlot."

It's a lesson in watching your step because evidently it's hard to shake a bad reputation, even after four thousand years.

Actually, we also know that the eunuch was an important guy in charge of the treasury of Ethiopia and that he was a converted Jew, because he was going up to Jerusalem to worship. He even had a copy of the book of Isaiah, which was probably hard to come by back in those days. Tougher than tickets to the Stones.

So the eunuch is confused about a passage in Isaiah, and Phillip explains how it's talking about Jesus and before you know it, the eunuch is asking to be baptized in a creek they happen to pass.

Then the Spirit whisks Phil off to Azotus, which must have freaked out the eunuch.

Although Dad's style could not have been more anti-climatic compared to the Right Reverend Williams, Elrick seemed to be engrossed in the methodical way that Dad worked through the weight of scripture as it pointed to Jesus as the Messiah. In places where his church would have shouted out an "Amen" or "Come on!" Elrick grunted his agreement.

I had never dismissed Dad's sermons, but in the past decade I had heard four or five hundred of them, and for me the bloom was definitely off the rose. But this time I listened through Elrick's ears and realized that, in his own way Dad, could stand next to the Right Reverend Williams without apology.

Dad ended the sermon by pointing out that from the very beginning the church accepted anyone who believed. Cast the big tent, as it were.

After the sermon, we had a final song, and as per tradition, Dad asked Harlan to deliver the final prayer while he slipped down the aisle past all the bowed heads to his post-sermon position at the door for the purpose of shaking hands as the congregation left.

When Harlan said "Amen" I looked over at Elrick and he looked at me.

He smiled. "Didn't think I would come, did you?"

"No." I didn't think it would be neighborly to say I had hoped he wouldn't.

"A Williams never backs down from a challenge."

I wasn't sure I could say the same thing for a Cloud. At least not for this Cloud.

We got in the line of folks filing out and eventually made it to Dad, who grabbed Elrick's hand with both of his.

"Elrick, I hope you get a chance to come back and visit us again."

"Thank you, Reverend Cloud," Elrick said. "But my father said he could spare me just this once."

Dad glanced at me and back to Elrick. "I understand. But we're glad you made it this time."

Claire walked with him to an old pickup truck. A few people greeted Elrick on the way and then he left. Claire looked back at me and then headed back to the house on foot.

Bubba elbowed me. "See, you were worried for nothing."

As I turned to him, my eye caught a black LTD sitting in the parking lot. It was running, but the driver's seat was empty. Mrs. Fry sat in the passenger seat reading a magazine.

"Or maybe not." I looked at the door. Dad was shaking the hands of the last person to leave, and it wasn't Deacon Fry. It suddenly occurred to me that this was the last Sunday of the month, the day I collected my wages. I had the distinct impression that I wouldn't get paid today.

Dad disappeared inside the church. I abandoned Bubba, scurried to the door, and slipped into the foyer. The swinging doors to the sanctuary were settling into position from Dad passing through. I stepped up and peeked through the window.

Deacon Fry stood up front, his hands on his hips, his back to the door, looking at the fake flowers on the communion table as if inspecting them for dust.

I slipped through the swinging door and behind a vinyl accordion door that was used to separate off the back corner for the adult Sunday school classes. If I positioned myself just right, I could see Deacon Fry through the slit between the edge of the door and the frame.

"I agree," Dad said as he approached.

Deacon Fry wheeled around, scanned the room to make sure they were alone, and focused his deadliest stare on Dad. "What?"

"Maybe we should consider fresh flowers. We could probably get a bargain from Farmer."

That was the funeral home in downtown Silsbee.

"I ain't here about flowers, and you know it. That boy of yours has gone too far."

I knew it. Bubba was amazingly naive for someone who grew up with Jolene.

Dad and Deacon Fry faced each other ten feet apart like two gunslingers at high noon. I couldn't see them both through the narrow gap, so I had to sway back and forth like a praying mantis to follow the conversation.

Dad sighed heavily, something he was not prone to do. He wasn't completely successful at making it look natural. "What's he done this time? Forget to clean the toilets?"

"You know full well what he's done. He brung that nigra in here."

I sucked in my breath so loudly that I was afraid it had given me away. I hadn't thought that even Deacon Fry would put it so bluntly.

"Oh, you mean he's gone too far by inviting one of our brothers in Christ to a service?"

"It weren't his place to do any such."

"Ulysses, remind me of the section and paragraph in the church bylaws that stipulate restrictions on who is authorized to invite people to a church service."

Good one. I wished I could come up with lines like that when Hannah hit me with a zinger.

"Never needed any," Deacon Fry said. "Common sense was enough. Until you come."

"If you would, could you explain exactly why Elrick should not come to our services?"

221

"He's got his own church over in Warren. Ain't no need for him to come here."

"I'm afraid that doesn't clear anything up. We have visitors from other churches all the time. You've never left your wife sitting in the car to complain about it before."

Deacon Fry flushed and took a step toward Dad. "Don't play the fool with me, Pastor. You know a nigra don't belong in this church."

I wanted to shout "It wasn't me!" but it would blow my cover.

Dad matched Fry's step forward, but his voice remained calm. "Let me make sure I understand you clearly. You're saying that because Elrick is a Negro and we're white, we should not welcome him as a brother in Christ?"

"You're a grown man, Pastor, not some fool teenage hippie that only uses his head for growing hair. We both know it ain't nothing but trouble for us to mix."

"And you base this claim on—"

"Common sense," Fry yelled.

"On what scripture?" Dad continued with a little more volume and intensity.

"The scripture is good for some things, but it don't tell me when to plant my corn or change my oil. The good Lord gave us a brain and he expects us to use it."

"I see," Dad said slowly. "Like when he interrupted a revival in Samaria where hundreds were turning to Christ and sent Phillip out to testify to one lone nigra in the desert?" He leaned into the term like a rapier thrust.

"Sure he might have converted him, but he didn't invite him to church."

"He didn't have to. The Ethiopian was already on his way to church in Jerusalem, where he was welcome."

"Pastor, you can use your seminary learning to twist the scriptures around to justify your tomfool ideas, but it don't make it right."

"Well, then, Fry," Dad said, his voice louder and higher pitched. "Perhaps you can help me untwist this scripture. 'There is neither Jew nor Gentile, neither slave nor free, nor is there male and female, for you are all one in Christ Jesus.'"

Ha! I was waiting for him to pull that one out. I swung a fist to register the direct hit.

"I never said they weren't Christian."

"But they should just stay on their side of the tracks. Is that what you're saying?"

"You just keep a tighter rein on that boy of yours is what I'm saying. Since you're so fond of verses, here's one for you. 'If a man know not how to rule his own house, how shall he take care of the church of God?'"

I knew he'd eventually get to that one. It was the dreaded passage, the one that haunts every PK. Trust Deacon Fry to have it memorized and near to hand for any occasion.

Dad took another step toward Deacon Fry. They were now close enough that I could see them both through the slit. Close enough for one to reach out and punch the other.

"I'm quite aware of that verse, but if you think that verse has anything to do with Mark inviting a brother in Christ to church, you're the one who is twisting scriptures to suit your own prejudice."

Deacon Fry's head lit up to reflect his mood and he halved the distance between them. "I'll say this one more time for your benefit, Pastor. Watch your step. This ain't no lifetime appointment like the pope. You been skating on thin ice turning this church into a circus and there's plenty besides me that won't stand for it."

He strode past Dad, his boots echoing in the empty sanctuary, and slammed through the foyer doors.

Dad turned to watch him go, breathing heavily. I stepped out from behind the accordion doors. Dad turned to me.

"I didn't invite him," I said.

"Why not?" Dad answered.

We walked to the door and watched the black LTD redistribute the gravel in the parking lot as Deacon Fry slalomed out onto the highway.

"I was watching my step," I said.

"If you watch your step by backing off of the gospel, then I've failed," Dad replied.

It was a nice day for a walk back to the house and I took it. By the time I got there, Sunday dinner was on the table. Afterward I retreated to the sanctuary where I seemed to spend most of my time these days. I was so used to writing poems during every spare moment that I opened the notebook out of habit and tried to think of something to write.

But my mind kept drifting back to the church service. Deacon Fry had taken off the gloves and declared his intentions, and I had been the catalyst. Well, actually it was all because of Bubba, but that was quibbling. I was the pawn on the board, the foil for Fry's nefarious schemes.

And Dad had as much as told me to rub Fry's face in it, hadn't he? In fact, Dad had started it back on Christmas Eve with that unseasonal sermon about Jesus tweaking the nose of the Pharisees and then again today with the sermon about Phillip and the Ethiopian eunuch.

But back in November, when Deacon Fry had called Dad to tell him I had been drinking beer on a hunting trip and consorting with a known bootlegger, Dad had said that I should abstain from all appearance of evil, especially in the immediate proximity of Deacon Fry or anyone related to him or anyone who might talk to anyone related to him. Which was pretty much everyone in Tyler county and probably the surrounding counties as well.

In the aftermath of Elrick's visit and the showdown in the center aisle, a question occurred to me. Whose yardstick was I to use when deciding what to call evil?

The beer thing was fairly obvious. It was on Dad's list too. The question of hanging with Vernon was not as black and white. And the question of inviting a black guy to a white church was black to Fry and white to Dad. I needed a scorecard to keep up with how to play any given situation.

As I was thus engaged, Claire's blonde head poked up through the scuttle hole.

"Is this a private party or are heathens allowed?"

"Come on up," I said. I opened up the secret compartment, handed her the pack of Virginia Slims, set the elephant out on a crate, and fired up two incense cones. I even held the lighter out for her like they did in the black-and-white movies. It wasn't consonant with my policy, but this was a day for turning things upside down.

Then I caught a whiff of the smell of stale perfume, as Three Dog Night said. "Hey, is that—"

"Cool your jets, Dudley Do-Right. I found an orphan joint in a pair of socks when I was getting dressed this morning, and it seemed like the right day to burn the crop."

I fixed a gimlet eye on her.

She held up a hand in a Boy Scout salute. "I swear on Roger's patents. I forgot I even had it. That's why I went to the stash a couple of weeks ago and cornered you up here with that stupid note."

I wasn't convinced. Given my experience with Claire, she could be telling the truth or she could have cracked the riddle and recovered her cache from the pit. Either way, she had violated the agreement.

"That wasn't the deal. You have no right—"

"Seriously. It was the last one, and now it's gone too," she said with a mixture of resignation and pique. "Your precious reputation is not in danger."

I stood up, ready to march into the house, wake Dad up from his nap, and push the red button.

"No, wait." Claire stood and put her free hand on my arm. "I didn't mean that. I came up here to apologize."

"You . . . what?"

"I've been doing a lot of thinking in the last week. You were right. I've been ungrateful. Actually, I've been a spoiled brat."

"You . . . what?"

Claire smiled. "If you're going to keep repeating yourself, we should sit back down." She resumed her seat on the crate and waited.

I stared at her for a good two minutes while she smoked her cigarette. Should I allow myself to be duped by her once again? On the other hand, I couldn't remember a single time she had apologized. Well, there was that one time in the Pontiac when she apologized for being rude. But this was different. I sat down.

Claire lit a new cigarette off the first and stubbed it out. "Once I calmed down, I did a lot of thinking, like I said. It kind of came together this morning in Sunday school."

"Really?" I'd never heard of Sunday school doing anything other than putting kids to sleep.

"I was thinking about last Sunday. Do unto others. You said that last week, but I didn't really think about what it meant." A hint of a smile fluttered across her face. "I was too mad."

I nodded.

"But what Bubba said connected the dots for me. Think about what the other person wants, or needs, and then do it for them."

Her voice cracked on the last phrase, and she paused. I waited, curious as to what would come next.

"That's what Uncle Matt and Aunt Elizabeth did for me. What you guys did for me." She blinked back the moisture in her eyes. "I mean, who wants some messed up teenager to move in with them? I know I wouldn't."

I considered the possibility that Mom did it for her sister, not for Claire, but I kept that to myself.

"So, I just wanted to tell you that I really do appreciate what y'all did. And I haven't made it easy on anyone. You deserve better."

"Wow." I didn't know what else to say. That seemed to cover it.

"Yeah. Wow. It's crazy, right?"

"And then you went out and smoked a joint?"

She shrugged. "Well, it was my last one. Seemed a shame to flush it."

I thought back through what she had said, looking for the loophole, but couldn't find one. It was airtight. A nice, neat package. Just what I would expect from Claire.

But a little voice whispered the question I had come to dread. What would Jesus do? With this confession. With this girl who seemed to have shed her wolf skin to find the lamb underneath.

"So you've turned over a new leaf?"

"A total change."

"What about the cigarettes?"

Claire looked at me like I'd asked her to swear off breathing. "Don't expect a miracle."

I looked back at her wondering if I'd already witnessed one.

CHAPTER THIRTY-EIGHT

On Monday Claire bounced through school like the happiness fairy At lunch she hung on C.J.'s arm and laughed at everything everyone said. She actually did several good deeds like a Girl Scout working on a merit badge. She even kissed Jimbo on the forehead, although she had to stand on a chair to do it.

It seemed she really had turned a corner. She had always been a friend magnet, but this went beyond her usual affability to genuine interest. If she didn't watch out, she might end up being the Dogwood Queen next year. Or being sent home to Houston because she had been cured.

I wondered if the change would take or if it was like church camp, where everyone came home vowing to be a witness for Jesus in school but fell back into their normal rut before Homecoming.

Bubba watched C.J. and Claire walk out the back door to the smoker's compound arm in arm and turned to me. "What's with her?"

"I think she's got religion, or something close."

"How? When? We haven't had a revival since last summer."

"Evidently you created a mini-revival in Sunday school last week with your comments about the golden rule."

"Really?" His gaze drifted off into space as he considered this revelation. "Me?" He smiled. "Wow, that's cool."

It was, actually. I mean, when you think about it, how many times do you get a chance to make a difference in someone's life?

Bubba's euphoria was interrupted by Elrick sitting down at the table. "Hey, man, what's this postcard thing you got going on?"

"Uh . . ."

"Two months ago you're hitting me up for romantic advice and now you're the expert solving everyone's problems?"

I shrugged. "I just wrote a few postcards for a few people. No big deal."

"How does it work? Ralph said it was ten dollars with a money-back guarantee."

Bubba suddenly developed a singular interest in the conversation. "Ten bucks? What's on these postcards? Some kind of love potion?"

"Think about it, man," Elrick said. "If your woman is mad at you, how much would you pay to fix it?"

Bubba nodded thoughtfully and turned to me. "So, is he right, you can fix it with a postcard?"

I held up my hands, palms forward. "Hey, wait a minute. It doesn't always work."

"That's where the guarantee comes in," Elrick said. "If it doesn't work, it doesn't cost me anything, but if it does, it's money well spent."

The ghost of a business plan formed in my head. I could stick with the five dollar rate Ralph had established with no guarantee, or double my rate with the risk of having to return the entire amount. It came down to how much confidence I had in my work.

So far with Claire and Ralph I was batting a thousand. "Right. So really, there's no risk for you."

Elrick slapped the table. "I'm down for it. There's this chick in Dallas—"

"Me too," Bubba said. He pulled two fives from his wallet and tossed them on my tray.

I frowned at him. "You?"

"Well," Bubba said. "There was this little thing I said that Mary didn't take kindly and—"

Elrick thumped a twenty on the table and took Bubba's fives. "I was here first."

I pondered the situation for a full ten milliseconds before I snatched the twenty and shoved it in my pocket. If this worked out, I could have enough money for another date by the end of the month. If I ever got another girlfriend.

Then I realized I could expand beyond damage control to the preemptive strike. Maybe I could write a card to Becky that would cause her to realize that I might be a better option than number 86 on the football team.

I pulled out my notebook, flipped it open to a blank page, and picked up my pen. "Okay, so tell me what happened. And don't leave anything out. The slightest detail could be the key to the whole thing."

Elrick told his story. I spent twenty minutes crafting a poem customized to his situation. The bell rang as he was copying it out.

"Hey, what about me?" Bubba said.

"We'll take care of it on the bus this afternoon."

When the bell rang at the end of the last period, I left the band hall and ran into Claire putting her Home Ec book in her locker. She pulled out her backpack. It was bulging.

"Wow, that's a lot of homework," I said.

"Yeah." She shouldered it and walked off.

That puzzled me because we had the same classes all day except the last period. I jogged to catch up. "A big Home Ec project?"

"Yeah." She avoided my eyes and picked up the pace.

I matched her stride. "You'll never guess what happened. I have a new business writing postcards for star-crossed lovers."

"That's great," she said in a tone that didn't sound so great.

I pushed open the door and veered to our bus. She veered the other direction toward the front of the school. I corrected my course and caught up.

"Where're you going?"

She didn't answer. We rounded the corner and she angled toward a black Datsun 240Z.

"Hey, you're going to miss the bus."

Claire stopped and turned to me. "No, you're going to miss the bus."

She tried to keep a blank expression but something leaked through. I wasn't sure what it was, but it wasn't good. I glanced at the 240Z. A guy got out of the driver's side and looked over the top of the car.

"Who is that?"

Claire glanced at him and then looked away.

Suddenly I knew. "It's Jeff, isn't it?" I squinted at him. Jeff, the cradle-robbing boyfriend who bought underaged girls drinks. Who stole sixteen-year-old girls away from boarding schools for a weekend. Of course he would have a 240Z. "What's he doing here?"

"We're going to get a burger," Claire said without meeting my eyes.

"Cool. I could use a burger." I pulled the twenty from my pocket. "I'll buy."

"It's a coupe. Only two seats."

I reached out to Claire's arm. "Dad's not going to like this. He'll probably ground you."

"Yeah. But I haven't seen Jeff in three months." Her eyes pleaded with me.

"Claire? You coming?" Jeff yelled over the roof of the car.

"When will you be home? They're going to ask me."

"If they ask, you don't know anything about it. Just tell them I wasn't on the bus."

"Claire?" Jeff yelled.

"Where's the fire?" I yelled back at him.

"Coming." Claire hugged me. "Don't worry, Mark," She whispered into my ear. "I'll be fine."

Something about this didn't feel right. Who was I kidding? Everything about this didn't feel right. "Let's just get on the bus. He can pick you up in Fred and you can have your date."

She pulled away. "I have to go. Thanks for everything, Mark." She turned to leave, but hesitated. "I love you," she said without looking back, and then ran to Jeff's car, threw her backpack over the seat, and climbed in.

"Hey, Mark," Bubba yelled to me from the window of the bus, which was inching forward. "You coming?"

The 240Z raced out of the circular drive, Claire watching me until they turned the corner and I couldn't see her anymore.

She'd never said she loved me before. Never said anything like it to anyone in my family as far as I knew. I sprinted to the bus and banged on the door.

The driver stopped and opened the door. "Get in if you're coming."

I trotted down the aisle and dropped into the seat next to Bubba. "What was that all about?" he asked.

I stared out the window at the spot where the 240Z disappeared around the corner. "I don't know."

Hannah dropped into the seat in front of me. "Where's Claire?"

"She left with her boyfriend."

"C.J.?"

"No, her real boyfriend. From Houston."

"Where are they going?"

"To get a burger."

"Really?"

"What do you think?"

Her eyes opened as big as the dog's in the fairy tale of the tinderbox. "What are you going to do?"

"Hide and watch."

Hannah waited for more information, but I just turned and looked out the window. Eventually she went up front with her friends.

CHAPTER THIRTY-NINE

When I got home, I found Mom doing cross-stitch. "Where's Dad?"

"At the church office," she answered without looking up from counting squares.

I got my bike and took the route through the school property to the bridge over the creek. At the side door of the church I tossed down the bike and burst into Dad's office.

He looked up from the three reference books open in front of him.

I dropped into a chair. "Do you know about Jeff?"

He peered over his Buddy Holly glasses. "Mutt and Jeff?"

"Claire's boyfriend Jeff."

"Ah, that Jeff. Yes, her parents told me about him. And Claire and I talked about him when I got the phone bill. Not a good influence, to say the least."

"She didn't get on the bus after school. She got in a car with Jeff. Said they were going to get a burger."

Dad's calm demeanor melted away. His eyes glinted as he focused on me.

"I told her she would probably be grounded when she gets home."

"At least somebody around here has a grasp of the obvious."

"But I don't think she's coming back."

He dropped the pen. "How so?"

"Before she got in the car, she hugged me and said she loved me."

The significance of this anomaly was not lost on Dad. He picked up the receiver on the phone. "Did you tell your mother about this?"

"No, I came straight here."

He dialed our home number. "What kind of car was it?" he asked as it rang.

"A black Datsun 240Z. I didn't get the plate."

His attention turned to the phone as Mom answered. He gave her the news, asked for Uncle Roger's phone number, and hung up. "I have some phone calls to make. You should probably go on home."

I stood. "Yes, sir."

He picked up the phone and paused. "And thanks for letting me know right away."

"Sure." I rode back to the house and ascended into the Fortress to contemplate life and green things in general.

On the bus after writing Bubba's postcard, I had considered the situation from all angles and come to the conclusion that she was running off with Jeff. Maybe she had finally decided he was The One. And she was seventeen, above the age of consent in Texas. She could marry him if she wanted to. And maybe she did want to.

I thought about the backpack. Obviously it didn't contain materials for a Home Ec project. Probably a change of clothes, maybe a few packs of Virginia slims. Maybe . . .

At that thought I shot straight up from the crate, scrambled down the ladder, and got the shovel from the pump house. At the bottom of the trash pit, I dug frantically past the two layers of trash I'd burned in the last two weeks and through four years of geological layers until I heard the satisfying clunk of metal against metal.

I cleared the debris and pried the ammunition box out of the clay. After I wiped off the latch with my shirttail, I flipped open the lid. Four baggies of dope looked back up at me.

A sigh of relief escaped my lips and I slammed the lid shut. I was pretty sure that Claire, being a heathen, didn't know that Gehenna, the Hebrew word for hell, referred to a valley south of Jerusalem where the Jews burned their trash. I had literally told her that the pot was buried in the trash pit. For the first time since Claire got in the car with Jeff, I smiled.

But I was left with the question of what to do with the dope. Now that Claire had abandoned it, I could dispose of it properly.

As I climbed out of the pit with the case, a thought weaseled its way into my brain. Back to the sixties when we lived in Ohio. Back to when I first heard of hippies. I found many things about them curious, but the whole drug thing fascinated me.

I had heard of people hearing colors and seeing smells and tasting music. As a kid in elementary school I wanted desperately to find out what that was like, but stories of bad trips and acid flashbacks added a darker, menacing tone to the magical stories.

It had been years since I even thought about it, but now I was in possession of a sufficient quantity of pot to find out many times over. It wasn't acid. It wouldn't reroute my brain so I could experience the synesthesia that had enticed me, but it also wouldn't terrify me or seduce me into flying off the top of a skyscraper. And it wasn't addictive. As far as experimentation went, it was the most benign option available.

But if I was going to experiment, I couldn't do it here or anywhere close to here. I transferred the contraband to my backpack, hopped on my bike, and pedaled two miles to a secret spot half a mile off the road on a timber lease.

It took me awhile to locate it. I hadn't visited the place since junior high. In the middle of a dense pine forest, I finally located the magnolia tree that formed an umbrella touching the ground on all sides. I burrowed into the secret circle eight feet in diameter. Although it was still full daylight, an eternal gloom nestled in this vernal sanctuary.

I pulled out the Zig Zag papers and the half-full baggie. I'd seen enough geezers rolling their own Bugler cigarettes to know the basic process, but it wasn't as easy as it looked. I curled a paper into a U, sprinkled in a generous amount of pot, and tried to close the gap. Most of the pot ended up on the ground.

A second attempt produced a minor improvement. Before long, the ground around me was littered with pot and I had a soggy, misshapen lump of paper that not even the most experienced stoner would have recognized as a joint. It would have to do.

I lodged the joint between my lips and flicked the lighter. The flame stood straight in the still air of my lair. As I raised it to the joint, that unwelcome, bothersome question leapt into my mind.

What would Jesus do? Would he burn one down?

Maybe. He drank wine, didn't he, and weed wasn't much different. A mild intoxicant. Nothing more.

Okay, if that's so, then why aren't you in here trying a sip of wine? The answer was obvious. I couldn't buy wine. It was illegal.

Ha! And so is marijuana.

At this point, I dropped the lighter because I had held it so long that the metal lever had burned my thumb. The joint dropped to the ground as I put my thumb in my mouth to cool it.

What would Jesus do? He would consider the circumstance from the perspective of other people and act in their best interest. Other people like Dad and Mom and Hannah and Heidi. And Claire when I thought about it.

If she were here right now, would I be lighting up a joint? Absolutely not. I was only doing this because I thought no one could see me. I had pedaled a bike two miles on a dirt road and hiked half a mile through dense woods to crawl into this place of half-light to do this thing in secret. That should tell me something about what I was doing.

I shoved everything into the backpack, hiked to my bike, and headed home. I got there at sunset and went inside.

Mom was in the kitchen. "Where have you been?"

"Riding my bike," I said as I walked through the kitchen back to the master bedroom.

I gathered the trash from all the rooms and headed out to the pit. In the twilight, I dumped the garbage in the hole and set it on fire. When it was going good, I pulled out the four baggies of weed and the two packs of Virginia Slims and threw them on the fire.

The plastic melted away and the dope caught fire. A familiar smell of strange perfume wafted up on the air currents. I watched the fire purge all the evidence of Claire's misdeeds. This was one thing at least that wouldn't come back to haunt her. Or me.

"What are you burning?" a voice right behind me asked.

I jumped. A hand grabbed my belt and pulled me back from falling into the pit.

"Sorry, I shouldn't have sneaked up on you like that."

I turned around to see Dad standing behind me. He must have walked back from the church.

He looked down at the fire. "What's that smell?"

"Something from the trash. Maybe something from Claire's room. It was pretty full. She must have cleaned up last night." It was as close as I planned on coming to the truth.

"It smells like her incense."

I shrugged. "Could be."

"Come on, supper's ready."

Supper was pretty quiet. During the blessing, Dad prayed for Claire's safety and quick return. I was down with the first thing but wasn't holding my breath on the second. It all depended on tracking down Jeff's car, but that could prove problematic. It could be a car he just got at an auction that wasn't registered to him yet, so good luck finding the plate number.

And even if they found him, they couldn't legally force Claire to come home if she didn't want to.

But one thing bugged me, and I finally put it on the agenda. "So, about this whole do unto others thing."

Everyone looked at me. I wasn't sure how to put it.

"Well?" Hannah asked.

"Well, we took in Claire, or at least you guys took her in. We didn't have much choice in the matter."

Dad nodded.

"And then she does all this stuff."

"We knew going in it wasn't going to be easy," Mom said.

"It says to do things for the good of others, to consider others as more important than yourself. So you do that and then they just take advantage of you."

"Yeah," Hannah said.

"I mean, she's not here a week before she basically steals our car and drives to Houston and back. And not only that, she gets copies made of the keys and she does it again."

"So that's how she did it," Dad said. "How did she get the copies?"

I told him about Jeff's job. "So from the beginning, she was planning ahead to steal the car again. And here we were, just going along being nice to her while she was taking advantage of us."

"Yeah, like all those long distance calls," Hannah said. "And hiding cigarettes in the tree house. She didn't even care what anybody said."

"So you think Jesus got it wrong?" Dad asked.

Maybe I did, but obviously I couldn't say that. "Well . . . it doesn't say 'Do unto others and let them do it to you.'" Actually, there was that whole turn-the-other-cheek thing, but maybe he wouldn't think of it.

"Perhaps we should change it to 'Do unto others as you would have them do unto you, except when they don't appreciate it, in which case get even.'"

"Like it is now, it might as well say, 'Thou shalt be a sucker.'"

"How oft shall my brother sin against me, and I forgive him? Till seven times?" Dad said with a gleam in his eye.

"But when Claire ran up the phone bill, you grounded her until she paid it back." With her parent's money, which was an even bigger insult than running up the bill, in my mind.

"Sin has consequences, but it's not about what happens to the one who sinned against you. It's about what you do with it," Dad said.

It wasn't as easy as all that. Not for me, anyway. "But what about what the other person did to you?"

"You let it go. You know the saying. 'Holding onto anger is like drinking poison and expecting the other person to die.' I'm not saying it's easy to forgive. Sometimes it's the hardest thing you could do. But it's also the healthiest thing you can do."

"Honey," Mom said. "The gospel is about loving the unlovable. God loved us even while we treated him like an enemy."

"If you're feeling like it's unfair, you're right," Dad said. "The gospel is inherently unfair, but in our favor. We deserve hell, but instead God gives us love. That's not fair. It's not what we deserve. That's why it's the good news."

I knew all that. I was a PK after all. But it was unreasonable to expect a human to actually do it.

"It might help to think of it this way," Dad said. "The Romans tortured Jesus and then they murdered him, but even while he was dying, he forgave them. Compared to that, what Claire has done is nothing. Less than nothing."

There it was again. What would Jesus do? The hardest thing in the world. "So we just let people take advantage of us?"

"That's where 'Be wise as serpents and gentle as doves' comes in. But if you're going to be salt and light to the world, prepare to be taken advantage of."

What a pleasant thought.

"Worse things could happen. You could be without God in the world."

"Who wants dessert?" Mom asked. "I've been saving some Blue Bell for a special occasion."

"We're celebrating the fact that Claire ran away with a twenty-four-year-old guy?" Hannah asked.

"She's in God's hands, honey," Mom said. "It's the best place she could be."

"I'm all for some Blue Bell," I said, suddenly hungry for some reason.

CHAPTER FORTY

The next day in Spanish class, the door opened as the teacher was taking attendance. Tiny Tim walked to the front of the class and whispered something to her. She glanced at her roster then at me. Or rather, at the desk behind me.

"She's not here."

Tiny Tim said something else and walked out of the classroom.

"Mark," the teacher said, "Vice Principal Timmons needs to see you in his office."

I frowned, unable to recall any grievous sins in the recent past, and took a step toward the door.

"He said you should take your things."

I froze for a second at these words. I'd be gone for at least an hour? Very conscious that all eyes were on me, I got my books and walked out the door.

Tiny Tim waited in the hall. "Follow me."

We walked through the halls in silence, my eyes on his snakeskin cowboy boots, the heels slightly taller than the average boot. As we walked through the office, conversations died.

Through the door of Tiny Tim's office, I glimpsed another set of cowboy boots and brown trousers that had an official look. We went inside. Tiny Tim closed the door behind me and pointed to a chair facing the desk. I had to walk around a policeman who frowned at me as I passed. He smelled like cigars and looked like the sheriff in that Dodge Challenger commercial. I was in a heap of trouble.

"She's not here, Deputy Higgins, but this is her cousin," Tiny Tim said to the officer. "She lives with his family."

The deputy turned to me. "Claire Foxe lives with you?" he asked in a voice that sounded like he gargled with nails and battery acid.

"Yes, sir."

"Where is she?"

"I don't know."

He didn't care for this answer.

"Answer the question, Cloud," Tiny Tim said.

"Yesterday after school she got in a car with a guy. We haven't heard from her since."

Tiny Tim and Higgins exchanged a glance that doubled my unease.

"What guy?" Tiny Tim asked.

"Jeff somebody. From Houston."

Higgins pulled out a notebook and flipped it open. "Did you get the plate number?"

"No, sir. He's her boyfriend. Didn't see any reason to."

"But you don't know his last name?"

"Never met him before. He's from Houston," I added in case he missed it the first time.

"Make and model?"

"What?"

Higgins looked up from his notebook with an expression that made me wish I had run away too. "The car."

"Oh, Datsun 240Z."

"Color?"

"Black."

"Race?"

I frowned. "I don't know if he races it. I doubt it."

Here was that expression again. "The suspect."

"White."

"Hair color?"

"Uh . . . dark."

"Brown or black?"

"He was like twenty yards away with his back to the sun."

"Eyes."

"He was wearing sunglasses."

"Height?"

"Well . . . the roof hit him just under the ribs."

"Weight?"

"He wasn't skinny, but he wasn't fat either. About medium."

Higgins made a note, flipped the notebook closed, and stuffed it back in his pocket. "What do you know about the drugs?"

"Drugs?"

"We have someone in custody who says he bought marijuana from Claire Foxe. She lives in your house."

She was dealing out of our house? I wondered if Dad would revise his position when he found this out. "I don't know anything about Claire selling drugs. Or anyone else."

Higgins focused the full force of his baleful gaze upon me. It reminded me of being cornered by Jimbo, only with ten times the authority. "You're telling me this girl lived in your house, sold marijuana to your classmates, and you knew nothing about it?"

"Yes, sir," I replied in a voice that sounded more like an apologetic hamster than I would have wished. "I've never even tried pot, must less sold it." I was thankful I'd taken a shower after burning the trash last night.

"His father is the Baptist preacher in Fred," Tiny Tim said.

Higgins didn't bother to look at him. "Don't make me no never mind. I've arrested preacher's kids with pot before."

"I don't even smoke cigarettes." I blinked twice. "Sir," I added for good measure.

Higgins continued to impale me with his iron gaze for a minute that felt like an hour. "Let's get the pastor on the line," he finally said.

Tiny Tim picked up the phone. I gave him the number. He dialed and gave the phone to Higgins. The ensuing conversation didn't add to the store of knowledge that Higgins had already amassed, other than the fact that Claire's parents had been notified.

He handed the receiver back to Tiny Tim and turned to me. "If she turns up, or even if she just contacts you, you let me know immediately."

"Yes, sir."

Higgins handed me a business card. "Now get back to class. And don't tell anyone what we talked about."

I grabbed my books and shot out of the office like a greyhound that has just seen the mechanical rabbit stroll past on its day off and thinks he might finally get a chance to catch it. The period was half-way over, but I had no desire to walk the gauntlet back to my desk in Spanish class. I stalked through the halls, found the back door, and wandered out behind the band hall.

Jimbo stood off school property just outside the gate, smoking a cigarette. I spun around to make a hasty retreat, but he saw me. "Mark."

I turned back to face him. "Jimbo," I said with more enthusiasm than I felt. My time had come to turn the other cheek. Or perhaps duck.

"Claire sick?"

"Not that I know of."

"Didn't see her get off the bus."

I suddenly remembered Claire's statement when she was trying to decide what to do with the pot I had confiscated. Before she realized she wasn't going to recover it. Jimbo was cool. How cool?

Steeling myself for a possible pounding, I sauntered over to the gate and leaned against it. "Were you expecting her for some reason?"

"Same as I expected you. Never missed school before now."

"You guys shared cigarettes."

Jimbo frowned. "So?"

"Ever share anything else? Herbal cigarettes maybe?"

His frown deepened. "What is that?"

"You know. She said you were cool."

It took awhile for his expression to morph from confusion to suspicion. "What is this?"

I inched back onto school property. "Just asking."

Jimbo stepped up to the gate, towered over me, and spoke in a fierce whisper. "Look here, Cloud. I know ya stole that stuff from Claire, and I know ya been in there talking to the law. I ain't buying anything from a narc."

I backed away, spreading my hands in denial. "I'm not trying to sell you drugs."

"Sure."

"And I'm not a narc."

"Right."

The bell rang. "Hey, Jimbo, I'd love to stay and chat, but I have to get to class."

Jimbo graced me with a menacing grunt.

I sprinted back to the school, somewhat disturbed by the knowledge that Jimbo knew entirely too much about my activities. Clearly Claire was still astoundingly clueless about flying under the radar.

For the rest of the day, I fielded questions about my office visit by saying that they wanted more information to track down Claire as a runaway. I didn't mention the dealer part. But I did wonder if she left because she knew she had been ratted out.

When I got home, Dad called me back into his study. He'd already reclaimed the area. Claire's stuff was packed in boxes in a corner. Dad sat in the swivel chair in his oil-stained work clothes. I took grandma's arm chair in the corner and propped my feet on the ottoman.

"Were you aware of this situation with Claire?" he asked.

"I had no idea she was selling drugs," I replied, hoping it would satisfy.

He sat silent for a while, which made me nervous. He finally spoke. "I'm afraid she might be in more trouble than we thought."

I nodded.

"That smell last night," he said. "When you were burning the garbage. It occurs to me that it might not have been incense."

"You mean . . . ?" A bit disingenuous, but when it came to staying under the radar, this was the granddaddy.

But Dad wasn't fooled. "Did you try it?"

"No, sir," I said too quickly. "I thought about it, but I decided the best thing was just to get rid of it."

"How did you end up with it?"

I told him the story of finding it in my bedroom, omitting the detail about the hidey-hole. That might come in handy one day. When I got to the part about the riddle, he actually smiled.

"She never figured it out, so she left without it."

"Why didn't you tell me?"

"I was trying to give her a chance to repent. Then, when she left, I figured it didn't matter anymore."

"If you had brought it to me, we might have had a chance to intervene and maybe she would still be here."

"How?"

"I realize you thought it was the right thing to do, but people don't learn to make good choices when you shield them from the consequences of bad choices. "

I hadn't considered that angle. I was beginning to realize just how bad I was at figuring these things out.

"And now you've put yourself in the middle of it."

"Technically, all I did was confiscate an illegal substance and destroy it."

"Exactly. You destroyed evidence of a felony."

Dang! I couldn't win for losing on this one. I dreaded the answer to my next question. "So what do we do now?"

Dad studied me for a while. "I'll have to think about it." He stood up. "But right now something else requires our attention."

"What?" I viewed him with suspicion. Something about the coveralls he wore filled me with a different kind of dread.

He smiled. "I got the pistons out of the tractor and the new rings installed, but putting them back into the block is a two-man job."

I consoled myself with the thought that overhauling an engine was better than an interview with Sheriff Higgins and possible jail time. Slightly. Plus, it was a nice day and it was only four o'clock. I wouldn't be consigned to the most boring job in the world, holding the light while he did all the work.

After a change of clothes, I joined Dad in the garage. He had pulled both cars into the driveway. The tractor sat in the center of the garage, the component parts of the engine spread all over the floor in groups, their proximity indicating the order of removal. When it came to overhauling an engine, and we had done it a few times on the cars, he worked with all the precision of a surgeon.

My job was to lie under the tractor and guide the piston rods onto the crankshaft as he squeezed the rings and tapped the piston into the cylinder. We were on the second piston when the noise of a car in the driveway distracted us.

I glanced down between my feet, which stuck out from under the tractor toward the driveway, and saw a black LTD stop abruptly in a small cloud of dust. The door opened and Deacon Fry climbed out with the determination of a sheriff headed to a hanging.

Dad straightened up from hunching over the engine, a ball-peen hammer in one hand, a block of wood in the other. "Ulysses. To what do we owe the honor?"

Good question. In the five years we had been in Fred, I didn't remember a single time he had come to the parsonage. Maybe he had been there for the pounding on the day we moved in, but I was only twelve then and didn't have a reason to single him out from the herd as a man to be watched and feared.

Deacon Fry stepped into the garage and took in the organized chaos scattered around the floor. "Pastor, your chickens have finally come home to roost. You made your bed and now you have to lie in it."

Dad set his tools aside, picked up a shop rag, and wiped his hands. "It's certainly possible, but it'll have to wait until I get this tractor running."

"You only have yourself to blame."

I wondered how many more folksy sayings he would inflict on us before he explained himself.

"Deacon Fry, your conversation is always a pleasure, but perhaps you could make your meaning more clear. I'd like to have this tractor mowing grass before sundown."

"I'll be plain. As if we haven't had to endure enough insult and embarrassment since you come, you had to bring a drug dealer into our church."

At the shock of that statement, I sat up abruptly. But in my distress, I had forgotten where I was and banged my head on the crankshaft. I flopped back down, rubbing my forehead with an oil-stained hand. At least it was fresh oil.

"Ah," Dad said. "I see that you are curiously well-informed, Deacon Fry."

Yeah, I thought, as I rolled on the floor suppressing my moans. The guy must have spies everywhere searching out any little transgression to amass in his campaign. The question on my mind was just how informed was he? I didn't figure that Jimbo was among his roster of stool pigeons, but who else knew? How long until it got back to Higgins, and eventually Fry?

I envisioned him as Saruman in his tower in Isengard sending out his crows to plague the fellowship. Only in his case, given his general physiognomy, it would be owls.

"There is nothing covered that shall not be revealed; and hid, that shall not be known," Fry said.

Leave it to him to have a verse ready for the occasion. I slid out from under the tractor and sat up.

"True," Dad said. "It is a lesson to us all to walk uprightly before the Lord."

"So you say, and yet you take into your own home, the parsonage this church built with our own hands, a wastrel, a wanton woman."

"Be careful of your words, Ulysses. The Bible has strong things to say about gossip and slander."

"What else can she be when she insults the very people who have taken her in and runs off with a man ten years older?"

"Seven," I said.

"What?" Fry said, turning his terrible gaze onto me.

"He's seven years older," I answered, regretting that I had abandoned my position as a bystander.

Fry disregarded me as he would a yapping dog. "The facts of the matter are these, pastor. This wayward girl who has disrespected her own parents, who you brought into your home, is wanted for selling drugs to schoolchildren."

"That's what I hear, but even the courts have enough grace to consider someone innocent until proven guilty. How can we call ourselves followers of Jesus if the secular courts extend more grace to the sinner than we do?"

If I thought Fry had bristled before, I was sorely mistaken. Now he bristled like an over-caffeinated porcupine. "You ain't the only one who's studied his Bible, pastor. It was Jesus who said, 'Give not that which is holy unto the dogs, neither cast ye your pearls before swine, lest they trample them under their feet.' There's such a thing as repentance."

"Yes, and as Paul tells us, it is God's kindness, not condemnation, that leads us to repentance."

"Grace," Deacon Fry spat. "That's all we hear from you. Cheap grace. We need a pastor who will preach the truth!"

"Grace is truth, Ulysses. It's the unbelievable truth, the good news that is the gospel. With the apostle Paul, on the grace of God I stand. I can do no other."

"Well, you won't be standing here much longer, if I have anything to do with it."

"Fry, if the good people of this church see fit to send me packing because I took in a troubled girl in need of love and understanding, believe me, I'll go gladly and never look back."

"Then I'd start packing if I was you, 'cause we ain't going to stand for it no more."

The door opened and Mom stepped out with two glasses of iced tea. "I thought y'all might . . . Deacon Fry, I didn't realize you were here. Would you like a glass of tea?" She held one out to him.

Fry turned on the heel of his boot and strode out of the garage like a conquering king. We watched him barrel out of the driveway in a furious cloud of dust.

"Should I have offered coffee?" Mom asked.

"Should I start packing?" I asked.

Dad took a glass of tea and turned back to the mess in the garage. "Not before we get this tractor running."

Chapter Forty-One

On the Day of Fools, the skies cleared, which just made me mad. A lesser man might have cursed the sun for shining when life was so obviously filled with pain and darkness, but I just shrugged. I was used to being out of sync with the rest of the world. Why should the weather make an exception?

I walked past the Fortress and across the creek. I had been a little slow getting ready and the gang had left for church without me.

I carried with me a letter that came in the mail the day before. The envelope had a St. Louis postmark and no return address, but I recognized Claire's handwriting even if no one else did. I read the letter one more time as I walked through the wisps of vapor lurking between the pines.

Dear Mark,

I'm sorry. I thought I could make a clean getaway, but I should have known you're too sweet to make it easy for me. I know you're worried about me, but don't worry. I'll be okay. Tell Aunt Elizabeth and Uncle Matt thank you for everything they did for me. And Hannah. And if you see him, tell Roger he can, well, you know.

Love,
Claire

I didn't think twice about telling anyone else about the letter. I figured she would be no worse off with Jeff than she was in Houston. Maybe better. What did I know?

I powered through Sunday school. Then Dad preached a sermon on the prodigal son and the loving father who received his wayward son with a party and rejoicing. Leave it to him to take Deacon Fry head on from the pulpit. I sat behind the good deacon and watched the red creep up his neck and scalp like a thermometer in July. For some reason, I didn't find it as disturbing as I had in the past.

After church I hung around the vestibule as Dad shook hands and did all that stuff that came along with being a preacher, vowing that I would never be a preacher if I had anything to do with it. Too much drama, and for what? For hidebound Neanderthals to hunt you down and nail you to a tree. They'd been doing it for two millennia and who was to stop them now?

I was about to buzz off for the house when Deacon Fry approached the end of the line. His appearance reminded me that I still hadn't been paid for March. One look at him convinced me that this was not the time to raise the issue.

"Pastor, the deacons have requested an ad hoc meeting," Fry growled.

"Have they?" Dad asked. "When?"

"Now."

Dad regarded him with an assessing gaze. "It's a bit irregular."

"These are irregular times."

I looked across the lawn to the parking lot. Deacon Fry's black LTD sat empty. Brenda, Scooter's wife, escorted Mrs. Fry to her car, surrounded by her kids. Something was definitely afoot.

Dad had also noted this detail. He looked at Fry. "If you make it quick. I'll meet you in the office."

Deacon Fry grunted his assent and walked back into the church. I walked up to Dad. "Can I come?"

"Why?"

"It's got to be about Claire. I want to be there."

Dad nodded. "Wait for me here." He delivered the car keys to Mom, returned, and placed a hand on my shoulder. "Once more unto the breach, dear friends, once more."

In his office, Dad walked the gauntlet of the deacons sitting in the chairs that lined the walls between the desk and the door. He took a seat at his desk, which sat at the back of the room facing the door. I took the chair closest to the door.

"What's he doing here?" Deacon Fry asked with a harrowing glance in my direction.

Dad surveyed the four deacons and let his gaze rest on Fry. "Evening the odds."

"He ain't a deacon."

"No, but he is a member."

Deacon Fry grunted. "I'll allow it as long as he keeps his mouth shut."

That was fine with me. I had no intention of turning myself into a target by saying something.

An eyebrow crept up toward Dad's receding hairline. "That's quite generous of you, Ulysses. Now, what is so important that it's keeping all you fine gentlemen from your Sunday dinner?"

"Perhaps we should open with prayer," Deacon Fry said.

"As you wish," Dad said.

Deacon Fry did the honors with a long, rambling, King James pidgin prayer that incorporated multiple verses regarding the responsibilities of leaders and the high standards to which they should be held. It had two effects on me—one to make me glad I wasn't a church leader and would never be, the other to make my stomach grumble as I reconsidered my decision. He finished with a growling amen and opened his eyes.

"Pastor, as the leaders in this church, the deacons are concerned about this business of a member of your own family and a resident in the parsonage being wanted for selling drugs to schoolchildren."

Dad frowned. "Of course you are. So am I."

"And that it is just the most recent example of how, since you come here five years ago, you done more damage to the reputation of this church than anyone in its history."

"Help me understand this, Ulysses. It is the considered opinion of the entire board of deacons that taking in a troubled girl in need of guidance is a stain on the reputation of this church? Is that right, Elmer?"

Elmer flinched as his name was called. He was tall, thin, and frail and wore his pants three inches below his armpits. He snuffled loudly as was his custom, but mercifully spared us a hawking session. "Well, no, that ain't rightly so. That's as may be a credit to your generous nature, but it is troublesome when the law comes investigating your own pastor and there has been talk." A snort and a cough signaled that Elmer was done.

Uh oh. What kind of talk? About destroying evidence?

"Just to clarify," Dad said. "I am not under investigation and haven't been suspected of, must less charged with, anything. No law officer has even been to the parsonage."

Elmer glanced at Deacon Fry warily and settled back down into his chair.

I let out the breath I had been holding. I might escape this skirmish unscathed yet.

Fry took the offensive. "This girl, far from being a poor, misunderstood innocent, began mocking the scriptures from her first day here."

"That's true, Pastor Matt," Scooter said. "First thing she made inappropriate comments saying the spies at Jericho went straight to a . . . well, you know, to Rahab the harlot."

I thought I detected the shadow of a smile lurking in the general vicinity of Dad's face. "Weldon, you got anything to add to this turkey shoot before we all go home to our dinners?"

Weldon was retired and usually wore overalls to everything except Sunday morning services. Didn't talk much, but had a sense of humor. He shrugged. "Only that I do think some consideration should be given to the image of the church."

"I couldn't agree more, Weldon. I'm thinking of that reputation that Jesus said would characterize his church, that we would be known for our love for one another."

Deacon Fry started talking before the last few words were out of Dad's mouth. "The problem here isn't loving one another. It's the bad judgment you showed by exposing this church to compromise and slander by taking in an unrepentant mocker and letting her run wild. A man like that should not be given a place of authority over the church. Not even as deacon, much less pastor."

He turned to his fellow deacons. "I would like to propose that we call a business meeting this evening and present the body with a recommendation to rescind our call to Pastor Matt."

"Judas," I yelled out from the edge of my seat by the door.

All eyes turned to me, especially Dad's.

"Jesus took Judas in as a disciple and never kicked him out, not even at the end, knowing what he had done. Talk about bad judgment."

Dad smiled.

Deacon Fry talked over me, holding out a shaking finger. "You have no say in this meeting."

I didn't miss a beat. "I guess if you had been one of the disciples, you would have proposed a recommendation to fire Jesus before he screwed everything up."

"Pastor, control your son," Fry demanded.

"Mark, where are you manners?" Dad scolded. "Don't interrupt when someone is talking over you."

I stared at Deacon Fry. He looked more like an overripe persimmon than ever before. I settled back down into my chair.

"Do you need to see anything else?" Fry demanded of his fellow deacons. "I can draw up the recommendation this afternoon and bring it around for you to sign."

I closed my eyes and mentally started packing my room. If only I had kept my mouth shut.

"Well, now," Weldon said. "Don't think it's come to that. We just come to express our concern, not to ride Pastor Matt out on a rail."

My eyes popped open and focused on Deacon Fry, who glared from me to Weldon.

"How can you say that after what you just saw? The man can't even control his own family."

Weldon glanced at me. "He just expressed an opinion. Might not be Robert's Rules, but it didn't hurt no one."

Fry scowled and went to the next in line. "What say you, Elmer?"

Elmer shuddered, hawked something into his hankie, folded it up neatly, and shoved it back in his pocket. "Don't know that such a thing is called for quite yet."

"Scooter?"

The Sunday school teacher squirmed in his seat. "You didn't say anything about firing anyone. Just if I was concerned and willing to say so and I was and I did."

Deacon Fry snarled his contempt for the cowards before him.

Dad stood. "Well, then, I'm glad we had this little talk, but I can't keep the missus waiting too long or I'll get in trouble for drying out the roast." He walked around his desk to the door. "And I'm sure you all would like to get to your Sunday dinner too."

He motioned to me. I walked out first and he followed. We didn't talk until we were out of the church and halfway across the pasture to the creek.

"What if they had all agreed with him?" I asked.

"Then I guess it would have been put up to a vote."

"But you could have lost your job."

"Not much of a loss to be kicked out of a church that cares more for its image than for the gospel." He jumped across the creek and started up the hill. "But we did learn one thing. Deacon Fry has a superabundance of bark but a severe deficiency of bite."

"Yeah," I said. "I guess we don't have to worry about him anymore."

"Oh, he's not going to give up and slink away into the night defeated. In fact, he probably won't rest until one or the other of us is gone, and I don't see him leaving any time soon. His family has been here for generations."

"Seriously?"

We walked past the Fortress, and I thought of the last time I had talked to Claire, of her apology. Was it real or was she still up to her old tricks? If she was, at least she wasn't here to make things worse.

"Maybe Claire did us a favor by running away," I said.

Dad stopped under the Fortress and considered this for a second. "Are you saying she took one for the team? Decided she was causing too much trouble and left to spare us?"

That wasn't what I was saying, but it brought to mind her apology. Admitting she hadn't made things easy. Maybe she did leave on purpose for our sake. "If she was here, she'd probably be in jail right now. Then what?"

"Then that meeting might have gone a different direction."

"So it's a good thing she's gone, right?"

Dad studied me. "What if she was here and in jail?"

I thought for a long time. It wasn't a simple question. So many ways to answer wrong and disappoint him. But I also thought Claire had a lot to answer for. "At some point you have to let her reap the consequences, don't you?"

"You don't think she's had to do that since she's been here?"

True, she had been grounded until she paid the phone bill. And she definitely reaped the consequences of hiding her dope in my closet.

"But selling drugs, going to jail, that's pretty big. Don't you have to draw the line eventually?"

"Like God does with us?"

I heard the unspoken question. Did I even hear the sermon this morning about the prodigal son? I studied his face, really looked at him for the first time in this conversation. The Buddy Holly glasses, the forehead that didn't know when to stop, the eyes that redeemed everything.

What was it like to be a pastor, to stand up there and preach the good news, and wonder if anybody got it, even your own son?

In the shade of the Fortress, I thought of the sonnet I sent to Anna. And the sonnet that spawned mine. Sonnet 116.

Love is not love which alters when it alteration finds.

That was the love Dad was talking about, that Jesus was talking about when he told that story, the one about the father who daily searched the horizon for the return of the son who had disrespected him.

O no! it is an ever-fixed mark
That looks on tempests and is never shaken;
It is the star to every wandering bark

If ever there was a wandering bark, a ship lost at sea, it was Claire. And where was her star in this world? Her parents? Certainly not Uncle Roger. Evidently not me. I was ready to throw her under the bus to keep Fry off my back. To keep from being played for a sucker.

It put a different spin on old Bill's poem. I had been so focused on Anna and the Valentine's Day Massacre that I had never considered that it might have a different, perhaps more important application. Instead of writing sonnets for a lost cause, maybe I should have been looking for a lost sheep.

I considered Claire's apology a week ago up in the Fortress, the letter from yesterday that I hadn't shown anyone. To take the time to write a letter when you're on the run, it wasn't a small thing. Had to buy pen and paper, buy a stamp, find a mailbox. You didn't bother with all that unless you really wanted to.

What if the prodigal son had come home a changed man, repentant, only to find that his father had decided to draw the line, to write him off? Out of outrage. Out of self-preservation. For some completely justifiable reason that nobody would fault him for, especially not Deacon Fry.

You think about what the other person wants, or needs, and that's what you do.

But if you really tried to do that, to do what Jesus would do, it got complicated pretty quick. Picking your way through the options was like walking through a minefield.

"So, what if she comes back tonight?" I asked. "What do we do?"

Dad didn't hesitate. "We fix her dinner if she needs it, call her parents to let them know she's safe, and call the sheriff. In that order."

"That's what Jesus would do? Turn her over to the cops?"

"God doesn't save us from the consequences of our sins, but he doesn't disown us either."

That made sense, but I thought that it ought to be easier to answer the question of what Jesus would do, although Dad seemed to have a handle on it. Maybe it got easier after a few decades.

Dad patted me on the back. "Let's go before the roast dries out and your mother blows a fuse."

We walked away from the Fortress.

"At least we'll have something to talk about over lunch," I said.

"Amazing how interesting it is to live on a dirt road in a hick town."

I wondered how Uncle Roger was dealing with a runaway daughter who was wanted for selling drugs. Would he blame us for making it worse, or would he be glad it didn't happen on his watch? I shuddered to think of his caustic comments the next time we crossed paths.

Dad was thinking of something else. "So, you spent more time with Claire than the rest of us. How do you think she's doing?"

I thought again of the apology and the letter. "There's one thing I forgot to tell you."

"What's that?" Dad asked in a guarded tone.

"She said to tell you and Mom and Hannah thank you for everything you did for her."

"Did she?" He smiled and picked up the pace.

"You know," I said. "I think she's going to be okay."

Chapter Forty-Two

While Dad told the tale of the meeting during Sunday dinner, my thoughts turned to Anna and the postcard. All my attempts to find out if she got the postcard had been thwarted by her gatekeepers. I could see only one way of talking to her directly and that was to storm the castle.

I blew through the meal like a horde of locusts crashing Pharaoh's party and asked for the keys to the lesser of the family vehicles, the one with the door Mick Jagger had yet to paint black.

"Thought I'd get in the first swim of the season at Toodlum Creek." I turned to Dad. "Some decompression time."

Dad looked at me skeptically. Mom said, "Honey, it's too cold."

"It's in the high seventies," I replied, hoping that the fact that it was April Fool's Day would count for something when I pulled a Claire and took the Falcon to Woodville instead of the swimming hole.

"I'll even fill up the car."

Dad shrugged. "It's your nickel." He turned to his ice cream and paused. "Just don't drown."

"Deal." I raced back to my room, threw on cutoffs and a T-shirt, and grabbed a towel for verisimilitude.

I saluted the dirt road that turned off FM 1943 toward the creek as I passed it. Maybe I'd stop there on the way back so I could come home suitably damp and sandy.

On the radio "Oh! Darling" on the Beaumont station competed with "Walk Through This World With Me" on the Woodville station. The closer I got to Woodville, the more George Jones dominated The Beatles. Not a condition I would typically endorse, but in this case, I took it as a good sign.

As I turned north onto Highway 69, I thought about the postcard. It had been approved by a diverse range of experts ranging from Hannah to Vernon. Surely something that appealed to such a wide spectrum of humanity couldn't fail to speak to one who had thought I was The One mere weeks ago.

Assuming Anna had read it. Perhaps Mrs. Courtney had hung up on me because the postmistress was wrong and the card hadn't yet been delivered.

My foot eased off the accelerator as I considered this disturbing scenario. In that case, I was driving into hostile territory, attempting to harvest before I had planted. I shuddered as I envisioned the minefield I might be walking into.

A pickup whipping around me in a no-passing zone brought my attention to the fact I was coasting at thirty in a sixty. I pressed down the accelerator and pressed on to my destination. If she had not received the card, I would recite it to her. What could be more romantic than that?

But as I cruised through the streets of Woodville, past the corner where a year ago I nearly ran down a dog during the driving test to get my license, my confidence faltered.

Maybe, as Hannah seemed to think, I had devised the ultimate weapon in the war to reclaim the promised land. Or maybe I was delusional. Maybe I was just a short skinny kid with stringy blond hair hanging in his eyes, driving along in a T-shirt, cutoffs, and flops to the house of a jewel in whom there was no flaw, hoping to undo Pearl Harbor with a dozen-plus lines of half-baked verse.

Before I could scrap the mission and shred the files, I found myself in Anna's driveway. It was two in the afternoon, the time you would be most likely to find the traditional Southern Baptist in his native habitat, snoring away in the easy chair in front of a game of some kind on television.

I sat in the car staring at the front door for approximately the length of time it takes sunlight to reach Pluto, or perhaps as long as it takes a bird to wear away a rock a hundred miles high and a hundred miles wide by sharpening its beak on it. I wasn't exactly keeping track.

I finally got the nerve up to open the red door and step out of the car. I was halfway to the porch when the front door to the house opened. Reverend Courtney appeared in the gloom of the entryway, his pale face paler than usual, his red tonsure pixelated by the mesh of the screen door, looking more like a manic clown than ever. Evidently he had been awakened from a nap to deal with the crisis.

"Son, what are you doing here?"

"Uh . . . hi. I was hoping to talk to Anna."

He shook his head. "She doesn't want to talk to you." He moved to close the door but paused for a final word. "Ever. So stop calling."

"Wait!" I sprinted to the porch without stepping up on it. "Reverend Courtney, I just need to know if she got the card."

"The card?" The crack in his voice made him sound like The Hose. "Oh, yes, we got the card. But perhaps in your case something more than spurs might be required. Maybe a bullwhip would be more appropriate."

I wasn't prepared for the sarcasm in his voice, and half of what he said made no sense. The card was not designed to induce such a reaction. He might find it juvenile, pedantic, derivative, overbearing, or even cloying, but contemptible? Disgusting? I refused to believe it.

"Could I talk to her for just one minute? I drove all the way here."

"Should have called first. Would have told you not to bother."

No analysis of this situation could be interpreted as going according to plan. A movement in a window caught my eye. A hand pulled the curtain aside and Anna's face appeared. She had cut her hair like Dorothy Hamill. I had not thought it possible that she could have gotten any cuter, but here she had gone and done it.

"A speed bump need not become a barricade," I shouted out.

Reverend Courtney flinched at the volume of my voice. "What?"

"A detour need not lead to a dead end." I held my arms out in supplication, or perhaps offering myself as a target.

"What are you talking about?"

"Too much has passed between us to persuade me that it is over, or to pretend that what we shared was a common thing, a lark—"

"Oh, it's over. Now get off my property before I call the sheriff. I think you've already met him."

"A crush, a phase we leave behind," I continued, louder. "And not a ticket to a time machine to take us to a place where stars align and worlds collide." I had never spoken with more earnest purpose.

Behind the glass, Anna stared at me like I was some kind of phantasm, a mythical beast suddenly come to life.

Reverend Courtney pushed the screen door open and stepped out onto the porch.

I took a step forward and held up a hand as if asking for the next dance. "If you can look beyond the words that, spoken, cannot be unsaid, and setting them aside, instead respond not to the past but to what lies ahead, then we can lay to rest what has been done and see that each of us has found The One."

Anna's face disappeared from the window as the curtain fell back into place.

Reverend Courtney closed the distance between us with three steps and twirled me around as if he had taken me up on my offer of a dance. He frog-marched me to the red door and released me with a shove.

"If I even hear a whisper of a rumor that you are within a mile of my daughter, you will regret ever hearing of me. Now git. Don't call. Don't come back. Ever."

I stood, bewildered. This was not the way it was supposed to end. In fact, it wasn't supposed to end at all. This was supposed to be the new beginning. I looked around, wondering if there were any witnesses to verify that I hadn't lost my mind.

Reverend Courtney leaned in. I jumped into the car and locked the door. He glared at me until I started the engine. Then he stormed back inside and slammed the door. After a few seconds, the door inched open and Mrs. Courtney looked out. She locked eyes with me and slammed the door.

All I could think was that I had indeed lost my mind. I had lost it the moment I saw Anna. And now I had lost all hope. There was no escalation of affinities, no next level to which I could take the assault. It was a war of attrition and I was the attritee.

I sat there with the car running for an indeterminate length of time, attempting to regain some semblance of a hold on reality. Then I backed out of the driveway and drove off. As I pulled up to the stop sign at the corner, a figure stepped out from behind a tree.

It was Anna. She was still in her church clothes, a light V-neck floral-print dress with a pleated skirt that flared as she walked around the front of the car and slid into the passenger seat.

"Hey," she said.

"Anna, what's going on? Your dad went crazy."

"I just have one question. Are you doing drugs?"

"What? No!"

A horn sent me into a spasm. I caught the glimpse of a car in the rearview and pulled forward reflexively.

"The church," Anna said.

I drove the block to her church, pulled around the back between the bus and the oak grove, and killed the engine.

"Mark, I'm sorry about how I acted at the Valentine's banquet. I was upset, but that's no excuse."

It had been six weeks since we'd talked, much less been together. I wanted to kiss her, to tangle my fingers in her thick, bobbed hair, to step into the time machine that made all this disappear, that took us to the place where I was The One for her and she was The One for me.

For a second I thought that might work, that somehow one kiss could undo all that had been done. I leaned toward her, resting my arm on the seat back, reaching for her hair, but she pushed me away.

"That's not why I came."

Then why was she here, taunting me with her proximity, looking twice as cute as allowed by state law?

"We heard that Claire was selling pot. That you were part of it."

"And you believed it?"

Anna looked away, through the windshield at the rose window in the back wall of the sanctuary. "It doesn't matter if I believe it."

"It matters to me."

"Daddy believes it."

"What happened to innocent until proven guilty?"

"You know how it is for us, Mark. Avoid all appearance of evil."

I knew how it was. If I forgot for even a nanosecond, I had Deacon Fry around to remind me. But I wasn't willing to leave it there. "The kingdom of heaven is like a merchant seeking beautiful pearls, who, when he had found one pearl of great price, went and sold all that he had and bought it."

"Matthew thirteen, forty-five and forty-six."

She whispered it like the words hurt as she spoke them. I wasn't wrong about her.

"How many times has this happened to you?"

"What?"

"Finding The One."

"Never," she said just above a whisper. "Until now."

"You don't turn your back on The One because of some stupid rumor that isn't even true. You risk everything to get the pearl of great price."

Anna's eyes brimmed. "You know it's not that simple. Not for us."

"But it's worth it. You're worth it."

She responded with words that pained us both. "Honor your father and your mother, that your days may be long upon the land which the Lord your God is giving you."

It was my turn. "Exodus twenty something."

"Twenty twelve."

"So what then? I'm just collateral damage?"

Anna was crying now. "Mark, you know this can't work without our parents' blessing."

This was all Claire's fault. Her selfishness. Her refusal to see how her actions would affect the very people who sacrificed to try to help her.

Anna touched my arm. "I'm sorry, Mark."

Before I could respond, she slipped out of the car and walked away. I watched her step into the oak grove, her skirt billowing like a figure skater's, as she turned toward home.

CHAPTER FORTY-THREE

The next time I looked up, I was approaching the cutoff to Toodlum Creek. I didn't remember starting the car, taking the turns on the city streets out to Highway 69, driving south to Warren, or turning east on FM 1943.

The heat of the afternoon was at its height, approaching eighty, and I had no pressing engagements such as spending time with a girlfriend. Why not drown my sorrows in Toodlum Creek?

I turned left and drove the five miles to the creek along a road that could more accurately be described as a meandering collection of sand pits to the break in the roadside brush that marked the entrance to the swimming hole. Everyone called it Toodlum Creek, despite the fact that the county map labeled it as Theuvenins Creek.

It was early in the season, and the swimming hole was as deserted as I expected it to be, redolent with the aroma of fresh mud and rotting wood. It was thirty feet across, had a three-foot bank on one side, and a ten-foot bank on the other. A giant oak tree hung out over the water with a rope tied twenty feet up on the first available limb. A rope of that length hanging a third of the way across the creek made for a great arc, particularly since the launching point was four feet above the water. You could do flips off the rope if you had a mind to.

It was typical muddy creek water, home to its share of fish, turtles, and snakes, but the critters usually left you alone, especially if you made lots of noise.

The water level was up due to the rains of the past week. The last swimmer had not bothered to drape the rope across the trunk of the oak, so I waded out into the water and flung it back over the trunk. I climbed back up the bank, grabbed the rope, and launched myself into the ether with abandon, not caring how I landed.

When I hit flat on my belly, I started caring right quick. The next time, I took care to hit feet first. For the third I did a half gainer and broke the water with my fingertips. Due to the rains, I had plenty of space to pull up without plowing sand on the bottom.

On the fourth dive, I swung out as far as I could to hit the deep water. Nobody was sure exactly how deep it went, but I figured it was at least twenty feet. No need to pull up.

I pushed as deep as I could on the momentum of the dive and then stroked deeper, shooting for the bottom. After five strokes I still hadn't hit it and considered that I might not want to find out what lurked down there.

Rather than turn back to the surface, I curled into a ball until my momentum faded. Then I stretched out spread-eagled and allowed my body to find the surface in a dead man's float.

As I drifted through the thermal layers from the cold of the bottom to the chill of the surface, I let my mind drift over how I came to be here on an April Fool's Sunday afternoon.

I had drifted from infatuation to certainty by slow degrees. I had been sidetracked by the vexing question of what Jesus would do on a date. Then I had abandoned that question as meaningless, too fraught with self-interest to be answered with any degree of certainty. Finally I had come to the realization that I had indeed found The One, an unexpected combination of beauty and brains and, most important, mutual attraction.

And then it all fell apart. How exactly? That was the question.

I wanted more than anything to blame it all on Claire, but I knew that was the easy way out. When I vowed to live by the inconvenient question, I had committed to asking the hard questions. And I had to take the hard answers, no matter how painful.

I replayed the scenario from the beginning in my oxygen-starved brain as I floated to the surface. Anna had complained about The Hose and I had piled on, venting all the frustrations I had harbored against him from the day I met him, the foremost of which was that he was a consummate geek.

From some remote crevice in my brain, Bubba's words replayed themselves. "It's only stupid if you use it stupid." You don't think what you want and then do it to the other person. You take the trouble to understand what they want.

Anna didn't want me to join her in trashing her brother. Like Hannah said, she wanted someone to sympathize with her frustration. If I had bothered to sympathize, I never would have had to apologize.

Which is exactly what Jesus would have done. The question wasn't as irrelevant as I had assumed. Now that I had this piece of the puzzle, all my other struggles were suddenly simplified.

What would Jesus do on a date, a situation completely foreign to his cultural context? He would consider each circumstance from the perspective of the other person and act in their best interest, not react out of desperation and desire.

And if I had done that, it might not have changed the ultimate end, but at least I would have had six more glorious weeks with The One before tragedy struck. And who knew but that it could have been enough time for the Reverend and the Missus to get to know me well enough to dismiss the rumors, or at least give me a chance to explain.

Nice to know, but as usual I was late to the party.

After what seemed like an eternity of meditation but must have been only a minute, I reached the surface and floated there, face down. A second later, I was electrified by a scream cutting through the fog of my reflections.

I thrashed in the water, sucked in a lungful of air, and looked for the source of the noise.

On the bank by the oak with the rope, the Beau sisters stared at me with their eyes and mouths wide open.

"What?" I yelled.

They screamed again.

I looked around but found nothing to scream about. I turned back to them.

"You're not dead," Raine said.

"Not yet." I was fairly confident on this particular point, but I was open to discussion. I swam to the bank and climbed up.

The Beau sisters, Raine, Ella, and Flo, were skinny stair-step Cajuns, looking like anorexic Russian nesting dolls in their floral-print bikinis. Bo, the brother, stood by in his cutoffs.

"Hey," I said.

Bo nodded.

I grabbed my towel and dried off. "See you in the funny papers," I said as I trotted down the sand path to the car.

As I drove home, I replayed the scene of the crash in Anna's front yard. One thing puzzled me. Her dad said that spurs weren't good enough for me, that a bullwhip would be more appropriate.

Spurs. It sounded familiar. I had heard that word recently. No, I had used that word recently. In fact, I had written it down recently. On a postcard.

In a panic, I pressed the accelerator to the floor. It couldn't be. Surely after weeks of torturous labor, my fate had not been sealed by a simple error. It was like a moon launch being scrubbed because someone locked the keys to the Saturn-V in the capsule with the windows up.

The speedometer on the Falcon went up to one-twenty. I pegged it on the straightaways and dropped down to ninety on the corners. At the house, I skidded up to the garage in my best Darnell Ray impression and jumped out of the car, leaving the door open.

I raced through an empty den and kitchen, down the hallway past bedrooms likely filled with napping Baptists, and to my closet. The notebook lay on my dresser, and I rifled through the pages too fast to actually see anything. Changing tactics, I grabbed the covers and shook it like a crooked cop trying to beat a confession out of a thug.

A half-dozen cards fell out. I flipped them over and tossed them aside one by one until I came to the last card. With a shaking hand, I turned it over and read the first line.

A speed bump need not be a barricade.

No! I flung the postcard away from me like it was a black mamba. This could not be happening. I had matriculated in the academy of experience and worked toward my master's degree, one rejected phone call at a time, one poet at a time, one tongue-lashing from Hannah at a time for six long weeks.

Dropping to my knees, I scooped up the other cards, searching for a clever but completely inadequate sentence about spurs, but I was pumping a dry well. No wonder the postmistress had smiled. It was a funny card. Funny, but deadly.

I snatched up the card I should have mailed and jumped to my feet to get to the post office before five, but then realized today was Sunday. Closed.

The injustice of it brought me to the verge of tears. I had been sweating blood, reading and writing and honing and perfecting, only to be judged not by my published masterpiece but by my first draft.

The notebook bounced off the wall as I unleashed my outrage at the unfairness of the universe. I threw open the sliding door, stormed through the pine trees, and holed up in the Fortress of Solitude to lick my wounds. A mere three minutes later, Hannah emerged from the scuttle hole and took a seat on a crate.

My unfocused stare converged on her face. "How did you know I was here?"

"Something hit the wall and then the sliding door bounced open."

I responded with a single nod and resumed my thousand-yard gaze into the abyss.

"Did she get the card?"

A questioning expression was all I could muster.

"If you were really going to Toodlum, you would have said you were meeting Ralph or Darnell or somebody. Nobody goes to a swimming hole by themselves."

I conceded the point with a flicker of my eyebrows.

"Based on your Neanderthal conversational skills I'd say she didn't get the card."

"Oh, she got the card all right. Or she got a card."

"Not the card?"

I shook my head. "Evidently there was a slight mix-up in delivery."

"And?"

"You remember the first card I wrote?"

Hannah stared off into space as she flipped back through the last few weeks. Then she turned to me in horror. "Oh, no! Not . . ."

"Yee-ha! I love you, baby, but could you please take off those spurs?" The bacon-wrapped fillet of postcards.

"No!"

"Oh, yes. Eight times yes, one for each level of hell and a custom level designed just for me."

"Oh, Mark." She placed a hand on my arm.

Such was the degree of my distress that I allowed it to remain until she removed it a few moments later.

"Well, maybe," she started, but then stopped.

"There is no maybe."

"Maybe it's for the best. Maybe God put the wrong postcard in your hand. Maybe he's telling you she isn't The One after all."

I bristled. "What? After all you said about—"

"Yeah, I know, but this is just too crazy to be a coincidence. I mean, really."

It was tempting to blame it all on God, but I felt she might have underestimated my incompetence.

"I mean, she took it pretty far. It's one thing to teach a guy a lesson. It's another to leave him hanging for a month."

"Well, it wasn't exactly like that."

"What was it like, then?"

I told her about the rumor.

"Claire," Hannah spat out. "I wish she had never come here."

I tended toward agreeing with her on this one, but something told me I had more thinking to do on that topic.

"I'm sorry, Mark."

She wasn't the only one. I nodded my thanks, and she disappeared down the scuttle hole. I looked around the Fortress as if it could somehow provide me with some solace. I popped open the secret compartment. Claire's cigarettes and incense looked back at me. I fired up some incense.

As much as I hated to admit it, I missed Claire's company, not only for the entertainment value she always brought to the table, but also because I wanted to get to know the new Claire, the one who recognized her shortcomings and treated people like fellow travelers rather than resources to be manipulated for her nefarious purposes. I realized that she might not have changed at all, that she could have been playing us all again, but her transformation had felt real and, like Mom and Dad, I chose to believe it until I had a reason to think otherwise.

That was what you did when you were doing unto others. You gave people the benefit of the doubt like you hoped they would do for you. Not blindly in denial of the evidence, but charitably, believing in the possibility that lay in each individual.

Who knew when this might be the time it all came together and the moment of change arrived? And who wouldn't feel like a heel if they sabotaged true repentance? After all, we had a God of second chances. No, that wasn't right. A God of seventy-times-seven chances. Who was I to keep track, waiting for the moment to write Claire off? That was Deacon Fry's job.

But I couldn't deny that Claire had gone off somewhere, following a path I couldn't begin to imagine, toward a goal I didn't understand. Or that she had opened Pandora's box and then left us to explain to Deacon Fry and his minions the evils that had escaped. She had failed to comprehend the consequences of becoming a blip on his radar. But I cut her some slack. It took a lifetime of training as a PK to acquire such nuanced skills.

I reluctantly acknowledged that if I had gone to Dad the second I found the drugs instead of trying to teach Claire a lesson, things might have turned out differently. She might still be here and the rumors that cost me the pearl of great price might never have metastasized to do their irrevocable damage.

As the incense sputtered out, a voice came up from the pine straw floor.

"How was Toodlum Creek?"

I peered over the edge. Dad stood below, his receding hairline accentuated from this perspective. He had his Bible and notebook. I suddenly realized two things. It was time for the Sunday evening service, Training Union followed by a sermon. And that was the last place I wanted to be, especially since Deacon Fry would doubtlessly be there.

"Instructive," I replied.

He nodded as if he understood, but I didn't see how he could.

"Hey, what if I didn't go to church tonight?" I asked.

He considered the question for a handful of seconds. "I think we would be able to soldier on without you."

"Thanks."

He proceeded on to the church, and I scrambled down the ladder to my bike. Twenty minutes later, I coasted up to Vernon's Pontiac. A visit on Sunday was unprecedented, but he still handed me a sweating can of Coke when I slid into the passenger seat.

The porch swing of the house across the road was empty, but I didn't comment on it. The girl would have to work out her own salvation with fear and trembling, without benefit of my third-hand speculation and commentary.

After ten minutes or so, Vernon broke the silence. "She get that postcard?"

I didn't relish explaining that particular disaster. "Sort of." I sensed his inspection from the corner of his eye.

He slapped his hand over his mouth, took in a lungful of smoke, and blew it out through his nose. "Don't rightly know how a gal sort of gets a card. Either she does or she don't."

"Well, I did mail a postcard," I conceded. "But it wasn't the one I told you about."

"You come up with something better?" His voice betrayed an understandable incredulity.

"No, I pulled the wrong card out of my notebook."

He grunted and took a long pull from his Coke. "Was it a good'un?"

"Not good enough."

Vernon took some time to increase the alcohol level of his drink and sample it. With a nod of satisfaction, he turned and spoke directly to me. "What did it say?"

"Yee-ha! I love you, baby, but could you please take off those spurs?"

The silence stretched through the shushing of the wind tossing around the tops of the pines that surrounded the clearing.

"I don't reckon she took that well," Vernon finally said.

"It was mainly her dad who failed to appreciate it, but that was enough." I didn't have the strength to explain the whole thing. If he realized that his part in connecting Claire with a supplier played a significant role in the debacle, he might feel guilty. Plus, he had no context for the nuances of the PK angle that drove the final nail in the coffin.

"Well, then."

We spent the next quarter-hour contemplating the descent of the sun past the level of the chimney down to the tree line.

"The one that got away," Vernon said. "That can set a feller back fer a good spell. Careful it don't wreck ya."

"According to your calculations, there is only one in Texas for me, maybe two. What are the odds I get another shot at it?"

"Ya can't think about the odds, Mark boy. That there's what'll wreck ya."

He was right about that part, but it was all I could think about.

"Just remember what I told ya. Yer time is gonna come."

"What if it already did?"

"Looks like that now maybe, but life has a way of throwing us a bone when we need it. Yer daddy would say it's God, and he might be right." He took a long slug from his Coke. "I been in some bad places, and all I know is things are never as bad as they seem when yer in the middle of them."

He caught my eye and held it. "Yer a good kid, no matter what ya might think right now. Yer time is gonna come. Count on it."

Somehow I thought he might be right about that. I would just have to wait and see.

{ A NOVEL }

"Whittington spins an enjoyable,
literary story and is
definitely a novelist to watch."
PUBLISHERS WEEKLY

ESCAPE
FROM
FRED

ESCAPE FROM FRED

CHAPTER ONE

I awoke in the dark, unsure where I was. The pain in my back indicated that wherever I was, it wasn't at home in bed.

I pulled myself up by what appeared to be the arms of a chair. My fingers settled into the smooth grooves of wooden hand rests. I swung my right arm around and banged against the vertical shaft of a floor lamp and followed it up to the switch.

I was sitting in an armchair with brown upholstery, matching ottoman at my feet. A bed lay to my right, unmolested, made with military corners. Against the far wall, a roll-top desk with swivel chair, IBM Selectric blocking the pigeonholes, a gray wooden file cabinet to the right. To the other side of the bed—a door, shower and toilet visible within.

I exhaled and settled back into my grandmother's chair. I was in Dad's study in Fred, Texas. I checked my watch. Three a.m. The midnight of the soul as Bradbury called it. A fading echo of images from my dreams swirled in my brain—a pale woman clothed like Godiva, hand outstretched, a red dirt hill, a white steeple against a cobalt sky, the ferric taste of blood, the musty scent of pine pitch, the sensation of pine needles pressed into my cheek. My hand reflexively stroked the pale scars on my face.

"The mark," I heard myself whisper into the thickness of the silence.

The patches of vapor cleared, and I recalled why I was here. The phone call from Heidi, the rushed arrangement of flights, arriving in Houston, driving to Fred.

He was already gone by the time I arrived. The next morning Heidi, Hannah, and I drove to Farmer Funeral Home in Silsbee for the viewing. Then we spent the day going through the house. I took the study, a job worth several other rooms for the filing cabinet alone. I remembered cleaning the desk and looked around. The small black three-ring binder I found lay on the floor next to me, one tab for each letter.

I picked it up and flipped through it. The first entry for the letter F leapt out at me.

> Faith, n:
>   —Ambrose Bierce's definition: Belief without evidence in what is told by one who speaks without knowledge, of things without parallel.
>   —Paul's definition: The substance of things hoped for, the evidence of things not seen.
>   —Matthew Cloud Lexicon definition: The determination to believe that which resonates in the soul, particularly when it ceases to resonate. See: life.

I fell back and wondered what had awakened me. I felt the suggestion of a door snapping closed. No telling who looked in. I was glad whoever it was saw fit to leave me alone. I didn't need anyone telling me to go to bed.

Dad. Faith. My mind worked back to the time when the entry was likely written. The year Patty Hearst was convicted, Apple Computer was formed, Son of Sam began shooting people, and Viking 1 landed on Mars. The year of the bicentennial.

It was the year that changed my life. The watershed year that divided all that came before from all that came after. The time leading up to that year began innocently enough. It wasn't until much later that the wheels came off.

CHAPTER TWO

"Feagin Hall? They named the guy's dorm Feagin Hall?" I looked back at Bubba.

He set his suitcase on the sidewalk and examined his fingernails. A semicircle of stairs led to thirty-foot white columns along the outer edge of a half-moon porch. The gabled roof three stories up was labeled in Roman letters.

I was undeterred by his studied disinterest. "It's not spelled the same, but I bet it's pronounced the same."

Bubba scuffed the taps on his cowboy boots against the sidewalk. "Do you know who Fagin was?"

"Can't say I've had the pleasure."

"He took in young boys and trained them to be pickpockets and sneak thieves. Oliver Twist." Silence from Bubba. "Charles Dickens."

"Never met him either."

Bubba ranked fourth in our graduating class, a fact he kept hidden from the gang like a shameful secret. He knew Charles Dickens. But during the drive from Fred to Marshall, a strained formality developed between us. Perhaps I was too vocal about his pigheaded obsession with the welfare of his Corvair convertible. He doubled our travel time to five hours by driving 30 mph the entire trip. Before we left, Darnell Ray told him the head gasket was very iffy. I scoffed at the diagnosis, a fatal mistake that destroyed my credibility. We both knew it was more likely that Donny and Marie would marry each other than Darnell would be wrong about an engine.

But few things are more unnerving than creeping along a two-lane farm-to-market road while pickups and LTDs pulling bass boats stack up behind. On the straightaways they screamed past en masse, hurling obscene words, gestures, and fast food containers. I didn't endure it gracefully. My reflections on Feagin Hall were the first words uttered in thirty miles.

"If the guy behind the desk introduces himself as the Artful Dodger, don't say anything. Just follow me back out."

Bubba snorted. I walked up the steps. He picked up his suitcase and followed. The lobby was littered with easy chairs and couches facing an old console television. The ceiling was two stories up. A balcony overlooked a grand piano and a set of more delicate-looking chairs. To the right, a half-door revealed a guy with blond hair that swept down across one eye and flipped up at his collar. Much like mine.

I walked to the door and dropped my suitcase. The guy didn't even look up.

"Name?"

"Twist. Oliver Twist. This here's Bill Sykes." I nodded at Bubba. He rolled his eyes.

The guy flipped through a roster on a clipboard.

"Don't see no Twist. Or Sykes. How do you spell that?" He glanced up for a second and flipped a few more pages.

Bubba pushed me aside and leaned on the counter. "I'm Bubba Culpepper. C-U-L-pepper."

The guy flipped back to the first page. "Culpepper, B. Got it." He looked at me. "But we ain't got no Twist."

"He's Mark Cloud. Probably right above my name."

"Here it is." He eyed me. "Wise guy, huh?" I batted my eyes sweetly. His eyes narrowed. "Hmm. I think we have a room for you on the third floor." He consulted a floor plan. "Yes, Room 320. You'll love it." He turned to the wall and grabbed a key and a piece of paper. "Here, sign this."

"Sure." I stepped to the window. "Where's the elevator?"

"Right there." He pointed to the stairs.

"Great." I signed my name and grabbed the key.

He went back to the clipboard. "Let's see. Culpepper. Looks like . . . looks like you're roommates with Oliver Twist." He winced. "Sorry about that."

"Is it too late to change?" Bubba asked.

He gave Bubba a sympathetic look. "Yep, 'fraid so. We got a full house."

Thirty minutes later the Corvair was empty and Room 320 was full. Such as it was.

From the door, a narrow hallway opened into a small rectangle of floor space. At each end, a writing desk with chair sat below a bookcase hanging on the wall. Two beds were end-to-end under the windows on the far wall. Actually, the term bed was too generous for what we beheld. In reality, a plywood platform three feet deep and two feet high ran the length of the room. A two-by-six split the platform in the middle. On each half lay an institutional pinstripe mattress with the density of a collapsed star.

We made the beds, placing the pillows at opposite ends. I plopped on my bed, the one that allowed me to look down the short passage to the room across the hall, adjusted the pillow, and leaned against the wall. Bubba took the bed by the door to the bathroom that was shared by the adjoining room.

I looked at Bubba, who was arranging the reference books Dad gave him as a graduation present, and then out the window to the porch three floors below. "Hey, you need the exercise anyway."

His lack of response was relieved by the bathroom door opening. A light-brown Brillo-head poked into the room. A tall, slender body followed.

"Hey, you must be our suite-mates."

Bubba whirled around, knocking a Strong's Concordance to the floor. "Sweet mates?"

"Yeah." Brillo Head stepped into the room and held out his hand. "Phil Moore."

"Bubba." He looked at the hand, evidently reluctant to shake hands with a sweet mate.

"Bubba what?"

"Bubba Culpepper."

"Hey, Bubba Culpepper."

I waved from the corner. "I'm Mark."

"Mark what?" he said, crossing the room in two strides.

"Mark Cloud."

"Hey, Mark Cloud. Phil Moore."

"Fillmore what?" I asked, shaking hands.

"That's it. Just Phil Moore."

"Just Fillmore?"

"Yep, no middle name."

"What about a last name?"

"Last name is Moore," he said, puzzled.

"Fillmore Moore?"

"No, just Phil Moore."

We were interrupted by a short dark-haired guy entering from the bathroom door. "Hey, just checking to see who's here. I'm in the next room."

Phil was next to him in an instant. "Then we must be roommates." He grabbed the dark guy's hand, towering over him. "Phil Moore."

The dark guy looked puzzled, his arm going up and down like a pump handle. "No, Phil Lancaster."

"Nope, I'm definitely Phil Moore."

"You're Phil Moore?"

"Yep."

"I'm Phil Lancaster."

Bubba's laughter startled everyone. "Phil and Phil."

"This could be a problem," Phil said.

"Yep," Phil said.

"Looks like we have our fill of Phils," I said. Bubba smiled. The Phils didn't.

"We could go by our last names," Phil said.

"Moore and Lancaster?" Phil asked.

"Or Lancaster and Moore," Phil answered.

"Too long," Phil said. "I don't want to have to say 'Lancaster' every time I call you."

"Then don't call me."

"Might I make a suggestion?" The Phils turned to me. "How about Thing One and Thing Two?" Blank stares. "Theodore Geisel." Blank stares. "Dr. Seuss. Cat in the Hat."

"How about Phil One and Phil Two?" Phil suggested.

"Which one is One?" Phil challenged.

Then it hit me. I leapt from my bed to the center of the room and held one finger aloft. "Since there is more to Phil Moore, we call him Phil-more. And, as there is less to Phil Lancaster, we call him Phil-less."

"Phyllis?" Phil roared. The short one.

"Fillmore. I like it," Phil said. The tall one.

"No way," Phil said.

"Let's vote," Phil said. "All in favor." Bubba and I held up our hands. So did Phil. The tall one. "All opposed." Phil scowled. The short one. "Abstaining? Looks like it passes. Fillmore and Phyllis it is."

Phyllis muttered a curse and disappeared into Room 322. Fill-more shrugged.

Monday night a group of sophomore sadists rounded up the fresh-man guys, known as Fish, for a forced march to the freshman girls' dorm where we were obliged to serenade the inmates. The next night we were lounging in Room 320 when the door slammed open and Captain Kangaroo burst in.

It wasn't actually Captain Kangaroo, but the guy could have been his kid brother. He had the same blond Dutch Boy haircut and bristle brush mustache. Before we could protest, he raced to the windows.

"This will hardly do. The screens are still on." He leaned over my legs as I lay on the bed, punched the screen out of the window, caught it just before it fell, and hauled it into the room. "Here." He dropped it in my lap and did the same to Bubba's screen.

"What are you doing?" I demanded.

"I understand your alarm, but expedience must take precedence over propriety," The Captain boomed. "Take these and fill them with water from the sink." He dropped a bag of twenty-five party balloons on the screen. He pointed at Bubba. "You, sir. Clear the immediate vicinity of all screens and mattresses."

I knocked the screen off my lap. "What are you talking about? And who are you?"

"Allow me to lay the essential facts before you. In a mere three minutes that porch will be teeming with freshman girls singing the school song in dulcet tones. Doubtless they will have an encore planned, perhaps 'Bicycle Built for Two' or 'Purple Polka Dot Bikini.'"

In anticipation of their arrival, I propose that we prepare a minimum of one hundred water balloons." He began dragging the mattress off my bed with me on it. "So let us now secure these mattresses in the shower and fill the balloons."

Bubba leaped from his bed and wrestled his mattress to the shower.

"I approve of your prompt response," The Captain called over his shoulder to Bubba as he dumped me on the floor and shoved my mattress toward the bathroom. The Phils appeared in the bathroom, demanding an explanation.

I finally grasped the plan. I grabbed the pack of balloons. "Do you have more of these?" I asked The Captain.

"Indubitably." He pulled out a handful.

I grabbed two bags and cornered the Phils. "Remember our serenade last night?" They nodded. "The girls are coming here to return the favor. They will be crammed onto the porch." I pointed to the windows. "Before they get here, we need lots of water balloons."

I tossed a package to Bubba. He tore it open and wrapped a balloon over the bathroom faucet. "One person fills, the other ties. I'll help Bubba." I shoved a package into Fillmore's hands. "Take these across the hall and get whoever is there to help you." I turned to The Captain. "Next door, 324. Phyllis, you take 318."

By the time we heard the sounds of a crowd gathering below the windows, Bubba and I had twenty balloons stacked on the plywood. I left Bubba to fill the last five. I dragged the mattresses off the Phils' beds, removed their screens, and took a pillowcase to the neighboring rooms to harvest the crop.

As the girls began warming up with the school song, The Captain slapped the light switch and marshaled our forces in the gloom. Bubba and I, the two Phils, and three accomplices from the other rooms lined up along the beds.

"First, I want everyone to wave to the ladies." We leaned over the balloons and looked out. More than a hundred girls were packed into the half-circle of the porch twenty-five feet below us like cattle at the stockyards in Ft. Worth. More pressed in from the steps. We smiled and waved. The ones who could wrest an arm free waved back, oblivious to their fate.

"I shall now reveal the plan. Four to a room, two to a window. Starting from this end you shall consider yourself numbered 1, 2, 1,

2, 1, 2, 1, 2. Do you apprehend me?" We all nodded. "In front of you find two rows of six balloons, one row for each hand. When I call out your number, eject two balloons through the window and acquire another set. They will emerge eight at a time. Before the first set reaches its intended victims, there will be a dozen more in the air. When the little dears realize their predicament, a hundred water balloons will be descending upon them."

The light spilling through the windows from the porch cast upside-down shadows on our faces, transforming our smiles into macabre leers.

"Gentlemen, to your positions." When all was ready, he began repeating "one, two" in a steady rhythm and it was just as he said. Before the first squeals broke through the melody of "I'm Looking Over a Four-Leaf Clover," a third of the balloons were airborne. We unloaded the whole nine yards on them, poked our heads out, and waved again. Some girls returned fire with the handful of balloons that didn't break, but we easily fended off the few that made it to the window. The rest assaulted us with unmaidenly verbal abuse, hair plastered to their Fish heads. We smiled and waved before tumbling back into the room in an orgy of laughter.

I looked around the room. The Captain had disappeared.

After the soggy girls departed, I put "Dark Side of the Moon" in the tape deck and leaned back against my pillow, watching Bubba put his mattress back in place and fuss over the arrangement of his shaving mug and aftershave collection.

It would be interesting rooming with the twin brother of Jolene Culpepper, the beautiful but incurable practical joker who humiliated every eligible male in a thirty-mile radius of Fred. One might think that Bubba would have partnered with his evil twin at an early age and shared in a reign of hilarity and terror. One would be wrong. Jolene used Bubba as a target for many years before dating widened her scope. By the time I met him in 1968, he was reduced to a cautious misogynist who flinched at loud noises like a Weight Watcher on a midnight refrigerator raid. It was a wonder he was still sane.

Then in 1972, a white-shoed, saliva-spewing evangelist swept through Fred like a wildfire, burning away the chaff. Bubba was set ablaze, to the astonishment of many. His photographic memory and voracious reading gained him a reputation for having a ready scripture for any occasion. His popcorn delivery of verses startled many of his old friends, but after awhile, no one flinched.

Unbeknownst to the gang, the following year he pounced on Dad at frequent intervals and quizzed him about all manner of doctrinal and theological issues, often trapping him in his study at the church on Saturdays. Had we known, it might not have come as such a shock when he announced after graduation that he was going to college to become a preacher.

Bubba arrived on campus with the fire still burning, although perhaps not at the white-hot intensity that characterized the early days. The coals were banked, prepared to burn through the night.

By contrast, I traveled a more rocky terrain. As a preacher's kid I was inoculated with the virus of faith at an early age, and as often happens in such cases, it served as a vaccination, sufficient to safeguard against any serious case of religion, even when most of my classmates succumbed to the epidemic of revival that claimed Bubba.

However, the Hound of Heaven stalked and eventually overwhelmed me in the California desert. I attempted a practical implementation of the gospel with the bumbling intensity of adolescence. In the process, I formed an unlikely bond with a WWII vet and caused the deacon board to demand Dad's resignation.

Graduation and a summer job at the lumberyard in Silsbee tempered my passion. By the time I arrived on campus, spiritual matters were of less consequence to me than starting a fresh era with a clean slate. I wanted the chance to live outside the PK straightjacket, to be taken for who I was and not what people thought I should be. I asked only for anonymity and the chance to experience life. Bubba and Heidi knew I was a PK. I saw no need to publicize it to a larger audience.

CHAPTER THREE

After a week of orientation, it was a relief to be initiated into the mystical rites of registration. Heidi provided the instruction with the double whammy of the condescension of a junior lecturing lowly freshman and the mother-hen played as only a big sister can. She took Bubba and me aside at dinner and briefed us on the arcane mysteries of bureaucracy, the triplicate form, the #2 pencil, and filling in the oval completely without stray marks.

She asked me about orientation week. I told her of carpet-bombing the serenading female Fish, which she found amusing until she heard that The Captain instigated it.

"You shouldn't hang around that guy," she said.

"Why?"

"He's a drama major, for one thing."

"And?"

"They're just weird. And they end up on academic probation a lot. Ernest was on probation last spring. I guess he came back a week early from Florida."

"Ernest?"

"That's his name. He's not a captain, you know."

"Yes, I know; he just plays one on TV."

"What?"

"I can take care of myself."

"Just be careful, is all I'm saying. Nobody knows you up here, so you'll be judged by who you hang out with. Drama majors are weird. You'll get a reputation."

"Yeah, yeah."

"I'm just trying to help. Here." She shoved a parcel into my hands. "Mom sent you a care package."

"Cool." I ignored the advice but accepted the loot. We had chocolate chip cookies in Room 320 that night.

The next day Bubba and I occasionally crossed paths in the maze of lines for financial aid, counseling, degree plans, parking stickers, meal tickets, and scheduling. I was in the line for people not sure of which line to stand in next when I saw a notice for a photographer for the school newspaper, *The Compass*.

Several lines and hours later I had a decent schedule and some spare time. I left Bubba discussing the merits of hermeneutics and exegesis with a skinny cowboy and located the office on the flier. It was on the second floor at the end of an empty hallway. A wooden door with a frosted glass pane stood ajar. I pushed it open tentatively. An empty reception area lay beyond.

"Hello?" I crept across the room to the next doorway and peeked in. A short man in a tweed jacket and a fringe of unruly hair stood with his hands clasped behind his back, staring out the window. "Dr. Fulton?"

He turned his thousand-yard stare on me without speaking. I held up the notice. "You looking for a photographer?"

"Ah," he said, slowly emerging from reverie. "Ah, yes. *The Compass*." He took the flier and reviewed it as if it were my resumé. "You want the job, then?"

"Sure."

"You have a camera, I take it."

"Yes. An Argus C-3."

"A C-3. Yes, then. An Argus C-3. I expect it will do. It's three hundred dollars a semester against tuition. Any surplus can be drawn from the registrar's office." He turned back to the window, rolling up the flier as if to swat flies.

"Uh, do I need to sign anything?" Dr. Fulton looked back as if surprised to see me still there. "I mean, don't you need my name at least? For the paycheck? And who do I talk to about what pictures to take and what to do with them?"

"Ah, yes. I suspect you're right. Write your name on the pad on the receptionist's desk. I'll have it taken care of."

I doubtfully took my leave and wrote my name, room number, and "Compass Photographer" on the pad.

A few days later I was at my writing desk, attempting to wrap my brain around a calculus problem. Bubba was reclining on his bed, working through a sizable Survey of Civilization text. Phyllis was crossways on my bed, leaning against the window and flicking the ashes from his cigarette onto the porch. Fillmore was sitting in the other chair, playing chromatic scales at a blinding speed on an Alvarez acoustic guitar.

Phyllis pulled his hand to his mouth as if it took all his strength, took a long drag on the cigarette, and blew the smoke out slowly while draping his arm back out the window.

"The cafeteria menu tonight is sauerkraut and weenies," he said for the second time. Nobody responded. "And Reuben sandwiches."

Bubba looked over his book. "A what sandwich?"

"Reuben."

"What's that?"

"Beats me."

I slammed my pencil down on the desk and protested the difficulty of doing calculus under such oppressive conditions when The Captain strolled through the open hallway door.

"Gentlemen, I fear we failed to make proper introductions last week. I have come to rectify that omission and further your education on the revered traditions of this esteemed institution of higher learning." He held his hand out to me. "Ernest Lee Franks at your service."

I shook his hand. "Mark Cloud. That's my roommate Bubba."

Bubba said, "Howdy, Captain." The Captain nodded.

"And these guys have the other room. Fillmore and Phyllis."

The Captain narrowed his eyes at Phyllis. "Phyllis?"

"Don't listen to that dingleberry. I'm Phil Lancaster."

The Captain looked at me. "Phyllis?"

"We have two Phils and need to distinguish them. Hence Phil-more and Phil-less."

"A most excellent resolution." The Captain's eyes twinkled. "Now, to the issue at hand. Doubtlessly you have seen tonight's dinner menu."

Phyllis snapped his fingers. "Just what I was saying."

The Captain regarded him with a doubtful eye. "A degree of refinement unexpected in one of your lowly aspect."

"What is that supposed to mean?" Phyllis bristled.

"And what is a Reuben sandwich, anyway?" Bubba asked.

"A monstrosity constructed with sauerkraut, corned beef, rye bread, and Swiss cheese." The Captain shuddered, pulled a cigarette from the pack of Marlboros laying on the edge of the bed, and lighted it.

"Hey, those are mine," Phyllis said, starting up from the windowsill.

"Very gracious of you, sir. Most gracious." He blew out a stream of smoke with satisfaction.

Phyllis looked around to see if we noticed this bold-faced act of larceny. "Just who do you think you—" he began, but was drowned out by The Captain's stentorian voice.

"Let us not dwell on the Reuben sandwich. We shall be delivered from it by the tradition of which I previously spoke."

"I wasn't dwelling on the sandwich," Phyllis said.

"It is the tradition during the first week of classes that the Fish shall treat an upperclassman to dinner. Rather than see my comrades in combat suffer by being paired with a beneficiary of lesser eminence, I have come here to grant you that special honor."

Phyllis broke the stunned silence. "You're going to let us buy you dinner?"

"You apprehend me precisely, sir. There is a charming little establishment on Grand known by the habitués as Neely's Sandwich Shop. There we may find a repast to charm the most discriminating palate. I can personally recommend the premier item on the menu, the Brown Pig. Most delectable."

"Do you get this guy?" Phyllis asked.

The Captain smoked, unperturbed, as we sat speechless, staring at each other. Even Fillmore looked around with a half-smile, his scales forgotten. The Captain flicked his ash into Bubba's shaving mug.

"All that remains is to determine the mode of transportation. I assume one of you is in possession of an automobile. There are only five of us; one vehicle will do."

"Bubba's got a car," Fillmore blurted out.

"Excellent. By tradition, one who contributes transportation is excused from providing cash."

"It's a Corvair," Phyllis said, with evident satisfaction.

"Hmmm. Most unfortunate." He regarded Bubba through a rising ribbon of cigarette smoke. "And most unexpected, I might add."

The silence was broken by a soft rap on the open door. A stocky guy in a flannel shirt and jeans stepped into the room. He looked old for a college student, with short black hair and a goatee streaked with gray. "Mark Cloud?" He looked around, uncertain in the unnatural silence. He nodded at The Captain. "'Lo, Franks. Fleecing the lambs?"

The Captain shifted uncomfortably and moved his cigarette to the other hand. "What brings you here, Wise Guy?"

I raised my hand. "I'm Mark."

"Henry Weissman, Compass editor. I'd like to get started planning the first edition. We can talk over a Reuben sandwich."

"What exactly is a Reuben sandwich?" Bubba asked.

Weissman glanced around. "Corned beef, sauerkraut, Swiss on rye. Toasted. The food service guy does them right. He's from New York."

I grabbed a notebook. As I left with Weissman, I heard The Captain's voice. "The Corvair will accommodate our needs after all. Shall we, gentlemen?"

One tentative bite of Reuben confirmed Weissman's evaluation. He nodded at my appreciative grunt.

"So, Cloud, how long've you been shooting?"

"Shooting?"

"Pictures."

"Oh. A couple of years."

"Darkroom?"

"A little, for the annual."

"It's a start. We have a small darkroom in the basement of the admin building. The school has a deal with the local paper. We use the *News-Messenger* facilities after hours to do headlines and layout. If we leave copy in the basket, they'll set it for the next night."

"OK," I said, letting him assume I knew what he was talking about. I flipped open the notebook I had brought along. It was a portfolio of sorts, a collection of things I thought were good. "Here's some of my stuff."

He glanced at a few pages. "You know we're not doing an art magazine. We're doing a newspaper. Headshots and sports pictures. Nothing fancy."

"Yes, sir."

"Sir? What do you think this is, a military academy?"

"No, sir."

"Then drop the 'sir' stuff."

"Yes, sir. I mean, OK."

"Only thing you need to know is F8 and be there." No doubt my blank look failed to instill confidence. "Set the F-stop on the camera at F8 for plenty of depth of field and get the picture."

"Ah." I took another bite of Reuben in self-defense. Weissman did likewise and flipped through the book, occasionally stopping.

"Where was this taken?" he asked through a mouthful of chips. Light streaming through the framework of a window created an angular cross of shadow on a warped wooden floor littered with detritus.

"An abandoned shack I found in the woods."

He flipped a few more pages. "What about this?" It was a shot of a gas pump.

"Fred Grocery."

"Fred's Grocery?"

"No. Fred Grocery. In Fred, Texas."

"That sounds familiar." He took a reflective sip of water. "Is that down by Beaumont?"

"Pretty close. On 92."

"Yes, yes. I hitched through there. There's a lake near there, right? A dam and everything."

"Right. Dam B."

"Dam B. Yes, yes. About ten years ago a very uptight Johnny Law in Jasper made it clear that I should keep moving. Made his point with the help of a rifle butt. Completely unnecessary. I was moving through as fast as I could. Then a cat in a Vette took me up next to Texarkana."

"A cat and a vet?"

"A guy in a Corvette."

"You hitchhiked through Fred? Where were you going?"

"I was getting out of Mexico."

"Mexico? Where are you from?"

"All over."

I wanted to tell him to cut to the chase, but I wasn't sure how he fit in. He was an upperclassman at the least. He looked old enough to be my dad. I didn't want to make the mistake of insulting a member of the faculty.

"So, are you a professor?"

Weissman choked. "A professor? Do I look like a professor?"

"Not really, but you look a lot older than the other students."

"That's because I am older. Thirty-three."

"So, you're a student?"

"Bingo. Got it in one."

"What year?"

"Third."

"What's your major?"

"Religion."

"You're a preacher boy? I mean . . . uh . . ." This was the less-than-flattering term used to identify religion majors, those studying to be preachers, like Bubba.

"You're two for two. No need to apologize. I'm not ashamed of it."

"How did you end up here?"

"It's a long story."

"Maybe you should start at the beginning."

"I grew up in Baltimore, left home when I was sixteen. Hit just about every major city in the U.S., Mexico, Canada, and Europe."

"What did you do, join the Navy?"

He laughed. "No, I joined the Beats."

"The beats?"

"The Beat Generation. Jack Kerouac." He looked at me. I shrugged. "William Burroughs?"

"Didn't he write *Tarzan*?"

"That was Edgar Rice Burroughs. Allen Ginsberg?"

I snapped and pointed at him. "The Watergate hearings!"

Weissman shook his head. "Give up. I read *On the Road* and decided that was the life for me. I went to New York and found the other Beats and from there it was all over the world. I even ran into Jack in Mexico City in '61."

"Jack?"

"Kerouac. *On the Road*. You're not paying attention."

"How do you spell that?"

"J-A-C-K."

"How do you spell Kerouac?"

"Just like it sounds."

The next morning Bubba told me about dinner at Neely's. As the evening wore on, Phyllis took greater umbrage to The Captain's condescending manner, the brunt of which seemed to be focused on Phyllis. By the end of the meal, he was a mound of fuming silence. Then a strange thing happened, Bubba told me. Phyllis suddenly looked at The Captain and smiled. He said it wasn't a very nice smile. In fact, it was on the scary side. Didn't say anything, just smiled.

After breakfast I was crossing the Quad when I saw what seemed to be a huddle of girls stumbling drunkenly by the fountain. A closer look revealed three girls attempting to edge a fourth girl into the fountain. The victim was smaller than the other three, but they still had difficulty moving her even a foot. I also noticed that she was as cute as a bug's ear, if not twice as cute.

"Hey," I hollered. "What's going on?"

The cute girl called out through teeth clenched with effort. "Please help me. These mean girls want to throw me in the fountain."

"Stay out of it," one of the other girls yelled. She was tall and wiry and had buckteeth. "It's none of your business."

"Please, kind sir. Save me from these mean girls!"

"If you come over here, you're next," another girl called. She was very wide, and I had no doubt that she could single-handedly make good on her threat. The fourth girl appeared to be her twin.

I opted for Plan B. I set the camera to F8 and proceeded to take pictures of the crime in progress. I began with a long shot that took in a good portion of the Quad and the fountain. Then I stepped in closer and got tighter shots of the struggle with the edge of the fountain in the background.

The quartet neared the fountain in stumbling lurches punctuated by moments of stasis. Finally they tumbled to the edge in a rush and the short girl toppled in, dragging the tall girl halfway in after her. The twins jumped back as the short girl splashed water in their direction.

I continued to take pictures, but backed to a safe distance after she soaked my legs. I inspected her through the viewfinder. Her shoulder-length blonde hair hung in wet clumps. Her jeans and softball jersey clung to her body, revealing an athletic build—broad shoulders, muscular legs. I found myself being drawn through the viewfinder, out of my comfortable and accustomed role as observer, desiring to become a participant, especially in whatever she might be doing. I lowered the camera and gestured.

"OK, everybody together for a group shot."

They didn't rush together. "Group shot?" the tall girl asked. "What for?"

"The school paper. This is the biggest thing that has happened all week. It'll probably make the front page."

They immediately lined up. The short girl climbed from the fountain and slogged over to the group, pushing into the middle and hugging two girls close to her. They protested and struggled to escape.

I moved with my back to the sun, counted to three, and took a few pictures. Then I pulled out a notebook. "I'll need all your names for the caption." I wrote them all down, but I underlined "Lori Street."

I pointed to Lori. "You're in Merle Bruce Hall, right?" She nodded. "You know, there's a play tonight over there in the theater. *Barefoot in the Park*. Starts at eight. I can get tickets. Wanna go?"

"Sure," Lori said.

"Yeah," the tall skinny girl said.

"Oh, yes," the twins said together.

"Uh," I said. Then they all ran off to Merle Bruce Hall.

Brad Whittington

ACKNOWLEDGEMENTS

Thanks first to you, the readers who have stuck with Mark Cloud on his journey to enlightenment. If somehow you missed the earlier legs of the journey, you owe it to yourself to start at the beginning.

Thanks to The Woman for coming up with an idea that made me willing to actually return to Fred.

Thanks to The Good Daughter for helping me brainstorm Claire and to Jeremy for additional story development.

Thanks to Ian Rogers for the tick on the June bug.

Thanks to Donece and Michael Gregory for info on how the Dogwood Festival works.

Thanks to Lanny Hall for a few law enforcement details.

Thanks to critique groups NIP and El Gee for feedback, Rebecca Leach, Leila Oliver, and Charlene Good for making the inside better, and Amanda Cobb for making the outside look good.

— BRAD WHITTINGTON —

Sign up for the newsletter to get other sneak peeks and freebies.

BradWhittington.com

ABOUT THE AUTHOR

Brad Whittington was born in Fort Worth, Texas, on James Taylor's eighth birthday and Jack Kerouac's thirty-fourth birthday and is old enough to know better. He lives in Austin, Texas with The Woman. Previously he has been known to inhabit Hawaii, Ohio, South Carolina, Arizona, and Colorado, annoying people as a janitor, math teacher, field hand, computer programmer, brickyard worker, editor, resident Gentile in a Conservative synagogue, IT director, weed-cutter, and in a number of influential positions in other less notable professions. He is greatly loved and admired by all right-thinking citizens and enjoys a complete absence of cats and dogs at home.

BradWhittington.com

88039249R00185

Made in the USA
Lexington, KY
05 May 2018